ARKHAM TALES

Legends of the Haunted City

Call of Cthulhu® Fiction

Call of Cthulhu® Fiction

ARKHAM TALES

New Terrors Threaten Arkham

James Ambuehl
Jason Andrew
Matthew Baugh
Bill Bilstad
Tony Campbell
David Conyers
Michael Dziesinski
Cody Goodfellow
John Goodrich
Pat Harringan
C.J. Henderson
Scott Lette
Michael Minnis
Ron Shiflet
Brian Sammons
Robert Vaughn
Lee Clarke Zumpe

Edited and Introduced by Williams Jones
Cover Art by Steven Gilberts

A Chaosium Book
2006

CHAOSIUM
INC.

Arkham Tales is published by Chaosium Inc.

This book is copyright © 2006 by Chaosium Inc.; all rights reserved.

Cover art ©2006 by Steven Gilberts; all rights reserved. Cover and interior layout by Charlie Krank. Edited by William Jones; Editor-in-Chief Lynn Willis.

Similarities between characters in this book and persons living or dead are strictly coincidental.

Reproduction of material from within this book for the purposes of personal or corporate profit, by photographic, digital, or other means of storage and retrieval is prohibited.

Out web site is updated monthly; see **www.chaosium.com**.

This book is printed on 100% acid-free paper.

FIRST EDITION

10 9 8 7 6 5 4 3 2 1

Chaosium Publication 6038. Published in 2006.

ISBN 1-56882-185-9

Printed in Canada.

Contents

Introduction to Arkham Tales

For many years Chaosium has produced an outstanding series of Lovecraftian and Mythos fiction that has expanded and inspired the imaginations of the entire world. Certainly, those of us who are aware of their role-playing game, *Call of Cthulhu*, have found countless resources hidden in the various anthologies and collections produced over the years. But one aspect that has not been previously explored is the fiction inspired by Chaosium's award winning game itself.

How is this collection of writings different from Chaosium's other fiction books? The answer isn't as easy or clear-cut as it might seem. There is more at work in the realm of "Mythos" fiction than the writings of H. P. Lovecraft. A vast number of authors from the past and present form the Chaosium canon. Some of these authors influenced the development of the RPG *Call of Cthulhu*, while others found their muse after being exposed to the game. Like Lovecraft's style of blurring fiction and reality, the boundaries of "game" and fiction are erased here. Instead, what is given life in this book is the vivid world that has been created in the *Call of Cthulhu* role-playing universe. This is a backdrop fashioned by those who heard a call, those who desired to engage the eldritch world through the imagination, exploring it, expanding it, and keeping it alive.

Each story in this collection is realized in Chaosium's adaptation of the cosmic horror sub-genre. For those unfamiliar with the role-playing game, the landscape is a familiar one, and capable of standing alone. However, to those readers initiated to the secrets of the RPG, the terrain is not only recognizable, it is nostalgic—a return home, a return to Arkham.

While many readers have ventured down the familiar streets of Arkham, it is doubtful that this mysterious city has previously been so well explored as it is here. Readers will find familiar locations and characters, ancient threats and new terrors. The haunted city's secrets are uncovered in a cohesive fashion, as the authors of theses stories drew their material from the various compendiums that provide a coherent history of Arkham, a source that is distinctly Chaosium's creation; yet it is sewn together by myriad imaginations and previous writings.

Welcome to Arkham, the legend-haunted city.

—William Jones
April 7th, 2006

Mysterious Dan's Legacy

By Matthew Baugh

I arrived in Arkham, Massachusetts in the late afternoon one day in September, 1873. I'd ridden on four trains in three days since leaving Kansas, and the ride had taken a toll on me. I was sorely in need of a meal, a bed, a bath, and a shave.

As I stepped onto the platform a man caught my eye. He was unusually tall, and unusually ugly. I thought for a moment he might have been staring at me, then I saw that he was walleyed. One eye looked in my direction while the other was pointed at the rear of the caboose.

"Mr. Daniel Hawkins?"

I shifted my gaze to a young fellow in a suit and long coat.

"I'm Hawkins," I said. "Though mostly I just go by Dan."

"Jasper Thorne, sir. It's a real pleasure to meet you." We shook hands and I noticed a bulge in the armpit of his coat.

"I've got a buggy out front." Jasper continued, "Mr. Henshaw was hoping to see you tomorrow. In the meanwhile he's made arrangements for you at a boarding house in town."

"That's very good of him." I replied.

We loaded my bag into the back of Jasper's buggy. I realized it was his exuberant manner made me think of him as a kid. He was about twenty, just a couple of years younger than me.

As we climbed in, I noticed a dime novel on the seat. Jasper blushed and tucked the thing in his coat.

"I love reading about the 'Wild West,'" he explained. "I guess I don't need to tell you about it though, you being from Dodge City."

"That one of Mr. Buntline's books?"

"Yes, it is!" he beamed. "It's about Wild Bill Hickok's adventures as Marshal of Abilene."

I nodded. I'd read a couple of Ned Buntline's stories so I knew what they were like. Jasper was probably saw Wild Bill as fearlessly arresting desperados and shooting the pistols out of their hands if they resisted. From what I'd heard, the real Hickok had spent most of his time in Abilene gambling. He'd been fired by the city council two years back after he accidentally shot and killed his own deputy. That wasn't a story the dime novels were ever going to tell.

"Did you ever meet any of the famous pistoleers?" Jasper asked, "Wild Bill or Ben Thompson?"

"I suppose the most famous I've known was Dave Rudabaugh." I replied.

"I haven't heard of him. Is he fast?"

"I suppose so." I answered. "I've never seen him in a quick-draw. He is good at hitting what he shoots at, anyway.

"I'm surprised you aren't carrying a gun, considering where you come from." Jasper said.

"I didn't think it would be seemly to carry one in Arkham." I answered, "That's why I'm surprised by that shoulder rig you're wearing."

He looked startled, then grinned his boyish grin.

"Mr. Henshaw's orders. He says working for him can get dangerous at times." He reached in his coat and withdrew a short-barreled .32 revolver.

"You ever need to use it?"

"Not yet," Jasper said. "But I've been practicing. I'm pretty fast. Maybe I could show you my draw sometime?"

"Maybe."

We rode for a bit with Jasper keeping up a stream of talk. I mostly keep my own counsel, even when I'm not bone-weary, so my end of the conversation lagged a bit. As he talked, Jasper guided the carriage onto the Garrison Street Bridge and across the Miskatonic River. We continued on Garrison past the University and finally turned onto Pickman Street.

The boarding house was a proud looking two-story building. Jasper explained that it was run by the widow of a sea captain, and that the house dated back to the mid-1700s. I collected my bag and Jasper knocked on the door.

The widow was not what I had expected. She was very pretty and not yet thirty. She dressed with a propriety that would have pleased my Puritan ancestors, but there was a kind of boldness in her gaze that they would not have approved of.

"Mr. Hawkins," she offered me her hand primly. "I am Katherine Maynard. I am pleased to have you as my guest. As you no doubt know, Mr. Henshaw has arranged to cover all your expenses while you are with us. The rules of the house are simple. I allow no drinking, cards, visitors, foul language, or any other wicked behavior. I serve dinner promptly at seven."

"Yes ma'am," I agreed. "Would there be any chance of a bath and a shave before dinner? I've been traveling a long way and am hardly fit for human company."

She smiled a tight little smile.

"Of course, Mr. Hawkins. I'll draw your bath right away. You'll have to shave yourself as I will be busy preparing dinner.

◆ ◆ ◆

Mrs. Maynard was an indifferent cook but her meal was still a fine change from the fare on the trains. Her other boarders were a drummer named Mr. Kensington, and a silver-haired man named Woolcot.

"Hawkins?" Mr. Woolcot had asked, "Are you related to the famous Massachusetts Hawkins family?"

I admitted I was.

"The Hawkins were a great line of preachers," he continued in his orator's voice. "Richard Hawkins and his son were two of the leading lights in old New England. Richard's grandson Israel Hawkins is perhaps best known of all, if only because of his association with the infamous witch trials. You're not a preacher yourself, are you, Mr. Hawkins?"

"I have never had that inclination," I replied.

"Perhaps you haven't," Woolcot said. "But that is my vocation. I am an ordained minister of the Starry Wisdom Church."

"I'm afraid I haven't heard of it."

"That's not surprising," he said, "Our movement is still in its infancy and is little known outside of Rhode Island. I have come to Arkham to plant the seed of our sect in Massachusetts and Mrs. Maynard has been generous enough to allow us to use her home for meetings."

"Reverend Woolcot's sermons are so inspiring," Katherine Maynard added. "Perhaps you'll be with us long enough to attend a meeting, Mr. Hawkins?"

"I can't say ma'am," I replied. "I'll be leaving as soon as my business with Mr. Henshaw is concluded."

"What is your business Mr. Hawkins?" Woolcot asked. "If it is not rude of me to inquire."

"Not at all," I said. "A distant cousin died recently and left me a legacy. I don't really know what it is, but Mr. Henshaw is the executor and he made arrangements for me to come here to receive it."

"I suppose both sympathies and congratulations are in order," he replied.

◆ ◆ ◆

After dinner I took a walk down Pickman Street. I have never been much for idle conversation and wanted a break from the garrulous Woolcot. It also gave me a chance to admire the old stone buildings that lined the cobblestone streets and the glorious colors of the Autumn leaves which were starting to fall. I had been born and raised in Westbrook, Connecticut and the sights brought back childhood memories.

When I returned to the house I found the tall man from the railroad station sitting on the porch swing. I rose as he approached, smiling with a mouth that seemed too wide for his face.

"Daniel Hawkins?"

"Do I know you, Mister?"

"Mr. Pumblechook," the man replied. He had a slow, deliberate way of speaking. "I understand you are to receive a family legacy tomorrow. Part of that legacy is a book for which I am prepared to pay you handsomely."

"How is it you know so much about me?" I demanded.

Mr. Pumblechook fixed one dull, black eye on me while the other looked at something down the street. Up close he was even uglier than I had first realized. He was mostly bald, though a fringe of curly black hair ringed his massive head. His nose was very small and his chin non-existent. His skin hung in folds from his over-sized mouth to his collar.

"I am prepared to offer you ten thousand dollars," he said, ignoring my question.

I wet my lips. What about my legacy could possibly worth such a large amount?

"I expect I'll have to see the book before I give you an answer Mr. Pumblechook. Now, if you'll excuse me, I'd like to retire."

Pumblechook stared at me for several seconds and it occurred to me how big he was. He must have been close to seven feet tall and was not lightly built. I tensed myself in case the strange man became violent. Despite what I had said to Jasper earlier, I had a Derringer in my waistband. I hoped I wouldn't need to use it.

I didn't. After a moment Mr. Pumblechook gave a curt nod and walked into the night. I watched him go, feeling confused.

◆ ◆ ◆

The bed was comfortable but, despite my weariness, I found it hard to sleep. I couldn't stop thinking about Pumblechook and his strange offer. I placed my Derringer under the pillow. It held only two shots, but they were powerful .45s. Its presence relaxed me a little.

I was still awake around ten thirty when I heard a soft knock on the door. I opened it to find Katherine Maynard with a candle in her hand. Her dark hair was unbound and she wore a long robe.

"May I come in?"

I opened the door wide. She swept past me and placed the candle on the table.

"Is everything all right?" I asked.

She smiled. It was as wanton a look as I've ever seen on the face a woman in Dodge. She opened her robe and let it slip to her feet.

"Mercy me," I whispered.

◆ ◆ ◆

"You were wonderful," she sighed sometime later. "You must have been in a woman's bed before."

"No ma'am," I answered. That was a half-truth as I saw it. I had been in with some sporting women in Dodge and other places, but I didn't expect that she wanted to hear about that. Anyway, this was the first time a woman had given herself to me without charging.

"That's pleasing to hear," she said, snuggling her warm body close against me. "I would have thought a handsome young man like you would have had many lovers, especially in a wicked place like Dodge City."

She said "wicked" like the taste of the word was sweet in her mouth. It was hard for me to imagine that this was the same proper lady I had met a few hours earlier. My Puritan ancestors certainly wouldn't approve of her now. Or of me either.

I winced a bit as she rubbed her hand across my belly.

"What is it?" she asked. "I feel a scar."

"A fellow cut me open in a knife fight a couple of months back," I replied. "Doc McCarty sewed me up but it still pains me a little."

"What a wild town it must be," she said, and giggled. "I wonder how I would thrive in a place like that. I hate New England and the way I'm expected to act as a 'respectable' widow."

"If you were to come to Dodge, you'd have a friend there," I offered.

"That's sweet of you." Her voice was soft. "Perhaps one day I shall. For now, we have only a short time before you must go home. I would like to spend as much of it with you as I can. Tomorrow I'll pack us a picnic supper. We can row up the river to a place I know. I used to go there as a girl."

"Won't you be missed?" I asked. "If we're both away the others are bound to gossip."

"There's a woman I can hire to come and serve dinner," she replied. "I'll just say that my aunt in Dunwich is ailing and that I have to visit her. You can tell them that lawyer Henshaw invited you to take dinner with him."

It seemed to me that she had planned this out with remarkable thoroughness. It made me wonder how often she took gentlemen boarders to her place in the woods. It was past one in the morning when she left me. I had twice as much to wonder about as before, but I found it easy now to drift off to sleep.

◆ ◆ ◆

Horace Henshaw was out when I arrived at his office. Jasper asked me to wait inside and said his employer would be back momentarily. It was on the a second floor of a building on Crowninshield Place. From the window I could see the ocean.

The door opened and a burly man entered. He was in his late forties, though he moved like a much older man and the lines around his eyes gave him a haggard look.

"Good afternoon, Mr. Hawkins," he said. "I apologize for my tardiness. Something came up that I couldn't ignore."

I shrugged.

"I was just admiring the view. I haven't seen the ocean in a long time."

"It must bring back many memories."

"Not all good ones," I answered. "My little brother and I ran away to sea when we were kids. We didn't like it much."

He nodded, gesturing for me to sit.

"You're here about the legacy of course."

"Yes, sir," I admitted. "I was surprised to hear of it. I've never had many dealings with my father's people. Ulysseus Hawkins abandoned my mother and us when I was little."

"There's more to it than that then you might realize," the lawyer said. "Ulysseus Hawkins was a hunted man. He left your mother for her safety and for yours."

That had an odd sound to it, but I couldn't contradict it. Ma had never talked much about my father, especially after she remarried.

"What manner of danger was he afraid of?" I asked.

"The Hawkins family has had powerful enemies for three hundred years," Henshaw replied. "Ever since the time of your ancestor, Israel Hawkins."

"What kind of enemies does a preacher make?"

"Israel Hawkins was much more than an ordinary minister," Henshaw said. "He was a consultant at the witch trials in Massachusetts, and especially in Salem. His book, *The Secrets of the World Beyond*, was a great influence on those proceedings, and he personally dealt with especially malign cases."

"Are you saying my family has witches for enemies?"

The idea seemed laughable in the daylight of a civilized place like Arkham.

The lawyer frowned and chewed his lip for a moment. He looked like a man who knew what he wanted to say, but wasn't too clear on how to say it.

"Not witches in the prosaic sense of course. The witch trials were largely a delusion. When there were bad crops, or sick cattle, or a rash of miscarriages, people looked for someone to blame. Most of the people tried for witchcraft were innocent scapegoats. Israel Hawkins advised the judges to be careful in sorting out the spurious cases from genuine black magic."

"There are people among us who are not human, Mr. Hawkins." The lawyer's voice had grown quieter and something in it chilled me. "Call them demons, or devils, or fallen angels if you will. Your ancestor used those names and they fit as well as any. They live unseen in the sky above us, in the oceans, in the cavernous spaces beneath the earth. These beings don't care about humanity. They don't even care enough to hate us. We're just some minor irritation to be brushed away as they make ready for their plans. They will stoop to use human beings sometimes. They make them do unspeakable things to prove their loyalty, then reward them with great powers. It is these human agents that your ancestor called 'witches.'

"Israel Hawkins gathered all the information he could about these dark forces and their human agents. He spent much of his life fighting them. When he died, he passed that legacy to another Hawkins, and another, until it came to your father. I was a young man then, but I was there when my predecessor told Ulysseus Hawkins the same story I'm telling you. He was reluctant to carry on the struggle at first. He had only recently married your mother and had a promising career as a ship's master. He finally agreed, and we taught him all that

Israel Hawkins had written. He learned how to recognize the signs of the creatures and their abominable followers.

"Ulysseus hoped he would never need to use his training, but he found some worshippers on a voyage to the South Seas. They prayed to a 'winged octopus' they called *Ku-hool-tu*, and they committed acts of piracy in his name. Your father struck the pirates a deadly blow, but he brought himself to the attention of the dark forces that ruled them. The next year his ship, the St. Bernard was lost in the waters off Bermuda with a full cargo. It was their way of striking back."

"They sank his ship?" I asked. "How?"

"That's the damnable part of it." Henshaw said, "There was no sign of any human sabotage. The ship just went down one night in March. The weather was rough, but nothing unusual. The board of directors ruled that it was Ulysseus' error in judgment. They ignored the crew's stories of the sounds, of something huge chewing at the hull. After that your father became aware that he was often followed. He decided it was too dangerous for his wife and sons. That is why he left you."

The story was outrageous, but there was something about the man I trusted. Maybe I just wanted to trust him. I had so little memory of my father, and this heroic story was a lot more comforting than the tale of the shiftless ne'er-do-well I had always heard.

"How do I know all this is true?" I asked.

"Do you know how your father died?" he countered.

"When I was fourteen, we got word he'd been killed in Shanghai. The story I remember was that he'd gotten into a fight with the ship's Chinese cook and been stabbed to death."

Henshaw nodded.

"That's true as far as it goes," he said. The lawyer opened the desk drawer and pulled out a wrapped bundle, about fifteen inches long.

"My firm went to considerable trouble getting the murder weapon from the Shanghai authorities."

He passed the bundle to me, and I took it with shaking hands. That startled me because my hands are normally steady. Steady hands are a life-saver, Dave Rudabaugh had told me. He would have been disappointed that a little thing like the knife that had killed my father would upset me so.

I unwrapped the bundle. The knife was strange. The blade wasn't straight; it undulated like waves on water. But, it was the handle that froze my blood. It was made of dark wood, carved in a shape that looked vaguely like an octopus with wings.

"On your father's death, the legacy was to have passed onto you," Henshaw said. "However, on your father's instructions it went to your cousin Joshua Hawkins instead. With Joshua's passing it reverts to you again."

"What happened to cousin Joshua?"

"He drowned," Henshaw replied. "He went for a walk in town one night and his body washed up on the beach three days later. He was still fully clothed."

"Suicide?"

"That was the coroner's opinion, but I have known Joshua for many years and I do not believe it."

"What is this legacy that is causing so much stir?"

Horace Henshaw opened the desk drawer again and pulled out a deep teakwood box about eighteen inches by twelve. He handed the box to me and I opened it. There were a number of charms and talismans within, some Christian and others with a heathenish look to them. The biggest object was a book wrapped in silk.

I unwrapped the book. It was leather bound with pages written in a careful hand. The title page read:

Darker Secrets of the World Beyond:
Observations As well Historical as Theological,
* upon the Nature, the Number, and the Operations of*
the Devils, Witches, and all their Kith and Kin,

*Including Methods for the Recognizing and Combatting Thereof.
By Israel Hawkins*

◆ ◆ ◆

I opened the book and scanned the pages. They were filled with commentary, prayers, and strange drawings.

"These are Israel Hawkins' personal notes," Henshaw said. "The book is filled with all of the secret knowledge he dared not publish. It is the single greatest tool for fighting the dark powers that I know."

"What would you say if I told you that a man had offered me ten thousand dollars for this book?" I asked.

"I would not be surprised." The lawyer looked grim. "The enemies of the Hawkins family would give a great deal more than that to see that book destroyed."

◆ ◆ ◆

There were streetcars in Arkham, but the horses didn't pull them much faster than a man could walk, and I was in the mood for solitude. I was less than a block from the lawyer's office when Pumblechook stepped out in front of me.

"Mr. Hawkins," he said, smiling his grotesque smile. "I believe we have some business to transact."

He fished in his pocket and brought out a wad of newly minted bills.

"What if I don't want to sell?"

He frowned. The effect was actually an improvement on the smile.

"Why would you want to do that?" he asked.

"Maybe because I don't like your face, you ugly bastard!"

He snarled and sprang at me, arms thrown wide. I noticed that the webbing between his fingers was more pronounced than in anyone I had ever seen, and his fingernails were unusually long and sharp.

I had my derringer out in an instant, and pointed it as his tiny nose.

"Try it!" I growled, "I'd really like to see what would come out of the holes I'd make in your head!"

He stopped cold and looked me over with that walleyed stare of his, then he walked away. No threats or curses, he just walked away.

I caught the next streetcar to Pickman Street.

◆ ◆ ◆

Katherine slipped into my room as I was getting ready.

"Aren't you afraid someone will see us together?"

"The house is empty for the moment," she said, then pressed her body against mine and kissed me.

"What is that?" Her hand brushed against the derringer in my waistband.

I revealed the weapon.

"I can't stand guns!" she said. "Please don't bring that with you."

I nodded. It occurred to me that someone who didn't like guns would have a struggle living in Dodge, but I didn't say so. I put the pistol in the top drawer of the bureau.

"I'll meet you down at the riverfront," she said. "It wouldn't do to be seen walking together."

She left and I recovered the derringer. I tucked it in the top of my boot where she wasn't likely to come across it again. I also got out my big knife from my luggage, and strapped it to my belt.

◆ ◆ ◆

"What's in the box?" Katherine asked as I rowed the small boat up the river. It was slow going, even keeping to the shallows where the water was still.

"My legacy."

"May I see?"

I nodded, and she opened the box.

"Why, it's only an old book and some trinkets."

"It's a valuable book," I replied. "A man's already offered me ten thousand dollars for it."

"Are you serious?" Her eyes were wide.

"Sure," I said. "But I told him no. I didn't like his face."

She burst out laughing.

"Daniel Hawkins, you are a terrible tease." She leaned back and closed the lid of the box. "Is it really valuable? Is that why you're wearing that big knife?"

"It's called an 'Arkansas toothpick' where I'm from," I answered. "And yes, that's why I'm carrying it."

The sun was going down when I tied up the boat. It would be dark coming back, but there was a full moon, and Katherine said it would be romantic.

"We can build a fire in the glade to keep warm. They say the local Indians used to dance naked around their fires at night. Perhaps I'll dance for you."

She had that wanton look in her eyes again and I thought she fit perfectly into this wild place.

It was a short walk to the glade. The woods were thick but Katherine knew the trail. When we reached the clearing I saw that there were two figures there already, hunched over their own campfire.

"Sorry to come up on you folks in the dark," I said, then froze. One of men at the fire was the Reverend Woolcot.

"What is this?"

"Why, it's just a gathering of friends," the minister said in his stentorian voice.

The other figure at the fire rose also, until it stood a full head taller than Woolcot. It smiled inhumanly.

"Pumblechook!"

"That's not quite all of us," said a voice behind me. I heard the sound of a revolver being cocked.

"That you Jasper?" I asked.

"It is," the young man replied. "Now why don't you let that knife drop?"

I pulled the big knife from its sheath, dropping it. The point lodged in a fallen tree limb.

I felt a tug. It was Katherine pulling the legacy box out of my grip. She took it to Woolcot and kissed him.

"All of you?" I was stunned. "How long have you been working together?"

"I've been working for poor Henshaw for nearly two years now," Jasper Thorne said as he circled around to join the others. The Hawkins have been a thorn in the side of the Starry Wisdom movement for some time. We knew that I would find an opportunity to strike back if I was there long enough. When Henshaw sent you the invitation, we recruited Katherine. The Starry Wisdom can offer a woman the power to be what she wants and to love whom she will."

"What about you?" I said to Pumblechook. "Are you a part of this Starry Wisdom too?"

"At this moment I am their ally," the ugly giant answered. "Your father did my people a great harm years ago on the island of Ral."

"You killed my father?"

"Not him," Jasper said. "But it was one of his people. You can find them near all the oceans of the world, and under the oceans as well."

I didn't understand what he meant, but at the moment I didn't care. Jasper had begun to use his hands to make dramatic gestures as he spoke. When his hands spread wide I dropped into a crouch and reached for my boot. The derringer was out and covering him before he had the chance to bring his gun back into line.

"Drop the gun!"

"Stupid woman!" Woolcot snarled at Katherine. "You were supposed to make certain he didn't have a gun!"

"I did. He . . . he must have lied to me."

Jasper had dropped the revolver.

"Put the box down and back away from it." I said, shifting my aim to Woolcot.

"Don't let him bluff you," Jasper said. "He's only got two bullets. It'll take that just to kill Pumblechook."

"I hit what I aim at," I replied. "I'll gutshoot the two of you and take my chances." I pulled my knife from the branch. Pumblechook may get a surprise if he comes too close.

Woolcot put the box down and they all backed away.

"This is your fault Jasper." The preacher sounded like an orator even when he was furious. "You and this stupid woman!"

I picked up the box and backed toward the woods. When I was nearly there I turned and ran. Jasper scooped up his gun and fired a couple of wild shots after me.

"Jasper, get him!" the Reverend commanded. "Pumblechook, stay with me. There is something we must do."

◆ ◆ ◆

Losing Jasper in the woods wasn't hard. He may have fancied himself a westerner, but no one had ever taught him how to follow a trail. I left him wandering and circled back to where I could see Woolcot and the others.

Katherine was tied to a tree. Pumblechook had torn strips from her skirt and had used them to lash her arms around the bole of a big maple. I could hear her crying.

"What are you doing?"

"We're summoning a hunter my dear," Woolcot replied. "That's a spell of the Starry Wisdom you've never seen before. Once we let it loose it will hunt down Hawkins. It will find him wherever he goes and none of his weapons will be able to stop it."

"But why are you doing this to me?" she sobbed. "I've been loyal. I would never betray you."

"I believe you," Woolcot said soothingly. "And I wouldn't do this, given the choice. It's just that, once the hunter is summoned it must be given a living victim. If you'd only been a little more efficient this wouldn't be necessary."

"You'd better go and help Jasper," the preacher said to Pumblechook. "It isn't a good idea to have any extra bodies around when the hunter comes. It might become confused and take the wrong sacrifice."

Pumblechook shambled off into the woods without a comment.

Woolcot began chanting in a language I had never heard before. I used the opportunity to creep as close to him as I could. I was still nearly ten yards away when the chanting stopped. I could have gotten closer, but what I saw froze me. A shadowy form was taking shape in the air above the reverend's head. It was long and thin like a serpent, but it had a pair of huge wings midway along the body and a head as big as a horse's torso.

Katherine started screaming as soon as she saw the thing. I understood why. I wanted to scream too. Instead, I raised the derringer and took careful aim.

The bullet punched a hole through Katherine's left cheekbone, ruining her pretty face on its way to her brain. She died instantly. The horror that Woolcot had summoned seemed to sense this. It nuzzled her once then made an unhappy noise.

"Wait!" Woolcot's voice was terrified. He pointed frantically in my direction. "He's over there! *He* is your prey! Kill him!"

The hunter crept toward the reverend. I closed my eyes, burying my face in my arms until the screaming had stopped.

There was no sign of the hunter, nor of Woolcot's body, when the silence came. Nevertheless, it was several moments before I could make myself go to where Katherine's body hung.

Had I her shot out of mercy, to give her a better death than the hunter would have? I wished I could believe that, but I knew that what I had done was to save my own life.

I used the knife to cut her down.

"A little late to play the gentleman, isn't it Dan?"

I turned to see Jasper standing there, his revolver trained on me.

"You've got one shot left in that toy," he said. "I don't doubt you'd beat me in a straight draw, but I've got six shots and I've already got a bead on you. Maybe you have a chance."

"You call it," I said.

"On three," he replied. "One . . . two . . ."

I shot him in the foot before he finished the count. He dropped his gun as he fell. I crossed the space between us in five running steps, kicking him hard across the face. Then I retrieved his revolver, jamming it in my belt.

I should have killed him then, but I couldn't bear to. Not after Katherine. I just walked away. I didn't go near the boat or the river, where Pumblechook might be waiting. I remembered what Woolcot had said about his people living "under the oceans" and the thought chilled me.

There was an easy trail back to Arkham through the moon-lit woods. Katherine would have said it was romantic.

◆ ◆ ◆

"Will you keep the legacy?"

I was standing in Henshaw's office, looking out the window at the distant waves and thinking of Pumblechook.

"I guess I'd better," I said. "They'll be after me now, won't they?"

"Yes, they will."

I shook my head. If I'd had a choice I would have passed the damned book along to someone else. I thought about killing someone I would rather have saved, and sparing someone I should have killed.

"Where will you go?" the lawyer asked.

I looked out at the sea, vast and bleak.

"Someplace dry."

END

Vaughn's Diary

by Robert Vaughn

Grandpa was a virile old geezer, if all the family records are straight. He fathered my dad at the ripe young age of 61, which in those days was almost unheard of. And dad was the oldest of five siblings. Must've been the clean air, red meat, and good country living. Grandpa was a real man, a man's man. Sometimes I think that's why dad loves to read so much. It lets him pretend to be half the man grandpa must've been. Reading that crap, Heinlein and Piers Anthony and whoever, is one of the things dad passed on to me. Sure, reading at an early age is great for kids. Harry Potter all the way. But I gotta think that all that stuff gave me some pretty skewed ways of looking at the world. Especially women. You know how it is in pulp stories. They all have perfect bodies, either keen intellects or endearing levels of naivete, and they all want to have sex with you, as much as possible. That's why I was surprised when Sarah asked me out. Shocked when she started dating me. Flabbergasted when she moved in. Y'see, Sarah was perfect. Straight out of a space opera . . . but without the laser guns.

◆ ◆ ◆

"Vaughn, I'm home!" Sarah stood in the doorway, a plaid green sundress highlighted by the bright sun outside. It made me feel bad for being inside all day. I tell myself to get out more. The dress made her look like a farm girl. She was pretty, prettier than any other girl I'd ever dated. With sandy blonde hair, and freckles, and skin that was just on the verge of being tan but still seemed soft and pale. And she was confident. She knew she was a hell of a lot more interesting than someone who spent two hours a day working out. Which made her sexier than anyone like that, even if she didn't have a supermodel's body.

See, I think it must be those books that even makes me say that. Who *does* have a supermodel's body? Supermodels, and that's about it. Most other girls are either fat or not fat, and if they're not fat then they're generally pretty cute. So, she was cute. I'd say gorgeous, but that's just me.

"I brought you something," she said cheerfully, coming in and standing next to my chair, rustling through her backpack as she walked. I had been doing some research. Not like you can trust the Internet. But still, it's easy.

"Weather Dangers?" she asked, looking at the laptop's screen. "Are you gonna be a storm chaser?"

"Nah," I answered, smiling up at her. "The pay's good, but the benefits suck. Kiss?"

"Better," she said, grinning back and wrinkling her nose. She bent down and kissed me anyway. She tasted like coffee and bookstores. Then she straightened up and stuck something under my nose. At first it was just a big blur, because she was holding it too close. My eyes started to cross as I tried to focus on it, so I stuck my hand out and pushed her hand away, hard. I guess I hit her wrist. I don't like it when things get too close to my face. It makes me nervous. It hurts my eyes.

Sarah exhaled and muttered something, holding her arm. She had a surprised and hurt look on her face. "That'll proba-bly bruise," I said, pursing my lips and looking at her forearm. "I'll get some ice." I didn't apologize. She knew I didn't like things too close to my face. But she didn't mean it. And she was amazing. So I should try not to be such an asshole. But I can't help it sometimes.

Then I realized that she was more hurt because I hadn't noticed what she had brought me. I looked down at her hand. She was holding a box . . . no, it was a book. For a second I was sure it was a box, with a face stamped on the cover. A confident guy, cleft in his chin, hawk nose, gray eyes, bushy eyebrows. I'd seen the picture before. But then I realized it was a book, leather-grained. No face. A trick of the light, I guess. But I still felt like it was looking at me. The book, not the face. There was a clasp, and metal bindings that might've been gold once, or silver. They had turned black. Some kind of metal turns black, I think it's silver.

I looked back at her, my brow furrowed. I didn't reach to take it. I needed to know what it was first.

"It's a diary, dumbass," she said, exasperated but forgiving. "It got sent to my history prof, the one that gets all hot and bothered by anything from Arkham. Miskatonic sent it. They say they found it in one of the old faculty apartments that had gotten sealed off. It probably would've gotten catalogued, but," and at this her enthusiasm returned, our brief accidental violence forgotten, "my prof noticed the name on it."

I loved her so much right then. She could deal with my moods. I was so goddamn lucky. Her freckled cheeks flushed a bit at the mention of her prof. She was excited by grad school. It made sense. A lot more exciting to be finding out new things, challenging your mind, than just earning cash. Not that I didn't like my job. GIS mapping for the state. It's pretty fun, and maps . . . well, it's just rewarding to make them. You take a piece of somewhere, an idea, and you define it for people so they can understand it. So they can see it. I like that. But it's not like going to school. You learn your set of tools and you use them. Sometimes you have to figure out how to make the software do what you want, and that's kind of new. But you don't expect to change the world of GIS mapping or anything.

As I pulled an ice tray from the freezer and broke a few onto a handcloth, I asked her whose diary it was. She told me to see for myself. So I came and stood behind her, putting both arms around her waist and applying the makeshift ice pack to her wrist. I kissed her once, chastely on the neck, and gave a squeeze that I hoped conveyed "I'm sorry and I am very grateful to you for bringing me a surprise and I'll love you forever," and then I finally looked at the name stamped in eroded gold leaf on the spine. Timothy Erasmus Vaughn I.

Grandpa.

◆ ◆ ◆

After giving Sarah a very pleasant and nicely sweaty thank-you for the diary, I threw on some boxer shorts, puttered out to my reading chair by the window, and cracked it open (gently, of course). The first entry read as follows:

> *April 14th, 1922—In order to keep an objective record of my findings and hopefully continuing clear thought during this process, I will endeavor to keep this diary. My goal is to write in it every other day at a minimum. First, I believe it appropriate to describe my surroundings. I am currently keeping a room in one of the faculty apartments provided by Miskatonic University. It is spartan, but serviceable. I should wish for my own stove with which to make coffee, but the woman assigned to our feeding and cleaning downstairs assures me that she will provide beverages at need. We will see. At any rate, I foresee myself working into the late hours and I do hope that it isn't an inconvenience for her should I wish coffee after dinner.*
>
> *My reading spot (and preferred writing spot, in which I pen this entry) includes a window overlooking one of the campus quadrangles. I must admit to wondering about the students as they meander back and forth. One can certainly predict their patterns of movement based on the wear of the grass.*

*I think I will keep a record of the times, numbers, and man-
ner of their perambulations. I wonder if by such records I could
find a universal pattern to their movements. Perhaps even a
correlation between those movements and other factors.
Predicting average test scores, or dropout rates, or rules infrac-
tions. Even odds of their experiencing injury, or contracting
illness.*

*Yes. An interesting question. And the ultimate prediction,
of course, the average student's proximity to death. All determined by a recording of the times and natures of their walking. My, that is getting a bit optimistic. But hopes and
dreams, eh?*

*I should mention as well my posting at the university. I
have been asked to study a weaving written in a strange language that seems reminiscent of Basque but is not that language itself (I don't need to tell you how strange an occurrence
that is). There are a few unwholesome diagrams and images
included in the tapestry (for that is our best guess as to what
role the weaving played). I begin the work with a single
phrase that my predecessor left optimistic notes on as being
"most assuredly true": The Key and the Gate.*

I had figured out three things about Grandpa from that first
entry. First, that if he was ever a virile lady's man, it wasn't during this time in his life. Second, and closely related to that, he
was pretty damn boring, even for a guy in the 20s. Third, he was
one morbid son of a bitch. "The average student's proximity to
death?" *Give me a break.*

◆ ◆ ◆

The next day was the same-old same-old. I managed to get
out of bed after a dozen tags of the snooze button and one pissy
nudge from Sarah. Work was work. When I got home, the first
thing I did was call dad and tell him about the diary. He told me
it had to be a fake, that Grandpa didn't leave us anything, not

money and sure as hell not a journal. "And besides," he said, that officious grumble in his voice from too much smoking and too much time spent in the business world, "why would he put 'the first' after his name? My mother convinced him to name me a junior. He certainly didn't have it planned. Didn't you say the diary's first entry was in the 20s? Way before I was born."

"Maybe he was just kind of, y'know, nuts," I answered.

He wasn't amused. He was so goddamned serious.

"Listen to me, young man. I'm serious." I rolled my eyes. "I don't want you reading that thing. Give it back to that history teacher. Tell him you know it's a fake. Hell, have him do that carbon dating thing, I don't care. But someone is trying to pull one over on you, son. For all you know it's that Sarah girl."

"Right, dad. Got it." He had a few more comments, all things he categorized as "serious" and I categorized as unsolicited advice. I nodded a lot even though he couldn't see me, said "uh huh" a bunch of times, and hung up as soon as possible.

◆ ◆ ◆

April 23rd, 1922—I have not managed every other day, I'm afraid. It's a wonder I can even keep normal hours . . . my fears regarding the woman's coffee are confirmed. I feel I would also be able to make more headway in my work if all of the information regarding the weaving was revealed. For instance, my employers at the university have been hesitant to provide its place of origin, believing that it would unduly influence my studies.

So it was apparently not found in the hills of Spain, as I would have assumed. Could it be a fake? Is this a test of my own skills? On the one hand, I would be outrageously offended if this were true. On the other, I do find a good puzzle quite stimulating.

Well, if they won't give me enough to work on at my posting here, still I can keep myself entertained by my own little game. As can be seen in the charts on the following three pages, the number of perambulating students per evening has increased while their average speed as decreased. Comparing the rise in number of students walking from library to student center (the longest path on the quadrangle), I find that the rate of both the increase of the former and the decrease in the latter almost precisely matches the rate of the rise in temperature and the decrease in precipitation as spring arrives. I have also noticed a high concentration of walkers of the male gender to veer near the fountain in the southeastern corner of the quadrangle, which I have correlated with the ahem, penchant for members of the fairer sex to congregate there. Ha ha!

◆ ◆ ◆

"102 deaths this year," I told him as we pulled onto the beltway.

"What?" He grunted it more than said it.

"102 deaths," I repeated. "All from weather . . . snow, ice, heat, lightning."

"In the world?" he asked reflexively, not really caring.

"In the state," I answered, barely refraining from adding 'dumbass' onto the end of my response. Robert needed rides to and from work, so I drove him. He didn't give me gas money. He probably never even thought to offer it. I thought about it, though. All the time. Every damn day, as we pulled up to his mom's house, I'd wonder if he was going to offer. And the sick thing is, if he did, I probably wouldn't take it.

Every damn day.

But I get something out of it. I experiment on him. I say whatever the hell pops into my head, and see how he reacts. Normally I'd never do that: say what pops into my head, I mean. So it's like this little bubble, where I say stuff and he listens and says things back, but none of it matters. That's his gas money.

Even so, it usually takes me until we're halfway home, going 80 on the highway and weaving in and out of traffic, to get the balls to say whatever it is that I thought of. And then it doesn't even come out naturally. So it's a sucky experiment.

God, Sarah. If you could hear this shit.

Anyway, that's what I said that day. "102 deaths." I pulled the number out of my ass. I didn't even know what killed them. All the people, I mean. Not until he asked what I meant. Then I decided it would be the weather. It was always snowing here, or raining, or sleeting, or some goddamn Eskimo word for water falling from the sky. And the drivers. They didn't even know enough to move the hell over when they weren't passing, much less how to drive in the rain. You'd think they could deal with it. It's not like they moved here. Nobody moves here. They just stay here. That's New England for you. Or I guess, New Hampshire for you. Vermont's different, I hear.

It wasn't until that night that the number scared me. One hundred and two. On the nose.

◆ ◆ ◆

I made fajitas for Sarah and me, splattering my only good pants with hot grease and making a huge mess in the kitchen. Then we watched some TV, and I taught her a little more chess. She was good, but pouted when I beat her. What did she expect? I'd been playing for years. Then she was off to another group project meeting. Seemed like she was always having to go to a discussion group meeting or a presentation group session or something. That had to suck, working with a bunch of assholes, having to cover their slack. I didn't mind that she was gone. I like time to myself. It helps me concentrate. I tossed myself into my reading chair with Grandpa's diary in one hand and my laptop in the other.

While I skimmed the diary I shot an e-mail to my friend Chris; he's one of those analyst dweebs. I was still thinking about the conversation in the car with Robert. It got me to wondering if a weatherman could guess a death rate based on environmental factors. That's assuming the death/weather thing is causation rather than just correlation. Or maybe they can cause deaths by making us think bad weather is coming. They could certainly prevent it, right? Or maybe they're in league with National Undertakers of America.

It's shit like this that keeps me sane on boring nights when I can't sleep.

◆ ◆ ◆

May 8th, 1922—I have made further progress at deciphering the images and script used in the weaving. I have also confirmed that creases and smudges near its edges are appropriate for something that was rested on a flat, square surface at least 5 feet on a side and with slightly rounded edges. I do believe that this was nothing more exotic than a tablecloth! It is indeed from the refuse of the ancients that we learn their ways.

Oh! And I am obligated to mention that the calculations shown on the next few pages suggest that, based entirely on observation, coupled with my theories regarding student patterns of perambulation, weather, and the university's course schedule, 102 of the underclassmen will fall prey to illness this term serious enough to miss one or more days of class. I eagerly await the end of the term to conclude my findings.

◆ ◆ ◆

That made me snort in derision before I had a few seconds to think about the number he wrote, at which point I went from mocking to freaked. Then my laptop whispered "Hey, baby," in a lonely, hollow voice, and I spasmed in fear and just about went out the window. At least until my fight-or-flight reflex was overridden by the non-reptile part of my brain, reminding me that I had programmed that sound byte to play when I got an e-mail.

A little bit numb and bewildered, I read Chris's response. He had sent me a bunch of links pointing me to all kinds of statistician sites. There was the usual pseudo-science crap on chaos theory, global warming, El Niño. A few sites on actual weather patterns. I figured I had hit as close as I could get when I found a survey of last year's (and prediction of the next five) property damage in the state attributed to weather . . . but then I saw exactly what I'd been looking for. Last year's mortality rates in New Hampshire, with a breakdown of direct and indirect causes: 102 deaths attributed to extreme or hazardous weather.

Huh.

I got shivers. Coincidences always give me shivers.

"We—we being me and Sarah, aren't around. Here comes the tone."

BEEP!

"Son, it's your father. I was thinking about that diary. I guess nobody would make a fake. I'd really like to see it. You know how close I was to grandpa. It'd be nice to see what he had to say. Could you send it down to Orlando, please? Address it to the hotel, that way I'll be sure to get it. You know how it is trying to deliver to the apartment. Let me know how much it costs and I'll send you a check. UPS should be fine.

BEEP!

Stress at work was starting to mount up. I kept getting this floating blur in the corner of my eye. Like when you stare at a light for too long, and this blob of color gets burned on your retina. Like that. Must've been from my monitor at work.

The diary was a nice release. Not Grandpa's writing . . . I mean, that was funny shit, but the charts and stuff on the 'perambulations.' That still cracked me up. Anyway, I like math all right, and there's a good bit of it in mapping. But, y'know. Once you get it down for work, same thing every day. This stuff, though. It reminded me of honors trig. That was crazy hard, but when you got a problem figured out it was that much more rewarding. Anyway, figuring out Grandpa's charts and trying to make sense of his predictions had that same rewarding feeling. It was some weird stuff, too, pretty odd ways of doing calculations. It was like astrology crossed with migratory patterns. I kept waiting for him to talk about reading the future from sheep guts.

◆ ◆ ◆

June 19th, 1922—I have managed to pry from the lady librarian, who is quite fetching, the origin of the weaving, or at least the place that the university found it. Oddly, it was found here in New England, supposedly buried at the top of some hill known to have been a gathering for, of all things, cultists. Though how a bevy of New England occultists came across such an ancient item is beyond me.

The librarian seemed very shy and hesitant to speak of the matter, but I suppose I managed to win her trust by helping her carry a stack of books to her automobile. What was she to do once I had assisted her so gallantly and was standing at her side, refuse my questioning?

I believe I will take her to dinner some evening. She may be willing to say more about this "cult."

I have taken to staying up quite late in the evening to maintain accurate accounts of the students' perambulatory patterns, and following the instructions of the old shrew from downstairs, have not hesitated to knock upon her door at any time of night, even near unto midnight. I think I have woken her up several times. That will show the crone.

◆ ◆ ◆

"Hey, Vaughn?" Sarah again. Didn't she know I was stressed out? That color in the corner of my eye kept hovering. I thought about going to see an eye doctor. Ontologist? Something like that.

"What's up, babe?" I answered, still working away at Grandpa's equations. Doing that made me forget about work stress. If I worked at it enough I could forget about the blob of color . . . the stress blob, I had taken to calling it.

"What do we have planned this weekend? Anything important?"

"Nope," I said, without even thinking about it. Weekends were the time I could focus for a good, real chunk of time on Grandpa's equations.

"Okay, good, 'cause my advisor wants to take all the students in the department on a retreat. To his cabin in the Whites. And I figured, with you not feeling up to going out lately, you wouldn't mind if I was gone." She was leaning over me, hands on my shoulders, watching but not-watching my work. She smelled like chalk and apples. She smelled good. Good enough to snap me out of my flow.

I looked up at her with a real smile, the first one I'd given her in a while. I spun my chair around, accidentally knocking her thigh with it as I swiveled. She curled her lip in annoyance, but I figured I knew how to distract her from that. I tucked a hand around the small of her back and pulled her down to me, nuzzling her neck. She always loved that.

"Sure, babe. That's fine. But you're staying around tonight, right? My baby doll . . ." I started kissing her neck and she moaned, so I worked my lips down to her collarbone and moved my hand along her thigh. Those dresses she wears seem so simple and plain, but god, they're sexy. And perfect for pulling her on top of me when I'm sitting–

"Vaughn?"

I snapped out of my reverie. I had meant to do all that . . . the nuzzling, the hand, pulling her down onto me. But I . . . huh. I guess I'd just started thinking about it. And sat there. And did nothing. *Weird.*

She was just standing there, looking down at me. "What are you doing?"

I dropped my hands from their raised position, blushing. I stood up and tried to offer a smile, put my arms around her neck. "Sorry, baby. I've been feeling kinda crappy lately. Hey, whaddya say we . . ." and then I started to nuzzle her neck, for real this time.

She pushed me away. "Ugh. You stink, Vaughn. Take a shower."

The look on her face terrified me. She looked disgusted. Was I that gross? I had gotten up late, so I hadn't had time to shower before work. But seldom did she refuse my come-ons.

It seemed like a reasonable thing to ask about, so I asked.

"God, I don't know. You really just smell bad, okay? Jesus. Sorry. Look, I'm gonna go. I have to meet someone. Don't wait up."

Then she turned, and left. And instead of being indignant or coming up with something witty to say as she closed the door, I just kept thinking about how sexy she was. But that only made the rejection worse. And I was left standing, stinking, in a t-shirt stained with coffee and a pair of ratty boxers, alone except for that throbbing blob of color in the corner of my eye.

"We—we being me and Sarah, aren't around. Here comes the tone."

BEEP!

"Hey, I'm looking for a handsome devil that goes by the name of Vaughn. You there, son? It's dad. Honey, I haven't heard anything from you. Did you send that diary? Son, if you still have it, can you call me? Box it up or give it to Sarah and tell her to hold onto it for you and call me, okay? I'm—"

BEEP!

◆ ◆ ◆

June 25th, 1922—Further progress. I believe the images and script on the weaving to represent a prayer to some strange deity in order that it bless the food of a meal. "The dweller on the edge of all things come to us, and grant us your virility. Take this sacrifice of flesh and make of it your womb." That's a bit of an extrapolation, of course. I added the articles and meter to the translation. But I believe it's appropriate, given the seeming seriousness of the rite.

It is late, and the rain has kept most of the perambulators in their dorms. Poor cretins. They are missing the luscious image of my lady friend the librarian, rushing through the downpour across the quadrangle. Hmm. In a white blouse, no less.

I love wet, shivering flesh on a woman.

◆ ◆ ◆

It was a long weekend without her. I felt like crap. Sarah was right, I did stink. I was pathetic. Why did I think she had ever wanted me? It must've been pity. I was nearly done with Grandpa's diary, and I was scared of being done. Like a favorite book or a good series on DVD. It's escapism, and what do you do when your escape runs out? You have to go back to life. And life hurts, and it's scary, and I just wanted Sarah to make it better, but she wouldn't, not if I was pathetic and begging. I had to suck it up. I had to be a man. I had to tell her how things were going to be. I had to show her.

I walked in the rain. Thought about things. The blob of color was always there these days. It didn't even go away when I slept. That was okay. I couldn't screw it, but it was a constant. Everything changes and then you're dead. That's the way it was. Cars can kill you. Cancer can kill you. Hell, weather can kill you. Maybe I'd die in the rain, I thought. But then every time I got to feeling so shitty I couldn't take it, the blob of color seemed to kinda bounce. Like a dance. It did a dance. No, I made it do a dance. When you move your eyes around, the burnt part of the eye, the glowy blob, it moves with them. But I swear I didn't move my eyes.

What am I talking about? Some of the time I thought maybe the colors meant I was going blind. Which was just an excuse for a big pity-party for myself. But I kept thinking, then Sarah would have to take care of me. Pathetic, huh?

◆ ◆ ◆

July 10th, 1922—My jubilation is countered only by my embarrassment at my previous assumptions. Tablecloth! Hah. It is a tapestry, yes, and for a prayer, yes, but not for a meal! Well, for someone's meal, I suppose. For HIS. It is, of course, an alter cloth. It took some amount of questioning the locals from the county in which the cloth was found. They responded to patience, to compliments, and of course to money. The journalist was quite helpful when I offered him gossip about the faculty. He was truly my prize source. He even gave me transcripts of the cultists' ramblings, the ones that lived past the night of the police raid. And, yes, told me what the cloth had been used as. What sort of things were done to the woman that laid upon it. Which explains the "womb" reference, of course. I do feel quite daft. I had imagined harmless Bostonian gentlemen coming out to the country for a weekend and praying over a sloppily slaughtered pig so that its innards would take their false god's blessing and give them virility. Not gentlemen. And not needing in virility. No.

Not when they could plant their seed in the womb of time.

◆ ◆ ◆

When she came back from her weekend trip, I hugged her, and kissed her cheek. She asked if I'd been crying. I told her I was, and I told her I thought I was going blind, and I think she laughed. I mean, when I said it I knew I wasn't really going blind. I knew I was exaggerating. I wanted to make it a joke. Then I think she might've cried a little, too. I remember she asked me what my problem was. She said "what the hell." Just like I had asked her. *Huh.*

She said she was tired from her trip. She said she just wanted to go to sleep.

Then there was the phone call. That's when I figured it out.

"We—we being me and Sarah, aren't around. Here comes the tone."
BEEP!
"Sarah, it's Colfax! We missed you this weekend at the cabin. Hope your young man is enjoying that diary. It was quite a find. Say, I've heard from two of your discussion group partners . . . they both say you haven't been to discussion groups lately. Is everything all right? You know you can talk to me, young lady. Let me know."
BEEP!

I sat for a few minutes in silence. I didn't know what to do. Then the blob of color creeped in at the edge of my vision and it felt soft and cool. I had been practicing while Sarah was gone. I could separate it into a spectrum, control the threads, move them. I had gotten to like it. It was like a pet. I could teach it tricks.

Not like Sarah. She already knew tricks.

If she hadn't been at the cabin that weekend, where had she been? If she hadn't been with her study group these past weeks, where had she been? With someone else. That's where.

I stood up and the ribbons of color danced in my eyes. I walked to the bedroom. It was a mess. I bet she had been mad that I hadn't cleaned it. I started picking things up. I picked up something heavy. I walked over to the bed. I sat down on it.

Her eyes opened groggily. She had gone to sleep so quickly. She must have been very tired. Tired from being up all night. Up all weekend with someone else!

Her eyes widened as she saw me holding the heavy something.

"Tim? Tim, I love you . . ."

And then the colors covered everything, and I did something I don't remember. Something was bleeding in the bed. I would have to clean that up. Maybe in the morning.

◆ ◆ ◆

May 5th, 2005—You can imagine my confusion when the first stimulus I experienced after the rite was someone calling me by my given name, Tim. And it was a young woman lying before me, no less. Why, I thought the ritual had failed completely and that I was still in my old body, back in the 40s, standing above the sacrifice. Ha ha! But then of course I realized that my sniveling little son must have passed on the name, so the vessel I came to occupy was, indeed, named Tim. Timothy Erasmus Vaughn III. Amusing. The boy seemed about to strike a quite lovely young girl on the head with a marble bookend when I came to full awareness. Some level of dementia from the transition was to be expected, and unfortunately I could not restrain my new body from bringing down the blow. Poor, unbalanced boy. And my, she was quite fetching. I should have liked to bed her. But I'm afraid the bludgeoning was too severe. She died as I gathered together what passed for attire in this modern age. I simply hope I can master young Tim's automobile easily enough to get out of town and make contact with the law firm in Boston that I commissioned with managing my estate.

I believe this will be the last entry in this diary. It is time to start a new one.

END

The Orb

by Tony Campbell

622 Gedney Street, Arkham, Massachusetts

She introduced herself as Madam Babtista. Following a courteous bow, she justified her presence in Elijah's office by announcing her lineage carried an ancient prophetic legacy from the Romany King, Nathaniel Faw.

Elijah J. Fortune, primary legal researcher for Jedediah Marsh's renowned team of notaries, looked curiously over the black rims of his reading spectacles at the woman who'd invaded the morning's serenity. What might bring such an irregular traveller to the door of a reputable law firm?

"Although I'm not aware of Mr. Faw," the researcher said, politely. "I'm sure you are a woman of honor, and to that, I offer the services of Jedediah Marsh and Associates."

His guest nodded and smiled.

"So," Elijah quizzed, "what can we do for you today?"

The gypsy leaned forward across the desk and whispered, "I bring a warning." Her words were long, drawn out, as if she were auditioning for a part in The Scottish Play.

"A warning," Elijah repeated.

"For you, Mr Fortune. Your dreams are getting worse, aren't they?"

"How do you . . . ."

She silenced him with a hiss. "Permit me to finish." Elijah sank back into his chair, resigning himself to the imminent tirade.

Walk-ins, as he called them, were only ever after one thing: attempted litigations and scams worked best when the fraudster had the input of a reputable solicitor—she was fishing for some gratis legal aid.

"Alexander is in danger."

Elijah's composure crumbled, allowing a hidden vulnerability to surface. He sensed something more sinister in this woman. A flash of fury in those black eyes. Nevertheless, he attempted to interrupt again. "Now hold on just a minute . . . ."

Madam Babtista smashed her fist onto Elijah's desk, his favorite gold pen scuttling onto the floor. "*SILENCE!*" she screamed. "Heed my warning. Your son is in mortal danger. Twenty-four hours is all you have to change your fates."

Elijah stared at the gypsy as he might a defendant in a tribunal. She leaned even closer, droplets of saliva spraying from her lips as she spat the final part of her warning. "Save your son, Mr Fortune. Stop the Architect of our destruction before it's too late."

"Right," Elijah snapped. "That's enough." He stood up, stormed around the table and firmly placed his hand on Madam Babtista's shoulder. "If you leave right now, I won't call security."

The gypsy wriggled from his grip and shoved him across the room, pointing an accusatory finger at Elijah's head. "You'll come to me before this day is through, Elijah Fortune, and your apology then will be sufficient." With that, she dropped a piece of paper on his desk, spun around and swept through the door.

Elijah shivered. His dreams had been getting worse. More intense and frightening than ever before.

But how could this . . . this, old crone, know what's going on inside his head?

He had not shared his dreams with anyone since Mary's death ten years before. And even then, he couldn't bring himself to telling her the full story.

◆ ◆ ◆

As the morning drifted uneasily into lunchtime, Elijah's headache turned from a dull throb to a full-blown migraine. He needed rest, low light, and a drink.

Jedediah Marsh was a short, stocky man with a face like a bulldog. Standing next to Elijah's gaunt, rakish frame, it was obvious that the creator's moulds were diverse and plentiful.

"Don't worry," Jedediah said, "take the afternoon off. In fact," he said, flicking through his leather-bound diary, "you haven't got much on tomorrow. I'll tell you what: take the rest of the week as paid holiday."

"That's very kind," Elijah said. He'd always respected Jedediah's integrity and unsurpassed work ethic. If you were in the service of Jedediah Marsh, you were always treated fairly. "I'll see you Monday then, Mr Marsh."

"Have a good weekend, Elijah. And try and relax."

◆ ◆ ◆

Elijah's cottage was situated at the far side of town, down at the end of West River Street where the road forked off to Boston and Dunwich. He was only a stone's throw from the Miskatonic River and where on fine summer days he'd often enjoy a boat trip.

Earlier that morning, Alex had been so excited about his new job at the university he'd blatantly refused to eat breakfast, complaining of a nervous stomach ache only curable by getting to work. Elijah was a frequent visitor to the campus' extensive library and knew only too well that if Alex had any of his father's blood in his veins, *that* particular library would become his shrine.

So, Elijah had the house to himself and it didn't take long to decide the best course of action: a large glass of his favorite scotch whiskey and soda, a long soak in the tub and another go at Thomas Hardy's *Return of the Native*.

The bath water was piping hot and as relaxing as an opiate. Elijah felt his headache lift as the soporific currents generated by cascading water from the hot tap lapped across his body. Coupled with the pleasant warmth from the alcohol and a chapter of Hardy's flowery prose, it wasn't long before the weary researcher drifted into a deep, restful sleep.

◆ ◆ ◆

His eyes flicked open.

What was that?

The bath water sloshed around as he shifted uneasily in the tepid liquid. How long had he been asleep? The bright sunlight that had earlier flooded the bathroom now failed, replaced by an early evening cast of gray. A sodden Thomas Hardy floated about on his lap.

The he heard the sound again: a low rumble, a growl.

The researcher froze, gripped the cold edges of the iron tub tight until his knuckles where white.

A lion? No, get a grip, man.

Slowly, he turned his head and scanned the room. Nothing except the chair he'd laid his clothes upon.

It almost felt painful to strain his hearing so much, but there was no sound, not even a timber creak from the rapidly cooling thatched roof. He relaxed. "Imagination working over-time today," he muttered. "Mental note: no more scotch in the bath."

Nervously, he stepped from the tub, toweled himself dry, then dressed in casual evening wear.

He wandered to the living room, still spooked by the sound he'd heard, and picked his way over to the grate. He grabbed a handful of kindling and tossed it into the fireplace. Soon he had a blazing fire.

Perfect.

The next two hours passed uneventfully. Elijah settled back in his rocking chair and read yesterday's copy of the Arkham *Advertiser*. It seemed the world had turned dull. The headline concerned a businessman who had gone insane and burned down his storeroom—who was now seeking an appeal with the court, claiming he was the victim of a cultist conspiracy. Elijah grinned. It'll never stick.

He'd all but forgotten the earlier fright, dismissing it as imaginative fancy, when suddenly, from the hallway came a thump and a long, low growl.

Elijah's heart skipped. "Hello," he stammered. "Alex, is that you? It's not very funny scaring your old dad."

Another sound, louder. Then he heard the distinctive padding of an animal's feet against wood.

"Oh, sweet Jesus," Elijah stammered. He sprang from the chair, running toward the kitchen door.

He slammed the heavy door closed, then dragged a chair from the kitchen table over and jammed it under the door handle.

That was close.

Then the door shuddered under the intense pressure of whatever was repeatedly crashing into it from the other side. Elijah pushed his shoulder into the chair, making sure it held. Whatever this was, he certainly didn't intend to meet it.

Something's escaped from the zoo, he thought. I really hope Alex wasn't home.

Then, as quickly as the impacts had begun, they ceased.

Silence.

Then it spoke.

Elijah winced. This wasn't like any human voice he'd heard before. An unearthly wailing accompanied the words, the hoarseness of it as if it were being bubbled through some thick implacable liquid. Like screaming under water.

"Elijah," the voice said, impassively, "I am a messenger."

Elijah shuffled uneasily, his shoulder still pressed firmly against the chair. "Who are you?"

"Open the door."

"No chance," Elijah yelled. "Tell me from there."

"Please. Open the door."

"No way, how do I know I can trust you?"

"You do not, but you have no choice. If you wish to save your son's life, you'll have to trust me."

This was getting ridiculous. Twice in one day Elijah had received threats relating to Alex's well being. This morning had been bad enough with that mad old gypsy, but now he was speaking with some faceless demon through his kitchen door. "I can't," Elijah said. "Not without some security. What do you know about Alex?"

"*Often you have seen us in your dreams. You have encountered the one named Mh'ithrha, arch-lord of the Tindalos. We come from the farthest reaches of the universe, our strength drawn from the angles of time. Today, we seek council.*"

"Just leave me alone," Elijah wailed. "I've done nothing to you."

"*You can change your destiny by simply cooperating with us. We need your help and for that we are offering you a pardon.*"

Elijah's world collapsed. He began shaking uncontrollably, falling to his knees, tears flooding his eyes. For what seemed an eternity he convulsed, paying no attention to his surroundings. But as his sobs turned to sniffles, he became less confused and noticed the house has fallen silent.

Tentatively, he reached for the chair and yanked it from beneath the door handle. With a creak, he pulled it open and gazed into the room beyond. Whatever had been there was gone now.

The fire smoldered in the grate.

As his eyes adjusted to the gloom he noticed a gossamer mist spiralling from the corners of the room. He watched the tendrils coalesce, take shape, merge into some monstrous bear-like form in front of him. The hair on the back of his neck prickled under his collar. This wasn't a bear; it was a monstrous dog. A huge, lithe pincer with a head the size of a horse and teeth . . . Christ, it had teeth like the razor-sharp fangs of a shark.

The creature solidified, and it slowly turned its head, surveying the surroundings. Then it saw Elijah, and smiled.

Trembling and near mental collapse, Elijah backed off toward the kitchen. But it was too late. The beast sprang.

Elijah cringed as the massive animal propelled itself from the floor using its muscular hind legs. It flew effortlessly through the air towards him, saliva raining down from its gaping mouth.

Elijah screamed, hands automatically cradling his head, bracing for the terrible impact. But it didn't come. Instead he heard a demonic bay, a howl so sickening, so woeful, that the terror it conjured made his mind shut down, the room turning black around him.

◆ ◆ ◆

The device was a perfect sphere. The external shell was cast from an ancient alloy, unknown in 20th century, but the Architect knew how to make it—along with many other devices and concoctions he'd carried in his head from the earliest days of the Empire.

He smiled. His work neared completion. Almost there. Then he could sit back and reap the benefit.

The device was large enough to support the cradle containing the man-sized pod as its heart, the contraption held taut by a lattice of cables secured to the device's inner shell by heavy, iron clasps. Inside this pod sat a simple wooden seat and a control panel with a few switches. A doorway led from the outer shell to the inner shell and connected the exterior mounting platform with a wooden bridge leading to the pod's small access hatch. Outside the device was a supporting infrastructure of steel scaffolding, and a ramp leading up to the door.

The Architect checked his watch. His guest would be arriving any minute. He closed the door to the barn where the device sat dormant and strode towards the house.

Once inside, he removed his robe, hung it on a spike sticking out of the wall, and walked to the library. The house was huge. He'd bought it the previous summer and had not regretted it for a moment. The purchase had certainly been expensive in terms of the Architect's cash reserves, but the privacy the property extended to his current project meant there could be no compromise, and if he was honest, it was a bargain.

Disposal of the previous occupants had been no problem for someone of the Architect's means. The old gentleman, Mr Carnegie, needed only gentle persuasion to see that his life-long misery could be ended with the simple acquisition of a double-barreled shotgun.

The Arkham *Advertiser* had announced: *Local Madman Kills Wife, Then Turns Gun On Himself.*

An unexpected bonus the Architect hadn't considered was that he got the house at a bargain price. No one wanted to live in the so-called "murder house."

He was just about to check his watch again when he saw the faintest of mists appear in the corners of the room. He gazed as the mists thickened and joined, coalescing into a form that resembled a huge dog.

The Architect stepped forward and looked directly into the creature's crimson eyes.

It made an unearthly howl, then lowered its head as if preparing to pounce.

"Greetings," the Architect said.

"*Master,*" hissed the beast.

◆ ◆ ◆

Elijah's eyes flicked open.

The head of a giant dog, teeth bared, saliva oozing from its glistening incisors, hovered inches from his face.

He screamed.

Demented fear took hold as he squirmed away from this terrible visage of evil.

But the creature didn't pounce. Its head followed Elijah as he wriggled across the floor. As his back touched the wall, Elijah cowered, head in his hands, pleading for his life. "Please, I have a son . . . ."

"You think that would stop me?" the beast asked. "If I wanted to, I'd have done it when I first arrived. You were easy prey as you slept in the bath."

Elijah's eyes widened. *I didn't imagine it.* He was about to continue when his eyes caught sight of a large black object slumped against the kitchen table. "Alex," he yelled and scrambled to his feet. "What have you done?" He sprinted through the door and fell to his knees beside the black shape.

Then he realized his mistake.

"It's dead," the beast whispered. "I came to protect you."

Elijah stared at the dead animal. It was identical to the one in the living room, but this one had a black, studded collar around its neck and the mark of a branding iron burnt into its right temple.

"What's that," Elijah asked, pointing at the burnt flesh.

"*A glyph,*" the beast replied. "*It symbolizes ownership. This Ny'rela was cast in the service of a master.*"

"Ny'rela?" Elijah asked. "Ny'rela is this creature's name?"

"*Ny'rela is the name given to any Tindalos cast into servitude. This one maintains the pretext of an assassin.*"

"Sent here to kill me?" Elijah quizzed. "Why?"

"*We are uncertain, but we do know that the destiny of the universe is in your hands. You and your offspring have a part to play in the future of all things, and we are here to make sure you fulfill what's been prophesied."*

Elijah felt as though he were someplace else. "If this is a dream, I'm committing myself to the asylum the moment I wake."

"Your dreams have always troubled you," the beast said. *"When you were a young man, serving time through your scholarship in Edinburgh, you were present at a séance with a medium called Nathaniel Faw."*

Elijah felt an electric shock ripple down his spine. Nathaniel Faw. He'd heard that name before today. From the old gypsy. It had seemed familiar but he had attributed this déjà vu to some fleeting paragraph he might of read in a newspaper or perhaps something he'd heard from Alex during one of their conversations regarding his historical studies.

Nathaniel Faw. He remembered it now with stunning clarity. Nathaniel Faw, the spiritualist medium responsible for his best friend's death—and the beginning of Elijah's endless nightmares. He always assumed that the dog in his dreams, that ever-increasing threat from canine pursuit, was purely a symbol relating to his friend's death.

"You remember," the beast said. *"That night was when we first met. You saw into our world, and we saw into yours. We feed on souls and Faw brought them to us. In return, we gave him and his kin the gift of sight."*

"Why did the gypsy come to me today?"

"She can help," the beast said. *"She has information on the Architect's plans."*

"Right," Elijah said, regaining some composure. "And who's this Architect?"

"We don't know. We have searched through time and space to find the answer to the riddle. Faw is dead, but the vision of the end of everything was what he left us on his death bed. He foretold the demise of the Tindalos by the hand of an Architect."

Elijah stared at the beast. But what could *he* do?

"*Go to the gypsy,*" the beast said. "*Learn of the Architect. You have a role to play in all of this and the gypsy can help you decide on the right path.*"

Elijah looked back toward the slumped body of the dead Tindalos.

"And what of him?"

"*Given time, he will fade. His vapor will return to the collective of time and space. His choices brought his own demise, and for this he is doomed to drift forever without solid form.*"

"Like a ghost dog," Elijah said, grinning.

"*Go and see the gypsy,*" the beast growled.

With that, the beast's eyes glowed blood red, and it slowly faded to a fine mist that retreated into the corners of the room.

Elijah paused for beat. This was a lot to take in. The gypsy had the answers, and he needed to act quickly. He checked his coat pocket, found the piece of paper Madam Babtista had given him that morning; read the address.

As the door to the cottage clicked closed behind him, the dead Tindalos slowly faded, dispersing into the darkening room.

"Ok," Elijah said. "Out of the frying pan, into the fire."

◆ ◆ ◆

"So, Alex," Balthazar said in his dry, husky voice. "How are you enjoying your first day?"

Luke Balthazar was a portly man in his mid-seventies, so much a part of the library's furniture that he'd even developed his own wood-tarnish-complexion to perfectly match the countless rows of bookcases lining the halls of the university complex.

Alex Fortune smiled at the old man and nodded. "I love it, sir. As a visitor to the library on the odd occasion when I accompanied father, I thought it was awesome. Now that I've been in it for a day, I can't think of any place I'd rather be."

Balthazar gazed at the sixteen-year-old boy with a mixture of nostalgia and jealously. He remembered the first time he'd ventured into the bowels of this amazing palace of learning, remembering the switch that had flicked. "You're whole life is still in front of you, Alex. Here you are, planning the rest of your days in the depths of *this* place."

"That's how you've spent your life," Alex said.

"That's right, Alex, but I do have regrets. I may be well read in all the fields of academia, respected by the physical and metaphysical scholars of Miskatonic, but it's a sheltered life amongst these great texts. I have no family. I've never had a relationship with a woman. I haven't travelled, unless solely for the purposes of expanding the archives."

"Don't worry about me," Alex said with feigned compassion. He decided to try and change the subject. "So, what's left for me to do today?"

Balthazar glanced around the room. "Over there," he said, pointing at a neat pile of books stacked on a chair. "Take those down to the basement. They need returning to the Old Book repository. Once you're done you can call it a day."

"Thanks, sir."

◆ ◆ ◆

During the morning's orientation of the library's facilities, Alex hadn't noticed just how chilly the basement was. The gargantuan granite cave that housed the university's oldest and most obscure publications normally remained temperate. A shiver ran down Alex's spine. It was then that he also noticed a peculiar smell. Sulphurous. He hadn't noticed that this morning either. The fumes tickled the back of his throat and as he walked further into the cavernous room, it cloyed in his throat, making him choke.

A fire?

He shook as another bout of coughing racked him. The stack of books shifted, then one slipped from his arms, dropping to the floor.

Damn!

Alex hunkered down to pick up the stray text, securing the rest of the pile precariously beneath his chin.

Suddenly, from the shadows of the nearby heating plant, a black shape rushed him, growling, its head lowered in a bullish charge. Alex looked up just in time to see two piercing, blood red eyes. He fell to the floor, the impact knocking the wind from him.

As he struggled to catch his breath, the beast struck again. This time with greater ferocity. And Alex, for all his efforts not to, blacked out.

◆ ◆ ◆

Madame Babtista's caravan was easy to find. The piece of paper had read: *You'll find me in the field at the crossroads of Boundary and West Miskatonic Avenue.* It didn't take Elijah long to get there; the evening stroll actually invigorated him after the traumatic encounter in his cottage. He glanced up and saw faint stars beginning to speckle the canopy, and noted with interest that Polaris was particularly spectacular—faint hues of red, blue, and yellow pulsing from the distant giant.

"I knew you'd come," the gypsy said, inviting him inside the caravan.

"Live here long?" Elijah enquired. The best approach would be politeness after the morning's proceedings.

"Have they visited you?"

"Look," Elijah began. "I'm sorry about this morning. We get people like you coming in all the time—looking for gratis litigation."

She smiled and raised an eyebrow. "People like me?"

"Sorry. You know what I meant. I'm doing my best—it's been a long day."

She handed the researcher a cup of tea and sat down next to him.

"I need to know how to save my son. What can you tell me of this . . . Architect."

"The Architect is an ancient emissary. Cast from his own world, he ruled ours from his temple in ancient Egypt. You've heard of Ra?"

Elijah set the cup on the floor then slumped back on the bench. "This is getting complicated. You're telling me Ra, a god of ancient Egypt, is alive today and controlling a splinter group of time-travelling dogs wanting to overthrow the rest of their pals from Tindalos, and helping this Architect take over the world. And for this, they need Alex?"

"There's more to it than meets the eye. Alex has, within his soul, the key to our universe. The Architect Ra, Nyarlathotep from the ancient texts, knows of the chalice where this key is hidden. He knows how to use it, and he's constructing a device that will leverage this power to draw his servants to our dimension. If the gateway is opened, the whole of mankind is doomed to slavery forever."

"Why Alex?"

"Fate, Mr. Fortune. Simple fate."

◆ ◆ ◆

Alex woke with a start.

He was strapped to a small chair inside what appeared to be a spherical room.

What the hell's going on?

He strained his neck and looked at the contraption. There were buttons in front of him, simple binary controls for switching something from *off* to *on*.

The broadcast made him jump. "Alex!" A voice reverberated inside of the compartment, emanating from a small speaker in the dashboard.

"Where am I?" he yelled, struggling against his bonds.

"All in good time," the voice replied coldly. "All in good time."

◆ ◆ ◆

It didn't take long to find the fence that surrounded the Carnegie mansion. The gypsy had briefed him well, explaining the demise of the previous owners. He shuddered. *This Architect must have great power—and confidence in what he intends.*

The house loomed ahead like some cyclopean manor constructed from countless rough-cut stones. The overgrown gardens, rife with weeds and crawling tangles of vine, gave the place a feeling of desolation.

A light shone from one of the outbuildings past the house, in the trees. Elijah watched as the front door opened and a tall man with a trailing robe emerge and walk towards the barn. *The Architect.*

Elijah crept forward for a better view. Next, from the shadowed entrance of the mansion, two bear-like monstrosities emerged, padding after their master, sniffing the air, scouring the grounds with their burning, red eyes. Suddenly, one of the two Tindalos cocked its head toward Elijah. The researcher trembled and held his breath. The beast stopped. Sniffed.

Oh, Christ.

Seconds passed. Then, as if satisfied, the creature turned and followed the Architect into the entrance of the barn. The door closed behind.

It didn't take long for Elijah to locate a crack between the great beams of the barn wide enough to peer through. Inside was a construction of scaffolding, holding a metallic sphere. A gangway ran to an open door, and Elijah caught a final glimpse of the Architect as he stepped inside. Guarding outside, at the bottom of the gangway, stood the two bulky shapes of the Tindalos.

Where's Alex?

Elijah edged around the building until he was standing next to main door. There he stopped and listened.

Out of the silence, a loud electrical crackle erupted. Elijah felt the static pull at his hair. He stretched out a hand to open the door, but before he made contact, a long blue line of electricity streaked from his hand to the iron hinges. He screamed and fell forward, right into the barn.

The two hounds responded immediately. One went left and the other right, trapping him inside the building. But the researcher had no intention of leaving—not without Alex. He edged forward, head swinging back and forth, appraising the two creatures as they readied to spring.

Then he ran, faster than he'd ever run before.

As he reached the wooden gangway, the predators charged. Elijah launched himself across the last few yards and fell through the door as the first of the two beasts thundered into the wooden frame. He heard the crack of bone—or was it wood?

Then he was inside the doorway, slamming it shut with a swift kick. His adrenaline was really pumping now, his mind racing as he oriented himself. Then he saw it. In the center, suspended in a webbing of steel guy ropes, was a pod. And inside the pod, was the Architect. And there was Alex, bound to a chair.

The Architect turned, his eyes burning as they settled on Elijah. The researcher lurched toward the central pod.

A smile rolled across the Architect's face. "Mr. Fortune," he noted coldly, "you are just in time."

Elijah watched the man flip a switch, and suddenly the electric hum intensified to a deafening whine. Blue arcs spilled from the ends of the guy ropes and electricity flowed down their lengths into the pod. When Elijah had reached the doorway, he took a final leap, slamming into the Architect. The guy ropes snapped, leaving the pod perfectly suspended in mid air.

"Fool!" shouted the Architect, his face contorting from scholarly countenance to the twisted flesh of some unearthly thing. "We'll all be destroyed."

Elijah pulled back his arm and punched the Architect square in the jaw. It hurt like hell, but he did it again. And again. The Architect's flesh split beneath Elijah's pounding, and the man fell to the floor, screaming in agony.

In a flash, Elijah untied Alex and yanked open the door, revealing an electric blue curtain engulfing the pod. Elijah knew he had no choice. He shoved Alex through and jumped after him.

They both hit the base of the sphere with a terrible jolt. The whole construction was beginning to roll forward, slowly at first but picking up speed.

"Come on!" Elijah yelled. Alex didn't speak; he simply followed his father.

They positioned themselves beneath the outer doorway and ran on the spot as the sphere rolled beneath them. When the doorway had shifted beneath them and begun its ascent on the other side, Elijah yanked it open, dragging Alex through. Then they watched as the sphere rolled forward, burst through the barn door, and tumbled onward toward the house.

The Tindalos.

Elijah looked around. He spotted one of the beasts speared on a piece of scaffolding, its legs flailing in the air like an upturned tortoise. The second was crushed by the rolling orb. Sensing defeat the two huge beasts dematerialized, leaving this dimension behind to whatever fate would befall the Architect.

Ha!

"Come on," he said again, and they sprinted from the barn.

The sphere continued to roll until it collided with the house. Then, with a cataclysmic growl and brilliant flash, the sphere imploded dragging half of the mansion into the abyss.

"It's over," Elijah said.

Standing amongst the devastation, Elijah felt different, as if a great burden had been lifted from him. He couldn't sense that constant dread he'd felt since he was a young man in Scotland.

Instead, he felt exhilarated.

And he knew the Tindalos had kept their word. Now he was free.

END

The Nether Collection

by Cody Goodfellow

The old man in the atrocious disguise was waiting in the lobby of the Hotel Miskatonic when the cruiser from the Arkham Flying Squad rolled up out front.

The cobblestones were still slick with the early evening rain, throwing off the light of the street lamps like the scales of a serpent, an image given force by the drooping gambrel roofs crowding over West College Street like the walls of a grave. He seemed to be looking for grotesqueries in everything of late, or maybe it was just this town.

The young officer came round, opening the automobile's back door, and offered the seat. The officer then hopped in behind the wheel and took off at a livelier pace than the God-haunted Puritan engineers had intended for such roads.

"Beg pardon, sir, but I saw you in Boston, when I was twelve. You got out of that Chinese Water Torture thing? What a whizbang! My ma thought you were the very devil."

The old man tugged off the thick silver wig and put away the round spectacles that so cunningly distorted his face. His own hair was gray and thinning, and his eyesight was not so good. Soon, he would need no disguises to play an old man. "Officer, what is this about? The constable was vague, except for the urgency."

"Ayuh, they're all of a bother over it, whatever it is. Thought you might know already, sir, what with—"

"Young man, I'm not a mentalist, more's the pity. I was at the library myself all day until closing, and I witnessed nothing. At any rate, nothing worth getting out of bed on such a night . . . ."

The young policeman smiled at him over his shoulder, long enough that the old man fought the urge to reach over and seize the wheel. He had proved his valor in all descriptions of vehicle, from racing cars to planes, but he had never developed the courage to sit calmly in a backseat with an idiot at the wheel.

"Constable McNaughton says something happened in the library, and no more, sir. The boys who stood duty the last time something happened there still won't breathe a word about what they saw. No, the constable says any man who could get in or out of that library at night would have to be a magician. And then he sent me over to fetch you, Mr. Houdini."

◆ ◆ ◆

A gaggle of sleepy policemen loitered in the lobby of the Miskatonic University Library, even though the rest of the enormous old building was empty and still, aglow with lights, doors standing open. When he'd entered the library this morning it had been bustling with students and professors, and thrummed with the hushed sound of minds eating up ideas. But he'd spent the day alone in a blank cubicle, waiting in vain for permission to view the Special Collection, reading things that had kept him awake all night, cursing himself for having to know, and demanding more that they outright refused. When he came out at closing in a black fury, the rooms were all dark.

And now, with deepening dread, he followed the young cop through the silent galleries and stacks to the reading room outside the Special Collection. He wracked his fevered brain for some shred of a clue. Had he seen something today that might be important? Had he done something, unknowing, that had led to trouble?

The policeman led him into the room and immediately turned back the way they'd come, with a nod to Houdini.

Chief Constable McNaughton stood at the end of a long reading table, with the muddy toes of his shoes on the shore of a pool of tacky blood.

Houdini met the man only yesterday when he arrived in Arkham, got all the handshaking out of the way, and explained the purpose of his visit and why it was necessary for him to travel in disguise. McNaughton was tall and stocky, with a halo of agitated copper hair sticking out from his blunt skull, and outgrown mutton chops framing an uneasy grin.

"This is all we've found, Mr. Houdini, he said. "Your pardon for the strong arm, but we're in a fog, and when the head librarian said on the phone that you were here in town—"

"I don't have any especial skill at detection, Chief."

"But you are an escape artist, isn't that so, sir?"

"Of course, but I don't follow—"

"Well sir, if you had to escape from this room without alerting the guards, or the dogs outside, how would you do it?"

Houdini looked at the pool of blood. It was dark and scabbing over at the edges, so it wasn't fresh. McNaughton snapped his pocket watch open and closed a few times, prodding Houdini.

The magician busied himself with examining the room. It was more of a show than he let on, for he'd done just this as he waited for the senior librarian to reject his request. A gallery on the floor above overlooked the reading room, and high windows surrounded the room, but none were accessible without a ladder, and he saw wires and an alarm bell in each corner of the room. "None of the wires were cut?"

"No, and a guard was in the lobby all night. He called when he heard a man scream, but he never saw anything. There was a librarian on duty through the night as well," McNaughton knelt before the pool of blood. "But he's gone missing."

"This library is very secure but it would hardly be impossible to leave undetected, especially if one were familiar with the floor-plan. Are you quite sure the building is empty?"

"Well, it's a hell of a place to search, but I had seven men turn it over."

Houdini pointed at the heavy doors of the Special Collection. "Have you searched in there?"

McNaughton smirked. "Only Professor Armitage has the key. The others get deposited in a safe with a time lock. He's on his way over, right now."

"I'll have to thank him for recommending me to solve this case," Houdini joked. The chief constable glowered in response. No doubt he thought Houdini an egomaniac, and by any small-town standards, he supposed it was true. Well, it might just as easily be an accident or some ghastly misunderstanding, but the sooner solved, the sooner he could go to bed, and perhaps an hour of sleep.

He tested the doors to the Special Collection. Heavy oak, they had three Crest locks with rolling tumblers, and no workable crack in the frame. He'd seen payroll safes with more play in them. Glancing around the blank, walnut-paneled wall he thought: maybe he should have become a detective . . . .

He went to the adjacent wall, stooping before an iron grille. "Have you searched the ventilation shafts?"

"Why, no, but we looked them over. They're quite securely bolted in. They lead to the furnace, and the chimney opens on a peaked turret roof."

Houdini pressed one bolt with a thumbnail, then took hold of the heavy iron grille and tugged it out of the wall with minor effort.

"Well, I'll be damned. How'd you—"

Houdini showed him the stripped screws, the fake bolts made of wax and lead paint. "Someone went to a lot of trouble to make this look right so they could come and go as they pleased. You said a librarian was missing?"

"A graduate student, name of Gaston. Quiet, even for a librarian, but not a bother, or so they said."

"Well, he—or someone—had the run of the Special Collection, and—"

"Then they're still inside," McNaughton finished, drawing his revolver and bending to peer into the vent shaft.

The chief constable sent for another man, but Houdini didn't wait. Biting his lip as he knelt and squeezed into the low, narrow duct, Houdini could see only shadows as he inched out of sight.

The walls and floor of the duct were sheathed in galvanized aluminum plate, but the cold of the grave seeped through it, and the air that flowed out from it was chill and sour, as if the furnace had been smothered with moldy earth. Houdini crawled along until he saw a shuttered glow beside him. He pushed out another grille and stepped out into the dimly lit atrium of the Special Collection. After he'd caught his breath and mopped sweat from his brow, he unlocked the door and let McNaughton in. They passed through the unlocked door into the reading room.

Behind wire-reinforced glass on every wall stood shelves. McNaughton searched the room and the cubicles in the center, and shrugged. Houdini led him to a shelf. "The book I asked to look at today . . . it's gone." Houdini remembered the librarian—sallow and thin, stooped shouldered, long bony nose and deep set, elusive eyes. It must have been the missing man, Gaston.

The chief constable eyed the titles on the shelf, mouth drawing down at ugly names in unknown languages, at bindings of papyrus and crocodile and human leather, at scorched scrolls and obscene pictures scrawled in blood and worse.

"I don't wonder what a killer might want with books such as these. What I wonder, sir, is what *you* might have wanted with them? What the hell brought you to Arkham?"

"It was as I told you," Houdini snapped, looking over the books. "I came to sit with one of your infamous local mediums. While there, I chanced to overhear something that made me think I might find some answers here."

"So Mag Cooney's not a fake then?"

"I've never met a medium who was not a charlatan," Houdini retorted, pacing the perimeter of the vault-like room, eyes roving over the paneled walls and flagstone floor, observing the subtle but ornate arcane carvings on the beams framing the shelves and reading alcoves.

"I know there's a pretty coin to be made in such dealings, but why you'd want to go attacking folks just for believing in something—"

"I attack only false hope, sir. The shame is that I've found no other kind." A glint of reflected light under a desk caught Houdini's eye. "Chief Constable," he whispered, "come here. I think I've found it."

McNaughton bustled over and found Houdini squatting at the mouth of a gate-leg table wedged into a narrow, dark alcove. He reached in and touched the black stone that stood a good inch above its neighbors amidst the crumbly mortar. Its surface was slick with blood, but Houdini was able to pry it out of the floor and prop it up on a length of pipe, revealing a pit with no visible bottom. The moldy fetor of the duct gagged them. McNaughton produced a carbide-battery flashlight that, after some beating and shaking, gave a fitful yellow beam.

Houdini aimed it straight down. The shaft terminated in a floor of packed earth ten feet below, and handholds and jutting slabs of rock marked out a rude ladder down which Houdini climbed with little effort. McNaughton's ruddy face peered down at him from the lip of the pit. "What do you see?" he hissed.

Houdini shined the unsteady light around the space, and tried to put into words what he saw. "It's another library."

In pockets and niches hewn out of the walls he saw stacks of scrolls and moldering vellum folios, yellow as old bones, and numbering in the thousands. Crates—or coffins—choked the crypt, mounds of journals, ledgers and sheaves of letters spilling out onto the floor.

Houdini tried to get a sense of the size of the crypt, but the walls bent and turned on themselves, folding around warrens of shadow that might be blind alleys stuffed with books, or low tunnels that wound off into impenetrable darkness.

He followed the flickering light deeper into the crypt until he could hardly hear McNaughton calling after him. Houdini didn't reply.

He swept the light over the walls and a narrow niche before registering what he'd seen. With a gasp he jerked the light back to focus on a pair of lambent yellow eyes—then the lamp went dead in his hand. In the dark, something chuckled.

◆ ◆ ◆

Houdini crouched and took shelter behind a coffin.

A crash of thunder, and the whole crypt was illuminated by a flash from the barrel of a gun. In that instant, Houdini had burned into his sight the image of a black shape pinned in the air even as it leapt at him. It was something like a dog, and still more like a man, but even as he saw it his body convulsively threw itself backward and he flung up his arms.

The blow never fell. The darkness shivered with a gibbering cry like that of an Egyptian jackal. Books rustled and tumbled and claws raked the earth as something stole into the dark.

"Good lord!" McNaughton cried. "Houdini, are you all right?"

"I'm fine, but did you see that?" Remembering the flashlight in his hand, he shook it and revived the light.

A big black paw swiped it out of his hand, sending it across the crypt.

Houdini ran toward the chief constable—or so he hoped it was the right direction.

"Hold your fire!" Houdini yelled. The claws of the thing shredded the back of his coat as he dove to the ground. "Shoot now!"

McNaughton snapped off four more shots and Houdini crawled under the cracking gun, making for the exit. The big, bellowing policeman stabbed at the dark with his empty gun, but thought better of it and scrambled up the crude ladder, trailing Houdini.

Grateful to find the reading room still empty, Houdini strained to hear. He supposed McNaughton had killed *it*—whatever it was. Moments passed as he calmed himself. A reputation was heaviest when it was almost ready to plant in the ground.

Behind him, in the deeper shadow of the shaft, he noticed those glowing, mocking yellow eyes! A black paw shot out beneath the rock to snatch at his feet.

Houdini kicked at the rusty pipe that propped up the slab. It skidded out of its divot in the floor and flew aside. The stone slammed down like a guillotine. Houdini heard a faint hooting cry from the thing and shone the light at the slab. All the fabled courage he'd spent his life proving to the world he possessed welled in his throat like vomit, before he forced it down.

On the floor was a paw, like that of a wolf or a mastiff, black as an advanced cadaver, and bristling with dark, wiry hair, and gnarled, jagged talons. When Houdini kicked it over, he saw that it had a thumb.

◆ ◆ ◆

When Harry Houdini and McNaughton exited the reading room, they found Professor Armitage, the senior librarian, waiting in obvious agitation. The old librarian wore a long coat

over his nightshirt, and his hands nervously wrung out a cata-
log. "Mr. Houdini, I might've known."

Houdini shrugged out of his tattered overcoat. The blow
hadn't broken the skin, but it had knocked the wind out of
him. His heart raced more than he would admit in mixed company. "I had nothing to do with this, beyond coincidence–"

McNaughton added, "He's here to consult, sir. There's
been a burglary, maybe a murder."

"I know. And the collection itself has been penetrated."

"What book is missing? What's this got to do with them,
down there?" McNaughton demanded. Out of his pocket, he
dragged the paw, wrapped in a handkerchief, and showed it to
Armitage.

"You know passing well what it is, officer," Armitage
croaked. "You've lived here all your life, and heard the stories.
You know, but you've never had to believe. I never should have
trusted Gaston, but he came with excellent references from
Columbia. He took the *Cultes Des Goules*."

Houdini grinned bitterly. He was never a stupid man, but
his pride was an enormous, idiotic thing, and Armitage had
gored it. "I might've been of more assistance, had I been
allowed to view the book earlier–"

Armitage cut him off with a vehement wave of his hand.
"This incident should demonstrate even to your satisfaction the
serious nature of our collection, Mr. *Weiss*."

Houdini scowled at the old librarian. "What would have
made it so important now?"

"Ghouls are not as other species, according to the Comte
D'Erlette," Armitage remarked. "A master necromancer, he
had occasion to pen the definitive monograph on the ghouls
and their worshippers. It is possible, through extraordinary
acts, to transcend—or abandon—one's humanity, and become
a ghoul. You can see, then, how such secrets would be ill-used,
one way or another, in the hands of a stage magician."

"We may've found more than you lost, Professor," McNaughton said, and showed him a couple of crumbling books he'd snatched in their escape. "There's an annex down below."

Armitage pried open a stiff, curled roll of vellum sheets and puzzled over the crabbed, Colonial script in ominous dark brown ink. "Good heavens," he breathed, after a while. "This purports to be a testament of Prudence Goode, hanged as a witch here in Arkham, in 1666. But Prudence Goode never said a word at her trial, and no record remains of her crimes, which were stricken from the colonial records.

"And this," he gently opened a mold-bloated journal and scanned its flowery script, "is a diary of sorts, of Asaph Morgan, who died of unknown causes in the town square in 1826, and was believed to be a warlock. It's said lightning struck his house in the moment of his death, and burned the place to the ground. Why, if these are not ingenious forgeries, this is a secret history of Arkham, told in the diverse hands of the dead!"

◆ ◆ ◆

Someone had brought coffee and sandwiches to the library when they came out of the Special Collection room. Chief Constable McNaughton detailed men out into the night. Two were sent to watch Gaston's garret on Noyes Street, and a team was sent to parts unknown with shotguns and shovels. Houdini didn't need to eat and couldn't stomach coffee, so he was left to wonder why he was there.

No publicity could come of this stunt. Bess was in Albany, recovering from pneumonia. So far as she knew, Houdini was meeting with his lawyer in New York City. He smirked. They were supposed to be strategizing to fend off the wave of pending libel suits filed by all of the fraudulent mediums he'd unmasked. Instead, he'd lied to his wife and come to this dreary backwater town to expose Mag Cooney. For that he'd never before needed to lie to his wife of thirty years. Then why had he come?

From the start of his career as a "working act" among the freaks at Coney Island, he had learned that only by stepping off the stage to accept challenges from the outside world could he strike a chord in the minds of the audience. Jailers slapped him in manacles and straitjackets and threw the bolts on his cell, but he strolled out behind them before they could laugh at him twice. He had learned the picks and keys for sixty-one types of locks, and every form of human confinement. When a fiery Englishman named Hodgson set upon him with rigged locks and heavy chains, it took him hours and cost him yards of skin, but he emerged from behind the curtain a free man—and would've hung back to dash off a letter to Bess or his mother and heighten the suspense if he hadn't been bleeding so awfully much.

But these were a younger man's stories, and easier spun to a press agent or a ghostwriter for the pulps, than actually lived through. He'd heard so many Houdini stories that made him laugh at their absurdity, but then he would recall that he had whipped them up himself, and blush. He had turned his life inside out so that he would never be forgotten, but in these long, dog-tired days, he had become ensnared by darker dreams of mortality, and added stranger chapters to his pulp legend. Houdini would never die, but what would become of Ehrich Weiss?

When McNaughton startled him out of his brooding spell, he was stunned anew as the constable asked him about Mag Cooney.

"What does she have to do with this?" Houdini asked, thinking he might go back to the hotel, and not sleep there as well as here.

"Growing up we all heard the stories about her, Mr. Houdini. She was old then. We heard about the voices that come up from the ground, and how the things they said were never wrong. She never would read for outsiders, though."

"I came with a local man who wanted to hear from his mother. I came along disguised as his paternal uncle. I do believe she smelled me out, but she went ahead with her mummery, fishing for last tidbits to make the gaffe stick. But she asked only where his mother was buried. His mother spoke to us in what he swore was her own voice, and told him of the location of some papers and other items, and some shocking items of family lore which left him speechless. I was less moved, though, and flipped over the table and hoisted the trapdoor I found in the floor underneath."

Houdini took a cup of water and gulped it too fast for anyone to see the pills he palmed into his mouth.

"The tunnel went straight down into shadow," Houdini said. "Then curved off under the streets of Arkham, but I did not think of going down into it. The stench—you're well acquainted with it, by now—was overpowering. At the bottom of the pit, when I shined a candle down into it, I saw a scrap of cloth that might've been a gown, but there was nothing left of it, and anyway, the medium drove us out of her room."

"Her room, on Dunwood Road, was it?" McNaughton asked, and Houdini nodded.

"Small wonder she's never wrong, when she speaks to the dead. Dunwood is near one of Arkham's newest cemeteries."

A policeman burst into the room just then, streaming water and white with panic. Houdini recognized him as one of the two sent to the librarian's garret.

"We got attacked, sir! We never got off a shot—"

"What happened, damn it? Where's Borden?"

"Sir, they come up from the dark, and we never saw 'em, sir, and then they was all over Borden, and then they went down the sewer, dear God, sir, they just held me down and they took it, they took his hand off—"

Houdini leaned against the wall and, slumping to the floor, haunched on his heels. It was as clear as writing. Inside or out, they were not safe.

"Mr. Houdini, I'll have Oliver here run you back to your hotel now—"

But Houdini heard nothing. He looked under the long table that served as the spine of the big reading room, at the end of which lay the pool of blood and the entrance to the Special Collection. They must have looked under the table when they first searched the room, but there was nothing remarkable about the short stack of nursing texts beside the chair. They must not have looked at it from all angles though; they would have had to sit down in abject fear, as he had let himself, in order to see.

Houdini scrambled to his feet, shouting, "We have to go back, McNaughton! We must return to the tunnel now!"

The chief constable drew away from him as if Houdini had gone mad. And who could blame him for doubting an old Jew magician from Wisconsin, albeit a world-famous one. The constable was right to doubt, until Houdini took his arm and pulled him to the floor beside the books and showed him the pocketbook and the single shoe—there rested a white nurse's shoe with a splash of blood on it.

◆ ◆ ◆

They carried lanterns and shotguns, and not a man among them felt safe as they lifted the slab and climbed, one by one into the tunnel. Oliver went first, then McNaughton, then Houdini, then Tilyard, the young cop who saw Houdini in Boston when he was twelve.

Their feet slipped in something black on the floor of the crypt. Houdini spotted a trail of the noxious liquid winding among the coffins and burst crates to an alcove that wound down into darkness.

The walls closed in and the ceiling dropped low until Houdini and the others had to hunch over, turning one shoulder forward to pass. But he charged on without thought or doubt; as he had when he jumped into the North Sea and New York Harbor wreathed in shackles; as he had when he was buried alive, and entombed in safes and milk vats and iron maidens. Yet he thought, now that it was too late to turn back, there was never in any of those places something waiting for him.

The tunnel rose and descended, undulating with the softer clay stratum beneath the city. The walls became soft and fleshy and obscenely swollen with fungal rot. It sweated and dripped down their necks, and the trail disappeared among the puddles and perversely thirsty stones.

In the lead, Oliver halted to get his bearings. They all then heard a woman scream and instantly broke into a run.

Fingers of questing roots dangled from the ceiling now, and Houdini saw rotted rafter beams among the slime above their heads. Then he spied one splintered by something that brushed his face and was not a root at all; rather, it was the sleeve of a bony arm. In the front, Oliver crossed himself. McNaughton cocked his gun. They were beneath the cemetery.

Another scream, much louder, resounded down the tunnel. Oliver blindly dashed forward, leaving them to chase the stray flashes of his lantern. The floor broke up, forming a crude attempt at stairs. Then the walls fell away, and they were in a much larger space.

Though the ceiling was still so low that only Houdini could stand erect, the far wall was a jumble of loose earth and rocks and charnel debris that their lanterns could only just touch. The floor dropped sharply before them to form a steep bowl or arena. At the center of the cavern, a low altar made of shattered and lichen-crusted headstones reared up almost to the roof. . Splayed upon it was a young woman in a nurse's uniform. As the light revealed her youthful beauty, she came alive and cut

loose a piercing shriek as her regained sight revealed the skulk-
ing horde of monstrosities gathering about her.

Such a monstrous hybrid of man and jackal, subverting the
nobler elements of each, could not have been the intent of any
sane creator. Surely, nature did not make men to be food for
such as these, nor did these abominations have any business
devouring the mortal remains of humankind. For that, he saw,
all of an instant, was precisely what they did, these *ghouls* . . . .
for the floor of their den was buried in drifts of bones and
human litter, and all of it gnawed or shattered to yield up the
delicacies of marrow and heart and brain. The young constable,
Oliver, lay on the floor of the bowl with his head canted at an
odd angle, presumably where he'd fallen in his haste. In the
midst of this riot of necrophilic horror, the nurse screamed
again.

Houdini's age and fatigue fell away, consumed in a fiery
tide of outrage. He charged forward, but McNaughton elbow-
ed him back, firing his shotgun into the snarling pack.

Houdini turned to Tilyard, but the roof above the young
man's head bulged and burst, raining clods of grave mold and
worm-ridden carrion. Tilyard staggered under the flow, managing to stay upright even when a ghoul swung down from the
hole to hang, upside down before him, and rip his entire face
with its powerful jaws.

Houdini dropped his lantern, shouldered his shotgun and
gave the creature both barrels in the back. To his amazement,
the foul beast gave no sign that the pellets had penetrated its
leathery hide. It shook Tilyard back and forth by his face and
finally threw him across the room after unmasking his screaming red skull.

Houdini reached for the lantern, but something kicked it
over, plunging the cavern into darkness.

He called out, "McNaughton!" No response, except for the
chuckling of hyenas and the wet crackling of teeth on bone and
sinew.

Something slammed into him from behind and ripped the shotgun from his hands. He braced himself for the *coup de grace*, but instead a long, slimy-cold thing that must be a tongue slithered up the side of his face, tasting his sweat, his fear, his quivering, guttering life.

Whatever it tasted must have piqued its curiosity, for it bound his hands behind him, hogtied them with a rusty length of chain, and dragged him down the slope to the foot of the altar.

Too thick to break, they were so tight they chewed the soft flesh of his wrists. Yet he smiled, and pushed his terror into the pitch darkness where it would let him go to work.

The nurse choked back a sob as the creatures converged on her. Houdini struggled to keep his heart rate and breathing under control, pushing the innocent woman out of his thoughts until he could shift his weight onto his side and roll against his shoulder, dislocating it, folding against his chest.

Over the reek of decay he smelled the stinging fumes of kerosene. Oliver's lamp must have gone out, but now it was leaking. If he could find it in the dark and get it lit, he could find the girl and escape. He had no doubt the things could see in the gloom far better than he, and so he would have to act fast to disable them.

The chain went slack enough for him to get his other arm free and in a single motion; he leapt to one knee and lashed out at the dark with the chain over his head like a bullwhip.

It bit into something that yelped and kicked bones at him, then circled back to murder and eat him.

Houdini went for his pocket. He deplored tobacco more than any vice but carried a lighter always, for those who did not. He thumbed the wheel on the fine silver memento he'd received from the Berlin Chief of Police, and tossed it into the face of the fumes.

The light danced like scarves, sweeping away the blackness and encircling one of the ghastly fiends as it crouched on its haunches with its snout buried in poor Oliver. The flames washed over the ghoul's legs, which bent the wrong way and were corded with muscle like black, twitching serpents. Barking curses, it leapt out of the fire and toward Houdini, who stood rooted to the spot by the sight of the thing.

For in the fleeting noonday light of the flames, he'd seen the paws of the creature stretched out for him; or, rather, the paw, for its other extremity was all the more awful for its normalcy. It was a hand, scrubbed and pink where it wasn't begrimed with the offal upon which these monsters feasted, and it bore a signet ring such as Houdini had seen on the young officer, Tilyard. This one had cause to hate him, but it had taken another man's hand. Houdini threw himself backward as he brought the chain around and smashed it into the charging ghoul's snout.

The creature kicked at the air and fell back in its tracks, mortally wounded, if not dead. But it fell squarely on the flickering flames, smothering them, and plunging the cavern back into darkness.

Bones clattered and scraped, and throaty chuckling knitted around him. He whipped the chain around over his head and made for the sound of the weeping woman. "Are you all right, madame?" he called out.

"Oh, God! Help me, sir, please—"

Houdini threw the chain out and hit one of them, sending it howling back. It stumbled up the steps of the altar. Houndini reached out and his hand was caught by fine featured, slender fingers, and the nurse gave a grateful cry.

Hauling her off the rude sacrificial stones, he threw her over his shoulder and swung the chain wildly at the snarling dark.

They did not press him nearly so hard this time, but as he backed up against the slope, he heard their claws raking over bones and met their charge with flailing iron links. Sparks struck off a broken cavalry saber, lighting a cavern now choked with the seething tomb-horde, creeping ever closer, crushing him into a blind alley and certain death. The nurse wailed a frantic and heart-rending prayer, and Houdini bethought himself of the twists that had made him into such as deserved a death like this, a little man who ascended to greatness by standing on the shoulders of giants, and dancing on their graves.

He had erased all the names of the great magicians from the book of history—Cagliostro, Blackstone, even Robert Houdin—to make room for his own, but what would it say of him, when he could no longer rewrite it with his lies? He had come to tear down a childish dream, and found something he could not accept, something worse than these necromantic horrors. He found that somehow, someway, the dead could see, could speak, could judge–

No! He would fight, and die fighting! He might be old. He might even deserve this. But the woman on his quivering shoulder did not. Though his arms weakened and the chain was caught by a cackling ghoul, Houdini fought on. He lurched forward, through tearing claws and snapping teeth, twisting through their filth-caked arms and into pitch-blackness, perhaps in circles, to inevitable death, but still he moved.

Thunder struck.

A blast of orange light showed him the furious face of McNaughton emptying his shotgun and then his pistol into the riotous pack that had him cornered.

They parted and melted away into the warrens of tunnels beneath the cemetery. Behind McNaughton, the men he'd seen sent out into the night earlier knelt and fired into the ranks of monstrosities without seeing, without judging, except in lead.

Houdini raced past them and up the narrow rutted tunnel that led into a mausoleum in the corner of the cemetery on Dunwood Road. He faltered when he stepped into the light of lanterns held by the policemen, for he'd been about to collapse. Barely, but totally, he remembered himself. Houdini, the hero, had triumphed over death yet again, and snatched an innocent from its jaws.

Gently, he laid the woman down on the rain-flattened grass, and sat back, and began to feel sick.

There was no nurse.

A narrow, stoop-shouldered form lay on the grass before him, arms drawn to shield its face. "Is it safe? Oh, sir, you were so brave, thank you," came the voice, her voice, coming from this thing in a filth-caked gray suit.

It enraged him. "Stop it!" he cried, and battered the imposter's hands away from his face.

It was the librarian, Gaston. His beady, yellowing eyes at last laid themselves bare to Houdini, and a meek smile creased his blood-encrusted lips. Gray jelly and strands of red-blonde hair clogged his long teeth. "I was drunk," he slurred, and chuckled, "I forgot myself."

"Where's the nurse from the library, you fiend?" Houdini demanded. Gaston gagged, belched and laughed.

Behind them, McNaughton came out of the mausoleum behind him and laid down a badly mauled policeman. He waved to another group of men in rain slickers, with kegs and coils of detonator cord under their arms, and they went into the ground in their turn.

Houdini looked around, blurry clouds of vapor occluding his vision. The ghoul brushed his face with one hand, and Houdini slapped it away.

The ghoul tasted Houdini's blood, and smiled, as a gourmet savors the faceted taste of a particular vintage. "United in perfect happiness," the creature hissed at last. "That's what you want, isn't it?"

Houdini leaned closer. "What do you know?"

"We know . . . They know . . . all of those laid to rest in New York. They share them. Machpelah Cemetery, isn't it? They know . . . her. She lives in them. You could speak to her . . . We know . . . your mother . . . *and we will know you.*"

Houdini looked into those muddy yellow eyes, and saw what lived in them, what unholy glow of stolen life played itself out to slake the ghouls' lust for the same things Houdini himself had sought all his life, by means less savage but no less ruthless. It was not out of rage or revenge, but mercy, that Houdini looked around, and dashed out Gaston's brains with a rock. He then wandered away.

They did not trouble him for a statement at the hotel. They did not trouble him at all, until his cab came to take him to the train station at dawn. Only the darkness and the sounds of the unquiet October night troubled Houdini, and they followed him into the day and out of Arkham.

For all the hundreds of coffins he escaped, one would catch him in its cold embrace until they came. And when they devoured him, as they had his mother and father and all the bodies ever left in the ground by the forgotten twin of the human race, then would come the worst of it, and for this he wept. For all his success though, the name Houdini would be written forever in the heavens. For Ehrich Weiss, this would be all the heaven he could hope for.

END

Worms

by Pat Harrigan

*"All politics, my friends, is simply evolved out of fraud,
fear, greed, imagination, and poetry."*
—S. M.

As he would later didactically explain, when he went to bed on the 12th of August the world was a fine place; when he woke up again it had gone straight to the devil. The turn of phrase is key. McKinley had a grotesque religious imagination; as a child he claimed to have seen, returning from school one day, angels sitting in a tree, whispering in giggles about him.

But as abruptly as the world had gone to the devil, Simon McKinley didn't notice it at the time. He took the bus to work that day as he had done for the past three years, and after the first cup of what they called coffee sat down at his desk and checked his morning's emails.

The mythology would have this as the first moment of revelation, of impact. Truth was, the significance of it all wouldn't hit him until weeks later, if it ever truly did, but it made for a cleaner story if he collapsed it all into a single morning.

By the grace of genius hackers we now know the ephemera of the McKinley in-box: sixteen invitations to Nigeria, twelve shocking discoveries about housewives, two breathless testimonials for Cialis but only one for Viagra, three offers of cheap copy toner, three offers of even cheaper Caribbean vacations, and one Ballardesque come-hither that he paused over for a moment, which promised "abnormal privacy violations of Yasmine Bleeth."

Beyond these, there were the usual business emails, the generative structures of his day that he could now, coffee-enhanced, begin to contemplate. It was one of these that would cause such belated consternation and that would in later years be seen as the start of it all, a timid testament hammered into NWI's intranet like a protestation onto a church door.

The email was from Philip Wade in HR, addressed to Kendra Mason, the head of that department, and inadvertently cc'd to the rest of the Inns./Mass. branch of the company. It read as follows:

Kendra:

Thanks for your consideration the other day, in Taylor's exit interview. You appreciate that I'm new at this sort of thing, and to have you there to help out is *priceless*!!

I hope you won't think it too forward of me if I share a few concerns. Especially seeing that you'll soon be moving to corporate and I'll be left here at Ground Zero, so to speak.

Of course we can discuss these issues later, in fact I think of them as talking points more than issues, but just to organize my thoughts let me break them out like this:

• NWI has seen unprecedented growth, but turnover has still been remarkably high, or at least, for all I see, it seems so.

• Certain departments (Accounting, Production, Creative, International) have been evidently immune. I recommend a thorough comparative analysis to see what these guys are doing right. (Or if they're just threatening their new hires with torture and death?)

• But to be serious for a minute, I believe the issue may be in the broad NWI attitude. Speaking frankly, we're both aware of the vetting procedures and sometimes it seems like the hiring recommendations are deliberately perverse. The personality profiles of most of the new hires don't look like they'd be receptive to many of the usual techniques (retreats, T-groups, trust exercises, etc.). And for the most part they haven't been. They leave or have to be let go pretty quickly, within half a year on average.

• Between you and me, I think NWI has contributed to a culture of disdainfulness. Part of this is that NWI hiring policies seem unusually weighted to favor a specific demographic. I'm aware of the tax incentive for local hires, but does that really extend to sensitive management areas? I'm no bigot, but for the most part these people don't have the experience, education or background to perform adequately. And upper management doesn't seem inclined to provide the necessary training. Is it any surprise that they turn over so quickly? I can't see that we're doing them any favors. Six months here isn't going to look that great on a resume in any case, and what good does it do them back on the cod fishing boats, or wherever?

• What does NWI get out of it? Isn't long-term stability preferable to a succession of placeholders, Kendra?

◆ ◆ ◆

This was when Philip accidentally clicked "Send to list," and ended his own life.

McKinley, like the rest of the branch office, read the email with amusement, and a week later was not surprised to hear that Philip Wade had himself been replaced. In later days he claimed that this news provoked in him a deep stomach-sinking insecurity. To hear him speak of it, the radical destabilization of his life began in earnest that morning, although in the early days of the rising he would claim a more honest moment: a sunny lunch hour three weeks later, as he noshed a burger down at the marina. The glossy magazine he flipped through told him nothing he wanted to know about Angelina Jolie, but a local human interest piece did catch his attention.

The reporter had written three hundred words about the declining fortunes of the town's fishing trade. The theories given for the economic failure ranged from the over-fishing of the reef waters to excessive EPA regulations to localized climatic change. Maybe this was an inevitable tragedy of the 21st century, mused the reporter. Maybe there was no place for family businesses in this cold world of multinational monsters such as Coca-Cola, Disney, and NWI.

A lugubrious photo of a local family, the Bishops, accompanied the puff piece: father, two sons, and motherless granddaughter. The infant was held in her uncle Jonas' arms, and uncle Jonas, Simon realized with celebrity-spotting delight, had until recently worked with Simon on the NWI factory floor. This was the previous year, prior to Simon's move from the floor to the front office. Simon remembered the man as a diligent, reliable and—it had to be said—a not terribly bright young man who liked to talk about football and who had a somewhat scary fixation on the ex-*Baywatch* actress Carmen Electra. No, thought Simon, it was Yasmine Bleeth—and this coincidence brought his mind back to Philip's email of a few weeks before. Philip's comments began to make more sense: the "specific demographic" he

had complained about must have been this maritime commu-
nity—hence the derisive comment about cod fishing boats.

Simon considered tearing out the article and showing it
around his work pod, but he didn't know too many others who
would recognize Jonas, and in any case he didn't want to
parade around anything the least critical of the company.

But this wasn't the moment of destabilization. That came
a few minutes later, as he tossed his greasy trash into the
garbage can. Someone had left a pamphlet on the top of the
can; its title read:

Do You Know That What You Have to Lose is Priceless?

And then, in smaller type:

All that we see or seem
Is but a dream within a dream

The word "Priceless" brought him back yet again to
Philip's email, and Simon's first thought was to be thankful for
his job, a better job than cod fishing he supposed, certainly
preferable to the assembly line—a position so devoid of interest he could barely remember what they had been assembling.

The pamphlet seemed to concern his immortal soul, but
Simon's lunch hour was running out, so he flicked it into the
trash without reading it.

Just afterward, while walking along the embankment listening to the circling complaints of the gulls, Simon was struck
unexpectedly with a brief vertigo, as if the green water that
surged at the pilings under his feet was also swelling against his
brain. He felt pulled and pushed, and he stopped for a moment
to lean against the damp brick of a wedding chapel. At that
moment the bricks felt altogether more stable than he did. It
was the hamburger, he assumed. But it wasn't.

◆ ◆ ◆

At that time President Dexter had just delivered his contentious State of the Union address, in which he had promised the nation a "new fraternity of labor and business." Commentators on the right claimed this as an increased sign of support for small business, but leftist advocacy groups such as OAK saw it as another of Dexter's assaults on the working poor. OAK executed a new autumn initiative, attempting to counter what they viewed, increasingly, as the Old Deal come back again.

McKinley, to his shame in latter days, didn't join the group out of any reason so high-minded. His existential dislocation on the waterfront was weeks in the past, and its true meaning had not yet become apparent. He began to volunteer at OAK, working the phones in the evenings, for three hours every weeknight and four on Saturdays, because of a girl.

Her name, strangely, has not been discovered, though most other elements of McKinley's life and OAK's activities have been meticulously reconstructed. It's true that one of his NWI podmates heard McKinley occasionally mention a "Victoria" or "Veronica," but OAK's employment records show no one of those names volunteering there at that time. Indeed, if the name McKinley mentioned was Victoria, it may simply have been a misapprehension on the part of the pod-mate: McKinley is known to have been reading a biography of the well-known Jazz Age society hostess and arts patroness Victoria G–, and a casual reference to that woman may have been misunderstood.

In any case McKinley was good at the work. His position at NWI required little sociability, or indeed social contact, but he proved surprisingly adept at cold-calling for OAK. Within weeks he was in the field, door-knocking and helping to organize rallies and cocktail parties for the limousine liberals.

What was happening here, by his own later admission, was his transformation into a politically-engaged being. It was commonplace at this time to talk about the social anomie of the corporate workplace. But emotionally Simon hadn't believed in it; it wasn't true, or didn't feel true until, as he would say, "you turned a corner and saw it standing there, with the light hitting it at just the right angle. Then it was like, of course, I've lived in that big damn building my whole life, but I only ever looked at the blueprints."

◆ ◆ ◆

It was soon after this that NWI relocated him to the Kings./Mass. office group, there to work overseeing a newly-acquired bottling plant. In a flush of leftist paranoia McKinley initially thought that the transfer was NWI's reaction to his OAK activities. This was not the case, as far as the records tell, but it reaffirms an important lesson: that the logic of a corporation's decisions is not that of a human being's. Hirings, firings, transfers—these are the functions of a vastly different body than that of man's, and to try to decipher their purpose is to act as a cryptozoologist, slipping from observation into speculation and from there into sheer disrespectable imagination.

There was no OAK office in Kingsport, so he started one, working from his sterile apartment, running flyers off at the local copy shack. He found it exhilarating. He wrote his own agenda. He began organizing at the local bowling alleys and VFWs, and the reports show clearly that it was here he first manifested his remarkable oratorical skills.

"You were soldiers once," he began one evening, to a group of bemused veterans.

"We're soldiers now," came a voice from the back of the hall, not kindly.

"I should hope so," he said. "Because soldiers are what we need. There are wars now that your children or grandchildren fight, and I know that some of you have misgivings about these. By God, it's every man's obligation to have misgivings about war. But that's not what I'm here to talk about today.

I'm here to ask you a couple of questions about health care, and wages, and providing for your loved ones."

In later years these themes would be only the grace notes to a very different sort of speech, but here they were the point—and even at this early date Simon knew the counterpoint they would draw:

"Screw you, you–" and an obscenity. This from a different voice, close to the stage, and Simon knew he had won the day.

"Mister," he said. "Why don't you come up here with me and let's talk about who's doing the screwing."

◆ ◆ ◆

Time passed, and Simon grew more confident, and better informed. It was one of his axioms that no one understood the scope of the problem because no one could be bothered to read all the documentation. This is why he spent so much time in libraries and archives.

◆ ◆ ◆

"I want to tell you about a group of people called OAK," he began another of his talks, this one on the courtyard of the Kingsport Public Library, where several hundred people had gathered to hear him. This day proved notable for three reasons, or four. Simon stood at the podium in the rain, his hand straying unconsciously to the book in his coat pocket. The book had been removed from the library's circulation, and he had bought it for 25 cents. It was a stained, privately-printed reproduction of the diary of a man called Vaughn, and it is notable reason #1.

Notable reason #2 is Simon's arrest. It occurred directly after this part of his speech:

"OAK stands for 'Organizing Against' . . . well, I can never remember what the K stands for. Sometimes I think it stands for Katastrophe, or maybe it stands for Kaos, but anyway it stands for something that we're opposed to. I don't mean this to sound flip, because this is a serious business, this organizing against. And whether or not I can remember what the K stands for I think we all know what we're organizing against.

"There are those in the world who think they're above it. They do us harm, through callousness, or neglect, or disinterest. But we are not crawling things. We have dignity, and deserve fair treatment, and fair pay."

Then abruptly fell notable reason number 2, as the blue men descended from the sidelines to the podium and in the interests of public safety carted Simon off to jail.

They stripped him of his belt and shoelaces, but they left him Vaughn's diary and a newspaper containing notable reason #3. The newspaper was simple kindness, his solitary cell a mark of fascist insecurity—by this time no one in authority wanted Simon speaking to anyone with the smallest grievance against the system.

With the righteous fury of the reformist, Simon whistled the Internationale and used his thumbnail to carve into the crumbling stonework of the cell OAK's motto:

We have grown strong

This message impacted and splintered his nail, and he wrapped his bleeding thumb in a sheet of newspaper. As if patterned by some force—certainly not divine, thought Simon, perhaps instead that helpless angel of history—the tiny welling suppuration of blood soaked through one sheet of paper and left the most tenuous of marks on the obituary section. Here then, drawn by Simon's own blood, he saw notable item 3, the death notice of Philip Wade, late of Providence (where he had moved after his dismissal), survived by his parents, drowned tragically in Narragansett Bay while strolling with his loyal dog, unnamed.

There is a measurable drift to events, thought Simon, and a man wrecked on the waves might, before he was drowned, see the same flotsam circle by him many times. So Philip Wade was sucked beneath the water, and though he did not know it at the time, NWI's undertow was dragging at Simon too: some time during that night Simon's personnel file was stamped "Discharged," and re-filed in a special drawer. When he learned of his dismissal two days later, Simon was relieved—increasingly he had felt pulled in two directions by NWI and OAK. But this also meant that Simon was left unprotected by the NWI umbrella: that passive wardship that blanketed all NWI employees, from the lowest janitor to The Man himself.

◆ ◆ ◆

That night in the cell, Simon, insomniac, flipped through Vaughn's diary. Some friend of the family had published it, believing that the old crank had reflections worth preserving for posterity.

Vaughn had been a social parasite in the bad old days, dividing his time between New England and the Continent. He was a snob and a decadent, a devotee of Crowley and Carl Stanford, and fond of quoting Poe:

> *The play is the tragedy "Man"*
> *And its hero the Conqueror Worm.*

Vaughn had apparently spent the bulk of his time acquiring antiques: relics mostly from Egypt, Greece and Mesopotamia. When not traveling in pursuit of these he hosted or attended society parties of, Simon felt, interminable dullness. Simon had no idea why his lady friend had so excitedly pointed out the book the day before, as they browsed listlessly through the stacks, waiting for the rally to begin. But she had forced the book into his hands and kissed him with the words, "A real progressive, just like you."

Simon couldn't understand what she meant. It was another 50 badly typeset pages before he began to take any interest in the book. Here Vaughn, first name still aggravatingly unknown, began a run of particularly vicious gossip:

"As old as time itself, O.S. has nothing clever to say and can make one afternoon lunching in the casbah seem like a century spent eating sand and camel dung."

"N.B., a sallow little boy crying after his father."

"The Dunwich clan is happily dispersed. I've had more thrilling conversations with certain species of fungus."

The passage that most interested Simon was this:

"V.G. and I have many a tea, and I try to shock her by nibbling on the cakes in imitation of *that very thing which gnaws*, but she is unshockable as well as unbeddable. It may be that I should be beyond such thoughts by now, but the habits of mortality are hard to break. I confess I will miss this bubble of earth when the Days fall on us. The stars assure us that they will fall in the blink of an eye (V.G., the astrologess, claims 1926), but I wonder in my bleaker moments if we will ever be completely free of that miserable anthropic disease."

Simon began to sense that this volume had been excerpted from a longer diary, or series of diaries. Vaughn would sometimes, as in the above entry, drop hints of some theological or theosophist philosophy, but would never develop it to Simon's satisfaction. Or sometimes an entry would obliquely describe some appalling event—such as "Erickson, buried alive, circumstances unknown, naturally"—and the next might read, frustratingly, "Marmalade on toast to ensure a proper digestion. Cook's coffee is better, but find I still prefer tea in the mornings."

◆ ◆ ◆

The next morning Simon learned what it meant to be freed from the patronage of NWI. Before dawn he was awakened and led shivering down the corridor to the infirmary. There he was stripped, and he sat goosefleshed as an ageless doctor named Freygan examined each patch and crevice of him. Simon felt less violated by this than exhilarated. This was acting for *la causa*, this was resistance and sheer unpolluted progressivism.

He had never felt less alienated, and every atom of the wards' bleak empty beds and of the doctor's unlined face seemed to raise themselves into clarity like a new Braille vocabulary.

Freygan, phlegm-voiced and disinterested, pronounced him fit enough, and he was allowed to dress. Two silent guards led him past his cell and down a flight of stairs, through a steel gate that they unlocked with a thick steel key, across a mesh catwalk and down a final set of stairs. Through an unmarked wooden door Simon found a small office, barely bigger than a closet. An aged and cigarette-scorched wooden desk sat on the concrete floor and behind the desk he saw two men.

The taller of the men leaned with his back to the wall, smoking a cigar. The shorter, thicker one, an old man, sat behind the desk, hands folded on a blotter. The two guards left the room and Simon heard the door lock behind him.

"Sit," offered the old man. Simon scraped a chair back from the desk and sat.

"Do you know who I am?" asked the old man. His voice was like the very stones of the earth grinding together. A mountain talked or grumbled.

Simon shook his head. The standing man breathed out a lungful of blue smoke and said, "You never will."

"I've taken an interest in you," said the old man.

The other one said, "Lucky bastard."

The old man seemed not to hear. "You're passionate and committed and your heart's as big as your balls. So my employers feel you should probably be killed."

Simon tried to jump from his chair. But somehow the younger man was now behind him, pressing him back into his seat with a hand that felt heavy as a barbell. Simon felt the bones of his shoulder bend, and he gasped.

The old man raised his hand and the pressure stopped. "But my employers and I don't always look at things the same way. So I'm here to share a few ideas instead."

There was the creaking of a desk drawer, and the old man held something in his hand now. Simon tried to turn away, but a hand, irresistibly strong, turned his face to look. He squeezed shut his eyes and bit into the hand that was trying to force his jaws apart. The owner of the hand did not react except to press fingers further in and pry apart Simon's teeth.

He heard the old man rise from his chair and move near to him. Then there was an awful smell, something like swamp water and spoiled eggs. A soft mass, the size of a billiard ball, was pressed against his tongue. Simon felt its segmented, needle-like legs begin to force it forward, toward the back of his throat. The thousands of cilia, jellyfish-like, tickled the insides of his cheeks.

Swiftly, with sharp movements that made blood well into his mouth, the thing disappeared down his throat. The hands on Simon's face released suddenly and he bent forward and collapsed onto the floor. He sobbed and gagged and opened and closed his mouth weakly.

"You think he'll make it, Mister Blackwood?" The words seemed to come from the far side of the moon.

"Maybe." The old man's cracked voice faded. "It would be nice to see a fellow make it, for a change."

◆ ◆ ◆

It is generally agreed upon that Simon's radical eschatology dates from that night. He returned from that cell a man with newborn drive and focus, and a growing conviction that a more extreme form of protest was necessary. He connived and charmed his way onto a local news program, and though all tapes of this event have been officially destroyed, enough bootlegs still exist for the contents to be known.

It was here that he first announced the need for "a new program of change . . . the sort of direct action that hits the bastards through their creatures." There is something in the tone of his words here, an element of surprise almost, that has led many to wonder whether the moment of inspiration was exactly here, and Simon was shaping his philosophy to fit the new vessel formed by his words.

Eight days later, in the last dying hour before dawn, Simon and a small group of what the press termed "zealots" incinerated the Boston corporate office of NWI, using a delivery van packed with nitrate explosives. They killed three security guards on the way into the underground parking lot, and when the bomb exploded thirty-three more NWI employees died, mostly janitorial and housekeeping staff, but also Kendra Mason, formerly of the Inns./Mass. branch and only recently promoted to regional director. No one ever explained why she was at the office so late, except to speculate on her extraordinary commitment to her work.

◆ ◆ ◆

Simon's private conversation grew more cynical. Having committed it to memory, he burned Vaughn's diary and frequently quoted Poe: "I have no faith in human perfectibility. I think that human exertion will have no appreciable effect upon humanity. Man is now only more active—not more happy—nor more wise, than he was 6000 years ago." Simon disdained happiness and wisdom, but prized action above all things.

◆ ◆ ◆

By the spring OAK had repudiated him. Simon didn't form another group, but began holding ad hoc public rallies, all the while denying any involvement in the increasing acts of terror that had by then claimed the lives of over a hundred NWI employees. He talked less about health care and wages, and more about systemic abuses: racial, cultural, problems of class.

His enemies loved to paint him as controversial: during one rally on the steps of the New York Public Library he railed against "the racial profiling of corporate hires," but some interpreted the anger in his speech as being directed less against big business and more against certain (unnamed) ethnic groups. The next day the *Post* gleefully attacked him as a closet racist.

Simon was careful never to single out NWI during his speeches—in fact his verbal attacks began to grow more abstract, almost metaphysical, so that an untutored listener might be forgiven for not knowing whether Simon was railing against capitalism or God.

Inevitably these rallies were deeply penetrated by the FBI and O'Bannion Agency thugs, and probably by NWI security services as well, though there are no records extant to prove it. Certainly many photographs were taken, and many attendees blackmailed—if they weren't abused, beaten or arrested.

But still the numbers grew. Simon was arrested three more times before the end, the last time spending two weeks behind bars. When he was released, the number at the rallies routinely topped fifty thousand, and from those he chose twelve for special assignment.

Three of these died in Washington, bringing down a hotel and an office block, and damaging the Capitol.

One died in Arkham, attempting to bomb Miskatonic's famous library. Another two died in Kingsport and Innsmouth, destroying two of NWI's subsidiaries. Two more committed acts of terror in England's Severn Valley district, and another shot a dozen men in Wisconsin. Of the other three men there is no record; it is plausible that they were captured before they executed their tasks. A few believe they are still waiting for the proper moment to begin their missions, but this is unlikely – or if true, extremely belated.

The total number dead from this final campaign: one thousand two hundred and eighteen, with eighty-six missing.

◆ ◆ ◆

This level of outrage overwhelmed any lingering reservations held by the authorities. Police surrounded the Baltimore neighborhood where Simon had organized his final rally, trap-

ping the crowd, over a hundred thousand strong, behind barri-
cades. To his advisors Simon privately admitted he was giving
himself up after his speech. They begged him to resist, but
Simon was concerned about the mayhem that might erupt if he
did. Finally he pushed through the restraining hands and onto
the balcony.

This is how he ended his final speech:

"I'll be leaving soon, and they'll arrest me and stick me in
a room. I can guess the kind of room it'll be. Well, we all know
what's in that room. I figure I'll be unlucky, and they'll let me
out again. When they do, I suppose I'll say things I never
would have said before, things I don't believe and you should-
n't believe. But I have no doubt they'll be able to make me say
them. This is what they call the Winston Smith bait-and-
switch, after that old martyr with the soul of fiction.

"Because of this, I want to make my final testament here.

"These are the end of days, make no mistake about it.
Within a generation every human being on this earth will be
dead, and maybe the earth will be dead as well. This isn't fatal-
ism; it's fact.

"So what are we going to do about it? Let me tell you."

And he did. I was there. I heard the words, and though I
howled in agony over his decision, I remember.

So that now, after strange years that fell like eons, as the
stones of the cities darken, and the oceans thicken and congeal
and rub their new fingers across the skins of our continents, and
that which was dead has proved to be but dreaming, and the
mad auroras roll—well, I watch this bleak luster dim for a
moment, and this terror briefly recede, as mankind walks on
the coast of life, exposed and free for a moment, in its single
file, in our own step, in our last selected direction.

McKinley did emerge from that room and, at first subtly
and then with increasing heat, repudiated his extremist past.
There was nothing changed in his voice or bearing, but in his
words we could hear, like a man scratching at the inside of a

coffin, the demon tones of the crawling chaos, and for a short while we were afraid.

But now, as the years pass on, even old men have the resoluteness of the young. If the seaweed cities rise we will bomb them. The madmen who lead the people into Perdition—we kill them. We will corrupt their immortal youths and poison the bellies of their shrieking beasts.

They claim that the Old Ones are, and the Old Ones shall be—but for a few years, we lived too. Though death and dissolution take us, still this is so.

By the Key and the Gate and in no one's name, I swear this, and I affirm in these transient pages Simon McKinley's final truth: that there may be a tragedy of man, but there is no hero in the worm.

END

They Thrive in Darkness

by Ron Shiflet

Owen Blake sat amid the smoke and crowd of Abagail's Last Gasp and listened with growing irritation to the man on the barstool beside him. The club was morbidly named after an Arkham witch who had been hanged centuries earlier. The establishment was reputedly built on the exact location of her demise and even if not true, it made for an interesting story. The man had been going on for the better part of an hour about something he had discovered in his basement. Blake listened further, shaking his head in disgust. Turning to the balding, middle-aged man, he said, "Excuse me for butting in, but do you really expect anyone to believe that cock-and-bull story?"

Surprised by his candor, the man turned to Blake and sighed. "I suppose it does seem rather farfetched but I swear that it's true."

Blake lit a cigarette and stared closely at the man. "Isn't it likely that this door—or whatever it is—has always been there but you just haven't noticed it before?"

Wiping his brow with a napkin, the man stared at him and frowned. "I'm not drunk all the time. I think I would've noticed something like that as often as I go to and from my basement."

Blake sipped his beer and said nothing.

"Besides," said the man, "I didn't say that it was an ordinary door as such but more of the outline of one."

"The outline of a door in your basement wall?" Blake asked, sarcasm dripping from his tongue.

"Well, really more of a phosphorescent outline."

Blake snorted. "And how did you discover this? Do you prowl around your basement in the dark?"

Offended, the man replied, "The bulb burned out when I was down there, for Christ's sake! Those things happen you know. That's when I first noticed it."

Blake thought about it and found that part of the story at least plausible. "That makes sense," he said. "But what makes you think this outline signifies the existence of a door?"

"You wouldn't have to ask if you saw it," the man replied. "It's pretty damn obvious."

"Perhaps to you," answered Blake, expelling a blue plume of smoke. "Geeze," he muttered, "who's the idiot that played that song?"

Alice Cooper's "I Love the Dead" was playing on the jukebox and several rowdy drunks were boisterously singing along with the chorus.

"That's the only thing I don't like about this place," the man said.

"What's that?" Blake asked, straining to hear.

"The Friday night crowd here tends to be a bit noisy."

The bartender came over as Blake finished his beer. "Get you another?"

"No thanks," Blake answered. "It's getting a little loud in here for me."

The man beside him grinned, saying, "That's one thing we agree on. If you care to follow me home, I've got a refrigerator full of cold ones."

Blake glared.

"I'm not gay," said the man pointedly. "I'm not trying to pick you up if that's what you're afraid of. I just thought you might like to drink a couple more somewhere quieter . . . and allow me to prove you wrong about that basement door."

"I'll admit to being curious," said Blake. "Do you live nearby?"

"Not far," the man answered, extending his hand. "The name's Underhill. Vincent Underhill, dealer in rare books."

"Blake . . . Owen Blake. I unfortunately happen to be between jobs at the moment."

"Something'll turn up," Underhill said. "It always does."

"So, where do you live?"

"Just west of Miskatonic University, on Dunwood Street—you know, that property bordering the new cemetery."

"Yeah," Blake said, "I know the place. Not too many people around there. "

Underhill chuckled. "Not live ones anyway."

The bar's patrons were growing louder by the second and Blake asked, "Is your car in the lot?"

"What?" Underhill answered, straining to hear.

"Your car, is it in the lot?" Blake asked, louder.

Understanding dawned in Underhill's eyes. "Yes!" he shouted, struggling to be heard.

"Okay," Blake replied. "Lead the way and I'll follow you."

"Splendid!" Underhill exclaimed, rising from his barstool.

Blake and Underhill left the noisy din behind them and walked to the bar's parking area.

◆ ◆ ◆

Blake followed the silver Audi down West College Street, reassured to see that Underhill was driving in a competent manner. *Maybe he's not as drunk as I thought. Still, I'm not exactly sure what possessed me to take him up on his invitation.*

He continued driving, glancing at the old clock tower at Miskatonic University. It was only ten-fifteen and traffic was reasonably light for a Saturday night. The spring semester hadn't begun but Arkham's population would definitely increase in the coming days.

He watched Underhill signal a left turn on Dunwood Road and prepared to do likewise. After turning, he drove at a leisurely pace as the downtown lights of town receded in the distance. The road was dark and winding but Underhill drove only a short distance before signaling a right turn onto a private drive leading to his home. Blake again followed suit and in a couple of minutes, parked his Accord in the large circular driveway of a relatively new, two-story brick home. Underhill climbed from the Audi, and motioned for Blake to follow. Turning off the engine, Blake got out and walked to Underhill.

"See," Underhill said, "I told you it wasn't far."

Blake grinned, saying, "Nice house! A far cry from most of the homes in Arkham.

Underhill jangled his keychain and smiled. "Arkham's growing. Few things remain unchanged."

"That's for sure," Blake replied.

"Let me get this door open and we'll have that beer."

"And see that other door."

"Yes," Underhill laughed. "And see that other door."

Blake followed Underhill inside, commenting on the conservative and tasteful décor. "I expected you to have one of those tottering, gambrel-roofed affairs after learning you were a book dealer."

"Ah yes," Underhill sighed. "The old stereotypes die hard. Excuse me a moment and I'll get those beers. Samuel Adams okay?"

Blake grinned, saying "Any day of the week."

Underhill returned shortly and the two men drank and talked congenially. Blake was surprised at how comfortable he felt in the man's presence, regretting the sarcasm he had earlier directed at his host. Three beers and several interesting stories later, he said, "Look Vincent, I owe you and apology for the way I acted back at the bar. I'm afraid the noise was getting to me."

No need for apologies," Underhill said. "I can be a little much at times, especially when imbibing."

"You've been more than gracious," Blake said, slightly slurring his words. "I think I better be going, don't want to wear out my welcome."

"Don't be silly!" Underhill exclaimed. "You can't leave without seeing the door."

"Really, it isn't necessary," Blake answered. "I believe you."

Underhill's smile narrowed. "You might as well see it now that you're here. Humor me."

"Sure," Blake said, "if that's what you want."

"Yes, you really should since you're here. Perhaps you'll have some idea what's causing it."

Rising unsteadily, Blake said, "Lead the way."

◆ ◆ ◆

The basement was dimly lit by a single 100-watt bulb, hanging from the ceiling. This surprised Blake, given the outlay for the rest of the house. Underhill, as if sensing his thoughts, said, "There's quite a bit that still needs doing down here. Funds were tight and it wasn't a priority. I wouldn't trust storing my books here at any rate. This is more of a place to store unimportant junk. The basement was part of the original structure that stood here. It was destroyed by fire and I got a good deal on the property."

"Way to go Vincent!" Blake replied. "And thanks for suggesting I bring my jacket. It is rather damp and chilly down here."

"Yes, it gets into the bones," Underhill said, smiling. "Well, are you ready for the great unveiling?"

Blake lit a cigarette and smiled. "Whenever you are. It's near the corner on the north wall, correct?"

"That's right. Keep the flashlight handy . . . I don't want you breaking your neck in the dark."

"Will do," Blake replied. "Ready when you are."

Underhill placed his hand on the light switch and said, "Here goes."

The room was plunged into darkness and a brief time elapsed before Blake's eyes adjusted.

"Do you see it?" Underhill asked.

"I'll be damned," Blake whispered in amazement. "It does look like a door."

"I told you!" Underhill exclaimed, vindicated.

Blake walked forward, cautiously making his way to the glowing outline. Standing in front of it, he said, "You didn't paint these lines on here did you?"

"No, I swear it!" Underhill protested.

"Then this is a hell of a mystery." Placing his palms on the face of the phantom door, he said, "Do you have a hammer down here?"

"I think so," Underhill replied. "Why?"

"Bring it here and I'll show you."

"Shield your eyes," Underhill warned. "I'm switching on the light." Turning it on, he walked to a cabinet and produced a hammer. Handing the instrument to Blake, he asked: "What are you thinking?""How badly do you want to get to the bottom of this?"

Underhill's brow furrowed. "I *would* like to know what's causing it."

"If you're willing," Blake said, "we could knock out this section of sheetrock and see what's behind it."

Underhill thought for a moment, nodded and said, "Yes, let's do that. Sheetrock isn't expensive, so no great loss."

After receiving his host's permission, Blake took the hammer and went to work on the wall.

◆ ◆ ◆

Blake wiped the clammy perspiration from his forehead and gulped a swallow of beer. "Thanks Vincent, that worked up a thirst."

"You've earned it fellow," Underhill replied. "Look at that thing."

Smiling, Blake turned to the fungus-covered iron door. "Well, this probably explains the glowing outline. This crap apparently seeped into the wall in sufficient quantity to account for it. Any idea where this door leads?"

"Not a clue," Underhill answered. "Perhaps it was a secret escape route for smugglers or religious heretics of the Puritan era. This house has been renovated many times. The door was probably covered during past work." He shook his head, exhibiting astonishment at the find. In a conspiratorial tone, he asked, "Want to see what's behind it?"

"Hell yeah," Blake replied. "Wonder if it's locked."

"Try it and see," Underhill suggested. "Let me get you a towel to keep that unwholesome looking fungus from your hand."

"Good idea."

Blake finished the beer and grinned. *This is turning out to be a hell of an evening. Not at all what I expected.*

"Here you are," said Underhill, handing an old towel to Blake.

"Thanks."

Covering his palm with the stained cloth, Blake tried the door. It didn't budge. He tried again, cursing at his lack of success.

"Would a crowbar help?" Underhill asked.

"It might do the trick."

Underhill left briefly, returning with the tool after a couple of moments. Handing it to Blake, he said, "I knew there was one around here somewhere."

Blake took the crowbar and looked at his watch. "It's getting late. Are you sure you're up for this?"

"I'm game if you are."

"Then let's do it!" Blake said, hammering the tool into the area between door and frame. Straining mightily at the door, sweat ran down his face and muscles corded with his exertions. Cursing, he stopped once but immediately reapplied himself to the task.

Underhill watched with interest as the door groaned, signaling its inevitable capitulation. He watched Blake pause, take a deep breath, and give his all to the effort. With a titan groan, the door opened and both men cried out in triumph.

"Great work!" Underhill exclaimed. "I would never have managed it."

Breathing heavily, Blake could feel his heart pounding. "I'm lucky I didn't burst a vessel. Damn, I'm out of shape."

The two men shifted their focus to the open doorway, staring at what lay beyond it. "Jesus, would you look at that," Blake whispered. "Steps leading downward . . . and the walls are covered with glowing mold, fungus, or whatever the hell it is."

Underhill nodded. "Those stone steps seem free of it though. I wonder where this leads?"

"Care to do a little exploring?" Blake asked. "We could take the flashlight and go down for a short distance."

Frowning, Underhill said, "Do you think it's safe?"

"Probably not," said Blake, laughing. "But it hasn't fallen after all these years, and I'm willing to take the chance."

Underhill looked doubtful for a moment but finally assented to the reckless venture. "Okay, but hang on to that crowbar."

"What's the matter, Vincent? Afraid of running into smugglers?"

Underhill smiled. "I couldn't say what might be down there."

"Would you prefer that I lead the way?" Blake asked.

"Be my guest," said Underhill.

"Okay. You hang onto the flashlight and I'll keep the crow-bar." Turning to the doorway, Blake said, "Here goes," and stepped into the mysterious tunnel.

The going was relatively easy as they trod cautiously down the stone-topped steps. They had gone only twenty yards in the eerily lit passage when the steps ended and the path became more level. It remained that way for thirty yards and then veered to the north.

Blake looked past Underhill to where the basement door was still visible. If they continued, they would lose sight of the entrance. "What do you think?" Blake asked. "Do you want to chance going further?"

Mopping his head with a handkerchief, Underhill took a deep breath. "You're not the only one out of shape. I guess we could go a little further but I'd advise stopping if we come to any forks or passages leading off from the main path. Lord knows I don't fancy getting lost down here."

"Agreed," said Blake. After walking another fifty yards, he asked, "Where do you think this leads?"

"I don't know," Underhill answered. "Considering the distance and direction, I'd say we're somewhere beneath the cemetery."

"That's a cheery thought."

Taking the crowbar, Blake scraped a small area of mold from the wall. "This stuff really glows. Someone should market it."

"If it isn't poisonous," Underhill replied.

"I hope not, considering how much of it we're breathing."

"Well, we seem to be okay."

The men walked further in silence, growing increasingly uncomfortable in the claustrophobic environment. Blake had almost decided to call it a night when he noticed something ahead of them. Something moving.

"What's wrong?" Underhill asked, sensing Blake's tenseness.

"I see something," Blake whispered. "Dark shapes coming this direction."

Both men peered intently into the distance, their visual acuity lessened by the strange ambient light. The unidentified shadows floated and fluttered silently toward them, erratic in their flight. Blake gripped the crowbar tightly, trying to decide what course of action to take. "They're flying, whatever they are."

"Maybe they're bats," Underhill suggested, gripping Blake's shoulder. "I think we should get the hell out of here."

"I hear you, Vincent," Blake replied. "Let's go!"

The dark fluttering shapes increased their speed and were upon the two men before they got very far. The air was thick with the creatures that—to the men's horror—were not bats. They appeared moth-like but were as large as paper fans. Reeking of the sickly-sweet stench of rotting flesh, their wings filled the close confines of the passage with a fine powder that was both nauseating and disorienting.

Blake heard Underhill yelp as the things swarmed them. Swinging the crowbar at them, his heart quickened with fear as he felt himself being overcome by the thick, powdery haze. His vision blurred and his ears ached with an excruciating buzzing. Staggering blindly, he continued to swing the crowbar, yelling "Run Vincent! Get away!" No longer seeing Underhill through the storm of wings, he soon collapsed as the noxious powder overcame him.

◆ ◆ ◆

Blake awoke with a splitting headache and a foul taste in his mouth. Disoriented, he blinked his eyes, knowing immediately that something was wrong. *It's dark. I'm no longer in the tunnel.* "Vincent?" he whispered. "Are you here?" No answer.

Hearing the gurgle of running water, he surveyed his surroundings, relieved to discover that he wasn't in total darkness. Grotesque toadstools larger than a man emitted a violet glow, reminding him of black-lights—a faddish craze from years earlier. From these unnatural plants dripped a viscous red substance that pooled in small stone basins before overflowing into a nearby stream that ran parallel to the stone path on which he found himself. *Where in the hell am I?* He felt around beside him, elated to find the flashlight. Switching it on, he was relieved to find that it still worked. Aiming the beam in various directions, his relief diminished at his failure to find any sign of the tunnel where he had last been with Underhill. He pointed the light upward as well but it failed to reach the ceiling. *How far below ground am I? I've obviously been brought here . . . but how?*

Rising to his feet, Blake shone the light on the nearest toadstool-like form and shuddered. He was fairly well educated but had never heard of such things. Wishing for possession of the crowbar, he sighed, deciding to follow the rock-strewn path beside the stream. He had no desire to venture into the fungoid forest through which the water flowed. *God I hope this is some terrible, alcohol-fueled nightmare. I don't have a clue where I am but surely I can't have been brought very far.*

He walked warily down the dimly illuminated path, wondering what had become of Underhill. In a semi-state of shock, he had great difficulty in accepting the turn of events. Along the way, he looked for something to use as a makeshift weapon but found nothing suitable. In a daze, he shuffled along the path, desperately hoping to see something that might reorient his sense of direction. He looked upward several times, vainly hoping to see light. *How long was I out? Is it morning yet? I can't tell shit with this busted watch and don't have any idea how long I was unconscious.* Seeing nothing but dark fluttering shapes above him, he quickly extinguished the light, not wanting to bring attention to himself. He continued to walk, growing more afraid with each passing minute. Wiping his forehead, he grimaced at the lingering stench from his encounter with what he had come to think of as corpse-moths.

After further walking he stopped to catch his breath, wishing desperately for a drink of water. Knowing it was the last thing he needed, Blake fished a cigarette from his shirt pocket and started to light-up. Startled by a loud splash, he dropped the cigarette, his frayed nerves betraying him. A second splash was followed by a loud, wet splat and Blake stared in revulsion at the pale, flopping creature that had landed on the path in front of him. Possessing fins, it was snake-like in most other aspects. The thick, yard long thing was devoid of color except for its ochre-colored eyes that glared inhumanly at Blake before slithering back into the red-stained water of the stream.

Hurrying onward, he made a point of keeping greater distance between himself and the rocky bank of the stream. Peering to his left, he became aware of a thinning in the toadstool forest. During one brief rest interval, he heard a loud sucking sound and warily aimed his light in the direction from which it came. The light revealed another of the loathsome, ichor-dripping toadstools. A jagged gash ran across its cap and nasty-looking creatures—about the size of footballs—feasted greedily upon its glistening pulpy flesh. Blake stared in horror at the creatures, seeing that they appeared to be some hellish amalgamation of tick and crab. Running hurriedly ahead, he wondered if he had gone completely mad. *Such things can't exist . . . they're just hallucinations . . . something happened back in the tunnel . . . a blow to the head must be the cause of this.*

Near the point of collapse, he stopped, his side cramping and his breathing coming in gasps. Running his hands through his hair, he felt no tell-tale lump to indicate a blow to the head. Underhill and his damned door! *God, I wish I knew what to do. These freakish toadstools are less plentiful in this area and it's almost impossible to see now without the flashlight. I wonder how long I can depend on it to last?* Blake surveyed the area ahead, seeing a large boulder sitting a comfortably safe distance from the stream. He decided to rest against it for a while, dreading the thought of what might lie beyond it in the inky darkness. Walking toward it, he nearly stumbled over a large branch of petrified wood. He picked it up and smiled. *It was the size of a baseball bat and would serve as a weapon if needed. What I really need is water but I'm not drinking from that particular stream except as a last resort.*

Blake sat against the clammy boulder and turned off the light. Resting his makeshift weapon across his lap, he leaned his head back, closing his eyes. He wanted only to return above ground and go home, never speaking of his unplanned adventure. Smiling, he knew no one would believe him anyway. Before realizing what was happening, he fell into a dreamless sleep.

◆ ◆ ◆

Blake awoke with a start, completely disoriented and emotionally devastated once the reality of his surroundings dawned on him. *I don't guess it was a dream. I'm still here. Can't believe I actually fell asleep in this place.* He sensed a presence, the hairs on the back of his neck rising. Listening, he heard what sounded like furtive footsteps. Not knowing from which direction they came, he remained still, afraid to move and give away his presence to anything not already aware of it. Clutching the length of stone in his hands, he rose slowly to his feet, exercising as much stealth as possible. He crept slowly around the boulder, hoping to see and remain unseen. *Damn, there's not enough light!* Remaining motionless, he peered into the darkness, silently cursing in frustration. *Maybe it was only my imagination. I'm understandably overwrought . . . or insane.* Returning to his original resting spot, he switched on the flashlight and stared into the face of horror.

A mold-caked, crouching figure with eyes of crimson glared at him. The vaguely humanoid creature cocked its pointed ears and smiled inhumanly—if a flat-snouted, canine-faced thing could do such a thing—and scraped its bony, scale-covered claws on the damp ground. Blake stepped back, gripping the flashlight like a talisman, almost forgetting the weapon clutched in his other hand. *God help me! The horrors upon horrors in this place are more than I can bear.* Thick saliva dripped from the yellow fangs of the dog-faced creature, briefly distracted by the hundreds of black mites, writhing in its furry forearms.

Continuing his slow retreat, Blake stopped when the hellish creature growled threateningly at him. The monstrous figure unexpectedly raised its snout and howled. The sound echoed through the massive cavern—if such it was—and was returned in kind. Blake shuddered at the doom-laden sound and turned to flee. He had traveled no more than ten yards when he slipped, falling to his knees. Yelling in pain, he staggered to his feet, glancing behind him and seeing the slowly approaching creature. *I'll never outrun that thing. My only hope is to kill it. Yeah, the chances of that look swell.*

In the shadowy gloom, he hefted the length of petrified wood, drawing it back threateningly. "You want some of me, you son of a bitch?" he asked. "Well come and get it!"

The creature leered, seeming to grin, and shuffled forward. Blake noticed that the thing had hoofs instead of feet and grimaced at the stench of corruption that wafted toward him. "What's the matter, you foul-smelling bastard? Waiting for help?"

As if sensing Blake's taunt, the creature growled and rushed forward. Blake met the thing's arrival with a tremendous blow from his stone club. It connected solidly against the monster's shoulder, sending the thing sprawling onto the rocky ground. "Yes!" Blake shouted, hoping he had hurt the creature enough to deter another attack.

Blake sighed, his hopes dashed as the malodorous thing regained its balance and prepared for another charge. *This nightmare refuses to end.* Again hefting the weapon, he braced for another attack. His exhaustion was taking a toll on him and he barely had the strength to defend himself. But what choice did he have?

His attacker scratched at the ground in front of him and growled. Rushing forward, it stopped suddenly as Blake swung his weapon. The thing's arm shot forward, grasping the petrified tree limb before it could connect. Blake screamed as the creature easily jerked the weapon from his grasp. Tears of frustration rolled down his face as the creature snapped the weapon in half and emitted a guttural noise that might have been a laugh. Blake turned and ran, knowing that his fate was sealed but unable to ignore the survival instinct possessed by even the lowliest of creatures.

The dog-like horror followed him in his flight, able to catch him at any moment but apparently satisfied to follow along behind at a threatening distance. Blake ran relentlessly, expecting to succumb to a heart attack before finding freedom. His breathing came in ragged gasps and his entire body ached from his ordeal. *Death would be a blessing at this point. All is lost.* Suddenly, in the distance, Blake spotted a flickering orange glow, a fire of some kind. Throwing caution to the wind, he left the stone path and loped toward the light, feeling that nothing in the surrounding darkness could be more threatening than what followed on his heels. Glancing over his shoulder, he saw the dark shape of his pursuer and tried instead to focus on reaching the light in the distance. Stumbling over a rock, he barely managed to remain on his feet. He was getting closer to his goal though he had no idea what reaching it might accomplish. After what seemed an eternity, Blake was within a hundred yards of the light and realized it was indeed a large fire.

Near collapse, he stumbled forward, amazed to see Underhill standing calmly in the light of the dancing flames. "Underhill!" he screamed. "Help me, some *thing* is after me."

Underhill smiled, stepping forward to catch Blake as he started to fall. "Hurry," Blake gasped, "the thing is almost upon us!"

"It's okay, Blake," Underhill replied. "It's not going to hurt you."

"No . . . you don't understand . . . it's a monster . . . it'll kill us both . . . you must stop it."

"Please man, get a grip on yourself!"

Blake pushed Underhill away, noticing the other figure for the first time. Before him stood a large being, similar to the dog-like creature but possessing slightly more human attributes. It smiled at him from the shadows. The grotesque travesty rested on a large throne-like chair that was assembled from human bones. Underhill turned to the figure and said, "See Richard, I told you I would bring a fresh one."

Blake blanched as the truth dawned on him. "Good God man, you mean you know this thing?"

"Certainly," Underhill replied. "He's an old and distant relative . . . reasonably famous at one time. Actually, infamous would perhaps best describe him."

"What is he?" Blake asked.

"Have you ever heard of ghouls?" Underhill asked.

"But they only exist in stories!" Blake protested.

"Come now, Blake. Surely you don't doubt that which is in front of you."

Blake sighed and asked, "Where are we?"

"We're beneath Arkham," Underhill answered. "Not that far from the cemetery, only much deeper."

"Ghouls, don't they . . . ?"

"Yes they do," Underhill said. "Only sometimes the pickings are lean and other measures must be taken. The ghouls, like the unusually large toadstools you've come across down here, thrive in darkness. Their numbers are ever growing and soon they won't be content to eke out an existence beneath the surface."

As if on cue, many more of the ghouls stepped forward from the shadows. Most carried bits and pieces of swollen and blackened corpses. Blake's stomach heaved as the stench of dead flesh wafted through the air. "No . . . it isn't true . . . ."

"Oh but it is," Underhill said. "Remember that bus crash last week—the one carrying the folks from the Retirement Center? Well, this is all that remained. It hardly seems worth the trouble. Don't you agree?"

Blake's mind teetered on the abyss of madness. Remaining silent, he swayed unsteadily, his eyes darting wildly from Underhill to the corpse-carrying ghouls. He remained this way for some time until the terrible creatures surrounded him. At the end, his screams mingled with the hellish baying of the ghouls, echoing through the subterranean hell beneath Arkham.

END

What Sorrows May Come

by Lee Clark Zumpe

1.

YODER. Annie Mae, daughter of Noah and Lydia Cripe, born near Smithville, North Carolina, Nov. 16, 1894; died at St. Mary's Teaching Hospital Nov. 1, 1934, of acute Bright's disease; aged 39. United in marriage to Amos Yoder June 17, 1917, in Arkham. Two sons and one daughter were born to this union. One son (Orvel Clinton) passed away Sept. 29, 1929. Formerly a member of Old Order Mennonite Church where she faithfully and willingly lived out its teaching. In Arkham, she attended the First Unitarian Church with her family. She leaves her deeply bereaved husband and two children (Simon and Mattie), and her parents. Funeral services Aug. 28 at First Unitarian. Burial in Chirstchurch Cemetery.

Amos held the paper in his trembling hands. He had read the clipping a hundred times through tear-stained eyes—so many times the words echoed in his mind like a prayer committed to memory. Some nights, he still could not believe she had been taken from him.

Carefully, he folded the obituary and slipped it back between the pages of the Bible he kept in the bottom drawer of his nightstand—her family Bible. Its dog-eared, yellowed pages betrayed its great age. With margins embellished by notations his wife penned over the years in her mesmerizing handwriting, Amos more often read her comments and observations than he did the gospel. Scattered throughout the pages, he had also inserted her occasional love notes—mostly her starry-eyed responses to the letters he had written her in his youth during their courtship.

One particular letter he read often. She had penned it mere weeks before her death:

> *We are one; our souls merged in a union whose harmony makes the universe rife with envy. Nothing will sever the bond between us—not separation, not heartache and not death. Still, our fleeting immortality in this transitory corporeal existence eventually must render one of us temporarily unaccompanied. Do not for a moment believe that solitude should override reason and grant you sanction to seek a premature end. No matter what sorrows may come, what tragedies may afflict us we must always prevail and not yield to the enticement of relinquishing our responsibilities. Though it may be obscured by grief, there is always purpose.*

◆ ◆ ◆

Amos lay back against the pillow, allowing his gaze to drift out an open window and up into the starry skies overlooking the town of Arkham. He felt utterly detached from the universe, as remote as some distant, shunned world adrift in the darkness orbiting an extinguished star.

Regrets occupied these lonely hours, plaguing his conscience and depriving him of sleep. Had he not lost his teaching job at the college, he might have been able to afford better medical care for Annie Mae. Had he not been too proud to ask for financial help from her family, he might have been able to take her to see doctors in Boston. Had he not been so insistent upon working odd jobs at all hours of the night and day, he might have been more attentive to her needs, might have recognized the illness in her sooner, might have been able to do something.

Had he been a better man in some way, done something differently, Annie Mae might still be at his side—not resting in the bleak embrace of the cold and bitter earth in Christchurch Cemetery. Six months after her death, grief and guilt still suffocated him.

A knock at the door separated him from another unhealthy, self-induced immersion in remorse. Amos, in his night clothes and slippers, shambled across the floor, a blanket draped over his shoulders to shield him from the slight chill of the Arkham night. He cracked the door and peered out into the corridor.

"Sorry to disturb you at such a late hour, Mr. Yoder." Dr. Moamar Shalad, chairman of Miskatonic's Department of Oriental Studies, stood in the shadowed hallway of the apartment building. "I should have realized you would have retired for the evening," he paused, anxiously scanning the hallway with darting eyes. "It's just—I was working late in the library, and I have some concerns."

"Concerns?"

"Corrections, I should say." Shalad worked long hours taking every advantage of his appointment at Miskatonic, burying himself in ancient tomes, scrutinizing texts to produce accurate translations, gleaning shards of forgotten knowledge from complex and esoteric medieval occult treatises. "Corrections to my manuscript. Very important corrections I must convey at your earliest convenience."

"It will have to wait until morning," Amos said, resting his head against the door. "I won't have access to the material until then."

"Yes, morning is good." Shalad spoke with a British accent, punctuated with Arabic inflections. Mild-mannered and somewhat reclusive, Shalad slowly backed away from the doorway, bowing in unnecessary gratitude. His eyes still swept the darkness surrounding him, his head jerking unnaturally to accommodate his restlessly drifting gaze. "I will see you in the morning. And please," he added, clasping his hands as if preparing to plead, "Please—no more editing until I can indicate the changes to be made, yes? Yes, all right. Thank you."

Amos nodded and closed the door.

Shalad often came across as eccentric and compulsive but Amos had learned to appreciate his neighbor's unconventional idiosyncrasies. He was, in fact, friendlier than any of the other tenants in the residence.

With Simon away at school, and Mattie living with her grandparents in Smithville, Amos decided to rent out the two-story house on East Church St. where he and Annie Mae had raised the children. He collected his most treasured belongings, condensed them into a few boxes and packed everything else into the attic for safekeeping. He took a vacancy at the Guardian Apartments, a three-room apartment with various amenities including an icebox and a gas stove.

The financial woes of the nation had begun to fade, and jobs had become more plentiful in Arkham. Amos found steady work in a job which fit his professional credentials. Before the depression forced the college to thin its faculty, he had taught undergraduate composition as an adjunct at Miskatonic. Still waiting for a new teaching position to open, Amos ran into Malcolm Bunden of Bunden's Bindery who immediately offered him a salaried position as senior proofreader and copy editor.

Shalad's upcoming thesis currently demanded his attentions. Bunden had warned Amos that Shalad would pester him incessantly, constantly seeking to revise his work, adding passages, deleting references, expanding some sections while eliminating others. He had developed an infamous reputation at the bindery—a nitpicker, a dithering scholar, a man obsessed with precision working in a field filled with ambiguities and uncertainties.

Amos settled back into bed, shrugging off the intrusion and eventually yielding to sleep.

In the hours prior to dawn, his dreams afforded him neither comfort nor sanctuary. He dreamed of Annie Mae, alone and barefooted beneath a slivered moon stained crimson red. She shuffled aimlessly across a weedy meadow peppered with shrunken, wasted flowers and grim, gray headstones.

He swayed beneath a sycamore towering over the center of the glade, arms stretching towards her in an inconsolable embrace. His attempts to call to her failed—no matter how he tried, he could find no voice.

As he watched helplessly, the ground beneath her liquefied. Slowly, the earth swallowed her.

2.

Residents of Arkham first noticed the Stranger in early November, after the leaves had passed the peak of their annual spectacle and had been collected in compost heaps on the manicured lawns of residents. Seen only in the final hour before nightfall, as the sun slipped from the colorless skies in its daily abandonment of the city to the absolutism of twilight and the apathetic moon, he materialized most often along the narrow streets of the French Hill district. His fascination with certain edifices—particularly the wretchedly neglected and boarded-up Bayfriar's Church and the ill-famed rooming house at 197 East Pickman Street—caused local denizens to abandon their custom of relaxing on front porches in the evening and discussing the days events.

"You have seen him then?" Dr. Cameron, Dean of the School of Physical Sciences spoke softly, cautiously. He sat across from Dr. Upham, chair of Miskatonic's Department of Mathematics and Dr. Shalad in a conference room in Locksley Hall. "The similarity is certainly striking."

"I knew him well," Upham said, nervously nibbling on a pencil. "Well enough to recognize him even now, years later. But in the state he is in, it is hard to say." The Stranger bore an uncanny resemblance to a former mathematics student from

Haverhill. Described by his mentors as a genius, the undergraduate had become so obsessed with the complexities of
quantum physics and non-Euclidian geometry that he lost all
perception of reality. His descent into madness and his subse-
quent disappearance still troubled his counselors at the college,
and his fate remained something of a mystery. "This Stranger—
if it is him—why would he not approach us? Why has he
returned?"

"Llanfer swears he's been in the library after hours."
Cameron sipped his tea gracefully, a model of New England eti-
quette. "Perhaps you've seen him there during your studies, Dr.
Shalad."

"No," Shalad answered quickly. Though always quiet, his
reticence at the table during the current conversation far sur-
passed his usual reluctance to engage in dialogue. "I've not seen
him."

"Surely, you've heard others mention him," Upham said,
raising an eyebrow. "The Stranger—that's what the locals call
him—has been turning up all over Arkham."

Shalad shook his head and frowned. He stared at his hands,
hoping the others would not recognize the indignity in his eyes.

"It is his awful appearance that has people gossiping."
Cameron slanted forward over the table. "Short, dirty and
unkempt. Face unshaven and unclean, with wild eyes and an
angry scowl. Pale and emaciated. Clothes grubby, trousers tattered at the cuff, shirt untucked and soiled with sweat and
dirt." Cameron eased back into his chair, an uneasy smile blos-
soming on his face. "Hardly the student I remember. It must
be nothing more than coincidence."

"I hope you are right," Upham said.

"I hope you'll excuse me, gentlemen," Shalad said abruptly,
"I have forgotten an appointment this morning regarding my
manuscript." Shalad hastily gathered his belongings and left
the room without further explanation, leaving Cameron and
Upham staring after him with puzzled expressions.

3.

Shalad's manuscript had taken up residence in a corner of Amos Yoder's desk several weeks earlier. Like a mule-headed squatter, much of it loitered in the same untidy heap it had assumed upon its arrival, feigning indifference but secretly begging for attention. Amos loathed proofing translations—particularly those whose subject matter dated to times of antiquity. Still, he had found Shalad's work meticulous and accurate, and expected to find few errors to mark for correction.

"Sorry I am late," Shalad said, startling Amos as he approached his office unannounced. The proofreader's desk faced a drab, dull and windowless wall in a remote and quiet niche in bindery's basement. Aside from the desk and an uncomfortable chair, the only other piece of furniture the bindery could afford to offer Amos was a water-damaged, old bookcase which housed a variety of reference books. Shalad lingered in the doorway, unable to find a comfortable place to stand in the room. "It is almost noon—I was distracted by a student's inquiry during a morning class and . . . ."

"No need for apologies, Dr. Shalad." Amos patted Shalad's manuscript. "I've been busying myself with other projects, smaller in scope. I've only read about a quarter of your work."

"Oh, my," Shalad said, looking somewhat troubled, "That much already you have seen?"

"Roughly. And may I congratulate you on your attention to detail." Amos picked up a stack of typewritten pages he had already reviewed, leafing through them proudly. "No significant mistakes, no typographical errors—only a handful of my marks, mostly indicating spacing issues for the typesetters."

"Thank you, thank you," Shalad nodded courteously, but the concern lingered in his expression and in his voice. His eyes began darting around in their sockets again, his head twitched noticeably from side to side as if he expected to catch sight of something in his peripheral vision. "Have you," he said after an extended and unnerving pause, "Have you gotten to the section on 12th century necromantic philosophy?"

"No," Amos answered abruptly, hoping to relieve Shalad of his unspecified distress. "In fact, I think I left off just before your introduction to that portion of the text."

"That is exceptionally good news," Shalad cracked a nervous smile and scratched the dark whiskers of his beard. His apprehension shrank, but did not entirely evaporate as Amos had hoped. His persistent trepidation made Amos increasingly tense, as if his unexplained fear had become contagious. "I am afraid that upon reflection, I must make extensive revisions," he said repentantly, lowering his voice. In a whisper, he continued, "Mistakes were made. Most terrible mistakes."

"I doubt that," Amos said, though the solemnity with which Shalad had made his confession disconcerted him. "Your thoroughness is legendary. I'm sure whatever your oversights might be, they are more trivial than you believe."

"I only wish that were the case, dear friend." Shalad faltered, shivering as if touched by an icy hand. "My omissions are indeed dire, and have put at risk my career and my life alike." The professor began swaying from side to side, struggling to keep his balance and his consciousness. "I only hope I can make the necessary revisions before it is too late."

His cryptic revelation still floating in the cool air of the bindery basement, Shalad's apparent exhaustion and anxiety caught up with him in a moment of unguarded frailty. He suddenly slumped forward, eyes rolling back into his head as he collapsed in the doorway.

"Dr. Shalad? Moamar?" Amos caught the professor's wiry frame and lowered him to the floor carefully.

Amos started to call for help, to summon Malcolm Bunden whose own office was one floor up, its door always open. Something held his tongue—something instinctive prompted him to manage the situation single-handedly, without making a spectacle of it. Perhaps he did so out of empathy, appreciating

Shalad's private nature and recognizing the event as a potential source of social embarrassment for him. Then again, perhaps Shalad's own fear unconsciously motivated him not to call attention to the man's momentary debility.

Retrieving a bottle of smelling salts from his desk drawer, Amos roused Shalad from the fringes of oblivion.

"What," Shalad shuddered, his eyelids tentatively lifting. His face contorted with short-lived horror as though he faced a vision of his own death at the very moment of his awakening. Mumbling, he continued, rather cryptically, "This is not the time. We must consult in private."

"There's no one else here, Moamar." Amos knelt beside the professor, waiting for him to regain his composure and fix his shifting gaze. His assurance seemed of little impact, and he wondered for a moment if Shalad had been addressing him or some other imagined—or invisible—entity. Nonetheless, he repeated assertion and reminded his friend of his whereabouts. "We're in my office at the bindery. We're completely alone."

"Yes," Shalad said, "Yes, I remember." With his wits returning, Shalad's face grew flush with humiliation. "Mr. Yoder, forgive my infirmity. I have not been myself these last few weeks, suffering from spells and seizures." His admission dredged up memories of Annie Mae's last weeks. Before the malady claimed her, it plagued her with fainting spells and frightening convulsions. Amos had been forced to watch as her precious life withered, her vitality waned, her beauty and charm shriveled under the encumbrance of disease. "I should rest more, but there is much more work to be done."

"You can not accomplish your work if you are not fit," Amos said.

"Perhaps." Shalad awkwardly returned to his feet. "I will rest this afternoon. Would it be possible to delay our meeting until this evening?"

"I think it would be to your benefit."

"Agreed." Shalad eyed the manuscript on the desk. "I would like to take the section of my manuscript that is to be corrected."

"It is your manuscript," Amos said, smiling. He picked up the pages the professor had requested and handed them to him. "But I would hope you would spend more time relaxing than revising this afternoon."

"Your advice is well received, Mr. Yoder." Shalad carefully tucked the pages beneath his arm, holding them close against his chest. "This evening then, shortly after dinner?"

"Very well."

4.

The Stranger waited patiently inside the abandoned house of worship on East Church Street, the dimming light of day shining through gaps in the boards covering the windows. The place reeked of rats' nests and pigeon waste. The shadows swarmed with insects as the wind howled around the soot-tinged steeple creating a wailing whisper that filled the air with tangible melancholy.

Dr. Shalad gained access to Bayfriar's church through a forgotten doorway almost wholly concealed by thick vines.

"Have you brought it?"

"I have not," Shalad answered nervously. The Stranger realigned himself in the light revealing the pallid, lesion-covered flesh of his awful face and eyes half submerged in their sockets. "I will bring you the new translation tonight, after midnight." Shalad winced at the stench of death. Beneath the Stranger's tattered, rotting flesh, worms yet toiled devouring the remnants of his mortal coil. "You must wait here. Too many have seen you, you risk discovery."

"I have nothing left to risk," the Stranger said, scarcely concealing his aggravation. The madness and obsession he had wrestled with in life continued to plague him in death, and Shalad suspected he had wrought dark designs in his seclusion, planning to use his genius to assemble legions of hideous allies from unimagined worlds. "I will wait, because I can no longer summon the strength to do what must be done." He faltered a little, recoiling back into the shadows. His power waned, and Shalad could sense his growing infirmity. "Don't think I cannot carry out my threats against you, Shalad," he warned, authority returning to his voice. "You are responsible for this, and you will see to it that my reanimation is complete so that I may complete my work."

Shalad nodded in silent understanding. He vowed to finish the job before dawn stirred legend-haunted Arkham.

5.

Shalad failed to appear for some time after dinner. As the evening progressed, Amos visited his apartment several times. Each time he knocked on Shalad's door, he thought he heard sounds coming from inside, but the professor did not respond. He hoped Shalad had taken his recommendation and had spent the afternoon away from his studies.

Shortly after midnight, Amos felt safe in assuming Dr. Shalad had forgotten their appointment. He turned off all the lights in the apartment, cracked his bedroom window, sat on the edge of his bed, and reread Annie Mae's obituary—a ritual he carried out nightly.

On the nightstand, a straight razor waited quietly. It kept its thirst discreetly censored, stifling the urge to glimmer in the moonlight. It made no perceptible promises, offered no guarantees of being able to end suffering. Silence and persistence served as deadlier enticements to a man like Amos. For six months, he had let the blade remain at his bedside, collecting dust. He still needed the comfort of an accessible, dependable escape should his grief prove too much to bear.

On more than one occasion, the razor had found its way into his hands. Each time, he found some reason to put it aside again.

Amos managed a noble charade in public, always acting properly and politely around Malcolm Bunden and the bindery's clients; attending church services regularly; corresponding with his children and Annie Mae's relatives. He lived from day to day, surviving on the bare necessities, feigning interest in his work, his acquaintances, and his future.

In fact, his life had become hollow—a black void opened up at the heart of him the day he lost Annie Mae, and it grew larger each day. He rotted from the inside without the cold comfort of death. Without her, existence was meaningless. His children—both on the verge of adulthood—would be cared for by their grandparents and would, ultimately, be better off without the burden of having to watch a sad widower squander away his remaining years in misery and seclusion.

Amos felt his fingers caressing the razor, his warm touch contrasting with its icy proposition.

He placed the news clipping back into the Bible, set the Bible in the drawer and closed it.

He examined his wrist, the serpentine blue vein beneath the delicate veil of flesh. He considered that at his funeral, they would have to pull his sleeves low to conceal the scars—then realized his palms would be faced down, his arms folded over his stomach in a simulation of tranquility and dignity.

Death has no dignity, neither for the living nor the dead. Amos no longer knew whether to believe in paradise, purgatory or oblivion. Whatever waited on the other side of the barrier, it had to be better than the inane anguish of his inconsequential life.

He pressed the blade gently against his skin, depressing it until a tiny bead of blood appeared. Amos closed his eyes, taking the absence of pain as an omen.

Had the pounding at the door come a moment later, it would have been too late. Pulled back from the edge by fickle fate, Amos placed the razor back on the edge of the nightstand, tugged on the sleeve of his nightshirt and matted the smear of blood staining his wrist.

"My apologies again, Mr. Yoder," Shalad stood several paces from the door, enveloped in inky darkness. "I was kept from our meeting by circumstances beyond my control. My concern for your safety, however, necessitated this late visit." The professor leaned into the light spilling from the apartment. His eyes wide and teeming with angst, he clutched Amos' left arm and turned it upright, exposing the wound which continued to weep droplets of blood. "She told me to stop you," he said, "She told me to tell you that no matter what sorrows may come, what tragedies may afflict you; you must always prevail and not yield to the enticement of relinquishing your responsibilities."

Amos recognized the words immediately—though how they could have been uttered with such precision by Shalad he could not guess. As Amos wavered in disbelief, Shalad shot impatient glances down the corridor, unmistakably expecting to see someone—or something. After a few moments, he pushed Amos back into the apartment and followed, closing the door behind him.

"She told me you had come to this," Shalad said, grabbing Amos's arm.

"Annie Mae?" Amos followed Shalad's gaze down to his wrist. The telltale incision joined a dozen others that had not healed, each a reminder of how tenuous the barrier between life and death had become for Amos. "How?"

"Necromancy, of course." Shalad relinquished his grasp, and Amos' arm fell to his side. "The process is academic. It is the interpretation that challenges the novice and adept alike."

"You spoke with her?" Amos knew enough about the medieval divinatory practice Shalad and other Miskatonic scholars had examined in their writings, but he never knew them to admit to conducting such ceremonial rites. "You spoke with Annie Mae?"

"Yes, for some time this evening." Shalad's response came in a blunt tone that irritated Amos, filling him with both jealousy and distrust. "Well," he continued, "She spoke to me through myriad voices, entities which have helped me sort out certain discrepancies in my theories. Their guidance will allow me to revise my manuscript and rectify a situation my ignorance and zeal brought about."

"I don't understand."

"Nor could you, Mr. Yoder." Shalad gripped Amos' shoulder, realizing his sudden revelations must have sounded like utter madness. "You would not believe me if I told you that, given the proper variables, I could sketch a doorway with charcoal or some other writing implement, and cause it to become real simply by its design." Shalad scanned Amos' eyes, searching for a glimmer. He hoped not for comprehension but for an inkling of faith. "If I suggested that I could pass through a mirror into another world, you would surely see me committed to an asylum. And yet, the phenomenon is real, possessing a complex but rational scientific explanation.

"There are passages all around us, some occurring naturally, some created long ago and long ago abandoned. These conduits, used properly, can be used to communicate with entities that have passed beyond the mortal sphere and into other dimensions." He recalled with pride his first successful experiment, piercing the barrier separating dimensions. "At first, I thought I was speaking directly with the deceased. I made contact with relatives and friends, asked questions only they could answer. But I found they also answered questions they could not answer—possessed knowledge they should not possess. It was as if I was conversing with an amalgamation of higher beings, some part of which formerly comprised individuals I knew."

"And that is why you must revise your manuscript?"

"If only that proved to be my gravest mistake." Shalad shuddered, recalling the terrible Stranger awaiting him in Bayfriar's

Church. "My initial attempts led to an unfortunate consequence and unanticipated discovery—the channels by which communication is made possible may also be used to redistribute the energy of a life force. I unintentionally allowed such an essence to travel back to this world, to reanimate its former shell—and tonight, I must destroy it, once and for all."

6.

Against Dr. Moamar Shalad's implicit instructions, Amos Yoder felt compelled to forsake the moderate safety of his residence at the Guardian Apartments, cross the Miskatonic and take to the narrow, shadowed avenues of French Hill beneath the gloaming. Arkham had a reputation for being two different cities occupying the same patch of land in the valley. By day, Arkham exhibited a distinctly patrician air, denoting its proud scholarly institution and the principled decorum and respectability of its denizens. The moon displaced the dignified face of the city, kindling its cryptic secrets, highlighting its most disreputable neighborhoods, and dredging up its most notorious scandals and the many disgraces tarnishing its history.

Bayfriar's Church towered over the surrounding neighborhoods, maligned with neglect and haunted by some whispered wickedness of old. A shrine to all things secreted in Arkham, its boarded windows and padlocked doors fell far short of hiding its shame—particularly when the knowing twilight assessed its merits.

Amos found Shalad outside the old church, half-crouching in the weeds.

"He's taken it—he's taken the manuscript," Shalad said, coughing for air. "He had more strength than I thought."

"Who?" Amos helped Shalad to his feet.

"I will not speak his name—it might serve to increase his power." Shalad, in poor health and weakened further by exhaustion, struggled to stand. "He must not be allowed to complete the transference. He will become too dangerous."

"What can I do?"

"Go to the cemetery—follow him to Christchurch," Shalad said. Amos now noticed the blood and bruises covering his face. The Stranger had taken advantage of Shalad, convinced him of his frailty, lulling him into false confidence. "The portal remains open—go and call her, she will do what must be done."

Amos traced the winding path of Powder Mill Street, where decaying houses dating to the late 18th century leaned into the lane. Overcrowded and populated by the impoverished, the neighborhood boasted bloated shadows in blind alleys, malodorous filth in inadequate sewers, and the constant impression of ongoing veiled perversions in dingy, crumbling dwellings.

With every step, Amos felt as if the night air had been tinged with the passing of something awful, something menacing and incongruous—a degenerate pariah with appalling aspirations.

When he reached Christchurch Cemetery an eerie green glow drew him to its center, where the old sycamore stretched its weary arms as if it alone supported the starry canopy of the night sky. The Stranger, on his knees, worked frantically under the glow of some unearthly radiance—perhaps the glow of souls enslaved. With a twisted branch clenched by his flesh-ragged fist he scrawled unfamiliar symbols into the damp clay of the graveyard, representing forgotten formulae. His etchings resembled more a mathematician's chalkboard than a medieval wizard's mystic renderings.

Amos pressed himself against a nearby headstone, shielding himself from discovery amidst charnel shadows.

"All those secrets kept from me," the Stranger said, muttering to himself, "Now will be revealed."

The cemetery floor trembled with agitation and apprehension as if the dead writhed in their coffins. Amos felt it in his bones, the stirring of ancient things long banished, the barriers breaking down around him. Had he glanced overhead, he would have trembled as the stars, one by one, began to desert the sky. Instead, his gaze chanced downward, his eyes suddenly fixed to the inscription upon the stone sheltering him.

"Annie Mae," he said softly, as all the grief and sorrow in the world fell upon him.

Thunder immediately followed the flash of lightning as it struck the old sycamore, flooding the cemetery with blinding light. Flames sprouted from its uppermost limbs, dancing on the tips of wilting twigs and spreading from limb to limb. The fire ebbed promptly, though, as rain erupted from the cloudless sky.

The Stranger had been thrown to the ground and scrambled to complete his task. His labors proved futile as the downpour washed away all his efforts.

Amos watched from the distance, his chin resting on the headstone as tears sprang to his eyes. His anguish dissipated as he felt a gentle hand rest upon his shoulder.

"Whatever sorrows may come," Annie Mae said, whispering into his ear, "Be strong for me. There is always purpose. We will be reunited when the time comes."

Amos turned, hoping to see her face, hoping to look into her eyes one more time. He found nothing but empty air beside him. On the outskirts of the cemetery, he saw a shambling figure—Dr. Shalad had finally caught up with him.

Turning back toward the sycamore, Amos watched as a brightly lit entity appeared, towering over the weeping Stranger. The ground beneath them seemed to liquefy, and in an instant, the earth swallowed them both.

END

Arkham Pets

by James Ambuehl

The semi hauling up Massachusetts Highway 1 had to brake for the little boy in the dirty white sweatshirt with the bright black and yellow *Batman* emblem still visible in its center despite the caked on mud. The boy was evidently coming out of the swamps behind Billington's Woods. He watched idly as the kid crossed the road and ran toward the lone ramshackle house on the other side of the highway. The trucker was grateful for the diversion, since it detained him that much longer from his ultimate destination. Then, with a slight involuntary shudder, he stepped on the gas and accelerated again, heading north-east, toward Innsmouth. Ronny Akers was trying to sneak into the backdoor of the house, hiding something wrapped up in his sweatshirt, when Uncle Carl caught him and threatened to tan his hide but good.

"Boy, what you doin' home early from school? And what you got hid in yer sweatshirt?" Carl's angry voice boomed like thunder. "You got another one'a them freakin' THINGS?" He made a grab for the cloth-wrapped bundle, but Ronny tucked it into his stomach and blocked it with his back toward Carl, a move Ronny soon came to regret as Carl rained a fusillade of blows upon his back and shoulders. The force shook the bundle loose, and it fell to the floor. Something that looked like a frog but with a bunch of extra eyes and legs half-hopped, half-scampered into his mother's laundry room to disappear behind the dryer.

"Damn! That's one ugly lookin' critter!" Carl Gillis gulped in amazement, his anger momentarily forgotten. But that didn't last long as he soon turned his fury upon the twelve-year-old, but at least the beatings had stopped. For now.

"Been in th' swamps 'hind Billington's Woods again, ain'cha?" the man said darkly, more a statement than an actual question. "Out by that tree you think is part human, I'll bet. Boy, I done tol' you to leave them dam' things in the swamp, where they belong." He was yelling now, his voice slurred somewhat by a series of early-afternoon beers. He glowered down at the boy, who in turn glowered at the floor.

"And yet you continue to bring 'em into the house! Damn it, boy! Look at me when I'm talkin' to ya! An' wipe them freakin' tears off your face, 'fore I wipe 'em off for ya! Now help me move that dryer so's we can catch it, an' kill it."

"No, Uncle Carl! Don't kill it . . ." A new batch of tears welled in the boy's eyes. "It's my friend!"

"Dammit, kid, I ain't your uncle! I'm just your Ma's boyfriend, no matter what she tells you to call me, y'hear? It's just 'Carl.' Nothing else . . . 'Carl from Ballard & Sons Auto'. Even if those SOB's did lay me off." His voice trailed off, and he looked a bit bleary-eyed. He ran a hand through his shaggy brown hair. It stood on end where he touched it. Then he shook his head, as if to clear it. "Now go get me that Louisville Slugger I keep on the front porch. Now!"

Swallowing back a threatened new river of tears, Ronny went to do as he was bid. He considered telling Uncle Carl . . . no, 'Just Carl' that the bat had been stolen, but he knew he would find it wherever it was hid and his anger would explode once more, but even worse than before. So he prayed instead, hoping his little friend would have escaped through a rat hole or something by now, before Carl had a chance to harm it. And he must have prayed to the right gods, for when he returned, that's exactly what had happened.

Carl stood dumbly, looking at the freshly-gnawed rathole, then looked over at Ronny. "Uh, how come you ain't in school anyways?"

"Miz Whateley got sick—started sayin' weird words an' began barfin' up black goop. It was gross, but kinda cool! Anyways, there was no one else to teach the class." He saw the doubtful look in the man's eyes as he slowly backed away, hands splayed, saying: "It's true! God's truth!"

The man glowered again for a minute, but then he seemed to calm down, letting out a sigh. "Okay, kid. Your ma will be home soon to fix supper, so go on and clean your room or something, all right? I don't wanna see or hear you for a while. I mean it. But I don't want to catch you in that swamp again, mister, ya hear me?"

Ronny swallowed thickly, nodding. When Carl began to stride toward the living room to turn on the TV, the boy made his way swiftly up the stairs to his room.

Once inside his sanctuary, Ronny dug deep in his pockets until his hand closed on something *squelchy* and he extracted a slimy green thing that looked like a stick of broccoli but moved of its own accord. A multitude of eyes winked upon the entire expanse of the thing. He deposited it upon the top of his work desk, but the thing seemed to enjoy the proximity of his hand, and so he played with it a bit more, and it began to emit a soft *bwee-heet, bwee-heet* sound. He quickly scooped it up and shut it away in the top drawer, with the socks and underwear, and stood stock-still for a moment. Satisfied the TV was loud enough, he removed the tiny thing from its prison and placed it upon the desktop once more. Going over to his closet, he dug under a huge pile of dirty clothes until he found a mason jar. Unscrewing the lid, he poured a spiderish thing with a multitude of fan-shaped wings out next to the green broccoli-thing, and watched the two entities at eldritch play.

Watching them, he lost all track of time. The sound of his mother's step outside the door startled him. "Ronny," she called. "Time for supper." He dumped the pets gently into the drawer and slid it closed again. Then he clumped down stairs.

After supper, he rushed to resume his play. His little friends seemed happy at his return., Each sang to him. *Bwee-heet, bwee-heet* from the green one, and a soft *shhirr-thirrfft* from the winged spider-thing. The sounds were so soft and pleasing that Ronny was soon fast asleep, his head down solidly upon the desk near the critters.

He awoke to a short, sharp shock, and a jarring thud, as the bat slammed down upon the desk, just narrowly missing his head. But it didn't miss it's target, sad to say, for it crashed firmly upon the green broccoli-thing, smashing it flat with a squelch. The spider-thing whirred its wings and flew at the bat's wielder angrily, sending Carl toppling over backward with a crash. The thing landed on the side of his head and began digging its way into his skull, when shaking fingers snaked up to Ronny's desktop to seize upon the scissors in the pen-cup. They flew at the thing, snipping it neatly in two.

Carl Gillis stood, gasping, clutching the side of his bleeding head. "Boy . . . Ronny . . . augh . . . h-hek." He hawked a bloody wad of phlegm upon the desktop. "I . . . I thought . . . I told you about . . . play . . . playing with those damned swamp critters. I warned you, boy.

"Oh God, Susie!" he called down. "I'm bleedin' here! Call 9-1-1."

Strangely emboldened now, Ronny stood tall at last, and looked Carl Gillis in the eye. "I wasn't playing, Uncle Carl. I was working. Something you should try, fatass."

But Carl was too stunned to smack him now. "Working?" he spluttered. "For who?"

"I was working for them . . . taking care of their babies," he said proudly.

"Who . . .?" stammered Carl.

"The Old Ones," Ronnie said simply. "The Old Ones who live in the swamp. The Old Ones, whose babies you killed." He gave Carl a dark look. "They're angry with you for killing their babies." The boy smiled viciously. "And they're going to tan your hide but good."

And as the formerly still night air became drowned by the massive sound of squelching from the swamp behind the house, and the thunderous tread of many-legged feet, Carl knew in the last moments of his life that this was indeed true.

END

Small Ghost

by Michael Minnis

An old black Dodge Model DD made its slow way down Parsonage Street. The car's driver, E. Franklin Bierce, city health inspection officer, was searching for an address—625 Parsonage Street.

He had driven through Arkham's old Polish district twice now, hunting for the address, and was growing uncomfortable and impatient. The neighborhood he was in—French Hill—had never been particularly well favored. There was little in the way of money or prosperity. Streets were narrow, often no more than crazily winding alleys: maddening exercises in the arbitrary. The houses—and there were many, clustered close—he disliked even more. It was an architectural jumble of soot-stained 19th century brownstones and rotting Colonial monstrosities from an even earlier time.

He disliked the old buildings. The steep moss-crusted roofs; the smudged bulls-eye windows; the jungle-tangle of blackened chimney pots and cornices and ancient iron weather vanes—all of it, rotted, disagreeable. Why, one could almost see the crumbling piles exhaling moldy vapors of decay! Shameful! Historical preservation was one thing . . . but whole-sale stagnation, well, that was quite another matter.

Even the churches had seen better days. Bierce noted with sour irony that second-hand salvation stood on every corner: St. Michael's; the First Baptist Church of Arkham; St. Stanislaus on Walnut Street; deserted and most ominous of all, Bayfriar's Church, atop French Hill. Old Bayfriar's, with its boarded windows and its wheeling flocks of black croaking birds.

Damned thing should have been torn down years ago, he thought to himself. He decided to park the Dodge on Parsonage and search for 625 on foot.

It was late April, cool and rain-drenched, with the promise of still more rain to come. Green buds were just beginning to appear on black tree limbs. Clouds were moving swiftly through the sky. Fedora on head, trench coat buttoned closely, briefcase in one hand and umbrella in the other, Bierce looked and felt out of his element. Not that he was afraid—he was, after all, a tall man, wide through the shoulders. A full beard framed a face intelligent and knowing, bespectacled and very stern. He walked quickly. He did not dawdle and took little note of the few residents and passersby. They were, after all, Poles and Irish. He was a man of position, a Mason and government official, of old Arkham blood. They were immigrants. His day would end with a glass of scotch, a good cigar and The Wall Street Journal, theirs with sweat and shouts and the stink of boiled cabbage.

The Poles and Irish, however, did take note of him. A gnarled stump of an old woman sweeping her porch stoop watched curiously as he passed—likewise, a noisy knot of running children. Bierce ignored them.

On his right he passed an empty, barren lot, a conspicuous space among the crowded homes. Well, it wasn't completely empty. Last summer's weeds lay dead in the yard. There were a few bricks and stones left in the grass. Looking closely, one could just discern the foundations of the old Colonial structure the locals had dubbed a "witch-house", which had been leveled nearly fifteen years ago, following a March gale.

Well, he had found the place; this was the source of the complaints. In this case it was 'vermin', as defined by town zoning ordinances set up in 1915. Rats, if one was exacting, as was Bierce. It hardly surprised to him, given the general state of the neighborhood.

With a stick he prodded through the matted undergrowth and scattered debris. A brick kicked aside here, a rotting board overturned there, he searched for signs of rats. He glanced into the tiny backyards of other houses, the narrow alleys with their crates and barrels and corners and winding stairways. Nothing. He discovered a few droppings, an empty nest or two within several stacks of old newspaper, but little else.

Actually, Bierce wasn't looking for rats so much as a rat. Since January there had been reports and sightings of a particularly large brown sewer rat in the neighborhood, possibly of the Sumatran variety, usually in or near the empty lot.

By all accounts the rat was a thoroughly nasty, slippery fellow. He was never seen by day, though there was frequent evidence of his night-work: rifled garbage and tins licked clean, mice and smaller rats found dead and decapitated on doorsteps. Once he had badly bitten a dog and killed a cat—a former resident of 625 Parsonage.

The rat was clever, too. He had a liking for cellars, attics, crawlspaces, and drainpipes. Though he was quite plump, he could squeeze through the smallest of holes. On more than one occasion he had squirmed his way up a watercloset, to the disgust and horror of onlookers.

What struck Bierce as odd was the fear surrounding this particular rat, the atavistic dread it invoked among the Poles and Irish of French Hill. That it was big and cunning, he could accept. Rats, after all, were reasonably smart animals, able to learn from experiment and experience. But that these immigrants should invest this animal, *Rattus rattus*, with real intelligence and supernatural qualities was Old World superstition at its worst.

Yet it was all there: the rat was said to scuttle across rooftops and scratch at windows and doors in the dead of night. Heaven help those who left either open. They would find the thing nuzzling them under their bed-sheets. Neither poison nor traps were of any use—he was too clever for that nonsense. He spoke, but very rarely—his voice was said to be a loathsome, half-strangled titter, made nearly incomprehensible by an antique accent. (Bierce thought this a marvelous detail: it wasn't enough that the rat spoke, but that his diction be that of a New England Yankee, too.)

Of course the rat possessed hand-like paws, a long naked tail and cruelly caricatured, vaguely human cast to his bearded face. Witch's familiar, devil's pet, yes, all the old familiar elements were here. It might as well have been Salem, 1692.

As if to reinforce this hypothesis, Bierce noted that windows facing the lot were shuttered and blinded. Some of the residents had even go to the trouble of nailing religious icons to their shutters. On three sides—crosses, wooden crucifixes, tiny Virgin Marys, medallions winking with muted light in the dim afternoon.

Witch-House . . . devil-rat . . . was there anything these people didn't believe? Honestly, what need did anyone have for ghosts and goblins in the wake of World War I and the Depression?

The little horror even had a few nicknames. Most popular of these was Brown Jenkin, though the Irish referred to him as Long Tail, Mad Jack, and sometimes Tommy Toothsome—a reference to his long teeth, Bierce was told.

His inspection having revealed little, Bierce went to the house next door—625 Parsonage. The wind was high in the trees, a thunderous rush of sound. A cloud of fat, speckled birds burst forth from a hedge, startling him.

625 Parsonage was an ancient Colonial structure, well over a hundred years old. Bierce noted the high narrow lattice windows, the steep roof of wormy gray-green shingles, the

encroaching moss and withered ivy. The door, of heavy oak
planks, showed signs of rot.

Why doesn't anyone take care of things anymore?

He checked a scrap of paper kept in his pocket. Elena
Bronski, 625 Parsonage, it read. Old Widow Bronski.

Inwardly, he sighed. He was hardly anxious to meet Widow
Bronski, an opinionated, stubborn, old East European battleaxe. She was what he considered the worst sort of Old World
immigrant—one with notions of aristocracy. Who really cared?
Polish knights, dukes of the Grand Duchy, generals and
colonels: dusty old icons of a bygone era. Fitting that she
should live in a house as antiquated as her ideas.

She was forever the gadfly, petitioning City Hall with letters in crabbed longhand, a joke among city officials. Over the
years there had been countless letters. Arkham did not need a
reservoir. Prohibition should never have been repealed. There
were potholes on Parsonage. Roosevelt's New Deal was
"acronymic Bolshevism". Well-bred women did not wear pants.
The Wojekos' compost heap drew vermin. *Weird Tales* and other
such penny dreadfuls corrupted young minds. Why had City
Hall ceased to answer her letters?

He knocked twice, and then once again.

A lock clicked, and the door opened slightly. A seamed,
worn face appeared in the crack, a face like fruit gone soft with
age. But the eyes were dark and alert behind thick gold-wired
spectacles, and the thin-lipped mouth was tight and set.

"Mrs. Bronski?" Bierce asked. "I'm Franklin Bierce, from
the city health department. The board sent me here to discuss
your complaints concerning rats sighted in the area."

Widow Bronski smoothed back her hair, which was tied in
a bun of almost painful severity. The woman's expression
clouded, but briefly, and she said, "Oh, yes. But it is a rat, not
rats, Mr. Bierce. Please come in."

She stepped aside, leaning on a cane.

Inside the house was somewhat better preserved, but small, with small rooms, close and confined, paneled in dark wood. Underfoot the floor was lumpy and warped. The curtains were drawn. Elaborate webs of white lace were draped over every horizontal surface, it seemed. Dried flowers and wax fruit and candles and tiny daguerreotypes of the Old Country had like-wise propagated in every corner. On a drop leaf table sat an old phonograph. Widow Bronski bid him sit in an overstuffed couch the shade of dark wine. She sat in an antique high-backed chair. The air was scented faintly of powder, perfume and mold rot.

He glanced at the clock on the far wall: twelve minutes after four. He would be late for dinner, more than likely.

She folded her hands and waited for Bierce to speak. He removed his hat but not his coat. There was somewhat of a chill in the old house, despite the glowing embers in the fireplace.

"Would you like some tea, Mr. Bierce? I brewed some before you arrived."

"Uh, yes. Tea would be nice, thank you."

Widow Bronski left him alone in the room. He noticed it then; all about him the old Colonial house made sly stealthy noises, creaks and tiny squeals and bumps. Black branches, swaying in the April wind tapped and scratched at a window. He thought them rather like skeletal fingers, and wondered why he would think such a thing.

The Widow returned with two steaming china cups on a small silver platter. The tea was good, strong. Only delicate sipping disturbed the momentary thoughtful silence. Then the old woman asked, "On your way here to my house, Mr. Bierce, did you happen to notice the empty lot next door? A place that the neighbors draw their shutters upon and hang crosses in their windows?"

"Yes. I passed it on my way over here. The empty lot you mentioned in your last complaint. Quite an eyesore, if you ask me. I'd keep my shades drawn too, if I lived next door."

She continued, ignoring his little joke. "You know what once stood there, yes?"

Bierce nodded, though he could hardly see how this related to the matter concerned. He decided he would humor her for the moment, and then get down to business.

"From what I've been told, an old Colonial house stood there for many years. It was a boarding house for a time, until a windstorm tore the roof off, fourteen, fifteen years ago. Shame. A waste of historical architecture, if you ask me."

Not very different from what we have here . . . .

"And?" Mrs. Bronski asked knowingly.

"And what? Oh . . . and according to some, it was a 'witch-house' of some sort. There were murders there, I'm not sure how many, and some nonsense about sacrifices around Halloween. I really don't know very much about it, but I personally believe most of its bull– . . . stuff."

He flushed momentarily at this near slip of the tongue.

"Mr. Bierce," the old woman said, "my husband, God rest his soul, was one of the men who helped tear down that 'witch-house' in 1931. He was a good man, like you in some ways. He did not believe in certain things because they upset his little world. He was not a religious man. He laughed at the thought of witches and devils, and told me again and again, 'Elena, this is not the Old Country! We left all that far behind. In America there is no use for such ridiculous things. Do you want people to say, 'there goes Elena, the stupid Pole who believes in spirits and spooks?'

"There was a murder at the Witch-House. A nice young man died there years ago. I do not remember his name. He was a student at the University. Not long afterward the house was condemned, and then came the gale that collapsed the roof. Workers were sent in to clear out the debris. They found terrible things. The bones of children, hidden behind a partition in the attic. A long knife. Worst of all, the skeleton of a large deformed rat."

"Brown Jenkin, right?" Bierce asked knowingly. He had little patience with ghosts stories and old legends. "Long Tail? Or is it Mad Jack? Certainly well known for a rodent, wouldn't you agree?"

"The skeleton," the Widow continued, "was profoundly misshapen. The skull and hands were like those of a man, though the teeth and claws were those of a rat. It caused a great stir among all gathered—the workers, the police, and the men from the University."

"And . . . ."

"That night the workers lit candles at St. Stanislaus. The police, I am sure, filled out their reports. The University men took the skeleton with them to study. No doubt it sits in a closet now, gathering dust. And my husband was never quite so sure of himself again. Would you like more tea?"

"Mrs. Bronski," Bierce said, "I don't mean to be rude . . . but what you've just said makes no sense. This Brown Jenkin you're talking about, according to you, has been dead for at least five, six years. And even if it did survive somehow, I don't believe most rats live that long in the wild."

"He's much older than that, Mr. Bierce. And he's not a rat."

Bierce sighed. "All right. Then what we have here is a rat that is not a rat, which is dead but not dead. What, is it a ghost, then?"

"I don't know."

"Mrs. Bronski . . . let's examine the facts. Here in Arkham, however long ago, an old woman goes to the gallows on suspicion of witchcraft. It was common enough then. All one had to do was point a finger and accuse a neighbor, should their crops die or their cow go lame. Guilty until proven innocent, so to speak. More than likely, the old woman had a pet for company—a cat, which in legend later became a rat, then a rat with distinctly man-like features. Why? It makes for a good

tale. Since it was her pet, her familiar, it shared the same fate—
the gallows, stoning, burned at the stake.

"And so the story is passed down, generation to generation.
Facts are forgotten, are distorted. The old woman was a witch.
The cat was a nasty little devil-rat. Gradually, though, the story
loses hold of its audience. The house stands empty for years,
decades. But! But, let something occur anywhere near it—a
suicide or a murder, for example—and all the awful old stories
spring forth again. 'It was the ghost of the old witch that mur-
dered that nice young man!' That sort of thing."

"Are you saying that I'm crazy?"

"Absolutely not. What I am saying is that imagination has
taken hold. Because this rat—and it is a rat—is relatively
clever and bears a passing resemblance to this 'Brown Jenkin,'
he suddenly becomes 'Brown Jenkin'. He refuses poisoned bait.
Not that unusual. Rats aren't stupid. Soon people claim to see
him undoing latches and opening windows. Before long, he's
on rooftops singing Gregorian chants to the moon.

"Do you see my point? It isn't a ghost. It isn't a witch's
familiar. It's a large, brown, common rat."

"I see," Widow Bronski replied stiffly. "Would you care for
more tea, Mr. Bierce?"

"Uh, yes. Yes I would."

She went to the kitchen, leaving Bierce with his thoughts.
He glanced again at the clock, again reflected upon dinner.
Widow Bronski returned with a steaming copper teapot,
poured more tea.

"Mrs. Bronski," he said, "I've examined the empty lot as
you requested, likewise the alleys and backyards nearby. I
found a rat nest or two in some shredded newspaper, nothing
else."

"That is because he drove off the other rats sometime ago.
He's not a social creature."

"Yes, well, there's no evidence of him, either. Am I to assume he's clever enough to hide traces of his whereabouts, too?"

"Assume what you wish, Mr. Bierce."

Annoyed, Bierce opened his briefcase. He made a business of sorting through papers, straightening them, poring over them.

"All right, let's get on with things. In your complaint, you claim he killed your pet cat . . . Pil-sud-ski? Am I pronouncing that correctly? Pilsudski."

For the first time the old woman's reserve began to break, slightly.

"What happened, exactly?"

Widow Bronski sighed and looked away, past Bierce.

"It was . . . March. A very cold, blustery, gray day, toward dusk, I believe. The sun was setting through the trees. I was in the kitchen. From outside, behind the house, came a horrible, screeching racket. I thought it was Pilsudski, fighting with the Woljekos' cat. But when I went outside with a broom, I . . . I saw that thing and Pilsudski rolling on the ground, snarling and fighting. I couldn't tell which was which . . . so I hit them both with the broom and yelled, "Stop! Stop it!" Finally, they broke apart. They were both panting. Gray and brown tufts of hair were everywhere. Then I remembered that the Woljekos' cat was black, not brown.

"It was Brown Jenkin. His face was scratched and bloodied, but I knew it was him. He has a nasty, sneering, bearded little face, like that of a very cruel man, and tiny clawed hands. He saw me and his lips pulled back in a horrible, trembling bloody grin, his sides heaving. Then he lunged at Pilsudski again, and Pilsudski snarled and swatted at him, but he broke away and ran down an alley. I tried to follow . . . but he was too fast and I am too old. And besides, it was getting dark, and he is strongest in the dark and lonely places."

"Hmmm," Bierce replied, stroking his beard. "Then what?"

Widow Bronski sighed again. With a delicate spoon she stirred her tea. She was close to crying, and Bierce dreaded that the tears might start at any moment. A gust struck the windows a blow that made them shudder and the wind screamed high and thin. The skeletal branches swayed, tapping, scratching at the lattice-window, and Bierce thought of claws. The clock uttered a single solemn brass note: four-thirty. Speckles of rain appeared on the leaden glass.

"Then what, Mrs. Bronski?"

"I brought Pilsudski inside. He was hurt, and tufts of his fur had been pulled out in several places, and a small chunk had been taken out of his ear, but otherwise he wasn't badly injured. I tried to clean his wounds, but he wouldn't let me touch them, he was that upset and angry. Eventually I did manage to take him to the veterinarian's, where he was given shots for rabies and distemper. He recovered and was doing well, for a time . . . and then he simply disappeared one day."

"When?"

The old woman sobbed and produced a handkerchief, dabbing at her eyes. "I don't know. Two weeks later, I suppose, it was still March. No, wait . . . I do remember the date. It was the 21st of March. The vernal equinox, if I am correct."

"And you think this 'Brown Jenkin' is somehow responsible for the disappearance of your cat?"

Widow Bronski fixed him with a bleary, red-eyed stare and stated flatly: "I know he is responsible, Mr. Bierce. He is very evil. I can't imagine what he's done with my Pilsudski . . . ."

"But how do you know that this rat, thing, whatever, took your cat away? What if Pilsudski ran away? Animals will flee things that disturb or frighten them, or when the competition in a given area becomes too fierce."

She appeared to take some comfort in this suggestion.

"Perhaps. I'd like to think that, I assure you. But I'm sure that little bastard had something to do with it."

Bierce flinched in surprise. To hear the old woman swear was hardly short of astonishing. An awkward silence fell, as did more rain, harder now, running down the windows in rivulets. The room became even more dim and dismal. In the fireplace, the embers winked, red and malevolent. Widow Bronski stared at them and muttered something Bierce did not quite catch.

"Excuse me?"

"The embers. They are like his eyes. I saw them once, gleaming from a tiny window in the garage attic, when I was outside calling for Pilsudski. God . . . they were evil little points of light. Cold and unblinking. They saw me and went out, like snuffed candles. I was so frightened, I went inside and locked all the doors and windows.

"He lives there now. I know. I hear him at night sometimes, moving about, scratching, rustling. God knows what he does up there. Sometimes there are comings and goings. Twice now there have been flashes of light, like lightning, and a smell, both burned and sweet, like ozone. I've found dead birds and mice in the garage itself, arranged in what I know are patterns.

"Once, I thought I heard him talking in his awful, halting, tiny voice; it made my skin crawl to hear it. But that is not all—there were pauses in his speech, and what sounded like an answering voice, as if he were talking to someone, or something. An old woman, I think."

"Mrs. Bronski, please. Rats don't talk."

"And I told you he is not a rat!"

The sharp, strident note in the old woman's voice irritated Bierce even further. Once again, he began straightening his paperwork, and put it back into his briefcase.

"Then what is it, exactly?"

"I don't know."

"So what would you like me to do, then?"

"Lay down traps? Poison? Holy water? I don't know. He is up to something terrible. But he must be stopped, somehow. He must be killed."

Bierce looked to the clock again for salvation. It was a quarter to five. Outside, the rain had abated somewhat. It was time to be done with this business. His colleagues had been right; old Mrs. Bronski had been getting progressively crazier since her husband Stanislaus passed away three years ago.

"Wait. Where are you going?" Mrs. Bronski asked.

"I'm sorry, Mrs. Bronski," Bierce replied, as he rose and began buttoning his coat. "But it's a quarter to five, and I have pressing matters back at my office. Paperwork, files, that sort of thing. What I'll do is recommend that an exterminator be sent here by the morrow to lay some traps and poison in your garage. That should take care of the problem.

"Afterward, I'd suggest you go through the garage attic and remove anything that rats could use as nesting material: stacks of old newspapers and magazines, fabric, boxes, mattresses, old clothes, get rid of it. Seal up any rat-holes you see; this discourages any 'new visitors', so to speak. And if you have any trouble in the future with rats–"

"But he is not–"

"Fine, then, Mrs. Bronski. Then I suggest you get a priest. But I really must leave, if you'll pardon me."

Widow Bronski opened her mouth to say something, but only nodded and sighed. She gave him his hat and he went to the door, reminded her again that an exterminator would be by, tomorrow. He promised. And he was sure her cat would return sooner or later.

"I would like to believe that, Mr. Bierce."

Outside, the rain had ceased. Heavy clouds scudded across the sky and every branch dripped wet and black. Bierce looked about him, at the terribly old houses with their tiny windows and steep roofs, at the dark trees and mossy stone walls and, for a moment, witches and little devil-rats seemed not entirely impossible. He dismissed the idea. Nonsense. Bullshit, as he had almost said in Widow Bronski's parlor. Had he been a less polite man, he would have suggested she visit the Arkham Sanitarium. The quirky old woman was descending into madness. But then, that was an immigrant for you. Provide them with electricity, modern transportation, and gas heating, and they still thought and behaved like medieval peasants, seeing the designs of angels and devils in everything.

Out of curiosity, he rounded the corner of her house. There, set discreetly back from the street, half-lost behind an enormously overgrown oak, was the mentioned garage. It was an ugly plywood thing, cheap and paint peeling, its outlines blurred by dead creepers. The door was open and inside sat a Model A Ford, which probably hadn't moved since the day Stanislaus Bronski died. The roof rose to a peak, and above the door was a small circular window, divided into four panes: the attic.

There was a flash of something—small, red eyes. They disappeared instantly and the window was dark again.

A chill rippled through Bierce, skating down his spine.

Brown Jenkin! He thought.

No . . . that was foolishness. It was a rat, that was all. It was no devil. It was no ghost. It was no witch's familiar back from the dead and full of vengeance. It was a rat, nothing more, and he would prove this once and for all to Widow Bronski.

Slowly, he walked toward the garage, never looking away from the attic window, which remained empty. The eyes did not reappear. There was no smell of ozone, or brimstone for that matter—just old wood and dust. Inside the garage, he set his briefcase down, and cast about for a weapon of some sort. The clutter of the garage was astonishing. Small wonder that the king of rats should make it his throne room! Cobwebs, jars and cans on shelves, stacks of old newspapers, discarded furniture. From a row of tools hanging on the far wall he selected a short, rusty spade. One good blow, he thought, and Mister Rat meets his maker.

Bierce gave the ceiling an experimental thump with the spade. There was scrabbling, and then silence. He smiled to himself.

A short flight of stairs led to the attic. They squealed thinly underfoot. Dusty, leaden light poured in through a round, webbed window. The ceiling leaked in several places and water dripped on the uneven floor. He strained his eyes to see into the gloom: old birdcage, cabinet, picture frames, brass lamp, the forgotten odds and ends of a household.

Grimacing at the stink of mothballs, he took a step forward and nearly crushed underfoot the body of a dead, decapitated sparrow.

Further ahead were several other dead birds, and dead mice. Two blue jays, two more sparrows, a grackle, a finch, and three field mice. Their bodies, Bierce noted with growing dread, were arranged in a circular orbit of sorts, so that each corpse occupied a staggered point, facing inward. Three birds lay on their backs, wings spread. Three lay like the mice, on their bellies. It was a pattern, intelligently arranged, yes. No wait, there was something wrong, even worse. Their eyes— they were bloody and ruined. They had been gouged out—or eaten—by something, or someone.

It's her, Bierce thought. Widow Bronski's doing this. My God, she's not just crazy—she's insane, she's psychotic, she's certifiable!

There were brownish marks in the dust, deliberately drawn, and linked ominously to the pattern of dead birds and mice. There was an orbit, and what appeared to be angles, and angles within angles, cubes and prisms . . . designs and symbols he could not guess at . . . and names, too, in a spidery script. He crouched to read it, nearly toppled, and so lay the spade aside. He read the names silently, lips moving:

VARDAR . . . GANZIR . . . IÄ . . . IÄ
. . . YOG-SOTHOTH . . .

The light seemed to be dimming. In the corners of the attic, where his eyes strained to see but could not, he thought he sensed movement.

BUGG-SHOGGOG . . . AZAZU . . . TAWIL AT'UMR . . .

There it was again, a sudden stealthy scrabbling movement, a shadow. In that moment, he understood—of course! Widow Bronski, far from being the rat's victim, was its keeper! This was her work, the patterns in the dust, the dead bodies, the substance disturbingly like blood. Hell, she probably even thought she was the legendary witch who had terrorized Arkham over two hundred years ago.

An empty can clattered and rolled, and Bierce jerked to his feet. There, on top of the dusty old cabinet, a sleek, low, hunched shape, crouched. It was the rat! And Christ, he was big. Its tail lashed about in a fit of ill temper, its whiskers twitched.

Slowly, ever so carefully, Bierce reached for the spade's handle. One blow, was all that was needed—one good, solid, blow to the skull. Fading light glinted upon the thing's eyes, and they briefly smoldered reddish-orange, fearful and pitiless. He thought he could hear it growling at him, a faint throaty intonation, but full of threat.

"Just stay right there . . . ."

The spade was missing.

Shock sent his heart to pounding like a trip-hammer. No, that couldn't be—he had set it beside him! He rose, and someone was there who had not been there before.

At first he was sure it was Widow Bronski, that she had followed him quietly up the garage attic. But Widow Bronski, while old, was not ancient, as was this gnarled, bent and haggard thing, whose grayish flesh hung upon her bones insubstantial as webbing. She did not wear shapeless rags and hood of moth-eaten brown. Nor was Widow Bronski's face so sardonically hateful, lined as old linen and knotted as the bole of a tree, long of nose, hideous as that of a bat. Her cataract-clouded eyes went wide, and she grinned, revealing blackened gums and teeth worn to yellow-brown nubs.

In her spidery hands she clutched the spade.

"Fancy a row with my Brown Jenkin, do ye, then?" she asked.

She swung the spade with strength belied by her shriveled size, and the flat side connected with Bierce's temple, knocking off his hat and his spectacles askew. Blood flew in a brilliant spray through the dusty air. Bierce fell to his knees, stunned, ears ringing. The blow seemed to explode inside his skull. He tried to crawl away. Dim, shadowy movements hounded his progress. The witch cackled, dark crumbling rotten laughter.

He nearly reached the stairs, but before him squatted the rat, Brown Jenkin. Mrs. Bronski had been right . . . he really wasn't a rat at all. Yes, he did walk on four feet, and yes, he did bear fur and a long pinkish tail, but there the similarities began to fade. His thinly bearded face was an imperfect and yet cruelly accurate mockery of a madman—one who might bay at the moon or eat corpses. The whiskers twitched, the eyes burned blackly. The paws, Bierce saw, were very much like small human hands, knotted by corruption and murder.

"Just a rat," Bierce muttered.

Brown Jenkin hissed, a sound like the sulphurous scuff of a struck match. Gathering himself and baring long yellow fangs, he launched himself at Franklin Bierce's face.

◆ ◆ ◆

Pilsudski, as Bierce said he would, did come back—the following day, as it happened. He was, after all, a born fighter, an old campaigner and the namesake of General Pilsudski, who had defeated the Red Army before Warsaw in 1920.

He had fought the rat-thing no fewer than three times. But it had eventually proven too determined an adversary for him. So, at the dark of the moon, he had surrendered his old home and stolen away, to the fantastic and indescribable hiding places where cats retreat when forced by great and terrible events. Here he had bided his time patiently, like a general in exile.

Before long, he sensed the passing of the storm. His home was his, once again. The rat-thing had returned to whatever bleak universe claimed it, to its furtive scurrying and scratching and scrabbling at the corners of the waking world.

And so Pilsudski went forth, and entered first the garage, his oldest haunt, his summer home and winter retreat. Carefully he sniffed at everything: every box, every can, every cabinet, every corner. There was no sign of the rat-thing or any of its terrible allies. Cautiously he went upstairs, to the attic, on swift noiseless paws.

Again, he sniffed fastidiously, missing no detail, and again, nothing of the rat-thing was revealed. The stink of its fur, of its carrion breath, was gone. Gone were the dead birds and mice, gone too were the blasphemous names and fantastic markings upon the floor. All that remained were several curious brownish angles and intersecting marks drawn on the opposite wall, symbols that meant absolutely nothing to the cat.

Pilsudski, immensely pleased, rubbed up against a stool leg. His world was his again.

He noticed something then, upon the floor.

His curiosity peaked, he sniffed at the discarded object, a pair of expensive, wire-framed spectacles.

END

Burnt Tea

by Michael Dziesinski

Doctor Henry Armitage scratched his beard as he looked out the third-story window of Miskatonic's Liberal Arts Building. Down below, a hive of activity buzzed under the trees near the Copley Memorial Bell Tower. A dozen carpenters, craftsmen, and gardeners toiled around a squat building in the shape of a honeycomb. Around the wooden skeleton, a Zen garden with miniature bonsai trees had been transported stone by stone from Japan to Miskatonic's central campus. And that wasn't the only thing imported; most all of the workforce appeared to be of Asian extraction. Despite the industrious scene below, Armitage's attention was drawn back to this cramped office by the redolence of burning joss.

He scanned the crisp document in his hand, dated September 27th 1924, on the official letterhead of Japan's Washington D.C. Consulate. It also bore an ornate red seal of angular Chinese ideograms stamped near the bottom of the page. Henry Armitage puffed at his pipe, the burning tobacco filling the soft tissues of his lungs.

"Magnificent isn't it? The Kurosenke tea hut should be done by month's end."

Still puffing, Armitage faced the speaker.

In front of two worn desks, no doubt scrounged from some other department, a Japanese man in a finely tailored tweed suit of European design stood with impeccable posture. Arms crossed, the man's body language struck Armitage as supremely confident. He appeared an older man, and judging by his carefully combed silver hair, bushy eyebrows, and the deep wrinkles at the corners of his eyes, Armitage guessed him to be in his late fifties, though he could not be sure as the years had been kind to him.

"Doctor Toge is it? Your English is outstanding. And do I detect a British accent?"

The man inclined his head in a slight bow of acknowledgement.

"Actually, my family name is 'toh-gee'. Shinosuke Toji. But, you are correct, Doctor Armitage, I studied History at Cambridge for four years."

Armitage was intrigued. "How did that come to pass?"

"In Japan's push to modernize after the arrival of Commodore Perry's Black Ships, the Meiji Emperor sent out many promising young Japanese to study overseas—to bring that knowledge back for the betterment of Japan, if you will. I was one of those lucky few, but that was almost twenty years ago."

Armitage rubbed his shiny pate as he lifted the letter with his other hand. "A gift from the Emperor of Japan? Well, I don't know why you are building this structure in the middle of the campus, but if Miskatonic's President Wainscott has no problem with this construction—well, to be blunt, I don't see what this has to do with my library."

Armitage's brow furrowed at the third desk in the room. It was strewn with various half-translated documents in Arabic and Sanskrit. The disorder was quite unsettling to the scholar.

"Yes, well, I do hope that Doctor Shalad doesn't mind sharing his office with you. To be honest, I don't think President Wainscott *quite* knew what to do with you—though

I'm sure our esteemed leader found it hard to turn away such a generous endowment."

"Doctor Armitage, I'm a humble man of learning such as yourself. I have come to Miskatonic to conduct research in an open atmosphere of inquiry. Something I find...difficult...in the present political atmosphere of censorship in my country. You sound . . . what's the word I'm looking for . . . *suspicious* of my motives—"

Arimitage quickly cut in, "I meant no offense Doctor Toji, it's just that in my own personal experience, I find that good fortune is often an illusion hiding a truth that—"

A *click*. The door handle slowly turned, followed by a slight creak. Two shadows filled the shaft of growing light on the floor. An expression of momentary alarm flashed across Toji's features, though he relaxed when a middle-aged man and young woman entered the office.

Smiling with recognition, Toji gave a curt bow toward the newcomers. "Doctor Armitage," Toji said. "May I introduce Deputy Minster of Foreign Affairs, Kuno Tachibana, who is on loan from Washington to oversee the tea hut's construction. And of course, my niece, Hanako Uchida."

The two Japanese nationals bowed to Armitage who was awkwardly withdrawing an extended hand while also trying to reciprocate the bow. He ended up bowing with the hand still outstretched.

A short man, Minister Tachibana wore a tailored black suit and top hat, though they hardly softened his gaunt face and bulging eyes. The man's appearance caused Armitage to uncomfortably flash to memories of his own childhood. Toji's niece, Hanako, a svelte woman in her early twenties, was dressed in an elegantly cut green dress, her black hair shorn in the bobbed flapper style popular in Boston and New York. Hanako caught Armitage's lingering gaze and looked down to the floor, her face flush, though she quickly recovered to appear to be merely checking her fashionable wristwatch.

A predatory grin crept across Minister Tachibana's face. When he spoke, his words carried a thick accent. "Doctor Armitage," he chided. "You seem surprised by our attire. Did you expect Japanese women to be dressed in kimono? Do you take us Japanese as a backward people because we are from Asia?"

Surprised by Minister Tachibana's sudden confrontation, Armitage raised his hands in mock surrender. "Now see here, sir; if I must confess to any wrongdoing, truth be told, it is my amazement that your attire is so . . . contemporary . . . by comparison to those who live in our small town of Arkham."

Toji came to Armitage's rescue. "Minister Tachibana, how goes the work on the tea hut? I suppose our government's money is being spent efficiently and without waste?"

Derailed from what Toji knew would degenerate into a black tirade on the virtues of a modern and militarized Japan, Tachibana scowled at the interruption.

"Everything is on schedule. The tea hut's structure should be complete soon. Then I'll be able to return to Washington and devote my time to issues of import."

As the two men continued to trade barbs, Armitage sheepishly approached Hanako. "A tea hut? Ms. Uchida, what is a 'tea hut'?"

Hanako's eyes nervously darted to her Uncle, but she remained silent. To Armitage, she appeared to weigh the question with a great deal of deliberation.

Toji abruptly ended his sparring match with Tachibana. "Doctor Armitage, I'm afraid my niece is still learning English . . . ."

"Ah yes, I see. My apologies."

Hanako smiled warmly at Armitage.

"You could not have known, Doctor Armitage. But to answer your query, the tradition of tea has long been practiced in Asia. In the twelfth century, Japan took this pastime and made it uniquely Japanese with *matcha*, green tea—"

"By the thirteenth century," Tachibana interrupted, "the practice of serving tea blended with the Zen philosophy of the samurai warrior class who ritualized the ceremony using specific implements, materials, and atmosphere."

Toji tugged his waistcoat in annoyance. With a strained voice, he continued, "Over the centuries, several traditions have developed, each with a hereditary tea master who passes his knowledge to the next generation. I am a historian, but I am also a hereditary master of the Kurosenke School of Tea Ceremony."

"Yes, well, that is *debatable,* Shinosuke. There is no denying that the Toji family has samurai roots, explaining your privileged status and aid from the Emperor. Your *school* . . . well, I have my doubts it is legitimate."

Armitage, smelling a fresh argument brewing, fished out his timepiece. "Lady, Gentlemen, I have to get back to my duties at the library. There's no telling what the student assistants have done to my stacks. Doctor Toji, feel free to call when you have need of the Miskatonic libraries."

And with that, Armitage was gone.

Except for the steady tick of the wall clock, silence blighted the room. The men's eyes narrowed at each other, as two samurai of yore, waiting for an opening in which to cut down the enemy.

A sneer curled Tachibana's mouth as he dropped into Japanese. "You can put on this act of the innocent historian all you want with the Americans, Shinosuke, but the *Tokko* knows that you're up to something. When you slip up, I'll be there—and you'll soon discover what we do to those who speak against Imperial Japan."

Though his body trembled with rage, Toji's expression was a mask of calmness. "I should have known you were a Tokko thug! If the Imperial Secret Police had evidence of wrongdoing, you would not be here posturing, now would you? You can watch me with the closest of scrutiny and report everything to your Tokko masters for all I care. I am only interested in researching truths lost to time, and Arkham is simply a suitable resource."

"Watch your tone Shinosuke! Seeking out truth has its price—one we *all* must pay in due time. I could easily call my operatives concealed amongst the work crew and have you arrested right this moment."

Tachibana inched closer. "*Especially* when they hear that you have been tracing the mundane origins of Japan's Imperial Family! The Emperor is a living god! What arrogance!"

Both Toji and Hanako gasped with surprise.

"Oh yes, I know! The Toji family's ties to the Imperials won't protect you. I've spent the last three months tracking you down to this insignificant town in the Americas and now that I've found you—"

"Get OUT! Get out of my presence!" Toji's rage surged at this petty little man. He gripped the edge of the desk, knuckles turning white.

Tachibana languidly walked to his desk, sat down, and propped up his feet."Sorry old man. I have a report to wire to Washington."

Toji stormed from the office, only waiting long enough for Hanako. He slammed the door so hard that the glass window shattered; shards tinkled to the ground in the hallway.

At the top of the stairwell, Toji stopped to clutch the rail banister as a brutal series of deep coughs wracked his aging frame. Hanako pulled a silk cloth from her purse and rushed to his side. His chest heaving with each cough. Toji blindly reached out with one hand, covering his mouth with the cloth. Meanwhile, Hanako pulled a bottle of green medicine from her purse. Toji's heaving subsided with a final spasm. Painfully, he stood upright and pulled the handkerchief away. A splash of crimson blood covered the pristine white of the fabric. Its coppery scent just barely masked by the incense burning in the office down the hall.

"It's getting worse, isn't it Uncle?" Sadness lined Hanako's eyes.

Unable to speak for the moment, Toji's lips pursed into a knot. While taking shallow breaths, he nodded, using a sleeve to wipe the sweat from his face before accepting the bottle. He sipped the greenish liquid; his ragged breathing smoothed.

"All the more reason to get the tea hut finished and access to Armitage's libraries. I feel the key to my life's work is hidden in those tomes. I must know, Hanako. Before I die, I must know the truth! Even if those deluded military dogs see this knowledge as threatening to the sovereignty of the Emperor, truth is truth, and it must always be sought out. Remember that, Hanako. For if humanity hides in delusion, we are no better than beasts."

Hanako sighed with resignation. "Uncle, let's return to the boarding house so that you can rest."

"Hanako my child, at times like this, you remind me so much of my sister. I miss her so."

"As do I, uncle. As do I."

Toji's knew he'd revived the memory of her mother—a callous action, he chided himself. He could see the concern in her eyes. She wondered how long before he joined the ancestors. On that day, Hanako would be alone, the last of the family.

◆ ◆ ◆

It was a blissfully short walk for Toji and Hanako from the Liberal Arts Building to the Franklin Place. As they opened the door, the smell of roasting meat filled their senses.

Mrs. Franklin emerged from the kitchen, smiling cheerfully. "Ah, Doctor Toji, Ms. Uchida, welcome back! The cook tells me that dinner will be ready within the hour. Are you agreeable with roast beef and potatoes? I know that may not be your standard dietary fare . . . ."

Toji smiled wearily at her motherly concern. "That is fine, Mrs. Franklin. Occasionally, we do get nostalgic for food from Japan, but the cook's dishes are always a delight."

Mrs. Franklin brightened."Oh, Doctor Toji, it almost slipped my mind. You received several parcels at midday. Sizable I might add. I had the postman place them in your room."

Agitated, Toji immediately peered down the hallway. Uncle and niece exchanged looks and rushed in unison toward the room.

"Monsieur Helcimer indicated interest in speaking with you at dinner," Mrs. Franklin called after them, but the room's door was already closed. Mrs. Franklin shrugged and returned to the kitchen.

Arranged in the middle of the room were three large wooden crates, each covered with postal marks in Japanese. The only English was the address to the Franklin house.

"Do you think Saiyako got everything past the Imperial Censors?" Hanako reverently caressed the nearest crate.

Breathing shallow and fearing another coughing fit, Toji took a measured breath. "We shall see my child, we shall see."

He grabbed the crowbar left atop the middle crate and struggled with the box. After a moment, Hanako gently took the crowbar from his hands. Winded from even this slight effort, a wan Toji helplessly watched as Hanako continued.

Wood creaked as nails sounded sharp cracks from Hanako's efforts, and renewed pride welled up in Toji's chest at his unorthodox decision in naming Hanako as successor to the Kurosenke School of Tea. Truthfully, Hanako was the only soul he trusted with the school's secret rituals. Over the last five years, she had quickly mastered the intricate gestures and movements of the Kurosenke School's centuries-old Ceremony of the Black Tea.

Though only hinted at in the seven strange Chinese scrolls found at Tokyo Imperial University, Miskatonic's library collection might hold the key to the lost steps in the black tea's preparation. Then, the hollow Kurosenke rituals passed on for generations in his family would once again have purpose.

Hanako lifted the lid from the largest of the crates, a reinforced wooden trunk called a *chabako* specifically made for storing tea in an insulated, airtight environment. The minute the lid raised a cloyingly sweet aroma danced in the air, filling the room with its heavy musk. Toji's vision darkened, his eyes felt heavy, as the apparition of a massive black flower squirmed into his consciousness. Hanako, who had stood further away, seemed to be spared. The lid dropped with a loud thump as Toji groggily stumbled over to the room's window and opened it to the cold night air. "Ha-Hanako, o-open the door," his leaden tongue managed. "T-The pe-perfume of the Kuroi Hazu . . . ."

After the room was well ventilated, Toji inspected the chabako again. The point of origin indicated Leung, China. Strange claw-like gouges and dark blue stains marked the chabako's wood in various places. Toji grabbed a clean handkerchief and placed it over his nose while gesturing for Hanako to stand near the door as he reopened the chabako.

Per his specifications, the fleshy black rhizomes were wrapped to keep them as fresh as possible for transport. Each plant was wrapped in a moist mass of pink translucent hide of some sort. He guessed it to be porcine in origin until he looked closer . . . no. That couldn't be! Tufts of fine human hair still clung to the hide!

Nauseated, Toji quickly closed the lid with a rush of shame. His contacts with the Black Brotherhood in China had warned that the only access for this rare delivery was through a primitive tribe on the plateau, and their price would be steep. It was too high. What humans could do such a barbaric thing—

"Uncle . . . Uncle Shin, are you all right? Do you need more medicine?" Hanako asked, concern in her voice.

"You must never open this chabako without my supervision," Toji said. "Do you understand?"

"Why yes, Uncle, but I don't see—"

Toji rose to his full height. "*Do you understand?*"

Shocked at her Uncle's uncharacteristic sternness, Hanako responded with a simple, "Yes."

Hearing this, Toji's tension washed away. He waved her over. Hanako hesitantly returned to the center of the room. She searched his face for some explanation but found none. The corners of Toji's eyes softened as he patted Hanako's hand reassuringly. "Now let's see what else we have in the other boxes. Tea utensils I would guess."

◆ ◆ ◆

Over the last several weeks, chill autumn air turned the leaves on Arkham's trees into crowns of fiery reds and oranges. The contrast of the trees' vivid colors against the tea hut's colorless Zen rock garden was jarring to the senses. It set Henry Armitage ill at ease as he and his colleague walked across the campus.

"President Wainscott, Doctor Toji is hiding something—"

"Henry, you are too suspicious," Harvey Wainscott said, waving an invitation written in beautiful calligraphic script. "Do try to enjoy tonight."

They continued walking in silence for a moment; a gust of cold air rustled the leaves. "Toji's recounting of tea ceremony in Japan is true enough," Armitage said. "But my students can find no reference to the Kurosenke School."

Wainscott shrugged. "So? Maybe it's a small school?'

"Harvey, it means *the Black Way of Tea*. Sounds ominous. Or are you blinded by the possibilities of the Japanese Emperor's *generous* monetary endowment?"

"Don't start about the reorganization of Miskatonic. Do I have to hear this from *every* faculty member?" Wainscott looked at the clear crisp night sky with its twinkling panorama of distant fires. "Hmm. No moon."

"Japanese tea huts emphasize elegant simplicity, *sabi*, a reflection of the tea ceremony's Zen origins," Armitage continued undaunted. "Toji's tea hut is an eight-sided monstros—"

The librarian stopped as they arrived at the entrance. As he and Wainscott drew near, they were overwhelmed by the smell of burning charcoal and the fresh green straw of the hut's tatami mat floor.

Toji sat in the kneeling *seiza* position on the woven tatami straw mats just inside the hut's low door. He was clad in a black kimono; its only adornment was his family crest of a lotus blossom in a white circle on each shoulder.

Toji burned with anticipation as the first of the guests arrived. With the sight of Doctor Armitage, the tea master thought back to his good fortune several weeks previous at the Miskatonic Library. With Armitage absent, a student librarian helped Toji find the Latin text by Ludwig Prinn so that he could brew the *Kuroi Hazu* into the powered form for tonight's ritual. Toji's reverie broke as more guests arrived.

Tachibana and his Tokko thugs gave Toji a lingering glare as they entered the hut. Toji smiled. *Tonight he would open all of their eyes.* And then, the last of the guests arrived and the tea ceremony begun.

Toji and the guests sat in a circle facing inward, toward the center of the hut. In the middle, Hanako took a triangle of red cloth from the white obi sash of her orange silk kimono. She refolded the fabric into a square and used it to open a cylindrical container coated with red lacquer.

In a ritualized movement, Hanako picked up a bamboo scoop from the assembled utensils and dipped into the fine black granulated powder, carefully tapping one scoop into each ceramic tea bowl for the guests.

With liquid grace, Hanako dipped a long bamboo ladle into a roiling iron kettle that rested upon red-hot charcoals. She poured the hot water into each bowl. Applying a bamboo whisk, she mixed each bowl into a frothy black tea. A cloying aroma of burnt musk filled the hut.

Using measured gestures, Toji placed the bowls before each guest. When all were in position, he raised a bowl to his lips, and announced, "*Dozo itadaki-masu.*"

Everyone looked around, but as the Japanese guests copied Toji's gesture, the remaining people also raised the bowls of the black substance to drink.

Armitage looked in his bowl; within the inky blackness points of light glittered like the night sky. His eyes met Wainscot's and with a slight gesture, shook his head.

Toji tipped the bowl back, zealously imbibing the liquid midnight in one draft.

Existence wavered.

An invisible force squirmed through the substance of the walls and ate away at reality. Except for those in the circle, the hut was rapidly devoured into nothingness.

Hanako faded from view as expected, but also Armitage and Wainscott with bowls still poised at their lips. They all dissolved. Gone.

The remaining guests hovered surrounded by endless void. No. Not endless. Merely immense to human perception. Toji could discern the outline of an immense black lotus blossom below and around them spreading out in all directions.

And then the guests noticed the *other* effect of the tea— paralyzed, helpless, raw panic rippled through the group with the realization they could not move.

All was ready.

Toji bent his entire will to his life's purpose. His disembodied voice boomed in this non-locality, "Behold, the true origins of the Japanese people!"

Involuntarily, the group's thoughts focused on his odd statement. The void responded.

A soupy haze manifested. The briny smell of the sea washed across their senses. Then–

Screams.

Ear-piercing screeches of writhing agony, a gamut of fowl odors.

Gradually, the haze cleared before them. They sat on a rocky peninsula in the ocean. Coming toward them, a crush of Asiatic people in ripped and burned gossamer clothes, many matted with drying blood. Between the weeping and sobs, they spoke a strange tongue, though some parts were recognizable. Proto-Japanese?

Ecstatic, Toji examined the visages of those nearest. They looked undeniably Japanese, but all were cowed and frightened. They could not see his group. But what? Toji's eyes traced the stream of human refugees back to the horizon. In the distance, gouts of flames hungrily ate away at a once beautiful city of crystal spires and domes. Tidal surges slammed into the coast and chunks of the shoreline lurched to the foamy waters.

A predatory shadow enveloped the crystal city. Above, an inconceivably massive presence burrowed through the burning pillars of smoke.

Gone again.

A serpentine head burst from the smoke at the edge of the city. A spherical writhing mass of fleshy protuberances surrounded the jaws and continued down the white body that whipped behind it.

Toji recoiled at this corpulent predator. This dragon.

Such a being could not, should not exist.

Closer.

Coming closer.

The fell serpent dipped, opened it jaws, and devoured hundreds of human refugees.

Mere seconds, and they ceased to be.

Its mouth still open, a putrid stench of charred flesh, oily sulfur and worse filled the air. The massive entity undulated and banked back into the burning skies, skeletal wings beating, giving it altitude as pustulant, milky orbs trained on Toji's group.

It is aware of them.

It sees them!

Closing.

Disbelief.

Not possible.

Not true!

Toji's concentration slipped, the surroundings rapidly returned to the eternal nothingness. Relief spread through Toji and his guests.

Escape, but not home.

The hair on the back of Toji's neck stood on end—unbridled menace and corruption stalked into his consciousness. A primal wave of white-hot panic surged through his entire being as the meat and flesh instincts of prey seized his mind. The agitated expressions of the guests confirmed he was not alone in this dread.

Beyond, a strange tangle of corkscrew towers with non-Euclidian geometries had taken shape around them. The sky, endlessly black. It was no human city Toji knew of.

Something clawed at the edge of his awareness. A timeless malevolence holding enmity toward all of humanity dwelled in this bizarre necropolis outside of space and time.

Smothering Toji's spirit, a hideous malignancy, an impossible fetid hunger dripped unbidden into his consciousness. Finding its prey, burning eyes loped toward Toji's paralyzed form. His limited human senses, in a panicked Gestalt reflex, struggled desperately to rationalize this being. At the edge of his vision, the irrational fear of the hunted took a canine form, but he could not be sure— it was only an instant.

It stalked down an impossible staircase. No. *They* did— blue spittle from hungry maws spattered to the ground with a crackling hiss.

Toji's heartbeat raced, his breathing frantic, a deep racking cough erupted from his chest cavity. Paralyzed from the black tea's influence, Toji's wracking coughs soon yielded gouts of blood with each spasm of his diaphragm. Soon, he could only manage a wet gurgling sound.

Toji and his guests were seated again in the tea hut on the Miskatonic Campus. Toji continued to spasm, his kimono sleeve now drenched with blood. Hanako hurried for his medicine, while others held the convulsing man.

Long minutes later, Toji waved his hand and managed to rasp, "I'm s-s-sorry. Thank you my f-f-friends, but that's a-all for n-now. I n-need to retire." Toji noticed that Armitage and Wainscott were nowhere to be seen.

Gradually, the puzzled guests dissipated.

"I know what you tried to do here tonight," Tachibana leaned close and growled.

With a pained face, Toji looked at the man, blood covered his mouth.

A tight grimace stretched Tachibana's face. "I'll be wiring Tokyo about your treasonous actions tonight. Expect to be on a plane for travel tomorrow, Shinosuke."

Tachibana stood and walked toward the Liberal Arts Building with his two Tokko. Toji watched him leave, sitting long minutes in quiet before standing with Hanako's aid. Leaning on her for support, it took the pair a good quarter of an hour to arrive at Toji's office. There they found Armitage examining something on the floor.

"What's wrong, Doctor Armitage?"

As Armitage stood to face Toji, Tachibana's lifeless body could be seen. Hanako looked away in revulsion.

"I saw a bright white light in the office window and came to investigate."

Tachibana had a series of circular holes burrowed into his chest cavity and forehead. The areas were also coated in a blue ichor, with the surrounding flesh an angry red. Here and there, deep gouges like claws carved Tachibana's dead flesh.

Toji tried to process the horrid scene. He clutched his chest at a new wave of coughing, but Hanako quickly produced the medicine, and Toji gulped down the last of the bottle. Guilt gripped Toji. What had he done?

"Doctor Armitage," Hanako said. "My uncle needs rest. You know of our lodgings? You'll find us there if you have questions later." Clearly she was eager to leave.

Armitage was startled at her revelation, but his eyes never left the corpse. He absently nodded as he reached for the phone. Hanako gently put Toji's arm on her shoulder and they left.

◆ ◆ ◆

At the Franklin House, Hanako helped her uncle lean against the doorframe of their room. She was not entirely sure what transpired in the tea hut between the guests, but some unspeakable evil had been unleashed by her uncle. She was deeply disturbed by this, but had a more pressing concern.

"Uncle, I need to see the cook about refilling your medicine."

Toji wearily bowed his head with a waxen expression before stumbling into the room.

Half an hour passed as Hanako made arrangements with the cook and Mrs. Franklin.

"Do ya smell it?" the cook said, wrinkling her nose. "That burnin' smell? S'like rubber."

A foreboding gripped Hanako. Running back to the room, she found the door locked. Black smoke billowed from the narrow crack below the door. Hanako banged on the door with her fists but no response came from inside.

Abruptly, the door became taught in its frame, splintered, and exploded. The force slammed Hanako against Monsieur Helcimer's door. Long minutes passed, and Hanako did not move.

Then, a searing light radiated from the ruined door. Dazed, Hanako shakily drew herself up to see into the room, but could not distinguish any shape or form in the blinding white. The luminance dimmed. Uncle Shin was prone on the floor, in the center of the room. Next to him, the chabako crate blazed! But,

Uncle's full attention was on the far corner of the room. She followed his gaze. It was just two walls. What–?

There, in the seam, where the walls met, gaseous vapors poured forth. Monstrous evil clawed its way into existence. Hanako had never experienced anything so singularly hideous in both form and spirit; her mind felt numb, paralyzed—incoherent awe like prey in the moment before death. A ravenous doom filled the room, its entire focus—Shinosuke Toji.

A strangled shriek.

The tangy stench of the burning black lotus filled her nose and brought her to consciousness. It took Hanako several long seconds to realize that the person screaming, still screaming, was herself.

Several hands grabbed her. She panicked at first, until she realized they were helping her stand. The Franklins and their cook were at her side trying to calm her down.

In the room beyond, her uncle's busted body lay crumpled on the floor next to the scorched chabako of black lotus. Toji's face frozen in a mask of abject terror; his lifeless eyes focused on eternity. A cerulean excretion coated his entire body and dozens of circular punctures defiled his mortal shell.

Upon standing, Hanako noticed something on the floor scrawled in blood, in Japanese, and it ended at Toji's bloodied hand. Mrs. Franklin rubbed Hanako's arm in support, but Hanako could not feel her touch. Hanako's sanity was slipping. Disconnected. Shattering. Colors mute, smells metallic. Far in the distance, she heard Mrs. Franklin's voice ask, "What's it say, dear?"

Unblinking, Hanako mechanically intoned, "Truth's Price is Tindalos."

END

Arkham Rain

by John Goodrich

I am standing outside my brother's house, and the near-freezing November rain has already soaked through my denim jacket, but somehow the gun in my hand is colder still. It's like a chunk of ice, a frozen mass of hate; I don't know if my terrible intention is the lesser evil or not. The agony of my decision curls in my gut, and I uselessly ask a God I don't believe in why this is happening to me, why my grandfather had to die and take everything that I ever valued away from me.

I remember my grandfather Saltonstall as a gnarl-handed Yankee carpenter. In his small, dark, crowded house, he told my brother Ethan and I strange stories about the things that shared the world with us, lurking just out of sight. There was a certain light on his eyes as he told us of the mad doctor on Mount Moosilauke, Old Trickey the cursed sandman, the Devil and Jonathan Moulton, the invisible monster of Dunwich, and Indian tales of Old Slipperyskin, the bear that was smart like a man. It seemed that there wasn't a single corner of New England that didn't have some sort of haunt, monster, family curse, or strange religious sect lurking in it. And somehow our hometown of Arkham seemed to have more stories about it than anywhere else.

We watched him fade as we grew, my brother and I. As we got taller, and he seemed to shrink, arthritis twisted his hands until they resembled the branches of tortured trees rather than anything you might find on a human being. Despite this, he continued working as best he could, his tortured fingers fumbling with his carpenter's tools until, just over a month ago, he completely wore himself out.

What was there to say to the man who looked so small and vulnerable on a white hospital bed, an IV and a breathing mask just prolonging the inevitable? How could a man who had been so full of life and stories be so helpless, unable to do anything but mark time until the end? I sat down next to his bed, my hand held his hand, and he squinted at me through his murky vision.

"Loved you the best I . . . could." he said with slow labor, taking a tortured breath after each word, clear despite the oxygen mask covering his face. "Even if you ain't . . . natural."

The phrase snapped my head around. What was he talking about? "Save your strength," I encouraged him. I didn't know for what, though. It was just something I was supposed to say, something to cover my own emptiness at watching my grandfather slip into darkness.

"You . . . got to know." he said, his eyes staring at me. "What you are." He was very insistent, staring at me intently, his arthritic fingers gripping me with what little strength he had left.

"Innsmouth," he said, very distinctly. "The look. The change." His face twisted with a combination of anger and hatred I'd never seen in him before, and he gasped out the words as if they were dire maledictions. "Hell . . . take that sonofabitch . . . Ephraim Babson . . ." he choked out, shocking me with the first profanity I'd ever heard pass his lips.

"What are you talking about?" I asked, genuinely frightened. He'd never said anything like this before, and his grip was insistent. It wasn't until then that I heard the high-pitched scream of the cardio-monitor on a stopped heart. I tried to pull away to notify the nurse, but he held me with all his dying strength.

He seemed about to say something more when the door erupted, and I was surrounded by fast-moving figures in white. One nurse rushed me out of the room as the others swarmed around my grandfather, but I knew what the outcome would be. He'd delivered his message, his final secret. I sat outside, trying not to listen to the talk and confusion spilling out of his room. Less than ten minutes later a stony-faced doctor delivered the inevitable news.

The funeral was a simple but surprisingly well-attended affair, and his death left an emptiness that I had never known before. Grandfather Saltonstall had been the last piece of family I'd had outside of Ethan. We buried him in the Saltonstall plot in Christchurch Cemetery, next to his wife, near my parents, and I was the subject of a lot of condolences. All through the ceremony though, his last words haunted me. What about me was unnatural? Had he secretly hated my father for marrying his only daughter all those years ago? Did he blame this Babson man for her death? Did he blame me? I had two pieces of information to work with; the name Ephraim Babson, and something about the mythical village of Innsmouth.

Innsmouth at least was familiar. Every school kid in Arkham knows that Innsmouthers are polluted mutant freaks, but nobody ever agreed on where it was. Some kids said there really was an Innsmouth, but belief in the mythical village as the source of all that was disgusting and unholy eventually fell away along with Santa Claus, cooties, honest politicians, and the guy with a hook for a hand. Certainly my grandfather had never said anything about it, and he knew more about Arkham's history than anyone else I'd ever heard of. Why suddenly bring the place up?

The name Ephraim Babson, however, meant nothing. There weren't any Babsons listed in the Arkham phone book, and after making some calls, I discovered that the Babsons living in Ipswich, Asbury Grove, East Parish, and Glouchester hadn't had a Ephraim in their genealogy for more than a hundred years. I considered hiring a private detective and having him find out all he could about this guy, but I decided to pursue my other, and probably cheaper, line of inquiry first.

A web search on Innsmouth turned up rubbish—mostly rehashed stories I'd heard in the schoolyard about degenerate weirdos living in a diseased town that was rotting into oblivion. A few had some authentic-sounding bits of history, but many of the websites contradicted each other only where they obviously hadn't cut and pasted text from each other. If anything has ever convinced me that any idiot can put up a website, it was my Innsmouth search.

Having gotten exactly nowhere with that, I decided to talk to one of my grandfather's old tale-swapping buddies whom I'd met at the funeral. Bill Thurber was an anciently creaky New Englander with rheumy eyes and only a few teeth, living alone in a small, yellowed apartment on Gendey street. Despite his age, his greeting was friendly and his hospitality kind, if sparse. He was especially solicitous after my health, and invited me to share in his afternoon shot of whiskey. We talked for some time, as he smoked his foul pipe and wove stories about Arkham, Kingsport, and Dunwich.

"So," he said, laying his pipe aside after telling me a thoroughly disturbing story about the witch Keziah Mason and her rattish familiar. "What can I do for Jefferson Saltonstall's grandson? You don't look like you came here just to hear stories."

"I was wondering if you knew anything about Innsmouth?" I asked, figuring there wasn't much point to beating around the bush.

Instantly the charming demeanor faded, and the clear, storyteller's elocution degenerated into a distant mumble. "Nothing that concerns you," he said, not looking me in the eye.

"I'm just looking for some stories," I insisted gently, disturbed by his abruptly furtive manner.

"Innsmouth's got nothing to do with your family," he returned, a little more abruptly than he needed to. He was silent for a moment, then picked up his bottle of whiskey.

"I didn't ask about my family," I said, trying to keep the intensity out of my voice. "I just want to hear a thing or two about Innsmouth."

He poured a few fingers of the brownish alcohol into a shot glass, then downed it with a quick, almost guilty gesture.

"Stories like that aren't appropriate among friends," said the man who had told me about the horrible, child-murdering Brown Jenkin in disturbing detail. What about this topic disturbed him? What sort of family secret was he was keeping out of loyalty to the memory of my grandfather?

His evasions began to annoy me. What could possibly be so horrible about my heritage that I couldn't be told? I was gearing up to give him a piece of my mind when he looked up, and I saw not anger or resentment but a sad pity in his gaze, which brought me up short.

"Look in the newspapers, if you want answers," he said in a haunted whisper, as if afraid someone was going to overhear. "Round about the time Lizzie Borden died, those two Eye-talian anarchists, Sack-o and Van-centi, got the chair, and they put that damn stupid fish on the licence plates." His face contorted with some ill-defined emotion. "You better leave now. I expect you have things to do."

So abruptly dismissed, and without anything to say, I got up and left. Glancing back as I left, I saw Thurber hunched over, his whiskey bottle still clutched in a claw-like hand, watching me go. There might have been tears in his eyes.

The Arkham *Advertiser's* newspaper morgue was old-school, which is to say that an enormous volume of papers had been heaped more or less into decades in the little building's surprisingly-dry basement. And there, in the dry, duty air of my newspaper's basement, I started to unravel the mystery of my grandfather's last words.

Lizzie Borden had died in 1927; that piece of information was pretty easy to find, and I discovered that Italians anarchists Nicola Sacco and Bartolomeo Vanzetti had been executed in 1927 to tremendous public outcry. But there was little in the *Advertiser* about Innsmouth in 1927.

However, when I started looking through the 1928 papers, I found what I was looking for. Innsmouth, it turned out, had been a real town, but one that had died or been abandoned. Apparently, in 1928, the government had staged a major military operation on the town, citing rampant bootlegger activity. But the more I read about it, and delved into the history of this mysterious little village, the more I was inclined to take a different view. Innsmouth, the *Advertiser* reported, had been the site of a mysterious disease outbreak in 1846, one that was never particularly well explained. Reading about the dynamiting that was done around the town in 1928, I was reminded of the treatment the federal government gave to the Arms Textile Mill in Manchester, New Hampshire after some anthrax deaths in 1957. It was odd that they'd be so secretive about it, but it was only ten years after the 1918 influenza pandemic, and maybe the feds hadn't wanted to create panic.

The more I thought about it, the more my little theory made sense. Arkham kids considered Innsmouthers polluted mutant freaks, which could easily have grown from handed-down tales of sick or diseased people out of Innsmouth, passing on parents' admonitions to avoid Innsmouth folk for fear of some unnamed infection. This did not, however, make any sort of connection back to me. If my hypothetical Innsmouth Plague was real, how could I have possibly contracted it, and how could my grandfather know about it?

I never did find out anything about the licence plate fishes.

Not the least bit mollified, and becoming frustrated with my lack of answers, I walked through the streets, and Arkham enfolded me. After crossing the dark waters of the Miskatonic on the West Street bridge, I walked through the old merchant district until the gambrel roofs and Federalist facades of the University reared up, dark and aged, their brooding matching my own mood. It was here, with the dark, tottering houses broken only by the small-paned windows, that I could think the best. What should I do? I had little to go on but supposition and a few tiny threads that my grandfather had gasped out just before he'd died. I couldn't just ignore this. What could possibly have been so terrible that he had waited until the last possible moment to tell me? Something for which he did not want to live to see the consequences. My mind rebelled at the thought; Grandfather Saltonstall hadn't ducked responsibility for a single thing in his life.

I walked past the black iron fence that delineated the old campus, each section holding with a plaque green with verdigris marking it as a gift from successive classes, beginning in 1898. My grandfather's condemnation of Ephraim Babson had been unprecedentedly stern. Who was he, and what was his crime that my grandfather had used his last breath to spit out the first and last epithet I'd ever heard him use? For this, I had no precedent, and no leads, except for his assertion that I was unnatural.

It was the fact that the condemnation has ben so completely out of character for him that really bothered me. He'd loved me, and Ethan for that matter, and never had any difficult expressing it. The sudden about-face was not just a mystery to me, it was a slap in the face, an abrogation of everything he had ever said to me. What could possibly have prompted those words?

I was unable to stop obsessing about my grandfather's last words, they echoed in my mind. I wondered what I should do. Babson had turned out to be a stone wall, and I was out of ideas. So if I wanted to move forward with this, I was going to have to work some more on Innsmouth. I'd gathered a lot of information, but there was still a large gap between the town and myself. I wondered if there was anything left of the seaside village. There was enough talk about the cursed town, both by the local kids and the post-Blair Witch crowd, that I should be able to find out something about its location. Looked at the Neo-Gothic university buildings silhouetted black against the darkening sky, I decided I was going to take a trip to Innsmouth.

The following day, armed with what seemed like the least-unreliable map I could find off the internet, as well as a detailed map of the Massachusetts coastline provided by my local gas station, I set out in search of a myth. With European civilization settling and expanding over Massachusetts for over five hundred years, people seem to assume that there aren't any more out-of-the-way locations in this or any New England state. But you can still get lost in ridiculously isolated locations less than forty miles from Faneuil Hall, and find the strangest things on unnamed New England back roads. Going to a vacation spot in Maine, I once got turned around and drove through an active Shaker enclave. A friend in college said she'd been to Connecticut's lost village of Dudleytown. A surprising amount hides along winding New England back roads with the trees crowding close.

After two hours of driving back and forth on little-used roads, I had found nothing to indicate the reality of Innsmouth. The rutted and potholed road I was proceeding down couldn't have been paved less than forty years ago, and was littered with slippery October leaves. To my left, the East, lay a nameless and fetid swamp, the decomposing remains of long-abandoned tobacco barns passed by on my right. My internet map had proven worse than useless. I was cursing the idiot who had made it when a small gap in the forested swamp slid past me.

I made an illegal U-turn, grateful for the near-complete isolation of the pitted road, and slowly proceeded back to examine the gap. This path, since calling it a road was to pay it far too much compliment, wound its way through puddles, around unexpected boulders that lay half-submerged in stagnant water, and vanished into the swamp. It might have been an old fire break, although I didn't think that particularly likely, as wet as the ground was.

In the middle of the road, engine idling, I hesitated. How badly did I want to follow this tenuous link to my grandfather's dying words? Enough to possibly get my decidedly not-off-road car stuck in a swamp in the middle of nowhere? I looked down the path again, and at the sickly trees whose trunks stuck out of the water like naked bones from a shallow grave.

I pulled onto the muddy track, but only far enough to be off the paved road. I got out, locked my car, and walked down the old track on foot. No sense in getting my car stuck.

I walked a little way, and then realized that I'd left my sense of time behind with the car. With it out of sight, I had few landmarks to mark my progress; all of the sickly trees looked the same. Like most people born in a town, I didn't have much of an idea how quickly I could walk, either. My progress towards I knew not what was slow and torturous. This forgotten and overgrown swamp seemed a pocket of time that all civilization had neglected. I trudged forward, with the uncanny feeling that this was how the colonists had felt, lost amongst the tall trees and dark paths of a foreign continent, the world they had known inconceivably far away.

The scraggly, gnarled shapes of swamp maple and oak crowded close to the track, and mucky dirt sucked at my shoes. Little gurgling noises stalked me as my footprints slowly filled with dirty water. Where the track wasn't waterlogged, brambles and other scrub reached for my feet, and once nearly succeeded in removing one of my shoes. The further I went, the more the swamp filled my senses. The croaking dirge of large frogs I could at least identify, but mysterious splashes and odd cries filtered from in from across the

stagnant water reinforced my feelings of loneliness and isolation in the face of so much nature.

The long-legged marsh-birds observed my passing like
silent guardians standing in the fetid pools. I stopped and
watched one, some sort of greyish heron, as it stood motionless
in the water. Abruptly, the long neck swooped and came up
with a struggling frog. A few short, jerky movements and the
frog was gone, and the bird was still again. For whatever reason, I felt an unexpected surge of pity for the frog.

Lost in more than thought, I was actually in the midst of
Innsmouth before I noticed it. The trees had thinned out a little, allowing more sun to get through, and I left the dark water
of the marsh behind. I could barely make out the susurrus of
the ocean, and wet leaves lay in mounds and drifts underfoot.
The tottering remains of an abandoned house close to surren-
dering to the combined assault of scrub, rot, and tree told me
that I had finally arrived. There could be little doubt that this
was the legendary Innsmouth.

Further exploration told me that what was left of the abandoned town was little more than a rotting, forgotten heap that
had mostly been reclaimed by nature. All that was really left
were some cellar-holes, with the occasional chimney or larger
part of a house protruding through the smothering carpet of
wet leaves. Clearing some of them away, I could see that I was
now walking on what had been a cobblestone street, but many
of the cobbles had been pushed aside or enveloped by roots. In
this abandoned place, the air was surprisingly still, the only
sound the soft rush-rush of small Atlantic waves.

If people had lived in Innsmouth, trees inhabited it now.
What had been homes were now collapsed shacks, cellar holes,
and single walls leaning against trees for support. A few rusted
remains stuck out of the leaves here and there, but most of the
household items had returned to nature, or deliquesced into
foul-smelling sludge after decades of New England weather. I

thought I saw the Bakelite handle of an umbrella underfoot, but I was in no mood to pick through Innsmouth's trash.

I wandered, trying to discern the layout of the empty village. Even at its height it couldn't have been much of a place. I thought I could see a few roads meandering through the ruins; I doubted it had ever been home to more than five hundred people. Neglected remains of a few stone buildings remained, huddled together in what had probably once been the center of town. One was the broken husk of what had been a white-marble building, and the shattered remains of columns out in front of it confirmed that it had been a "fraternal order" building, of the sort so popular in New England at the beginning of the last century. Others looked like large brick structures that had to have been mills or other places of work, each in a different state of destruction and decomposition. One remained somewhat intact, while others were barely-distinguishable heaps of brick rubble. I wondered at the lack of graffiti. For a place as famous as Innsmouth was among Arkham children, I wondered that this wasn't a stoner hangout with heavy metal emblems sprayed on every available upright surface.

After some time in the quiet desolation, I remembered my original purpose. What answers had I thought I was going to find here? I had gone to this decayed wreck of a town, and for what? The secrets to why I wasn't 'natural'? My frustration mounted. What could this dilapidated, long-abandoned ruin of a town have told me? I wanted to be home, doing some work, grieving, finding a girlfriend, or just about anything else but wandering around in stupid, forgotten towns that kids told ghost stories about. There had been nothing for me in Innsmouth, and I still didn't know what the hell my grandfather had been thinking in his last moments. I must have been desperate for some sort of answers to have thought that going there would answer any sort of question.

I screamed out my wordless frustration and anger across the decaying town, and threw some sticks in random directions. It helped a little, and my rage quickly faded into a dull sort of despair. Mildly interesting as this forgotten dump was, it held no answers.

I thought that perhaps I could pick up enough impressions to do a soft-news piece for the Arkham *Advertiser*, maybe make some money on the side selling reprints to those hokey ghost-hunting magazines, and I cursed my stupidity at not bringing a camera. My anger resurfaced, this time at myself for being unprepared. I nevertheless had a pen and paper handy, so I walked towards the shore where I could hear the sigh of breakers, scribbling down occasional phrases to build an article on.

There was a movement off to my left, and the unmistakable sound of something being dragged across the ground.

"Who's there?" I shouted, brandishing my pen in front of me like a knife. There had been a bear sighting in Northboro just last year; this place would be ideal for a bear. But it was quickly clear that whatever was crawling towards me in the dark shadow of a free-standing stone wall was no bear.

I stood, not wanting to run, yet not knowing what was coming towards me. It made a harsh, rasping sound as it came, reminiscent of my grandfather's agonized breathing at the hospital. I steeled myself, not wanting to succumb to the superstitious terror that was licking up and down my limbs.

The . . . thing crawled half way into the light, and I saw that it had a face, and limbs—a person! But there was something terribly wrong with the features, the bulging eyes, the too-wide mouth, and the curious, yellow-pale hue to the thing's scabrous skin. Where before, I had steeled myself not to run, now I was rooted to the ground, staring at this twisted creature before me.

"Please," it begged in breathless, asthmatic gasps, its eyes protuberant under a rough and scabby forehead.

"Wh–who are you?" was all I managed to stammer out.

It broke down and wept, huddled under its tattered woolen coat. I was torn as to what to do. On the one hand, this was a human being that needed comfort, not two feet away from me. At the same time, I didn't want to touch it—him. What if this was the face of my Innsmouth Plague? If I already had it, then there wasn't much point in avoiding this person, but I still pulled away from the searching hand with the instinct of anyone avoiding the detestable.

"What happened to you?" I eventually asked, unable to take my eyes off the repulsive spectacle before me.

"The change," he rasped, and ripple of fear surged down my spine. The same words my grandfather had used. Here, in Innsmouth, I was about to find an answer, coming from the pitiful figure huddled figure at my feet. He looked up at me, and I was reminded of an abandoned puppy, desperately hungry for attention, yet at the same time terrified that the stranger would kick it.

"The change," I echoed back to him, some part of my mind struggling to make sense of the what I see. "How did it happen? What started it?"

"Father found me. Said I was special. Said . . . I'd know when go to . . . to Innsmouth." My mind reeled. Special? What sort of twisted individual would consider this condition to be special?

"Are you all alone?"

"Used to be others," the terrible gasps are coming faster. "They've all . . . gone to . . . the ocean."

"They drowned themselves?" By this point, I was numb with the overwhelming horror that was unfolding in my mind.

"Call of the sea. Getting stronger. Dreams of Him . . . in His . . . watery grave. Calling to all of us." Great, desperate eyes sought mine, and I saw the unfathomable fear and untold horror of this tortured individual's existence.

"I can feel . . . myself fading . . . away," he clutched at its head, rocking back and forth slightly. "Drowning in darkness . . . ." He reached out suddenly, drawing me close despite my reflexive and ineffectual attempt to pull away. He pulled me close with a hideous strength. "He calls."

A cold prickle worked its way down my spine; the utter conviction and desperation with which he spoke would not allow me to disbelieve him.

"Your father," I rasped with a terrible premonition. "What was his name?"

He let go of me and turned away, so I only heard the gasping voice,

"Ephraim . . . Babson . . . ."

I couldn't speak; my shock and revulsion were too great.

"Boasted of . . . spreading his seed." Diseased and deformed as he was, there was still someone this pitiable creature could look down on and hate. "Said he'd fathered . . . a lot of us . . . ."

He turned to me again, and for the first time, I saw his pale hands with moist webbing that came up between the knuckles, and the small claws that looked like no human nails.

"Come back . . . soon," he whispered. "With a pistol."

I'm not ashamed to say that I fled then, overcome with the horror of what I'd seen. Only the marsh-birds saw me running from that terrible, decrepit village. Once back in my car, a solid piece of the sane, rational twenty-first century, I sat behind the wheel and wept, overwhelmed with the horror I had experienced. I had come looking for answers, and now I couldn't face them. The childhood legends of Arkham were right; the Innsmouth Plague wasn't something you caught, it was genetic. Would that be my fate, to return to Innsmouth transformed, hideous and insane, only to drown myself?

I returned to Arkham, a cloud of despair hanging over me. I had seen my doom; I was a walking dead man, like someone diagnosed with terminal cancer. I bought a pistol, but I couldn't bring myself to suicide quite yet. But I did end the misery of the pathetic thing that thanked me in a wheezing voice, and then the marsh-birds rose, startled at the sudden retort. I sat for hours, staring at the sad corpse of the person who had broken my life, and I never knew his name.

Numbly, not knowing what else to do, I continued my investigation. I thought that if I looked hard enough, I might find a loophole and this wouldn't have happened. I had all the secrets of Innsmouth that I cared to, but I still didn't know anything about Ephraim Babson.

I thought of the pathetic thing's gasping voice, and about Ephraim Babson spreading his taint, and realized that I hadn't been thinking large enough. It took me two hours to drive to Boston, and the Boston *Globe's* newspaper morgue. I looked for articles on serial rapists, starting a year before my birth. It was a tricky search; the police don't want to talk about them, and the newspapers really don't want to make a report until the bastard is caught.

Hours passed, and I began to pick up the trail. Here and there, now and then, in between the constant articles on safety and not going out in Boston after dark, I saw a pattern that I could trace back at least as far back as seventy-six. One 'crime-beat' article confirmed my fears, discussing a number of common descriptors for a string of sexual assaults in areas surrounding Boston. Women described their assailant as 'fishy'-smelling and wide-mouthed, which had the police scouring a couple of the Oriental open-air fish markets for suspects, only to come up empty. Among others, one Ephraim Babson, address unknown, was wanted for questioning in relation to at least one of the linked assaults perpetrated in the Arkham area in nineteen eighty—a couple of months after I was born. Which would make it about eight months before Ethan had been born.

Simultaneously, I was dizzy with relief and yet my guts yawned with dread. Dying, his eyesight nearly gone, my grandfather had mistaken me for Ethan. I hated, still hate, the never-jangled relief that sat in my gut; my doom had passed onto another. To Ethan. How could I be happy knowing that my brother is going to mutate horribly into something like the pathetic thing in Innsmouth?

I haven't been able to sleep for the last three days; whenever I close my eyes I see Ethan, bloated, distorted, drowning in murky water, reaching out to me, and I would wake in a cold sweat. I have stopped going to my job, I stopped going out of my apartment at all. Ethan was doomed, and I wondered if I could even tell him. How could I burden my younger brother with the knowledge of what he is—of what I think he might be? And yet, would it be fair to not tell him?

The thoughts scrabbled incessantly around my head. I knew the lack of sleep was making it harder for me to focus. I could see no good way to end this, unless I was greatly mistaken, and this was all some sort of psychotic episode, or maybe I'd looked at all the evidence wrong. The question burned hot in my head, scratching at all my thoughts with tiny claws. What could I do? Babson was presumably long gone, and each of my trips to Innsmouth had been worse than the previous. Where can I go now, what could I possibly do? My hands shook with exhaustion, and I prayed for sleep, thinking that if I could just close my eyes for an hour or two without seeing Ethan's distorted, terrified face superimposed on that horror from Innsmouth that maybe I'd be able to think straight enough to solve this mess. The only solution I could find, the one my mind always came back to, was the pistol.

An hour ago, I decided to go see my brother.

The Arkham rain is freezing, and I am standing outside of Ethan's small house, shivering with the cold, and I still don't know if this is the right thing, or if I even have the strength to do it if I have to. A memory flashes through me, of Ethan and me hiding out on summer days in a fort made of construction leftovers we'd found in the trees beyond Meadow Hill. Another one hits me, of being old enough to bike all the way to Kingsport, and the two of us, full of energy and youth, staying so long at the rock beaches that we develop terrible cases of sun poisoning. My frenetic thoughts pass through me, and I think about how much I love my brother, and the bittersweet memories of all the things we have done do not strengthen my resolve. I press the doorbell with numb fingers, my knuckles aching from clutching the gun in the relentless, endless, Arkham rain. I think of my grandfather Saltonstall's gnarled fingers, I know how he must have felt at the end, unable to use his tools. Useless. Helpless. Hopeless.

Ethan opens the door. His expression immediately becomes concern when he sees me, soaking wet and shivering in the rain. I look at his familiar expression, and I remember the twinkle in his eyes when he said we should to go the abandoned island, and the way we fought off the three Wheeler brothers once. He is my brother, and I love him almost more than I can bear. I step into the house, and he closes the door behind me.

"Are you all right? Jesus, you look like shit," he says. My brother, always honest with me. He moves to take my denim jacket, and if he does I won't have recourse to my gun. I almost let him take it, but at the last moment I shake him off.

"It's been a tough couple of weeks," I croak at him, and he knows I'll tell him when I'm ready, and backs off. Instead, he moves to one of the windows and pushes the curtain back, and looks out into the hammering rain.

"When it's raining like this," Ethan said in a distant, dreamy voice. "I think this is what it must be like to live under the sea. Everything so wet and cold, and I keep thinking I'll see something swim by."

"Do you think about the sea a lot?" My voice is raw, but I think it conceals the emotions that battle each other like angry cats in my brain. How can I do this, and simultaneously, how can I not? How can I possibly let him slowly turn into that tormented thing from Innsmouth? And yet, how can I possibly use the pistol on the brother I love? I feel like my chest is going to rip itself apart.

He gives me an odd look, then turns back to looking at the rain streaming down the window. "Not really, but you know, I've got this urge to go down to the coast. Take a look at the stormy sea, or maybe a late vacation in a lighthouse in Maine or something."

A stillness descends on me, and there is no contradiction. Convulsively, my hand clenches around the pistol. There are no marsh-birds to startle with the sudden noise this time, and I am left numbly looking at the corpse that was my half-brother. At least now he won't have to hear the siren call of the ocean, and feel his mind slip slowly into darkness.

END

Regrowth

by David Conyers

From the third-story of the Science Hall, I looked down over the campus gardens of Miskatonic University to see a light shower casting rainbows in the morning mist. Amongst the droplet, the autumn colors of reds, yellows and gold, littered under all the trees as a fresh carpet. For some moments I watched as a group of finely dressed men, and a solitary woman, strolled across the grass. Of them I knew little, except that they were Japanese.

The world outside held no comparison to the laboratory where I now found myself; the comparison particularly began and ended with the bizarre tropical abnormality, squat and unmoving on the dissection bench between myself and the head of the School of Biology, Dr. Conrad Miller.

"At first I thought this new plant species sent to us from the Amazon, or more likely the Congo," explained the calm, rational professor who was about to hire me for twenty-five dollars a day plus expenses. "Then I realized this was some kind of misplaced hybrid, created in a test-tube by one of my very own staff."

The "growth" suggested a gnarled wooden root, coiled like a squid's tentacle. Moss overlaying its core was the color of pond slime, while hundreds of differently sized black pimples shaped like tadpole eggs set into the bark seemingly gazed at me. It was these pimples that disturbed me the most, because at first I thought they were eyes, and now I couldn't shake the sensation that they weren't . . . and that they were watching.

"If you aren't similarly convinced Mr. Kinsley, then you should take a look from where I am standing."

Holding my fedora tightly, afraid that if I let go I might feel inclined to touch the thing, I stood next to the Doctor and looked again.

Then I saw it, and stopped breathing for a moment.

From here the wood looked very much like a cat, a normal tabby but warped and mutated, as if the wood had been carved to suggest an animal flowing away . . . as if the cat had grown into the plant.

"Disturbing isn't it?"

I nodded, at last understanding why the university had sought out my services as a private investigator. Previously I'd been weighing up the possibility that one of Miller's underlings had taken a week off for a holiday down by the Cape, paid for by misappropriating M.U. funds. That would be a simple case. Now that I was seeing this "thing" in the flesh, so to speak, I knew that what my eyes examined could only be the end result of scientific mind that was unraveling, obsessing with the unreal and the psychotic.

"Doctor Hetfield has been in this department since 1922," explained Miller. "I regret to say it was I who personally hired him. He was a brilliant mind, once upon a time."

"Was?"

"Yes, of late he became very reclusive, started missing his lectures, failed to mark exams and basically . . . " Miller hesitated so I indicated with a shrug that he should continue. "He started stealing departmental supplies, Mr. Kinsley. But it wasn't until this thing," he pointed at it, stepping back as if sensing its dangers, "that I became really concerned. Doubly so now that Hetfield has been missing for over a week."

Miller walked backward to the far side of the laboratory, eyes still toward the anomaly—perhaps because he didn't want to lose sight of it, and I didn't blame him. When he returned, I was handed a stack of notebooks, which by Miller's expression, he wanted me to examine. I took them, placed the volumes on a clean bench and started flipping through the yellowing papers in chronological order.

Twelve books in total amounted to three years of journals detailing Hetfield's experiments and his results. His disturbed conjecture was obvious: all life, if modified on a cellular level, could be transformed into any other known species, plant or animal. Early notes were rational with neat handwriting, straight lined charts and explanations in an elegant language. Later, when he began referencing books held in the occult collection at the University Library, such as *Nameless Cults* and *The Revelations of Glaaki*, his style deteriorated, his conjecture became wild, and many of his paragraphs were wholly illegible. The last journal was the worst, with scrawls and scribbles which might have been sentences and charts, but were really nothing less than mad scratching. Toward the end, the only words that I could read were the often repeated "Shub-Niggurath" and his favorite, "Regrowth". That last word filling page after page after page.

"An unsettled mind," I said placing the last journal back down where I had found it. I hadn't yet accepted this case and to do so, to go to the other side of that choice, would give me a new and interesting investigation far more intriguing than cheating spouses and insurance scams. However, the hair on the back of my neck wouldn't sit down, and my stomach churned as if I hadn't eaten in days; signs telling me to walk away. But I couldn't think of any rational reason not to take the job. Miller hadn't bothered to argue down my initial price, there didn't seem any chance that I'd be involved in anything questionably legal, and most importantly I wouldn't be dealing with any criminal types. So why did I hesitate?

I was sure the thing on the table knew why.

"You should take those with you," Miller interrupted my thoughts, referring not to the abnormality my eyes couldn't stop watching, but to the journals he was now pointing to.

"Sure," I picked them up accepting the case. "But one more question before I leave, Dr. Miller. You said Hetfield was stealing supplies from the department. Can you tell me exactly what?"

"We suspect theft because we never found any of the missing items in his possession." Miller looked away, out the window toward autumn as if part of him, like me, hoped to escape the nightmare on the table, remembering that the rational and enlightened world in which we lived could still be glanced out there. "They all just vanished."

"But you suspect . . ." I led him on. "What went missing?"

He paused again, "We suspected him of stealing laboratory animals."

◆ ◆ ◆

Five years ago in 1919, I resigned my post as a detective with the Arkham Police, and at long last became my own boss. Within a month I'd established *Peter Kinsley, Private Investigations* on the sixth floor of the Tower Professional Building on West Armitage Street, the *only* address if I was going to attract high-paying clients. And I did! Somehow I did all right, making far more money than I had ever expected. That's because I'd never suspected Arkham to be the kind of sleepy old town that hid so many mysteries, each just itching to be unearthed— and mysteries were my bread and butter. Last year I had gathered so much work that I needed an extra pair of hands, and so hired a secretary to help out. I still remember the day Julie Gammell walked through the front door.

"How did it go?" she asked from behind the reception desk as I strode into the office, hung my overcoat and fedora on the coat stand as I always did.

"This will be an interesting case, different from the usual fare." I kissed her gently on the lips. Then her mouth was all over mine, and I was enjoying it too much to stop. Last month saw us engaged, and now she only promises to quit working when we are properly married so her attention can be directed toward raising a family. We didn't stop kissing for at least five minutes.

"I missed you Peter," she pulled away, gasping for breath And so was I.

"I've only been gone the morning."

"You should bring me with you; let me share some of the fun."

"I need you on the telephone," my eyes shifted toward Mr. Bell's contraption, as still and silent as that growth in the Life Science building. Once again the abnormality's unwholesome shape was in the forefront of my mind.

She scoffed, sat on the desk crossing her legs, knowing that the hem of her dress would rise. "You know perfectly well clients only telephone in the morning, or occasionally late at night. I've got nothing to do all day." Then she ran up to me, wrapped her arms around my shoulders, her beautiful deep blue eyes finding mine. "I'm bored, Peter. Take me with you."

I laughed, patted her on the back, and then stepped away to take in her shapely figure. Julie was my movie star, dressed up like a Louise Brooks and just as alluring, even the styling of her dark hair like a pageboy was the same inviting shape.

"Then you can start by going through these," I handed her the journals, all twelve.

Her cute smile transformed into a frown. "Always the boring paperwork. I want to see all those gangsters that you talk about, be your flapper sidekick at a speakeasy, and enjoy the excitement of a stake-out." She made the shape of a revolver with her hands, pretended to fire it over my shoulder as if she'd just saved my life from an unseen assailant. "It would be fun."

"It would also be dangerous." I opened the pages of the first and last journal while explaining this case to her, careful to demonstrate the rapid degeneration of Hetfield's mind over the last three years. "You want to help me Julie, then go through these with a fine tooth comb and see what you deduce. An address or two would be helpful"

She sat back, crossed her arms and scowled like a little girl who had just been told off by her mother. I knew Julie too well; if we didn't drop the subject now she would become incessantly more difficult to handle, so like all men dealing with relationship problems, I found my overcoat and fedora again and headed for the door.

"Where you going now, you've just got back?"

"Arkham Police Station, maybe they have something that might help."

She ran up to me, hugged me, trembling in my arms, and I was caught unaware. "You're not going to leave me, are you Peter?"

"I'll only be gone for an hour or two at the most."

She bit her lip nervously, "No, I mean . . . we're still going to be married aren't we? If you give me nothing to do here all day, then I at least want to know that I will be your wife, so I can give you babies and I'd feel important again"

The hardness of my face melted when the subtext of her words were finally revealed. This had nothing at all to do with her lack of involvement in my work, but a fear that something might stop us finding happiness together, as husband and wife. "No, sweetie, you're the world to me," I said taking her in my arms and holding her tight, feeling that if I didn't, I just might lose her forever. "We're going to be together for all time, no matter what."

"I hope so," she cried into my shoulder. "Because I'm holding you to that promise."

◆ ◆ ◆

Arkham Police Station was as drab and musty as I remembered where I found myself chatting with Detective Ray Stuckey. He just happened to be the main reason why I'd left the force in the first place. Stuckey was a good detective, but he was on the take, paid to look the other way when the local O'Bannion mob smuggled their shipments of illegally liquor into town. I was no bent cop and never would be, but I also didn't plan on taking any lead in the chest because my partner's interest rested somewhere other than upholding the law. That feeling was mutual and opposite; Stuckey didn't trust me because I was honest. Hard feelings die slow deaths, so today as expected I got nothing out of him.

"Nothing?"

"Where did you say he lived again?" Stuckey's gruff tone was its usual unhelpful self.

"Near West Curwen and Brown Street?"

He squinted, then shook his head vigorously. "Just some missing pets; cats and dogs, nothing unusual. A few people complain about strange sounds at night." He tried to imitate the sound. If I had to guess, I'd guess he failed. Still, he continued to *bwee-heet* away, as though I might know what kind of animal made such a noise.

That ended the conversation. I was so hot under the collar that I departed quickly before a gasket blew.

On the stroll back to my office, I gave myself time to do some deductive reasoning, starting with the best place of all—the facts. Miller believed his missing scientist was important enough to hire a professional to find him, but not important enough to involve the police? This suggested there was something going on that Miller didn't want Stuckey and Co. to undercover. Perhaps Hetfield was into some kind of illegal experimentation, and Miller knew about it. If I was right, then the thing on the table certainly fit the scenario. Only problem was, Miller didn't seem the type for collusion.

It was getting late, so instead of interviewing Miller again, I returned to my office only to find that Julie had left for the night and the rooms locked up. Hetfield's journals had departed with her, taken home for bedtime reading. One could say many things about Julie, good or bad, but no one could say she wasn't due diligent. Many a case would have taken longer to solve than they did if Julie hadn't worked the numbers in the background. Efficient and affectionate, how I loved that girl.

I sauntered back to my apartment where I called Julie, only to have her parents answer saying she wasn't home yet. So I left it at that, read a good book by the fire, and drifted off to sleep.

And then that thing came to visit me in my sleep . . . refusing to stop watching me . . . always crawling across the dissection table.

I shouldn't have taken this case.

◆ ◆ ◆

I woke with a startled cry, but in a half-dazed stupor, I realized all that I heard was the early morning squabbling of crows, and the sounds of automobiles rattling their drivers toward another day's pay. I needed to do the same, but not until I'd had a good wash, a clean shave, and slipped on a fresh suit. Only then did I feel like a crisp fifty-dollar bill, and ready to earn as much.

When I reached the office and hung my fedora and coat as I always did, I noticed Julie had yet to open up the office. Two hours later while I was still sorting through my badly out-of-date accounts, she still hadn't appeared, which was not like her at all. I telephoned her parents, they were angry suspecting that their daughter had spent the night with me, so I assured them that she had not. Then they became concerned that something terrible might have happened, and when they became worried, so did I.

"Let me make a few calls." I hung up before her father could abuse me further, and I dialed the exchange. A minute later I had Dr. Miller on the line.

"Did my fiancée . . . I mean did my secretary call this morning?" My voice was frantic.

"Well no, not this morning . . . but she did call last night"

"Nothing this morning?"

"No, why do you ask?"

"She's missing," I blurred, unsuccessful in my attempt not to appear panicked, but that was exactly how I felt right now so that was exactly how I sounded. "I'm sorry. I'm trying to piece together her recent movements, work out where she might be?"

"Oh," he sounded a little calmer now that he understood my intentions. "Perhaps I can help. She did ask me about an address."

"Address!?" I yelled, hoping he'd get to the point faster.

"Yes, she wanted to know if Hetfield owned a property in Billington Woods. Said it had something to do with the case"

I waited. He said nothing. "Well, does he?"

"You mean you weren't told, Mr. Kinsley? Why yes Hetfield does own such a property. I'm sorry if I sound confused, but your secretary informed me that you were heading out there last night? Am I mistaken?"

"Can I have the address please," I asked.

Once the number was committed to paper, I hung up without further pleasantries. I collected and loaded my .45 revolver, found my flashlight and then clambered into my Chevrolet. Speeding out of Arkham I left nothing but scattered autumn leaves to signal my departure.

◆ ◆ ◆

Billington Woods is a dark and foreboding forest grown wild on the outskirts of town. Much of it still untouched by axe or saw, and probably just as unexplored, at least it seemed that way whenever I'd driven past it in the night. By day it was only marginally better, suggestive that it was home to more of Arkham's numerous mysteries. Tangled and old, this wood had been owned by the Billington family since colonial times, and for some unknown reason no family member had lived there since the early 1800s. They probably knew what the rest of us suspected—that it was an unwholesome place. They probably knew why too.

The address that I'd been given was on the edge of Billington's property, just off Cabot Road near the creek of the same name. I turned the corner sharply, scattering dust and gravel winding my way further into the dingy pine trees that grew far to close together. I noticed how thickly the needles and branches intermingled as if they were one giant organism with many trunks. No wonder the wooded interior became nothing more than darkness as I was consumed by it.

Finally I came upon an old farmhouse overgrown with vines and moss, surprised by the different species of trees sprouting through the splintered planks of the porch as if it had always been like this.

And an attached greenhouse didn't surprise me either, although the state of it did. Many of its panes were dark with grime and molds, while others had long shattered against the explosion of rampant tropical plants pushing from the inside, probably so they could continue their sinister plans to overtake the rest of the woods. I saw banana and figs trees, palms, tropical vines and jungle creepers, all thriving in a temperate climate that should have killed them.

I knew I should have taken all this as a warning, but I didn't get the chance to turn away. There was a loud explosion and the front wheel of my Chevrolet deflated with a *pop*.

Gripping the steering wheel tightly, I tried to maintain control of the spinning automobile, but in the end a ditch betrayed me and I crashed straight into a heavy stack of new firewood. My head hit the wheel knocking me out for a moment, and I vaguely remember the windshield shattering. When I woke, glass fragments lay everywhere. More telling— if not seriously—my face and hands were bleeding.

Next, both barrels of a 12-gauge shotgun were wavering only a few inches from my face.

"Get out!" ordered a gruff voice.

I looked his way, expecting and confirming that this was the good Dr. Hetfield all right, only his left eye was twitching and his dirty hands trembled too much for my liking, especially since they were on the trigger of the loaded weapon pointed in my face. I couldn't imagine him lecturing in a respected university like Miskatonic; he was more hermit and bear-trapper now, ragged with clothes tattered and torn, and his stench was overpowering. If Miller thought Hetfield had been unsettled before he had disappeared, well I had news for him.

"I said get out!"

I did what I was told. He didn't see my .45 still holstered under my jacket, so I didn't offer it up. When I stepped out, I exaggerated my condition, staggering, feeling pain that wasn't real, while knowing that the blood on my hands and face would now work in my favor. This brought the desired effect, my foe relaxed somewhat, and I noticed that his eyes strayed from me more and more often as we walked away from my vehicle. Still he used the barrel as a prod to get me inside his house.

The stench of the interior assaulted me first, like an old nursing home catering not only to too many old folk, but for too many of their unnourished pets as well. It was easy to see why, for what had once been a lounge room was now a holding pen, with hundreds of wire cages packed hap-hazardly one on top of the other packed with frightened animals pacing and screaming from their confinement. More than a few were already dead or close to it, while those that lived were definitely starving. A few with lingering strength violently chewed or clawed to get free. I identified all kinds of domestic pets from rabbits, hamsters, cats, dogs, mice, and even rats. When they spotted us the rabble transformed into a riot, until a cage with a dog tipped, clanging to the wooden floor and stunning every creature into silence for a moment, but just a moment.

Now that we were inside, Hetfield locked the door behind us. Three times already I'd seen him look away long enough for me to draw a gun and shoot him, but I wanted to hear what he had to say first, and more importantly, lead me to Julie.

"Where's my fiancée?"

"What?" He looked genuinely confused, but then insane people often do.

"Julie is her name. She turned up here yesterday?"

"Oh her," he laughed far too manic for me to feel assured. "she's through there." With his shotgun he pointed to a doorway leading into the greenhouse where the smell grew worse.

I led the way, careful not to trip over the thick vines and creepers that grew around and beyond the entrance, until it seemed we were stepping into the middle of some fevered African jungle full of exotic and wild vegetation. Nothing looked real, that is to say, nothing looked to be like what a plant should. Everywhere I noticed the same gnarled, wooden roots covered in thick green moss, sprouting the same tentacle-shaped branches, and those seas of black eyes, some as large as a baseball all watching me. I muffled a cry when one rotated my way, looked at me, until I dismissed it as a trick of the light.

I could see this was the source of Hetfield's madness and not the other way around, for this was where the strange abnormality Dr. Miller had shown me yesterday had first found life. Here the abnormalities grew everywhere, dominating and consuming every other plant and tree that I had previously thought had been thriving in this greenhouse. Outside appearances in this case were definitely deceptive, for the *normal* plants were not thriving, they were food.

"So what is it Hetfield," I spoke as calmly as I could. "are you a biologist or a botanist?" I wanted to say butcher but held my tongue.

He smiled with a dirty mouth. "I'll be famous you know I've discovered the secret of regrowth. Only I know that all plant and animal matter are all one and the same. I know how they can be converted."

Feeling the pit of my stomach sink with despair, I remembered what I saw in the growth at Miskatonic University. Now I saw the same suggestions here; a hanging vine that might have been inspired by a strung cat, a root system half buried in the earth oddly shaped like a curled up dog, and hanging pods in their dozens uncannily reminding my of twisted rats. Wild-eyed and suddenly terrified I looked back at Hetfield, "Where is my wife?"

He laughed again. "Right behind you."

So I turned, seeing nothing but a tangle of mossy gnarled vines. Yet something wasn't quite right, so I stepped closer, looked again. What first appeared to be a leg was covered in bark and the rings of old wood, and just above an interlaced hand that instead of fingers sprouted mossy vines. I followed the shape upward, pushing aside the tangles that obscured more. Green flesh around the navel, pink flesh at the breasts, neck and face, half of her was mutated wooded plant, the other pale soft human skin.

Then those blue Louise Brooks eyes opened, and looked at me.

I feel backward, stumbling almost falling as I sought the breath to scream.

"The stupid fools," Hetfield gloated behind me. "Back at Miskatonic they think they understand science. All those professors with their walls of qualifications and honors, but let me tell you they know nothing. I've read *Nameless Cults* and *The Revelations of Glaaki*, and I've poured through every fable in *The Masked Messenger*, which even they don't know about. Only I know that these books tell the real truth, expose the real answers behind all of life's mysteries."

I stood up, anger flowing through every vein in my body. My fiancée, my love—this madman had forever taken her away from me. So if I couldn't be with Julie, love her, care for her, then I could still extract my revenge.

"They don't understand!" His monologue rattled on, his wild eyes no longer caring that I was advancing upon him, my fists clenching and unclenching as I did. "No one understands that Shub-Niggurath is the source of all life, that she is fertility, and that she is the regrowth which is stunted in all of us. Understand that and you understand where we all came from—how it is so easy to convert animal life into vegetation, and perhaps even understand our origins from a time when life on Earth was little more than seas of glorious algae."

I was upon him now. He didn't seem to notice; his attention drawn away pointing to a freshly prepared flask of thick green noxious fluid on a workbench. "Go on, drink of the blessed Mother Shub-Niggurath, and discover who you really are."

He didn't see me take out the .45 revolver and point it his way. I don't think he even realized that he had been shot until the second slug exploded through his lungs. Four more bullets ensured that he would never get up again.

With tears in my eyes, I returned to my fiancée's side. Julie Gammell had once been the woman who was going to be my wife and who was to bear the future generations of the Kinsley family. Now she was more plant than woman, a jungle vine that had grown from her shape, twisting her body as if she were a wet towel wrung to dry. I pulled my gun to take away any pain she might still be suffering. I tried to shoot her, only to realize I'd used all my rounds on Hetfield. So I sat down instead, rather fell, feeling the despair overwhelm me.

I'd always known that Arkham was a town of too many mysteries. I think that was why I was drawn here in the first place, but I'd never guessed for a moment that I'd be part of one. How stupid was I? Julie just wanted her freedom, and I'd done all that I could to cage her. So she had gone behind my

back, to prove what? That she could get herself killed? If only
I'd trusted her more, let her be part of my life, then I wouldn't
be alone right now with no future in sight. I'd lost everything.

"You promised."

I heard her voice, remembered our last conversation inside
my head. It seemed so real, and that made it so much worse
remembering.

"Peter?"

Her words were as clear as day, as if she was in the room
with me right now.

But she was in the room with me right now.

I turned, looked back to see those eyes, they were alive and
animated. Looking at me they were catching my stares, before
darting back at the bench with the noxious green fluid. When
I looked back, her blue eyes grew large with great urgency.
"You promised," she managed again through a mouth that was
more knotted wood than flesh.

Dumbfounded I watched her.

"A promise Peter . . . you promised . . ." She kept repeating
the words with a voice that was too unreal to believe.

It took a while, but finally I understood.

"I did promise, didn't I?"

◆ ◆ ◆

So here I am, about to drink Hetfield's "Milk of Shub-
Niggurath" as he calls it, but before I do I just wanted to com-
mit the rest of my story to paper, make it real so that if others
start down the same path that Julie and I so foolishly followed,
they won't become lost like we are.

How did it come to this? I don't really know. But how I got
here is no longer really important, not to me. The past is past
and that is where it belongs. It is my word to the one woman I
really care about, whom I love more than anything on this
earth. That is all that matters now.

So now that I've finished my sad little tale, I'll drink Hetfield's milk, and then I'm going to wrap my arms about my wife, and wait for the change.

And as I wait, she'll remind me again what I've already decided—that from this moment forward, we really are going to be together forever.

END

The Idea of Fear

by C.J. Henderson

"We are terrified by the idea of being terrified." –Nietzsche

He looked the house over from the street. Dark and old and tall and musty, like every other dilapidated dump in town, he knew. They were all the same, all creaking, all spongy—alive with mosses and spores and gas leaks—all filled with a thousand crinkling noises. The man stared out the window of his car and despaired dragging himself out onto the sidewalk.

Some detective, he thought. You sure aren't going to give Phil Marlowe a run for his money anytime soon in this town.

Franklin Nardi had left New York City after its police force had used up his strongest, bravest days. Many envied the life—work a job for a mere twenty years and retire with benefits beyond the dreams of most. With only the slightest of salaries on top of such a retirement package, it was said, a man could support a family in style.

Yeah, he thought, taking another long drag on his cigarette, and all it takes to earn those fine benefits is walking out the door with a target on your back. Every day. Every stinking, miserable day. For twenty goddamned years.

Frankie Nardi had no family. He did not lose them tragically, except in the sense that it was tragic they had never existed at all. Nardi did not by nature enjoy the company of women. He had witnessed the eternal grinding down of his father and his uncles, all men to be proud of, except when they ventured into the presence of women and their guts turned to cheese. He listened to them complain, watched them live their lives afraid to speak, afraid to contradict, afraid of what they might do to these women they loved if they ever stopped reining themselves in.

The detective was not afraid of women. He went out with them and played their games to the extent those rounds gave him what he wanted—flesh and momentary contact free from the rock-heavy drag of commitment.

"Ahhh, fuck," he snorted. He took another long look at his assignment for the night and then crushed his smoke out on the roof of his car, adding, "no one ever said life was easy."

Window up, bags grabbed from the back seat, car locked, up to the front door. Nardi assessed the ring of keys he had been given and with his usual skill picked the correct one on the first try. Throwing open the old door he threw his bags inside and surveyed his home for the evening. With a crunch of muscles he stretched his arms out, flexing his back and shoulders unconsciously. Even though he expected nothing more than a night's sleep, he was still a man who did his job.

After twenty years of not blinking, of watching over his shoulder, behind his back, of sizing up each and every human being that came near him, figuring their angle, investigating their souls in the split-second before contact, moving to Arkham was supposed to have been a breeze. The town was known for importing New York's finest. One supposed the New English hamlet would have preferred Bostonian coppers, but as the mayor of Arkham had put it to Nardi when he asked;

"This town has enough drunks with their hands out. We need real men. Manhattan is the attitude that goes over well here when people want protection."

It was true. New Yorkers took charge. Taking charge of his life, Nardi had left the city he simply could not stand any more and turned his back on it for trees and fields and runaway dogs. His idea was to open his own detective/security agency in Arkham with three other New York cops—one who had retired a year earlier, Tony Balnco, and two others, Sammy Galtoni and Mark Berkenwald, who were right behind him on the escape track. They had all agreed instantly—the one already retired fastest of all. In three months they were the fastest growing business in the city of Arkham, Massachusetts.

And why not? People cheated on their spouses in New England same as anywhere else. They stole from their bosses, needed background checks, wanted to find lost property or people from their pasts, required security like everyone else. Nardi had seen Bloods selling crack behind the playground at Allan Halsey Memorial High School the same way he had behind the playground at Thomas Jefferson High in Brooklyn, and every other high school throughout the five boroughs. There was no "safe" America anymore. The green was going to hell in all the same ways as the concrete—just a little slower, that was all.

Which is what had made Arkham perfect for Nardi and his pals. For five years they had built their business and life was good for them. They held the security contracts for nearly three/fifths of the businesses in town. They were the first contact point on the speed dial list of four/fifths of the town's lawyers. They had all the work they needed; which was what angered Nardi when Berkenwald took a job like the one he was stuck with that night.

"So?" he asked the house absently. "Let's make with the spooky noises. Let's get this over with."

In New York, Nardi had found plenty of opportunities to placate the wealthy. Those with money were always finding some new way to waste it. Years ago the slugs bleeding cash could not move into a new property without calling in a feng-shui master to make certain it was properly positioned in the universe. Now, in Arkham, the chic move was to have your home desensitized by a supernatural security team.

"What a crock of shit," muttered Nardi.

Berkenwald, getting wind of the new chump rage, had let it be known to only a few, close personal friends, mind you, that the agency had been called in to clear a few major hauntings back in New York. Hinted at terrible moments, let it be known they simply did not do that sort of work anymore. Too stressful. The hideous terrors that awaited the uninitiated . . . .

The suckers had begun throwing money at the agency immediately. Any new bride or social matron who heard a noise she did not like, felt a draft that seemed a little too frigid, awoke in a cold sweat, et cetera, knew what to do—buy some peace of mind.

But Berkenwald had booked more work for them that week than they could cover. And thus Frankie Nardi, himself, the owner of the company, who should have been working on his model railroad set-up in his basement at that very moment, and dreaming of a date with his hammock for the next day, was instead stuck doing a point-by-point sweep of some ancient rathole for ghosts.

Ghosts, for Christ's sake.

"Does it get any stupider than this? I don't think I want to know if it does."

"Don't tell me you want the world to smarten up, Nardi," a voice said from behind the detective. "That would lose you a lot of business."

"I'm retired, remember?" He threw the line over his shoulder to the woman coming in the doorway. "The more business I have the less I like it."

"I think you're just afraid to run into the Headless Horseman or one of his pals. Something like that would be hard work," she said with a bite in her voice as she dropped her bags heavily on the floor, "and we all know you're afraid of that."

"Yeah, nothin' with tits is a feminist when there's heavy-liftin' to do."

The woman was Madame Renee, her profession, medium. Born Brenda Goff, she had cultivated her over-whelmingly Middle Eastern looks until a nose too big and brows too bushy had begun to work in her favor. As her love of all things covered in, filled with, or simply made from sugar had stolen her figure, she had made her shape a badge and transformed herself once more. Dancers had a short shelf-life, she had told herself when she had traded her tights for a beaded curtain and a crystal ball. Fortune-tellers could work from a wheelchair.

"Sweet as ever, ain't ya?"

"Oh, don't crawl up my ass; I've got all the shit I can handle today, and this job is half of it."

"You're not a happy man, are you, Frank?"

Madame Renee reached out to touch the detective on the cheek but he ducked the contact, his glower showing open hostility. "Look," he told her curtly, "we're here to de-ghost this dump, and as stupid as I feel about this nonsense, a job is still a job. Mark told me you've got the checklist, so, if you do, then let's get to it. The faster we prove the Ghostly Trio isn't hiding up the chimney, the faster we get to go home."

With a shrug, the madame sighed and pulled out the official Nardi Security Occult Clearance Form from the large carpet bag she seemed to always keep with her. Without trying again to lighten the mood, she simply started calling off routines and posing questions while Nardi poked, prodded, and peeled back this and that part of the old house. Between them they searched every room for cold spots, listened carefully to each wall with their stethoscopes, made certain a mirror would reflect light in every room, and tested the air on every floor to make certain no unwanted chemicals, smells, gases or aromas were present.

They set up motion detectors in every passageway and sound-trigger tape recorders in every room. Powder was sprinkled around doorways and across table tops and mantlepieces to record the motion of any invisible forces. Hairs were secured across the doors of cupboards and the drawers of dressers with nothing more than a finger smear of saliva. If anything with the slightest physical presence moved within the old house outside the living room where Madame Renee and Nardi would be camped out for the night, it would be known.

The madame, of course, had her own bag of tricks to perform. She rolled her bones, did an open reading with the tarot deck she had made herself, and set herself to staring into the crystal shard she used for focus to reach out beyond herself to bind herself with the house's aura—searching for unwanted visitors. After that, as Nardi went room by room, setting his machines and traps, she pulled back into herself, and then opened her own aura to the building and to all and any that might be within it. Reaching deep within herself, she peeled back the layers of modern life, of concern over her daughter's college expenses, moved past the aches and pains a body some one hundred and sixty pounds past its medically approved weight-for-its-height felt constantly, dug down inward until she had found the pure essence of her inner being and revealed it completely and utterly.

By the end of the night the pair were utterly exhausted— Nardi from covering the old place attic to basement as well as every room of the three floors in between, Renee from having thrown herself open past all boundaries. She had poured her soul and heart into every bit of wire and plaster and mahogany the old home had to offer, placing herself out before it, helpless and beckoning, and had received nothing for her efforts.

This fact confused her greatly.

"What are you talkin' about?" asked Nardi. The detective desperately wanted to fall back into the recliner he had chosen as his bed and shut his eyes, but a job was a job and so he coaxed the woman further.

"Com'on, spill it."

Renee propped herself up on the couch with one of her massively fleshy elbows. Staring at Nardi, knowing he did not believe in anything they were doing, she struggled to find a way to voice her concern. Finally, she simply told him what was on her mind.

"Listen, I don't want to go around and around with you on this, so I'll just say it. I did several readings of the house before we got started—future glances, stability predictions—that kind of stuff. It's the low end of what I do for one of these things. Then I fired off the big guns, really put myself out there, bared my soul, big irresistible hunk of ectoplasm for anything nasty in the area and . . . I didn't get a bite."

"Disappointed?"

"No, you Italian shit. If you had a soul that could be touched by anything you'd know I was more than earning my fee here. If this was a spirit shanty, I would've paid a price, believe me."

"Then I don't get it," answered the detective honestly, stifling a yawn. "What's the problem?"

"The problem is that something should have come for me." When Nardi said nothing, she continued, explaining, "those early readings I did, they said this place is, I don't know, that something's going to happen here. Something . . . nasty, maybe, I don't know. I couldn't get a good sense of it. I didn't worry about it, because I figured I'd find something later that would point the way to the truth. But, the more we checked the place out the cleaner it seemed to get."

"And this is bad?"

"No; it's just confusing." Taking a tiny bit of pity on his temporary partner, and also knowing that placating her would allow him to get some sleep, he said; "Look, we're just here to do a job. If we don't turn up anything more, then that's what we tell the too-rich pair of country club snots who bought this museum. We give 'em the bad with the good, tip our hats, and we leave."

"I know," Renee answered. "It's just that I met the wife. She's young. She's in love. She's—" the sizable woman paused for a moment, then found the word for which she was looking.

"—She's nice. I don't want to just take their money. Not this time. Am I making any sense to you?"

Franklin Nardi did not like to reveal much about himself, especially to women. But, he was not heartless, and he let Madame Renee know that he did indeed understand her concern. He also told her that, tired as they were, if there was anything in this house waiting to play with their minds, this was the time they would do it.

"We both came extra tired. That's the deal. Our systems are as weakened as they can get without us bein' sick or something. We're as vulnerable as can be. If nothing bites our asses tonight, and we don't find any reactions in the morning, will you be happy?"

"Heavens," the large woman answered. "I've heard concern in the voice of Franklin Nardi. Why, I'm happy already."

The detective simply reached over and turned off the lights as Madame Renee chuckled softly.

◆ ◆ ◆

Despite his fatigue, from a long evening on top of a long day on top of a week where he had already worked two double shifts, Frankie Nardi could not sleep. Renee's words had stayed with him. As much as he was willing to trade quips with the woman, he respected her as a professional. To him, her tarot readings and the such were the hard evidence of her line of work. Opening herself up to her surroundings was subjective.

If her hard evidence told her one thing, and her subjective evidence told her another, he was wondering exactly what was wrong.

Did she just do a bad reading? Three different types? All wrong? Was that possible?

Nardi drummed the fingers of his left hand against the handrest of his recliner. Wide awake, he worried more and more over the problem before him. Although he did not like the de-ghosting part of his agency's business, it was not because he did not believe in the supernatural. No NYC cop lasted twenty years without hearing about the Zarnak files, the Thorner case loads, old Tommy Malone . . . .

"Damnit."

The whispered word hung in the living room air accusingly. Franklin Nardi was a good detective. He had been a good cop. He did not leave a job unfinished. All stones on his beat were turned over. His tongue pressed against his teeth, face a tight mask of skin and tension, he threw his jacket off himself and got up out of his chair.

"All right, house," he said, getting down on his knees. "You want something juicy, I got juicy for you."

Renee had done this kind of thing a hundred times. A thousand. Maybe that was where the problem was. Maybe whatever her readings had picked up wanted more than a few bites out of a pro who could reject their spectral advances. Maybe she had found something lurking in a corner that wanted to taste real fear.

Fine, he sneered within his head. Com'on, I gotta bellyful of it for you.

So saying, Nardi closed his eyes and began pulling off his clothing. A man who never went to the office without a tie and jacket, who did not like the beach, who showered strictly by himself, the detective peeled away his layers of protection and sat naked on the floor. Then, slowly, he began to peel away those mental walls he had built over the decades as well.

It was hard work for Nardi, mainly because like most people, he did not know where to begin, where the boundary lines were drawn. As he fumbled, the back of his mind whispered: *It's like George Carlin said, everyone driving slower than you is a moron, and anyone driving faster is an asshole.*

The detective knew what he was trying to tell himself. With the courage he had used to knock in the door of a known gun dealer, that he had used when he had charged straight into a hail of gunfire thrown at him by both sides of a gang war, he looked into his soul and tried to figure out why he had never had a serious relationship.

What was it about women that he dreaded so? He had watched his father and others all his young years. So there were fights? So what? People fight. So families split up. His hadn't. Some women cheated, but so did some men. His mother and father had been faithful. Everyone in his family had been as far as he knew. There were plenty of ugly rumors about who stole what from who, and who didn't bathe, and who drank too much, his one uncle—the one who stayed a confirmed bachelor until he died, left all his money to the church, all those video tapes they found, Lassie, Wonder Years, The Andy Griffith Show, anything with a young boy in the cast—he had heard it all, knew it all.

So what's your problem, Nardi?

The detective could feel the sweat flowing from his body. He thought of women he could have made a life with, remembered their faces, their bodies, the way they smelled in spring, the sound of their laughs, and he shuddered as one by one he remembered shoving them away from himself. Until it became easy. Until it became routine.

He thought of women with whom he had slept, those he had used as rough fun, for sex and satisfaction and nothing more. And he thought of others. His mind brought him pictures of dozens of girls, some he had slept with, others he had played around with, those he had merely kissed, and even women he had simply dreamed about.

And then he remembered Anna.

Anna, with her perfect hair. Anna, with the shoulders so straight, body so taut, legs so long, whose lips tasted of happiness and whose eyes could see into his lungs, could watch the oxygen in them reach his blood stream and rocket to his brain. Anna, who had laid beside him the night he got his acceptance papers to the Academy, who had surrendered herself to him, allowing him his ultimate conquest on his day of triumph, when he was a king who could not be denied.

Anna, who had been so shocked when he had rejected her when she told him she was pregnant. Anna, who he had sent to have an abortion. Anna, who he had ordered to murder his son, and then had blamed her for his death.

Anna, who had spit on his shadow and told him to rot in Hell, and who had found herself another.

Nardi sank to the floor and sputtered, tears pouring from his eyes, spittle bubbling on the carpeting. Afraid to face responsibility, afraid to be father to a thing like himself, he had instead poisoned his own life and then spent twenty years trying to throw it away. His gentle sobs turned into wails of despair, so violent a noise that he never even noticed when Madame Renee rose from the couch and covered him with her blanket.

◆ ◆ ◆

The next morning Nardi and Renee spoke at length. He explained what he had tried to do, and what the results had been. At first he thought he would be embarrassed, but he was too empty, too drained of anger and shame to care. For the first time in over a quarter of a century, he felt like a whole person and did not mind talking about it.

"So," he asked, shoveling in a large spoon of corn flakes, "where does this leave us?"

"I think it comes down to what you said last night. We went through the entire place this morning—not a tripped wire, not a bit of powder out of place . . ." when the detective corrected her, Renee laughed, "all right, so we have to tell the blushing bride her pantry has mice—and small mice at that.

But that's it. I'll offer to come back and do another reading after they move in, but that's it. This place is clean."

Madame Renee stared at the detective and marveled at what he had done. To throw himself open to such psychic damage, to be able to face his deepest fears, unaided, unprotected— this was a man, she told herself. A hell of a man.

"It has to be clean," she added.

And so, the two packed their machines and clothing and bits and pieces and piled them into their vehicles. Making certain he had both reactivated the security system and locked the front door, Nardi took one last look at the old house, then said;

"Well, no one can say the Nardi Security Team doesn't earn it's pay."

Renee made a surprisingly graceful bow of acknowledgement to his statement, then headed for her car. Nardi turned back to the house, tipped his baseball cap to its weathered roof, and then headed for his own.

And, inside the house, the foul presence which had spent the entire time of Nardi and Renee's visit suffering in exquisite anguish, allowed itself to burst forth once more from its thousand different hiding places. It was an elder, jaundiced thing, and its hate bounded from the walls as it unfolded itself.

The fat cow, she had been so easy to resist it was a thing of amusement to the cursed soul, a humor so gay it crippled the violent spirit. But the man, all that marvelous, seething, ever-so-fresh pain . . . .

That had been hard to ignore. Agonizingly hard. Oh, for just a tiny tongueful of his snivelling grief, the merest pin prick of his pain . . . .

But that would have alerted the pair of interlopers, set them upon it, forced it to fight back, wasted time, lost it the prize.

No, it purred, remembering the bride soon to be thrust into the bowels of its domain, the smell of her innocence, the drooling wonderfulness of her softness, the flesh to be touched, the love to be poisoned . . . .

What did they think it was, some inconsequential? Some mere nothing of mere human memory? Fools.

The thing which pulsed with the old house exploded with laughter. It had been sorely tempted, but it had won its prize. It had been afraid for a moment, the detective had almost snared it with the delicious aroma of his fear.

Almost.

But it knew a thing or two itself, about the idea of fear, and it had conquered its own.

Now, it mused, bring me something else to conquer.

The house laughed, and the trees shuddered, but there was no one there to hear.

Yet.

END

Disconnected

by Brian M. Sammons

click

the .45 bucked in my hand and my ears rang with
its report, and a new hole suddenly appeared in the
● ● ● thin wooden shutters that covered the back window. I think I hit the thing on the other side of the window
as I saw shadows shift and moonlight once again filter in
through the shutters. However, if I did hit it, it never once
made a sound. Not for a second did I think one lousy bullet,
not even from a .45, would kill one of those misshapen
nightmares, but perhaps it would keep them at bay for a little while.

No such luck.

One or more of them were at the front door once again. I
saw flickering colored lights seeping beneath the door even
before I heard claws on its wooden surface. The pale light illuminated the inside of the farmhouse in angry rainbow hues
and reflected wetly off the pile of debris that had once been
the person who lured me out here. Damn, I walked right into
that trap like a first year rookie on the force. How could I
have been so stupid? Now I was stuck in a deserted house on
the outskirts of . . .

click

. . . "Arkham? Where the hell is Arkham?" I asked as I poured myself a second cup-of-joe. For me the day didn't start until I had at least three cups.

"It's a little college town in Massachusetts. It's next to the Miskatonic River and the college is also called Miskatonic University. Other than that, I can't help you, so you're going to have to pick up a map or ask around or something. Jesus, Harry, you're a P.I. for Christ's sake. If you can't find an entire city, maybe you should just hang up the–"

"Ok, Bob. I was just asking. No need to bite my . . . "

click

. . . "head at?" I asked while not looking too closely at the stiff laying on the slab. Not that I was overly squeamish or nothing. Just some things didn't need to be seen if you can help it. Besides, I had a sinking feeling that I had once known this headless corpse and that made a greasy cold spot in the pit of my stomach.

The coroner replaced the sheet. "That's a good question, Mr. Martindale. The police have yet to find it. But a better question would be: What took the head off?" The old man smiled a gravedigger's grin. I knew that he was just numb to the death and gore like all coroners and homicide dicks, but I still wanted to belt him one for that smile. Not that "the deceased," as he was now called, and I were really close, but we were co-workers of a sort.

I took the bait. "What do you mean?"

"Well you see," his blood stained and eager hands went back to the sheet to pull it down again, "there was very little blood loss and I could see no striations indicative of a saw blade yet the bone was . . . uhm . . . rasped away, not cleaved through like you would expect an axe or other heavy blade to do. In addition, some of the surrounding tissue looks to have suffered frostbite, which is odd since it is late May. I must admit, I'm most thoroughly perplexed over this."

"That's fascinating, Doc, really it is, but let me just ask you: Without a head or any ID found with the body, how can you be sure that this is . . ."

click

. . . "Dennis Dillion? Yeah, I know Dennis. He works out of Boston. He's a pretty good guy, why do you ask?"

On the other end of the line I could hear Bob puffing on one of his stinking stogies. I swear, I wouldn't be surprised if the old man slept with one of those nasty things sticking out of his mouth. "Well he was the first one the agency called because he was closer. He went up there and met with Ms. Atwood concerning her uncle. Last we heard from him he was following the professor around and . . . well that's it. That was four days ago and it's not like Dennis not to report in at least every two or three days. So we contacted the local police, and they went to the boardinghouse where he was staying. They said it looked like someone had tossed the joint looking for something. To be on the safe side, the agency has decided to send you up there to find out what happened. So pack a bag and hop a train north, Harry. We expect you to be in Arkham in the morning. Give us a call when you make it in and keep us posted on what you find out."

"Sure thing, Bob. I'll call you when I'm in Arkham, talk to you then."

I hung up the phone and ran a hand over my chin covered in a day's growth of beard. I took one last drag off my cigarette before crushing it out, standing up, and walking to my open office door. The next room was where my secretary did all the paperwork and met the clients. This early in the morning she had had yet to . . .

click

. . . "Come in, Mr. Martindale," she said with a slight Boston accent. You could tell right off this dame wasn't from this sleepy town. She had miles of class and then some.

"Thank you Mrs. Atwood—"

"It's 'Miss', Detective. I'm not married. But please, call me Judy," She flashed a coy smile. She was a well-schooled flirt and probably a professional heartbreaker. Hell, with looks like hers, how could she not be?

"Yes, sorry about that, Ms. Atwood . . . Judy. I take it the Pinkertons called you to let you know I was picking up the case after Mr. Dillion?"

"Yes they did, Detective. May I call you Harry?"

I nodded as I took off my hat and Ms. Atwood lead me through the main hallway of the large Victorian house, into a sitting room. Everything in this joint screamed money, from the art on the walls to the antique furniture. I could tell two things about Judy Atwood right away: She had a lot of dough, and she wasn't afraid to show it off. A smile touched my lips as I thought that a less professional P. I. would have tried to take advantage of that, or hell, of the fine looking woman herself. But not me, no sir. "Professional" would be my middle name on this case. I couldn't afford another . . .

click

. . . "Lana Landerson, Mr. Martindale. It's a pleasure to meet you." She breathed in a husky whisper through wet, ruby red lips. She stood in the doorway of my office in a short red dress that was tight in all the right places she had long raven-black hair, an hourglass figure and legs that went all the way up. I knew right away that this dame would be trouble, but God help me, I thought she might be worth it.

"Mind if I smoke?" And before I could answer, she pulled a long-stemmed filter and a cigarette from her purse and lit up.

Man, just watching those perfect lips draw on that filter could have kept me entertained . . .

click

. . . forever? No, that is not possible. I have been here for a long time but not forever. That's crazy talk. But what is time here? All I know is the cold, although I can't feel it—and the black, although I can't see it. A total absence of everything that is nonetheless cold and black, cold and black, cold and black, cold and . . .

click

. . . "black," I answered and watched her pour me a cup-of-joe.

"So has there been any news about Dennis yet?" Miss Atwood asked as she walked back to my chair with steaming coffee. Not that I knew about such things, but at a guess I would say that the cup and saucer she handed to me were fine china.

"No, ma'am. I just got in town today. I'm sure Mr. Dillion is fine."

"I do hope so; he was a good man."

"Yes, he *is*," Was she already writing him off, or was that just a slip of speech? "Now Miss Atwood, I mean Judy, I got the basics of the case from Bob Gellman in New York, but I'd like to hear the whole story from you, so why don't you begin at the beginning and tell me everything."

"Very well, Harry. I'm worried about my uncle . . ."

click

. . . "Professor Wilmarth, what do the Pinkertons want with him?" asked Detective Harden. He was a big guy, old and weathered, with a bushy gray mustache and eyebrows that looked like a couple of shaggy caterpillars had crawled onto his face and died. He sort of reminded me of my uncle Paul, which wasn't a good thing.

"Well we don't really want anything with him; it's just his niece is worried about him, that's all. She says he's been acting strange ever since he can back from a trip to Vermont."

"Acting strange, how?"

"She said that he thought there might be people following him."

The detective rocked back in his chair, causing it to squeak plaintively beneath his bulk. "How come the professor didn't come to the police if he thought he was being followed? Why did he have to run to you Pinkertons? Didn't he think we could handle the problem?"

I knew that was coming. It was always the same with small town cops, hell it was the same with many big city cops as well. No lawman liked having their toes being stepped on, especially by "rented dicks" like me. So I had to snip this right in the bud. "Actually, Professor Willmarth didn't hire my agency, his niece did. As to why she didn't come to you, well she's new in town. Maybe she didn't know you very well? In any event, has there been any luck in finding out what happened to Dennis Dillion yet?" That's it, I had to get Detective Harden's mind off of his bruised ego before it began to fester like dirt in a wound.

"No, he's still missing and hasn't turned up yet. Last place anyone saw him was at the . . ."

click

. . . University wasn't the biggest college I had ever seen but it wasn't the smallest either. Located south of the river that gave it its name, it was geographically speaking, almost at the heart of Arkham. In every other way it *was* the heart of the town. While it was true that the entire town didn't depend upon the school for its livelihood, it was a sure thing that if Miskatonic University had never been built, then Arkham would only be a quarter of its current size.

I was sitting in my rented Packard on West College Street, which, as its name implied, ran parallel with the school's center campus. Across from me was the Liberal Arts Building, and in a corner room on the second floor is where Professor Wilmarth taught English. I brought up my binoculars and looked into the windows of Wilmarth's classroom. He was still in there, standing at the podium at the front of the class, giving a lecture or something. I lowered the glasses and checked the copy of the professor's schedule that I had made, and this class would be over at eleven, so I had over a half an hour to kill.

Taking a sip from my now cold coffee, I was reaching for the copy of the Arkham *Gazette* I had in the seat next to me, when I noticed that I wasn't the only one spying on the good professor. Across the commons was a young man sitting on a green iron bench. He looked like a student with his sweater in the school's colors, the stack of books next to him, and the expensive gold-rimmed glasses that were no doubt a gift from his parents, but something about him was just *off*. Maybe it was because he was craning his neck to look into Wilmarth's classroom, but besides drawing my attention he also drew my animosity. I'm never one to dislike somebody without a good reason. I wasn't sure *what* bothered me about this fellow.

I grabbed the binoculars and gave him a closer look. The kid sat stock still, like a blond, freckled-faced statue. I stared into his face for a good three minutes and never once saw him blink. He had something in his hand, a shiny silver object about the size of a baseball that I couldn't make out.

I put the binoculars down and continued to watch him for a bit. Checking my watch, I noticed that fifteen minutes had crept by and still the kid just sat on the bench, unmoving, staring into Professor Wilmarth's classroom. I was thinking about getting out of the car and approaching him when I felt that something was out of place. At this time of year, the campus was overrun with birds, mostly sparrows. The tiny brown things flapped and bounced about everywhere, but they paid special attention to the benches around the commons where students would sit, eat their lunch and often throw the winged beggars a crumb or two. Today was no different as around all the benches sparrows flocked and it didn't matter if the bench had human occupants or not. That is, the tiny birds gathered around all the benches except one, the one that "Mr. Curious" was sitting at.

I don't know why such a little thing as that unnerved me, but it did. So I decided to find out just who this kid was. Getting out of the Packard and jogging across the street, I glanced up to see that Wilmarth was still at the podium. Then I turned back just in time to see the kid turn his . . .

click

. . . head towards me with a look of almost comical surprise on his face. Then the German pulled his bayonet out of Mike's belly and began to chamber another round into his Mauser. I landed in the trench just two feet behind him and smiled at the Hun through bloody teeth. Before he could snap the bolt of his rifle closed, I pinned him through the back like a bug to the ground with my own bayonet. He thrashed and gurgled in the mud as I twisted the foot-long blade back and forth to work it free from him.

Another German was yelling a battle cry as he charged me, swinging an entrenching tool like it was a battleaxe. I brought my Springfield up and took a hip shot at the Hun. It tore a hole through his dirty gray coat and sent him sprawling backward. I chambered another round and tried to remember how many bullets I had left in the weapon, when two more Germans came out of the bunker to my left. I crouched down and shot at one, causing his face to disappear in a red mist when his buddy brought up a pistol and begin squeezing off shots at me in rapid succession. Ducking behind the bodies of Mike and the still twitching, I chambered another, then peeked over my gory cover and saw that the German was . . .

click

. . . running almost before I knew what he was doing, but the strange kid even ran wrong. His limbs flailed about like a badly controlled puppet whose strings had gotten all tangled. Unfortunately for me, no matter how awkward it looked, the kid was making good time.

"Hey, stop! I just want to talk to you," I shouted then began to give chase as I knew the kid wasn't going to listen.

The kid scrambled deeper into the campus commons causing both students and sparrows to scatter. It looked like he was making a beeline right to the bell tower that stood alone in the center of the campus. Then, all of a sudden the kid spun, raised his hand, and I saw a gleam of silvery metal in it.

Oh man, the kid's packing heat, I managed to think before I saw a bright flash of light, my vision began to blur and it felt like my head was . . .

click

. . . swimming, am I swimming? It feels like I'm swimming, like I'm weightless, but if I'm swimming why can't I feel the water? Why can't I feel anything? Or see or hear anything? Where am I? All I can see is blackness, but somehow I know I'm not seeing blackness at all. It's like my eyes are closed and I'm just not seeing anything, but it doesn't feel like my eyes are closed. Are they closed? Is this my voice or is this just something that I'm . . .

click

. . . "thinking that nothing is wrong but I know my uncle, he is a very private man and he would not have let his concerns slip if he wasn't really worried."

I sipped the weak coffee and looked at Judy Atwood for a while before replying. Despite my better judgment, I could feel myself falling for her in a big way. Not only was she drop-dead gorgeous with her shining golden hair, deep blue eyes, and smooth creamy skin, but she had a real sweet side to her as well. At first I thought she had to be a heartbreaker, but the longer I sat and listened to her the more I came to realize that she was just all heart.

In other words, she was the wrong kind of dame to get mixed up with a guy like me.

"So let me get this straight," I said as I put the now empty cup and saucer down on the table in front of me, "your uncle went up to Vermont last year and something happened to him there that he won't talk about. Even since coming back he has been secretive and acting frightened, almost bordering on paranoid. When you finally confronted him about it he broke down and told you that he had made some powerful enemies while in Vermont and that he was sure that their agents were following him. But the next day he telephoned you and said that he didn't know what he could have been thinking, that there was nothing wrong and no one following him but he nevertheless wanted you out of Arkham immediately. Is that about right?"

"Yes, that's right."

"Now while I agree that sounds pretty strange, the only thing I can do is what Mr. Dillion was doing for you, and that is follow your uncle around and see if anyone is tailing him. If I approach your uncle directly he's not likely to tell me anything, and then he'll be on the lookout for me which will make my job twice as hard."

"That's all I want, Harry. I want to know if my uncle is in danger or if he's just . . . well, troubled."

"Did Mr. Dillion come up with any evidence that your uncle might be in danger?"

"You mean besides Mr. Dillion suddenly disappearing without a trace?" she said without a hint of sarcasm which made my question sound all the more ridiculous.

I walked right into that one, I thought. "Yes, besides that."

"No. He kept all his findings, if he had any at all, to himself. I went out with him once when he first came to Arkham, to point out my uncle, his house, his classroom at the university and things like that. He did write a lot of stuff down in his notepad that he put into the glove compartment of his . . ."

click

. . . car over to the side of the road, killed the engine and got out. I jumped across the drainage ditch and into the field on the other side, feeling my shoes sink deep into the muddy earth. I then crouched and checked the road I had just come down. I saw no signs of life, which wasn't surprising way out here. I really wanted to strike a match and check my watch, but already my army training was coming back to me. I knew that an open flame made you a target, so I resisted that urge, instead going for the security of my gun. Yanking the .45 free of my shoulder holster, I pulled the slide back to chamber a round, but kept the safety on. It was only then that I felt ready to approach the old farmhouse in the distance and into something that may or may not be a trap.

I crossed the field in a low crouching jog and in the back of my mind I kept expecting a German to take a shot at me with a Mauser from somewhere in the darkness. About thirty yards from the ramshackle house I stopped and ducked behind a bush to catch my breath and give the area the once over. In the gloom I couldn't make out much, but I didn't see anyone lurking in the . . .

click

. . . *dark? When did it get dark?* I wondered as I blinked my eyes and stared up and the unexpected night sky. Then came the voice again, the one that must have snapped me out of whatever trance I had been in.

"Hey, mister. I said are you all right?"

I pivoted my head around, my stiff neck popping and creaking in the process, to see a young man off to my right. He was short, squat, dark haired, and staring at me with a look of confusion plastered on his face.

"What? Yeah, I'm fine, why?" My words stumbled over a tongue that felt too thick and dry.

"Well I've seen you standing here all day today. When I came out of my dorm to go to classes, when I came back, and now you're still here. Heck, you must have been standing out here for six hours or more." He said with a nervous laugh.

I shook my head and looked around, and it all came flooding back. I was at Miskatonic University and I was chasing a creepy kid that was spying on Professor Wilmarth. The kid had twirled around and pointed something at me, something silver that had flashed a bright light.

My hands moved on their own, patting me down, feeling for pain and blood. Then I realized what I was doing and stopped because if the kid had plugged me I would have known it by now. But when exactly was now? When I was chasing the kid it was just a little before eleven in the morning. Checking my watch I saw that it was now eight-forty in the evening. Nine hours! I had been standing here in the same spot for over nine hours, and I couldn't remember a thing that happened during that time.

I tried to take a step and collapsed. My whole lower body was one big cramp.

"You okay, mister? You want me to get the school doctor or something?" The kid asked.

"I'm ok," I panted. "Just a little stiff." Then I gritted my teeth against the pain and begin to bend my legs at the knees, slowly working the kinks and cramps out. Standing, unmoving, for such a long time had really done a number on me.

After a few minutes of painful flexing, I let the kid help me up and then sent him on his way with thanks and a promise that I was now . . .

click

. . . "fine, Mr. Martindale. Please tell my niece that and I am very sorry that she troubled you and the Pinkerton Detective Agency with this bit on nonsense, but really, I am in no trouble. So if you'd excuse me, I am in a hurry." Wilmarth tried to scurry past me but I was having none of that, not after what I went through last night. I grabbed his arm and squeezed a little too hard to make sure that I got his attention. The professor's face whipped around and he gazed at me. I saw that he was sweating and that his eyes were filled with fear, but I knew that no matter how tough I was acting that I was not the cause of his terror.

"Now listen to me, professor, and don't try giving me any of that bull. I know there's something strange going on, and I know that people are following you. I even know," I leaned in close so that the students that were passing us in the hall, and no doubt staring at us, couldn't hear what I said next. "I know that whatever they are, they aren't people. They can look like people or maybe they just . . . I don't know, *do things* to people to make them do their dirty work, but they are like nothing I've ever seen and mister, I have seen a lot."

"Please, Mr. Martindale," the old man pleaded. "For your own sake, and for the sake of my niece, just drop this inquiry. Despite what you may think, you have no idea of what you are getting involved with nor of the danger you are in. In fact, I would like to hire you to see that Judy safely leaves Arkham right now."

"Sorry professor, but I'm already on a case, and I won't take another until this one is finished. So I guess you're stuck with me." Then a dirty trick came to mind, good thing I'm not above playing dirty when I have to. "Of course, this means that without someone to watch over your niece she will have to stay in Arkham all alone and helpless until this thing plays out. Now if you would just cooperate, I'm sure we could get to the bottom of this in no time and then I'd be more than happy to–"

Professor Wilmarth interrupted me by yanking his arm out of my grip and glaring at me. His face was beat red, his jaw clenched so tight that the muscles twitched, and he was actually shaking with rage. Just as I thought, his niece was his weak spot. Later I could feel like a rat for poking him there, but right now I had to know what this tight-lipped little man knew about those strange creatures that had almost killed me. After all, next time I might not be so lucky to come out of it with just a gash on my . . .

click

. . . forehead slammed into the handrail as I dove for cover. Shaking my head to clear the stars, I saw that the stairs where I was standing only seconds before was now covered in slimy, foul smelling ice. I was sprawled out flat on my back several steps below them. I gingerly touch the spot on my head where it had collided with the rail and felt the blood and split flesh. Wanting to curse, but not having time to do so, I leapt to my feat and peaked around the curve of the tower stairs. The . . . *whatever* . . . it was that had sprayed the icy mist at me was gone. From up above I could still hear the strange whirling sound and smell the sickening stench I had not smelled since the war: The stink or burning flesh.

If I had guessed right, and the kid had fled to this bell tower after somehow rendering me unconscious in the university commons, then it was likely that the burning smell was coming from him since it sure wasn't coming from that thing with the ice-shooter. Now whether the kid was the one being burned or the one doing the burning I didn't know, just like I didn't know why he was still in this tower after having nine hours to get away or what the hell that ugly thing was that shot at me. But by God I intended to find out the answers to all those questions and more.

I sprinted up the winding stairs as quietly as I could and made it to the top without drawing the attention of the weird thing up there.

Better make that weird *things* as I saw two of the misshapen creatures up there scuttling between the wooden beams, thick ropes, and the Copley Memorial Bell. Because of the gloom, I could not see the creatures clearly, which was probably for the best. All I could make out of them was numerous spidery legs, an oblong head covered in tentacles, antenna, or both, and large, translucent, insect-like wings that sprouted out of their backs. A part of my mind was screaming, *my God, what are these things,* while the larger part of my mind was trying to keep everything together and was having me scan the area to make sure there wasn't a third of those freakish nightmares lurking up here somewhere. Thankfully there wasn't.

One of the creatures was standing near the tower's balcony that only led to the night sky or an eight-story drop to the university commons below. The other thing was fidgeting with something lying on the ground. It was from this creature the weird whirling sounds and burning smell was coming from. It was toward this creature that I slowly crept. I kept my .45 ready and cringed at every creak of the old floorboards as I inched closer to malformed beast. Whatever it was doing, it was focused on it because it never noticed me.

Unfortunately for me, I realized that I had made the same mistake when I head a rustling buzz come from above me. I whipped my head up and saw that there was a third creature in the bell tower. This one was hanging upside down from a cross-beam like a giant deformed bat. In two of its twisted arms it held a mass of golden tubes that it used to rain down a deadly stream of ice at me. I leapt forward, once again luckily dodging the misty spray, and tumbled right next to the creature that I had been creeping toward. Springing up, I got a good look at

what the thing had been doing ,but God help me, I sure wish
that I . . .

click

. . . didn't believe for a second that I was alone out here
despite not seeing or hearing anyone, or *anything*, else. Besides,
those creatures could come flying in here at a moment's notice
even if they were hiding at the edge of the wood line some two
hundred yards distant. But none of this changed a thing, so I
got out from behind the bushes and dashed to the farmhouse.
Once there I started sneaking closer to the front door when I
head movement inside. I thumbed the safety off of my .45 and
brought it up ready to open fire if I had to.

"Mr. Martindale, is that you?" came a whispered question
from within the house, and I paused before answering because
while I recognized the voice there was something *off* about it.
Maybe it was just fear that caused it to tremble oddly but it
hardly sounded like . . .

click

. . . "Judy, are you there? It's me, Harry. Open the door
please, this is important." My head was thumping where it was
gashed open and my mind was still reeling from what professor Wilmarth had told me. I looked nervously over each shoulder to make sure no one was watching me, then pounded on
the door once more. Still I got no reply, so I tried the doorknob
and found it unlocked.

Stepping inside I drew my piece when I saw the overturned
table in the front hall. Going deeper into the house, I found
everything in a shambles. But even after a thorough search, I
could find no sign of Judy Atwood. The entire house had been
tossed in a fevered search for something, but as for what the cul-
prits had been looking for I didn't have a clue. This also meant
that Judy might have been abducted by agents of those things,
or at best she was at the police station after coming . . .

click

. . . "home. Mommy I said I'm home!"

Mommy wouldn't answer me and I didn't like that. She always said, "How was school today, baby?" when I came home, but today she didn't say anything. Was she gone? Was I alone? I dropped my books by the still open door that led to the apartment building's hall. Just in case I had to run. Just in case there was something *bad* in here with me.

"Mommy, it's me; I'm home from school, you here?" I tippy-toed into our apartment and that's when I saw . . . when I saw my . . . my mommy! She was lying on the floor and not moving and there was so much . . .

click

. . . blood was pooled around the kid's head, or at least what was left of it. The top of the skull had been cut away from the eyebrows on up, and as I watched, thunderstruck and unmoving, I saw the creature scoop out the gray, jelly like mass of the kid's brain and place it in a large golden jar.

Then from behind I heard a thump and out of instinct I dodged to the side as the third monstrous thing tried to spray me with its ice gun. Tumbling away I smashed my knee into a support beam. I jumped up and starting blasting away with my Colt .45. Slugs tore into the mushy mass of the thing that had been trying to kill me, but I only heard it buzz in annoyance. Its ugly head glowed and pulsed in strange colors, but when my pistol was emptied, I saw that the thing was still scuttling toward me as if all the lead I had just pumped into it hadn't harmed it in the least.

I spun around, running in a crouch between support beams while reaching for a full magazine for my Colt, not that I thought it would do much good. Whipping behind a moldy beam with my pistol fully loaded and ready for business, I saw that the creatures were now ignoring me. The one that had removed the kid's brain was at the bell tower's balcony with the second one, and it was still clutching the now sealed gold jar. The third almost insect-like thing used its ice-spraying weapon to coat the kid's butchered body in a cold mist that instantly began to dissolve the corpse like it was covered in frozen acid. Then it too waddled next to the other creatures, and as I watched all three of them spread their wings and buzzed off into the night sky, illuminated only by a sliver of a moon and the . . .

click

. . . "stars, Mr. Martindale. A more precise location than that is the ninth planet in our solar system that the aliens call 'Yuggoth'."

I looked at the professor for a long hard minute. Only two days before I would have laughed at the man and threatened to belt him one if he kept talking nonsense, but after last night . . . "So, you saying those spider-crab things are Martians?"

"No, they don't come from Mars, although they may have a base or outpost on it somewhere. As I said, they have a large colony on the ninth planet of our solar system, a planet that we humans have yet to discover, I might add. However even that distant planet is not their home world. Where they actually hail from, I do not know, but I would guess that it would be very far and vastly different than any of the celestial bodies of which I'm aware." Professor Wilmarth took a look down both ends of the hall to make sure no one was within earshot of the little alcove we were in. "As for them being 'spider-crab things,' I don't think they are like any life forms found on our planet no matter how bizarre. I say this because these creatures have mastered inter- stellar flight without the aid of transports; they greatly unnerve all manner of animals by their very presence, and the fact that they cannot be photographed. I believe that these creatures' very essence, their cells and the like, exist outside of our scientific laws and therefore they exist both within and without–"

"Wait, wait, wait!" I was trying to keep up with what the professor was saying but it was just too much coming at me too fast. "This is all crazy talk, professor. You don't really believe this, do you?"

"Well don't you believe what you witnessed last night? Did you imagine those creatures, or that cut on your forehead, or what they were doing to that boy's brain?"

"What WERE they doing to that kid's brain?"

Wilmarth looked pale, and he swallowed hard before he answered. "They . . . harvest living human brains and place them in metal canisters where they can keep the mind of an individual alive for ages, perhaps forever. In such a vessel the mi-go can take the still living brains into outer space with them and transport them to untold alien worlds."

"Wait . . . what did you just call them?"

"Hmm, what? Oh, mi-go. It's not an official name, but one that I applied to them as I believe that they are responsible for the myths of the 'Abominable Snow-Men' of the Himalayans. The Nepalese call those creatures mi-go and well, it is the only name I have for them."

"So what do these . . . mi-go, want with human brains in . . ."

click

. . . canisters were sitting on a rickety table pushed up against the far side of the room. I counted nine of the shiny golden jars and listened to them softly click and hum for a few seconds before turning back to Judy.

"So how did you come all the way out here and find these things?" I asked, but I was already thinking that I wasn't going to like the . . .

click

. . . "answer me that!" I twisted my fists into Wilmarth's lapels, drawing him closer to me. I shook with rage and he shook with fear and this time I knew that I was the cause for his trembling.

"Please Mr. Martindale, calm yourself. I don't know all the answers as the motives of the mi-go are truly . . . well . . . alien. I know that they have been interested in humanity since they first came to Earth aeons ago. They have also experimented on us, paying particular attention to our developing minds and intellects. I believe that removing human brains and taking them to their laboratories back on Yuggoth is just one example of this."

"So is this why they never found Dennis Dillion's head? Do those damn things cut out his brain take it back to . . . *wherever* to do experiments on it?"

"Yes, that is one possibility. They also remove the brains of loyal human allies and promise them lifetimes of wonder and discovery. That is what happened to a friend of mine and what almost . . . well almost what happened to me." Professor Wilmarth had spoken the last part in a hushed whisper, and he had an odd look in his eyes. Yes, there was fear there but also something else, longing perhaps?

A sickening thought came to me then. "So tell me, what do you think happens when those mi-go take someone's brain that wasn't a 'loyal ally' to them? What do you suppose they do to that . . ."

click

. . . "brain is quite safe. In fact, it is in one of the cylinders right over there," Judy said in that odd, wavering voice and then smiled at me a joyless grin. She pointed with her left hand at the table with the golden mi-go brain jars on it. "You see, Mr. Martindale, we are not murderers. Judy Atwood is alive and well, in a matter of speaking."

"Judy, what the hell are you talking about?" I asked, not believing what the woman in front of me was saying. Not wanting to believe it.

She sighed and took a step closer to me. "What I'm trying to tell you, Mr. Martindale, is that I am not Judy Atwood. At least, my mind is not and that's what really matters, does it not? While this is her lovely young body, her brain has been surgically removed and placed in a hyperthermic cylinder for safekeeping. This was done so that I could be placed within her body as we thought that was the best and safest way to approach you."

The woman took another step toward me and I raised my .45, pointing it at her. "Stop right there . . . whoever you are. This is crazy! This is all crazy! If you are not Judy Atwood, then who the hell are you?"

The smile on Judy's face wavered the tinniest bit as she looked down the barrel of my pistol, then she continued her slow, confident advance. "Why I'm the young man you chased to the university belltower two nights back. Ane while in a different host body, I was the man investigator Dillion unwisely confronted in Billington's Woods. But before that, in my original prison of flesh and bone, I was known as Henry Akeley. I was the one who first lead Professor Wilmarth to Vermont and facilitated his first glimpse into the greater unknown when he met the amazing travelers from Yuggoth. Since that time I have had . . . well I have had a change of mind. Ha, several of them, in fact. My masters have no limit to their surgical skills. Wilmarth, on the other hand," at this Judy, or at least the insane thing that wore Judy's body like a tailored suit, clucked "her" tongue and shook her head, "he has been resolute in his defiance. He and his librarian friend have been poking their noses into matters best left alone, and so I have come here to offer professor one last chance at true immortality . . . or else."

"Immortality, you mean life as a brain floating in a jar, right?"

Henry Akeley laughed through Judy's lovely mouth, making an unnatural, cringe-inducing sound. "Oh Mr. Martindale, it is not as bad as all that. Look at me; I'm not in a jar right now, am I? I can be many people and live endless lifetimes and I will be privy to secrets that mankind could never hope to learn in a million years of scientific advancement. Now how does that sound bad to you?"

"And all you have to do for all that," I hissed at the *thing* in front of me, "is blindly follow your alien masters and do their dirty work when they command it, right?"

At that, the smile on Judy's face vanished and the man behind her eyes glared out at me. "What you have to come to turns with is the fact that no matter what, your brain will be leaving your body this night. You will be joining the travelers from Yuggoth. Now you can do so willingly and reap the rewards of being a good . . . ally, or you can defy them in which case they will be forced to punish you. To break your will and trust me, they are quite efficient at doing that."

"Is that what they did to you, or are you one of their 'willing' lackeys?"

The blazing in *its* eye died down to dull embers, and was overshadowed by the first hint at sadness I had seen from the willing slave in front of me. "It doesn't matter. Do you hear that . . . ?

click

. . . clicking coming from. *Click*, *click*, *click*, that's all I hear in the darkness. But do I really hear it? I know it's there, but I don't think I actually hear it. It's like I feel it but I know that's not right as I can't feel anything. Nevertheless its there, *click*, *click*, *click*, all the time, never stopping, a painful clicking that hurts even when I know it really doesn't. Oh God, make the clicking stop, just stop the clicking, the endless, ceaseless . . .

click

. . . "clicking coming from the brain cylinders in the other room?" Akeley asked me and I nodded. "That is the sound of electrical impulses being applied to exposed brain matter at strategic locations. The effect that has upon the human brain is simply amazing. It produces a prolonged state of unrest similar to sleep deprivation only a hundred times more severe and continuously repeating memories that go on and on and on for what seems like eternity, for time matters little to an immortal mind. Think of it as being trapped in an endlessly shifting, ever-confusing dream world forever. This is what the travelers from Yuggoth do to those who resist their will, and after only a matter of days of that, which feels like countless years to the one undergoing the 'treatment,' the once rebellious individual will either be sufficiently humbled, or incurably insane."

Henry Akeley forced Judy's mouth into a twitching, deathly grin, and I knew at once that Henry had had first hand knowledge of the events he was describing. I took a few shuffling steps backwardstoward the door, kept my piece trained on the beautiful woman in front of me, and let the insane mind within it to continue to rant.

"But even going mad does not stop the agony as the aliens are interested in all aspects of the human psyche, including dementia. Once upon the road to madness, the travelers from Yuggoth will push you further and further into the black abyss of insanity all in the name of what they call science. You'll never know peace, never again know reality. Trust me, Mr. Martindale I've . . . I've . . . I've *seen* it happen to . . . *others*."

That was when I hear a loud thump come from the roof of the little farmhouse and a second or two after that another thump-crunch from behind the shuttered windows at the back of the room. I knew that both sounds signaled the arrival of the mi-go.

Akeley was raising Judy's hand, and in it was the silver sphere I had seen Akeley's student body use on me. I pointed my .45 at her face and cocked the hammer back with an ominous . . .

click

. . . *CLICK!* I looked down stupidly at my .38 as if I did-
n't know what was wrong, but I knew all right. The little
revolver only had five shots as it was only for emergency
backup, and in all my years with it I had never once drawn it
from my ankle holster. Not until tonight, and those five shots
were now all gone, just like all the rounds for my Colt.

When one of the mi-go poked its mushy, misshapen, glowing head into the window, I threw the empty gun at it in defiance before spinning around and running into the room that
contained the brain jars. Slamming the door behind me, I ran
to the golden jars on the table and began to claw at them, desperately looking for a way to pry them open. I knew I didn't
have much time now but I wanted to find Judy's brain before
those things got me. I didn't know which jar held it, but I'd
search them all if I had to. I would find her brain and rip it
apart with my bare hands if I had to. She deserved better than
to exist like this. I could not save her life, and I was sure that
her uncle Wilmarth wasn't long for this earth either, but I
could at least . . .

click

. . . "do nothing, Mr. Martindale. All you will be doing is
killing Judy's lovely body. My friends outside will simply
retrieve my brain and place it back into its cylinder until they
need me again. You will accomplish nothing, except making
things worse for yourself," Akeley said, but I noticed that he
had stopped bringing up his hand with the silver knockout
weapon in it.

A smile of my own at last touched my lips as I heard the
first clawing at the farmhouse door and leveled off my Colt
right between Judy's deep blue eyes. "What if there's not much
of your brain left for those creatures to scoop up? What happens to your immortality then, Mr. Akeley?"

I got to give the man some credit; he tried to pull off the shot even though I had him dead to rights. Then again I guess he didn't have much of a choice. Before he could raise the sphere another inch, I squeezed the trigger and . . .

click

. . . the .45 bucked in my hand and my ears rang with its report, and a new hole suddenly appeared in the thin wooden shutters that covered the back window. I think hit the thing on the other side of the window as I saw shadows shift and moonlight once again filter in through the shutters. However, if I did hit it, it never once made a sound. Not for a second did I think one lousy bullet, not even from a .45, would kill one of those misshapen nightmares, but perhaps it would keep them at bay for a little while.

No such luck.

One or more of them were at the front door once again. I saw flickering colored lights seeping beneath the door even before I heard claws on its wooden surface. The pale light illuminated the inside of the farmhouse in angry rainbow hues and reflected wetly off the pile of debris that had once been the person who lured me out here. Damn, I walked right into that trap like a first year rookie on the force. How could I have been so stupid? Now I was stuck in a deserted house on the outskirts of . . .

click

click

click

END

The Lady in the Grove

by Scott Lette

I can see it on your face, Father.

You think that I am a murderer.

I know that you are worried in asking about it. I appreciate that deep down, you feel like all of this is somehow your fault.

I do not want absolution—what I did is ultimately between God and me. I believe in Him now, more than I ever did before this all started.

What I do want is for you to understand what happened, so that you can hear my side and understand what it is that I did. You deserve to know that much.

Tonight, I will tell you of those murders in Arkham.

◆ ◆ ◆

As an old boss used to say—Thank God for Temperance! Without it, the twenties would not have been as good to my family and me as they were. I do mean that sense of family in more ways than one, my wife back in the windy city and to my working brothers of that other important family. You have probably heard all sorts of cockamamie nonsense and read even more in the papers—stories about the Irish "White Hand"; bootlegging, gambling, prostitution and other sorts of shenanigans.

Most of the jobs I had taken in that year had been in or around Beantown; the Walshes and the Wallaces were good to me at a time where it was hard to get by. With them, you don't stop to ask too many questions beyond what needs to be done.

After finishing some business for them across the border, I managed a few good days with the wife. It was just like being married again; I left that Sunday night in a fuss, my suitcase on the street, the neighbors looking on as I screamed my way into the cab.

I took the long train ride back from Chicago to New York and a car from New York to Boston. I had a meeting with someone there, you don't need to know the who's or whys. Suffice to say that the job sounded simple enough; someone needed some muscle in a town to the north in blue-ribbon country.

I was assured that after this job I would be moving west, beyond Chicago to help with aspects of the operation that were more financial. At the time that was good enough for me. I wanted to move into something with a bit more class. I wasn't getting any older; I missed the wife despite our rows and wanted to see our baby son grow up. So I took the job, on the proviso that I'd never have to do this sort of thing again; no more favors, no more leg breaking, no more standover stuff.

That's what brought me to this town called Arkham.

◆ ◆ ◆

You don't see a lot when driving at night, especially if you're a passenger weary from a train ride. The parties involved had taken a few precautions, including sending a driver to discreetly pick me up from the train station. It was a nice enough car; one of those twenty-seven Model T's that everyone seemed to still be buying.

I managed to catch a few of the street names as we drove, a Pickman street here, a Church street there. And some street name called Miskatonic.

"That's not as uncommon as you think in these parts," the driver assured me. "The university here has got the same name. Hell, even the river through town does. Think it's a founding family here."

"So you don't say?" I said back. "It's a real stand-out name, that's all."

A few more minutes of silence later and I arrived outside of what I thought was the town hall. Like many buildings I'd seen here, it was a sandstone affair with three-stories and a fairly austere front entrance. There was also a tradesman's entrance to the side—that's where the car pulled up into and parked.

"They're waiting for you," said the driver.

I saw someone standing in the doorway of what I took to be a private entrance. He was just outside enough to smoke, inside enough not to catch the occasional drop of rain. Gray suit, nicely tailored vest, red and white pinstriped tie. He was shorter than I, but then most folks are. He sported his reddish moustache much as if I already imagined he tended his garden or stamp collection.

"Charles Quinn?" he asked, putting away his pipe.

"Who wants to know?" I said.

"The name is Royston Mallard. I'm a professor at Miskatonic University. Would you step inside, please?"

Royston escorted me through the mostly empty halls and up a few flights of stairs, into a darkened wood paneled room. Here a man waited.

"Charlie Quinn. By I live and breathe, so good of you to come see me!"

I hadn't seen Mickey Callaghan for some years now, not since the bad old days of the 400 Club. He was a hell of a gambler in his time, and had been a big favorite of Wallace until six or so years back. I now knew why he'd stop taking those frequent trips to Boston.

Callaghan made a big point of getting up from his desk as I entered, trailing himself and his lit cigar across the office, a heavy set arm up and over my shoulder.

"I see you've met the professor," he said.

"I have. Mind telling me what this is all about?" I wasn't really in the mood for an extended get-together. I was here to do a job and get out of the place as quick as I could.

"Ah. Fair enough then, Charlie. You're here to go to a party." Callaghan made it sound like a flight of whimsy.

"Is this some sort of joke?" I said.

"No joke, Charlie. You're to go to a party with the professor here. Just do what he says. If there's, well you know, then he'll let you know what to do." Mick demonstrated his civic mindedness by stubbing out the cigar in his tray, and turning his back to me for a moment.

You're probably wondering why I just didn't get up and walk out? Truth was that although I smelled a rat, I wasn't sure whose rat it was or who it was for. I was also quietly confident Wallace or Walsh would stand up for me if things like that had to count, so I let my suspicion simmer.

The professor had been quiet throughout our exchange, thumbing through a book of some kind, absently mumbling to himself. He decided to change that.

"I do not approve of this, Mayor. This man is a known associate of . . . ."

Callaghan was not one known for allowing others eloquence in his presence.

"It was you that complained to me about this. For Christ's sake Mallard, I don't pretend to understand half of this. But if there's any truth to what you say, I think we're in agreement you'll be needing a man like Charlie for his talents?"

Not one it seemed to argue with politicians, the good professor lit his pipe and started smoking right there and then.

"Whenever you're ready, Mister Quinn" Callaghan said.

◆ ◆ ◆

The professor had his own car parked in the back lot. By the time we left Quinn's office and were outside, it was dark proper. The moon was new, a few whisps of cloud here and there under a mostly dark sky. There had been a silence between us since his outburst in the Mayor's office.

"We will need to get you new clothes, Mister Quinn," he said. "There is a formal dress requirement for the party we must attend."

"I do own a coat and tails, you know. If someone had warned me . . . ," I said, letting the rest of the sentence trail off.

"This was all put together at the last minute. Evidence of their activities has only recently become known," said Mallard.

"Oh," I replied, playing it safe.

This was starting to sound a bit too cloak-and-dagger. Still, this I thought it must be exciting for old Royston—a little bit of skulduggery, as they say on the radio.

We were more than a few minutes into driving about town at this point when Mallard pulled over, parking his car carefully outside what looked like a three story apartment complex. As we entered, the doorman was kind enough to give us both the nod.

That was also a bit odd, seeing a doorman here in provincial Massachusetts. Still the professor hadn't struck me as a poor sort, so I wrote it off to a number of men like Mallard, living off inheritance.

Following Mallard's lead I went into the lobby and around to the side, instead of taking the escalator, we went up a few flights of stairs to the top floor, and down a hall to a door..

"Come in, Mister Quinn," someone said as the key was in the door.

Inside was a sprawled but wealthy mess. More books than I imagined a library might have, shelving occupying most of the wall space. There were books on the floor as well, scattered in among a few dainty looking cushions. To the far side of the room, closer to the window, a great Atlas looked onto us, bearing the weight of the world upon his shoulders.

I saw then why the good professor was not a married man.

"Look mister, I'm not in the mood for any of your funny rich games," I said.

The professor looked more annoyed than shocked at the implication.

"We don't have time for games, Mister Quinn," he said.

Right on cue, someone who must have served as a butler stepped out from a side room, a silver tray of scissors and measuring tape in hand.

"He's with the building," Mallard explained.

Having put down the tray and disappeared for a short while, the butler reappeared, pushing a wheeled rack of men's outfitting.

"There's bound to be something here, Mister Quinn. Just let Marcel take your measurements. It's merely a temporary fit," he said.

I did have to hand it to Marcel. While Mallard disappeared to another room, Marcel worked his magic, and in no less than ten or so minutes I found myself fitting into a dinner suit and jacket that were about my size, and even a nice pair of ruffles and even cuff-links monogrammed "GA."

"You are ready to go to, Mister Anthony," he said.

◆ ◆ ◆

"The Royston building. Named after you in a way?" I asked as the professor and me made our way past the doorman again, both of us carrying a full forearm's load of books. He didn't seem to pay either one of us any mind.

"My mother's side, Mister Quinn. They've lived here in Arkham since the days of the Civil War," he said.

"That's Mister Anthony, Roy," I said back. "Why are we taking these books to the party? "

"That's a good question, Charles," said Mallard.

"Charlie," I shot back. "It's Charlie."

I guess Royston had his reasons; he didn't see it fit to tell me what this was all about as yet. The .32 I'd re-holstered in the new jacket wasn't sitting quite right, but I did my best to adjust it without causing the professor any alarm.

"You might be needing that," he nodded toward the holstered gun as he drove.

"It doesn't worry you?" I asked.

"I wish it did, Charlie. I just hope that when this night is through you'll be one to still think that a Smith and Wesson pistol is your best defence against evil."

"I don't, Roy. That's God." I said.

"Mankind has never had the luxury of relying upon God in battle with our eternal enemies, Mister Quinn."

There was a solemnity in his tone that I'd heard not for some years, not since you, Father, when you lectured me on my association with Wallace, back in Beantown. I remember you telling me that unless I changed my ways that I too was on the road straight to Hell.

Both times, I should have listened.

We'd taken Federal out of town, the lights of the vehicle almost enough to see the road in front of us. Now and again a spattering of raindrops on the windshield, the sides of the road beyond blanketed in a shroud of a mist. Royston seemed to know the way; After a few minutes I could see our destination, a somewhat stately looking place with whitewashed walls and overstated columns in front. A dirt road made its way onto the property, and based on the number of cars parked on the side yard, it looked like the party was already in full swing. As we pulled up and let the valet take the car, music could be heard from the back, sounding like Irving Aaronson and his Commanders in their play. Back in twenty-nine, they had a few tunes that were quite popular with the social set.

We were confronted by two of the help at the front, not far from our car. Before they gave me a chance to speak, Royston produced a fine looking piece of paper. There was a nod or two from the men and then a "welcome to the party" nod.

We were in.

"Just mingle about for now; keep your eyes open," said Roy.

My eyes caught a flash of skirt.

"Sure thing, Roy. What's my first name?" I asked.

"Oh. You are Guy. Guy Anthony, a friend of mine from Boston. Well travelled and athletic," he said.

"That kind of friend?" I asked back.

"Not that kind of friend. Someone I travelled to Kathmandu with a few years back. He was a laconic, determined fellow."

"Cat-man-do what?" I just wasn't getting it.

"It's a place, Guy. A place," he said as he made eyes with someone. "In Nepal."

"Ah." I'm still not sure where Kathmandu exactly is, somewhere in the world where the mountains are high and the number of people speaking English is low.

I started to make my way around the party, to both sort out if I recognized anyone, as well as the general layout of the place. It was a big place; the front rooms opened up for the guests, most of the downstairs parlour, dining room and entertainment areas, side-balconies here and there, and a larger area leading out to a backyard gazebo and gardens.

It certainly was a wet party; they were not shy about the booze. Penguin men threaded their way about with trays of champagne and wine, each returning to a bar on one side of the dining room area.

I was still coming to terms with what seemed to be a relaxed yet confusing arrangement. I hoped Roy would make it clear what he was up to; I felt very out of place with these folks. I was not one to mingle when I was supposed to be on the job.

Then I noticed her in the far corner, having her ear corned by some Princeton precious. No more than twenty years by my reckoning, dark eyes trying hard not to encourage the gent in question to continue overstaying his welcome. I was always a sucker for a pretty face, and when she made a guarded look in my direction I knew we should have been playing from the same song sheet.

"I think they're playing your song," I ventured.

"Really? What song is that?" Princeton asked as he turned to face me.

"It's a real short ditty. It's called *scram!*" He was looking at me now, giving me a second glance.

He stood there for a few short moments, bowed like a bell-hop, mumbled something about talking to her later and made his way elsewhere into the party's fray.

"That was a bit harsh, don't you think?" she said.

"Yeah, it probably was," I conceded.

"Well, thank you all the same, Mister Anthony. I wasn't sure how much more of his career in football I could have endured."

"You don't say?" I said, looking about the room to see if Roy was going to leap in front of my love life like a desperate man in front of a moving train. "How do you know who I am, Miss—?"

"Miss Virginia Armstrong, Mister Anthony. You're Royston's mountaineering friend, aren't you? All rugged and tall," she said.

She certainly was coming out fresh. She'd already moved her eyes up and down me a few times, adjusting her own posture to keep me awake and alert. Somewhere at the back of my mind, I saw my suitcase on the pavement again and simply let go.

"Before you ask, Miss Armstrong, Roy's a friend. He ain't that dear though, if you catch my drift?"

"Oh, but I do, Mister Anthony. Can I offer you something to drink?"

◆ ◆ ◆

A few nice single malts later, Miss Vicki and I were out the back of the Armstrong place, talking and listening to the band near the gazebo. The band was starting to wind the party down, the clock's hands firmly wrapped around eleven. I've looked for the good professor a few times. Vicki's eyes meet mine now and again, and I was feeling my own attentions shift focus, wondering where the pair of us could spend some time getting more acquainted.

Then Royston finally decided to make an appearance. I caught him in the corner of my eye, near the back stairs, waving, indicating that he wanted me to come over. I fabricated an excuse to grab us both drinks and headed over to meet him by the rear-side porch.

"This had better be important, Roy."

"Just come back inside with me for a moment," he said as he took me by the shoulder and led me into the dining area again.

Once inside I spotted Vicki's father engaged in speaking with our good friend Callaghan. The pair of them were talking quietly in a corner, Callaghan nodding and even grinning to Armstrong as he took something from his hands that was wrapped in brown paper.

I was starting to get it.

"Okay Roy, I see the picture. You owe old Joe here a favor—maybe he's got some goods on you, I don't know. Are you even listening to me?"

Royston wasn't listening; his eyes were firmly fixed on something across the room. I could have sworn that just for a second the shadows on the back porch lengthened, the brazier beside us spluttered. That was probably still just my imagination, but I got the impression that Royston was spooked.

"Something is not right here, Charlie," he said.

"It's Guy, Roy."

"Of course. They should have revealed their presence by now. Is her psychic stain still around this place? I don't understand," he said.

"You're not the only one," I said as I watched Roy scan the room with desperation, looking between each of the guests in succession. For a reason I still cannot fathom, I decided that Roy was wasting my time and headed back to Vicki, grabbing some drinks on the way. I caught a glimpse of Roy heading into the party and tapping Callaghan on the shoulder, a man awash with confusion.

"Is something the matter, Guy?" Vicki asked.

"Nah. It's fine. Champagne, like you asked," I said.

"Isn't prohibition wonderful!" Vicki said in delightful mockery.

◆ ◆ ◆

Father, I have to confess that the next few hours are somewhat of a blur. You could say that some of the events were biblical, if you know what I mean. I've heard it called "congress" before, that name for it though sounds rather funny to my own ears.

But this is the part of the tale where everything ceases to be a laughing matter.

I awoke with a blinding headache. When I put my hand to the back of my head, I could feel that wet stickiness and smell something like copper. I found myself lying face-up, outside; the chill of the night air around me, darker shades from distant lights playing across where I lay.

"Vicki?" I cried out. I almost passed out as I stood up and looked about. I soon made out the Armstrong's house in the distance; it looked like I had awoke in the copse of trees I'd spied while at the party. As I began to walk back toward the Armstrong place, I became increasingly aware of a smell. At first I thought it was on me, but as I started to get closer to the house, I came to realize that the odors were around me and not just on me.

They were a woman's smells, Father. The sort that you as a priest are meant to know little or naught about. Unlike that smell though, this smell was more; an overpowering kind, a terrible, dank, fetid smell. Like some sort of pregnant rot, this fragrance seemed to cling to every tree and blade of grass underfoot. Soon I found myself at a slow run through the woods.

Something hit me on the back of the head as I ran; something hard and wooden. I didn't see or even feel it coming. I was bowled over again like a nine pin on regular's night. I caught a flash of something dark in my eyes, someone running on the edge of my vision. I felt another blow, this one straight between the shoulder blades.

These were strong hits. I fought to stand, feeling another hard whack on my head from the side. This time I saw a figure in a dark-brown robe, dressed like a friar. He darted and circled about me. Unlike a monk though, this one was wearing some sort of mask; a horned goat etched in bronze.

I lashed out as best I could, catching the figure unaware with a solid blow to the midsection—like you taught me in school. It was a "she." That's right, Father. I heard a cry underneath the mask, a scream that resonated more with anger than fear. I caught yet another blow to my head from an unseen attacker and all became painfully dark once again.

◆ ◆ ◆

I heard their chanting long before I awoke, horrid and melodious chants coming to me much like song lyrics can come in dreams: *"Iä! We call to you now, Sister of Darkness. Iä! We call to you, Mother of our Night. Iä! We beseech you, Black Goat of the Woods. Iä! We call to you now All-Mother; your Children, your Beasts, your Young! Arise, Arise!"*

I awoke to a circle of blasphemy. I lay in the center of a clearing in the woods, surrounded by twelve brown-robed figures, each wearing the mask of an animal. My head and hair a mess, my left side puffed and bloody.

The thirteenth member, in purple robes, stood over me. All I could do is stare—into that darkness where a face should have been. Then there were eyes, dark and beautiful eyes, staring from beyond the hood and down at me.

"You are chosen, Charlie," she said. "It is a beautiful thing that you will do for us."

She leaned over me; I lay before all of them, bound and tied—helpless. In her arms was a large wooden box; she opened it to show me the contents.

A terrible fear came over me, the likes of which I had never known before.

"No! God no, Vicki. What are you doing?" I recalled screaming at her, over and over again.

The twelve behind her chanted more than they sung; some I swore danced, their shadows twisted in shape with the trees that surrounded us. All at once, I heard a terrible keening in the wind like a scream from a distant and shipwrecked shore, a wail from the damned-to-imagine.

Even in the relative dim starlight, I saw the flash of something, a reflection of light on metal.

A sound like a thunderbolt exploded in my ears, rousing me from my terrified state.

I heard their chanting stop at once; they too now joined me in cries of terror. In the shadows, I saw one of them fall, the body pulled from my sight and into the darkness they had so recklessly taunted. Blood misted, clouding my vision for a few seconds, then Virginia Armstrong fell across me—she was dead.

"I call you out, Shub-Niggarath! I call and cast you out. Cast your presence out of this circle! Obey that Unspeakable Oath, obey and begone from this place! Remember your pact with the Elder Ones—recongize their sign!" The voice was unmistakably that of Royston's.

On the edge of my vision, the other women began to run, their shrieks and cries all the more human now that fear had visited and tamed their minds.

On my lap, the body of Virginia writhed in some interminable agony, flopped then stopped as like the last moments of a dying fish out of water.

"Can you stand?" asked Roy as he appeared above me. In his other hand, he flourished an amulet of some kind, bearing the symbol of a tree with five branches on its side. I shook my head, indicating that I was still bound with ropes. Royston made short work of them, using the blade he found at Virginia's feet.

"That's Gertrude Armstrong."

"What?" I said, struggling with my senses.

"Gertrude Armstrong; born December 15th 1779. There never was a Virginia. I found your gun, Charlie. Let's get you out of here." I took Royston's hand and stood, turning my back to them both and to the not-so-distant lights of the house.

There was a sound, a terrible sound, like cold hamburger meat scraped from an overworked grill. I slowly turned to see Royston stopped in his tracks.

There, blanketed in the shadows of the grove was Gertrude Armstrong. Her hand—a tree-like appendage — reached forward and glistening in the starlight disappeared into Royston's back. There was a look on Roy's face, like a man who had decided to simply just let go.

He dropped the amulet of iron at my feet. Then the sound not unlike that of a butcher using his hands to rip fat from the bone of a carcass filled my ears.

I grabbed the amulet and ran.

Despite my prior injuries, I felt seized by certain clarity of purpose. Behind me, I heard a terrible wail rise from the grove. As I ran, the trees around me shook as if seized by the most potent of winds, yet the skies were still and dark. The cries from the woods rose in intensity as I cleared the wild area and shuffled into the back gardens of the Armstrong estate. Joseph Armstrong saw me coming from afar; he stood brandishing a shotgun beside the gazebo.

"She'll kill us all! By God, she'll kill us all!" His own eyes were seized by a madness, as if his life of secrets with Gertrude was free now and all his fears were both being realized and released. Our eyes met as I approached, but before he looked then he looked beyond me and screamed—a scream no man ever made before.

I found myself stumbling more than running, my feet a little slick from dew and blood, hearing the double discharge of Joe's weapon as I cleared the side and stumbled near the woodshed. Fortune favored me, as I stood from my fall; I found myself in the possession of a hefty wood axe.

I seized the weapon, feeling for the first time since I awoke a rising of a righteous anger. It is even harder for me now to recall the precise details of what came next.

I remember coiling the leather binds of the amulet around the head of the axe, tying and binding the iron symbol to face outward from the blunt end. I ran across and back to the gardens, seeing the ruin of Gertrude Armstrong entwined and both absorbing and choking her great grandson like a creeper does along side trellises. I recall seeing the remnants of her head twisting toward me, a travesty of monstrous resemblance that opened its mouth and into a scream. My own eyes unnervingly agape I swung that axe in time to that maddening precision, blunt and sharp blows alike showering myself and my surroundings until I and the twisted mockery could move or shriek no more.

◆ ◆ ◆

And that, Father, is why I am here now, on this day of execution. It is true what the papers say of me—I am a murderer.

Judge me though on my words here and not on the mockery of truth that was my trial. Prescribed as a sadist, refused access to legal counsel, their part denied in court by Mayor Callaghan and his driver. All a part in bringing me to their wretched town of rotting gables and testimonial sandstone.

Do not fear for me, or my soul Father. I know that I soon go to a better place. I have seen with my own eyes demons walk upon the earth and know that someday, this world will be theirs again; but not without a fight.

Pray for my swift execution, Father.

Let the good Lord know that one of His defenders is coming home.

END

On Leave To Arkham

Bill Bilstad

T he cross-shaped marker in Christchurch Cemetery was dated June 10, 1917. "Three years, five months . . ." mumbled Fred Giotto, placing the flowers on the grave. "I'll do something special for your birthday tomorrow. Aren't you excited, Jon?"

Jonathan said nothing. He had no desire to speak. Jonathan never did. The sanitarium's orderly pushed Jonathan's wheelchair back to the Peabody Avenue trolley car. Thirty minutes later, Jonathan heard a distant scream, the dull swish of his door being shut, the turn of the key in the lock. He was alone again with his cluttered thoughts, alone again in a roomful of his chaotic selves.

◆ ◆ ◆

"Private Winthrop, training is over! Save that vigor for when 1st Division is shipped to France!" The drill sergeant had been pleased, yet guarded.

Jonathan had towered over the straw-filled mannequin, the Springfield rifle heavy in his hands, its bayonet cutting deeply each time in rhythm to his pantings.

◆

Alaric Charles Winthrop spoke with the voice of an aging but still active man of fifty-six when his young grandchild came tearfully knocking on his door that chilly November day in 1909, on Jonathan's sixteenth birthday. Alaric could not refuse the panting and sincere pleadings for lodging. His own heart had long since grown cold to his own son, but Alaric pledged to offer Jonathan whatever fortunes life shared with him, be they for weal or for woe. Jonathan gratefully hugged his grandfather, unabashed tears of relief on the youth's face.

Alaric's face was an uncomfortable blending of joy and wariness as he explained to Jonathan the rules of his household.

◆ ◆ ◆

WELCOME TO ST. NAZAIRE had read the hand-painted sign, along with a long list of regulations concerning the barracks. The lieutenant had barked on about the Y.M.C.A., and the list of entertainments offered, but after disembarking from the ship, Jonathan had felt the first stirrings of homesickness, the sense of loss.

◆

The oilskin-wrapped scrolls were the last items to be hidden. Grandfather Winthrop clutched the pages one last time, squeezing them as if they were his beloved terrier Cleveland. Alaric finally relinquished his property to his sole grandchild and carrier of the Winthrop name; Jonathan apathetically accepted the charge of concealing them from his grandfather's sight. The weight of sins used to obtain these scrolls troubled Alaric Winthrop, for his grandson now was too familiar with the unconscious physical tremors that accompanied his grandfather's frequent confessions. The stories that his grandfather provides provided were no longer refreshing. The scrolls' texts no longer were a mystery to Alaric; he revealed to Jonathan the repulsive secrets that foretold a price too high to pay.

Jonathan fell asleep that night to the sounds of Alaric weeping, repeatedly singing a hymn.

◆ ◆ ◆

As they sang, the ruckus of male voices had overtaken the low rumblings of the troop train.

"Take me back to dear old Blighty,
Put me on a train for London town,
Just take over there
And drop me anywhere,
Manchester, Leeds, Birmingham,
I don't care."

The rhythmic clacking of the steel wheels over rails had lulled Jonathan back to sleep. The train from Orléans to the front had been crowded, but Jonathan was able to sleep, believing he heard his grandfather's voice mixing with the soldiers' voices'.

◆

Often Jonathan wondered why his grandfather displayed a Calcutta newspaper article prominently in the oaken trophy case against the back wall in Winthrop's Antiques & Orientalisms. Dated 15 October 1875, the article was about the discovery of the grisly robbery and murder of a *nagbob* outside the man's posh estate. Sir Richmond al-Wazeez not only lost his purse, he lost his jewels, his embroidered silk robes, and his heart was cut from his chest.

◆ ◆ ◆

The smartly dressed officer had been a spit-shined example of what the troops once looked like on the parade grounds in Tours a year ago. Jonathan and his company troops still were too exhausted from battle to understand they were on rotation to the rear. Jonathan had drifted away, then returned. ". . . the 'Y' sells cigarettes for 35 centimes, not cents. We are in France, after all."

A snort.

". . . which the canteen workers will not tolerate. Any reports of misconduct toward female Red Cross or 'Y' workers will be brought to my attention and . . ."

◆

Jonathan sidestepped into an alley off of South French Hill Street. He was out of breath. Shame and mortification were his two pillars of support, the legs that stopped him from toppling over and huddling in the dark. His grandfather had given him a Liberty silver dollar and an address to celebrate his eighteenth birthday at, an address he now ran away from. When Jonathan recited what he expected to happen, the prostitute slapped him and shrilled at him in a high-pitched scream. "Filthy pervert!" she hissed over and over again. Jonathan bundled his clothes as best he could as he skulked from the prostitute's unclean apartment.

Later that night, Jonathan cleaned his keen jackknife, watching the sheet-wrapped corpse being swallowed by the Miskatonic River. He had taken care of the naughty whore, just like his grandfather did with others in Arkham who earned his displeasure.

◆ ◆ ◆

"Winthrop, this is your bunk."

Jonathan had stared at disbelief in the muddy hole in the trench wall. "But, Sergeant, there isn't enough room for me and my gear!"

Exhausted, Sergeant Turner had snorted back at him, "You have a shovel, use it!" the exhuasted sergeant Turner snorted.

Jonathan was greatly displeased with his sergeant's callousness.

◆

Sixteen-year-old Jonathan was grateful for a warm and somewhat dry place, his newfound home in Arkham a place where he felt loved by its owner, a place where he would not be preached to in a dry and authoritarian tone, a place where joy and imagination were handmaidens to transgression and wickedness. Even brown-furred Cleveland adoringly accepted the once-removed scion of his master's loins. Alaric's wildly flaring mutton-chop whiskers amused Jonathan, embellishing the dramatic hand gestures his grandfather used while recalling his adventures in India and in Transvaal. Jonathan could listen to his grandfather's yarns all night, and sometimes he did. When this happened, Grandfather Winthrop would sing him and Cleveland to sleep with morose songs Alaric learned from his German and English neighbors on the Witwatersrand.

Alaric told Jonathan he would always be there for his only grandchild.

◆ ◆ ◆

17 June 1917

Dear Son,

I wish this missive would find you cause to celebrate as God intends, but it is with a sad heart that I that I bring this news of God's will.

Your grandfather, my father, died a week ago. He shall be judged, and God shall find Mr. Winthrop wanting. Your grandfather's will leaves me Winthrop's Antiques & Orientalisms, and I have sold it back to the City of Arkham, who will make sure no trace remains of his vile shop. There is a tombstone being constructed for his grave in Christchurch Cemetery, in Arkham. A Christian cross will mark the site of this Philistine. What is left of his tainted wealth after his burial expenses have been willed to you.

I do not know if you have been sent across the sea yet, but know that the offer of sanctuary in my home will be yours if you ever decide to quit the path of your dead grandfather.

Go with God,

N. A. Winthrop

◆

Alaric Charles Winthrop was born March 3, 1853, and married Austere Jane Smith on July 30, 1871. He left his wife and only child Nathaniel to find wealth in India in 1876. Alaric Winthrop left India in 1886; the opening of public lands of Witwatersrand in Transvaal lured him and many other fortune-seekers. The newfound South African Republic became overrun with "outlanders", *Uitlanders* in the Afrikaaner language of the Dutch settlers. The promise of wealth from gold mines became a reality for Mr. Winthrop.

When the second Boer War came, Alaric joined the British Army as a mercenary, fighting the kommandos whenever General French thought his unit would be of any use. Jonathan listened, enthralled, as Alaric whispered darkly of his own private war, one he began in India.

Jonathan knew the trophy case could not lie.

◆ ◆ ◆

"Private, you're dragging your feet!" barked out Sergeant Turner. "Do you want the Hun to think they fight a slovenly soldier? Look at Private Winthrop to see a proper soldier step lively!"

Company E grumbled and marched on.

◆

Young Jonathan had trod the marble steps of the Miskatonic University Library many times with his grandfather during his summer stays. They both always bid hello to the head librarian, and once the bespectacled gentleman had introduced Alaric and Jonathan to Dr. Henry Armitage, who had been the director of library for thirteen years. The librarian was seemingly pleasant in his inquiries of his grandfather's researches, but Mr. Winthrop evaded even the simplest of questions. Jonathan could not fathom why his grandfather was so evasive in his answers to the librarian. It was as if his grandfather was taking a roundabout way to the book he actually was looking for, a tome called the *Necronomicon*.

◆ ◆ ◆

Under their breath, several Sammies had muttered their own version as they marched:

> *"You're in the Army now,*
> *You're not hiding behind the plow,*
> *You'll never get rich,*
> *You son-of-a-bitch,*
> *You're in the Army now!"*

Jonathan had been eager to prove his love for country, his patriotism, that he was a "hundred-percenter," but when, he had wondered, when should he start his judgments? As he had spied glints of bone protruding from the earth, he had known the omens were becoming favorable.

◆ ◆ ◆ ◆ ◆ ◆

Sometimes Jonathan envisions his marches would take him along treacherous banks of the Miskatonic River; the path he takes is often outlined with white quartz rocks. The mud dapples his elegantly pressed trouser cuffs, and as much as Jonathan tries to shun the fetid debris, he cannot disengage the actions of the earth. His white suit and tie wear heavily upon his frame; his shoulders ache. Hordes of white squirrels cluster by him, crowd him, whispering their dark prophecies to him.

◆

"Damn, did you see the size of that bugger? Two-stone, I wager!"

"I think you exaggerate a bit, Hodge. I think that rat is only eight pounds at most."

"Bugger you! That's a monster if I ever saw one. And I'll bet the rats will be bigger next week, mark my words, Winthrop."

"Why do you say that?" Jonathan raised an eyebrow with reservation.

"You dunce, don't you know that's when we go o'er the top for the great push? The rats will feast on our twisted bodies in no-man's-land! Ha, ha, ha! Gnawing, getting fat on our fat!" Private Hodge swallowed another illegal mouthful of cheap French wine.

"Shut up, Hodge, just shut up."

◆

Jonathan spied the squirrels, too, as he and his grandfather wended their way along the gently sloping River Road. Protruding from the picnic basket that Jonathan carried was the single-shot .22 rifle that sometimes accompanied their journeys, a Quackenbush Bicycle rifle with a collapsible steel skeleton stock for ease of transport, and, as Jonathan learned from his grandfather, for ease of concealment.

"See how the squirrels cluster about that tree yonder?" taught said Alaric Winthrop, extending the stock from its oft-repaired housing. "They have a nest in yon oak. We shall eat good, for victuals are a-plenty this evening."

Glancing about down the length of the road, up and down to reassure themselves that they were alone, Jonathan took the rifle from his grandfather's calloused and trembling hands, fitting the lone bullet into the breech.

"How many shells be ye using? We need some to remain for the way home," admonished Grandfather Winthrop.

Jonathan patted his jacket pocket. "I have twenty some shells in my pocket yet."

Jonathan tugged the trigger, and then tugged again when he saw he missed.

◆ ◆ ◆

"Reload, private! Reload!"

The Springfield had long since ceased struggling in his hands, but Jonathan had still mechanically yanked the bolt open and shut between tugs on the trigger. Up, back, forward, down, pull. Up back, forward, down, pull . . . .

"Reload, private! Reload!"

◆

The river walks were maddeningly slow. Jonathan's legs ached to leap and spring, the youthful vigor he knew painfully mocked the steady but awkward amble of his grandfather. During his volunteer duty in South Africa, on October 21, 1899, Grandpa Winthrop's thighs were pierced by three rounds of German-made Mauser ammunition at the battle of Elandslaagte. His wounds were never treated adequately, and while he recuperated in a grimy British tent with injuries sustained for the glory of the Empire, Grandfather Winthrop suffered infection and fever. Strain and sweat crossed the elder Winthrop's brow in the heat of the August afternoon, but he shunned any attempts to be coddled. "This limp I have is naught compared to the fate of my evil companions I left behind on that plain in Transvaal. While I walk, I still live."

◆ ◆ ◆

Jonathan limped into the bunker. Captain Miller's face was creased even further in the pale kerosene light. "You are very fortunate, Private Winthrop, all others in your raiding party were killed. You say you heard the Germans kipping them all in the ambush?"

"Yes sir!" shouted Jonathan.

"Hmm. Turner was a good sergeant." The captain scribbled on his list. "Anything else to add to your report?"

Jonathan did not mention that his former comrades were wicked, wicked people, Turner and Hodge being the worst. Jonathan had the ears to prove it.

◆

When Jonathan was fourteen, Grandfather Winthrop showed his young grandchild the hidden compartment in his trophy case. Not the side where he stocked the public pride of his travels in India and South Africa, those mementoes of battle and struggles with his fellow humans were freely discussed, but the trophies Alaric never told anyone about. Alaric moved aside the well-maintained Mauser Model 1896 rifle, which was once the property of a Boer farmer, now some ten years a mound on the Transvaal plains. The stories behind the medal given to him by the governor of Calcutta, tainted and tinted with a splash of verdigris across its sullen face, nor the tulwar, notched, dulled, sheathed in rust, could hold Jonathan's attention anymore. For when Alaric inserted the key into the hidden lock, and the whole trophy case swung aside on well-oiled hinges, Jonathan could see the full truth behind his grandfather's alleged tales of prowess. The Boer cap, the smashed Foreign Service pith helmet, and fragments of the Union Jack flapped past the astounded Jonathan's face, then in their stead now gleamed wicked daggers that hung on metal spikes, daggers Alaric Winthrop convinced his sole grandchild each had tasted deep of yielding human flesh. Here also hung photographs, tattered and faded, along with their primitive cousins, the tintype, of sites and places that Alaric had visited in his younger age. Jonathan noted with a certain familial satisfaction his own resemblance to his grandfather's face in those pictures, his grandfather's mane not at all brushed with the distinguished gray of his elderhood, but smeared with the darkly glistening source of life.

Grandpa Winthrop did not exert prejudice against the race of his victims; Jonathan noted the even samplings of God's races in those horridly fascinating images from across time.

◆ ◆ ◆

Jonathan had added another bootlace to lengthen his necklace. His concealed collection of human ears had been growing. Company E had learned to shun his dull snickers.

◆

Alaric's voice snickered with pride as he spoke about his exploits. The strings of human ears were medals of his proficiencies, and he even allowed Jonathan to don the macabre necklace as Alaric did once upon the steps of some nameless temple in the jungles of India in 1874. Further proof did Alaric also offer: rings, passports, keepsakes, teeth; all wrested from wicked, wicked people whom Alaric deemed worthy to be rushed headlong into doom.

◆ ◆ ◆

The mud had clung to his boots, a fervent friend who pleaded in vain to halt this furious stampede of men. All was silent now, the ponderous thunder of the artillery having long since pounded his ears to deafness. The only intrusions in his mind's eye had been the flashes of light, white-hot sears of pain and torture across his eyes, daylight that rent the darkness like a ravenous lion ripping into its prey. He had been dimly aware that his rifle no longer worked, but he had mechanically trudged forth through the everlasting muck with it. Like phantoms from a flickering dream, figures in khaki-stained wool had paced him, urging him onward. Jonathan had begun to know he was invincible, that no power in heaven or on earth could have stopped his forward march. He had viewed with disdain at how the lesser beings around him were not made of the same caliber of supreme material as he was becoming. They had floundered in the mud, had sprawled into it, had become one with it.

Jonathan had comprehended suddenly he was favored by God. This sudden insight had enthused, yet terrified, him. Jonathan then had groveled in the holy ground, asking for His powers to shine forth.

The daylight of God had come upon him without warning. The ground had shaken, swayed, and in that revelation of God's sudden pronouncement, Jonathan had seen the shattered path before him lay clear. He had leaped into the trench-grave, a whir of steel-tipped wood seeking to redeem the devils in dim green. They had fled before his divine fury, dwarfen shadows that acknowledged his sole right to exist. Those who had stayed behind offered up their ears willingly to each hacking tug.

Another rush of daylight had sped into the trench, but this time with irate retribution. Jonathan's left leg had intensified in warmth, then had exploded with a deep, salty fire . . . .

◆

Jonathan licked his lips, tittering with further pleasure, as his grandfather opened still another covert panel in his trophy case. There, propped in the thin space between the mahogany wood frame and the blood-red velvet lining, lay a time-touched sheaf of coarse scrolls, scribed by hands unknown, in a language that neither Alaric nor Jonathan were familiar with. Grandfather Winthrop gingerly hugged these pages to his bosom, like he hugs his dog Cleveland, and swore that he would shatter the barrier of language and delve into the secrets of the pages; secrets, of which he was assured their veracity, under pain of torture from its former owners, that would enable him and his line to live forever, the key to understanding that would be found in the *Necronomicon*.

The interruption of Winthrop's Antiques & Orientalisms door chime startled them, bidding the pair to hush their unholy trophies back into their clandestine repose.

◆ ◆ ◆

Jonathan had lain curled, unseen, in the shell hole. He had never assumed he could welcome this much pain.

◆

Jonathan's curiosity over the intervening years grew into a steady will-o'-the-wisp, taunting him with every turn he took in the dismal swamp of life. What was on those scrolls that Grandfather cherished so much? And why were they so loathed as Grandfather drew closer to solving their secret, laboring in the university library?

◆ ◆ ◆

His world swayed. Faint grunts came from his four stretcher-bearers, the dim slosh of mud echoing with each sway. Jonathan's hearing was coming back. But his leg burned. Burned.

His sins were burned away and buried.

◆ ◆ ◆

In the spring of 1915, with much debate and spiritual trepidation, Grandfather Winthrop gathered his remaining fortunes, along with his secret trove of treasures and trophies, and extracted the solemn pledge of his able-bodied grandson to undertake missions that would take the pair around Arkham until completed.

Selecting trinkets that would fit with ease into their picnic basket, Alaric and Jonathan would stroll a predetermined section of town, and like the pirates of yore, they would surreptitiously bury their ill-gotten booty for future safekeeping. The British gold guineas were the first to be conscripted to silence, as they were entrusted to the care of a vast weeping willow that daunted the Miskatonic River along River Road. Hoisted into the tree's limbs with a stout canvas bag that vexed Jonathan with its weight, Grandfather watched with a certain melancholy as Jonathan nested the treasure in a hollow section of the tree trunk. Tossing up some river rocks, Alaric made sure Jonathan secured the sack into place with the stones.

Grandfather Winthrop made a scribbled entry in a black leather covered diary, and then returned the diary to its accustomed place in his thread-worn serge vest, next to his solid-gold Crescent Watch Case Company pocket watch.

"God forgives me," declared Alaric.

◆ ◆ ◆

Jonathan had felt his puttees being forcibly removed, the clotted blood and wool tearing the mangled flesh even more. There was no forgiveness

in the doctor's tone as he spoke, "That leg will have to come off. Poor lad.
Medic, more light here."

◆

It was May 2, 1917. While Grandfather Winthrop read the
Arkham *Advertiser* under the living room's gaslight, Jonathan
felt the compulsion to look upon the accursed scrolls, to hold
them for his very own, but his oath to his beloved grandfather
held sway. Jonathan made the journey to the Miskatonic
Library on the following Tuesday, where he quietly sifted the
paper bundles in with others in the chart and maps room on the
library's third floor. Entrusted now with the protection of his
grandfather's diary, Jonathan surreptitiously added a coded
notation of the concealment place of the papers, and returned
to his grandfather's apartment over the antique shop.

Jonathan finished backing his trunk. The black diary he
retained in his breast coat pocket. He came back downstairs.
"Grandfather," he began, "I have hidden the scrolls as I
promised. No more obligations tie me here. I leave now for
Boston to enlist with the United States Army Corps."

The elder Winthrop moaned, a rosary in his ague-rattled
fist. "God forgives me."

◆ ◆ ◆

While recuperating in London, feverish, Jonathan had read and
re-read the black leather diary, his grandfather's voice speaking to him
in his head as he pored over the pages. Tiny fang marks had gouged the
cracked cover, a playful memento from Cleveland when he had been a
teething puppy.

◆

In December 1913, when Grandfather's terrier, Cleveland,
had been shaking and refusing to eat, Jonathan took the ailing
pet to Doctor Pinter's, whose veterinary practice was located
across town at 184 East Saltonstall Avenue. Jonathan had

memorized the address directions his grandfather gave him, but he lost his way, and stumbled for blocks through the twisting narrow streets and alleyways, until finally, arms aching from his blanket-wrapped burden, he had worked up the courage to ask a stranger for help. But by then, it was too late, as Cleveland had succumbed to the cold.

◆ ◆ ◆

Jonathan curled deeper into his wool blankets, shivering. In time with each pitching of the troopship's movement westward, Jonathan's crutches clanked against the chilly bulkhead. He clutched his grandfather's diary, eyes open to the ceiling and beyond, dreaming of the treasures spelled out in the crabbed handwritings.

◆

Some of the more durable loot, the gold and silver coins minted from five differing nations, rings and other jewelry, along with a minute collection of South African diamonds, was stashed in an iron box, which was concealed in a rotting stanchion in the unused docks that lined the south shores of the Miskatonic River near the Peabody Bridge. Grandfather Winthrop placed his treasured necklace of detached ears in a rubberized canvas bag, and then on the Fourth of July on picnic in Christchurch Cemetery, had his grandson brazenly tip back a marble tombstone to place the bag into the worm-rotted soil under the memorial to Susan Dearkins, who passed from this mortal coil on April 23, 1907. Jonathan shrugged off his grandfather's odd laugh as he patted the mold-etched engravings.

"She'll be keeping my jewels safe, won't you, Miss Dearkins?" Alaric laughed and stretched his face to the sun. "God forgives me!"

Jonathan turned away in repugnance.

◆ ◆ ◆

In October, in Boston, his own father had refused to see him. Twenty-four-year-old Jonathan had fled once more to Arkham; only this time no one was there to welcome him home.

The argument turned violent. Jonathan slammed his fist onto the kitchen table. "I will sign up!"

◆

His father recoiled from the sudden outburst, but remained steadfast in his oration. "I don't know what stories your grand-dad has filled your ears with, but you are far too young, Son, for one thing. The Army does not accept sixteen-year-olds. But even if you were twenty-one, I'd still forbid it. I will have no son of mine breaking the Sixth Commandment!"

"But, Father, I want to be a soldier like, like . . . ."

"My father, Alaric? The very same heathen who left your grandmother and myself? The same man who sits now at the Devil's left hand, full of sin and inequity?"

"I don't care! He is a good man . . . ."

"He will burn for all eternity with the damned. If you go, I will have no son, no one who will enter into Heaven with me. I will be . . . all . . . alone." Nathaniel Asa Winthrop's voice cracked. "Please, please, son, don't . . . *God will punish you!*"

The impetuous Jonathan had already left. Initially rejected by the Army for being too young, Jonathan would have to wait. Until that time, he waited in his grandfather's dank apartment in a squalid section of Arkham.

◆ ◆ ◆

His soiled room is as cold as a tomb. Jonathan does not care. His mind is elsewhere, but familiar sounds draw him back. The squeak of a metal cart's wheel; the click of the key in the lock.

♦ ♦ ♦ ♦ ♦ ♦

Confused, Jonathan Winthrop imagines he celebrates his thirty-fourth birthday quietly with a white-frosted cake, then strolls through the town square during an unseasonable warm snap. He tips his white top hat to the Arkham residents he sees, but no one responds to his pleasantries. He expects little today, but a parade, a celebration, a band rehearsing somewhere in Arkham, any such gathering would Jonathan be willing to subvert inwardly as a gesture of his birthing anniversary. He is not sure what day of the week his birthday falls upon in 1927, but he always knows his birthday is on the eleventh day of the eleventh month.

Jonathan pompously marches through the downtown, moving into the Miskatonic University campus in a heartbeat. He even stops to pet the guard dog chained at the library's entrance, a white terrier named Cleveland. As he and his grandfather have done on many occasions, he climbs the white-streaked marble stairs that leads into the Miskatonic University Library. Once inside, he determinedly marches down the center hallway, up the thirty wide marble steps that eventually lead to the third floor. There he turns left down the corridor, past the mute secretaries as they type in mathematical unison, and stands outside the open doorway to the Rare Books Collection room, where the *Necronomicon* is kept, the book that shall solve all his woes. He repeats to himself "I shall succeed where my grandfather had stopped," with every hobnailed clomp of his left boot step.

But the secretaries flee before him as his steps echo through the now-deserted third floor. Jonathan hesitates outside the closed door to where the legendary book is kept. He wonders out loud, "Why did my grandfather abandon his quest?"

Jonathan stares at the endless rows of white-spined book stacks. "Why did he stop in his desire for eternal life?" His voice reverberates in the empty chambers. A sudden thought alarms Jonathan. Perhaps the idea of his grandfather's sins being with him for all eternity stops Alaric from completing his own mandate. Alaric kills, he covets, he is unrepentant. Jonathan surely follows his grandfather's life.

Jonathan sits on an iron bench in Independence Square's bandstand, rain beating down on him, wondering if his eternity will be spent like this, conjecturing, worrying about the misdeeds of his past. His AEF woolen uniform clings to him, itchy in the hot August humidity, and the phantom pain in his absent left leg telling him his puttees are wrapped too tightly, while his grandfather shakes his white mutton-chop whiskers in disgust as he shuffles past, dragging a pram, its steel wheels squeaking.

◆ ◆ ◆ ◆ ◆ ◆

The squeak of a metal cart's wheel, the click of the key in the lock.

◆

"Happy birthday, Jon!"

"This is silly, Fred. He can't hear you."

"Don't mind him, Jon, it's your birthday. You are twenty-seven-years old today. Do you want to open your present? Don't worry, I'll do it for you."

The gentle sounds of paper being torn.

"Fred, this is highly absurd. What if Doctor Hardstrom sees us? He isn't the most understanding type."

"Shush, Thomas. I feel sorry for Jon. This is no way for a veteran to live, locked away and forgotten."

"You think he knows today is his birthday, much less Armistice Day?"

"I doubt it. He was shipped back to the States two months before the war ended, shell-shocked, and he's been like this ever since."

"Hmm. What's that book you're giving him? It looks old."

"It was his grandpa's diary. Jon was clutching it when he first admitted. I figure it might be of comfort to him. His grandfather was very fond of him, according to it."

"Well, he does seem to smile now. Come on, Fred, let's not be tardy in our rounds."

The clank of a metal cart against the bed.

"Goodnight, Jon."

The dull swish of door being shut; the turn of the key in the lock.

Grandfather stands, the whites of eyes glowing bright. "Jonathan."

END

Geometry of the Soul

by Jason Andrew

Glancing through clippings from the past several years of the Arkham *Advertiser* and the Arkham *Gazette*, Jonathon Hunter decided that this small quaint town might pose a problem to his assignment. The files of the Pinkerton Detective Agency were famous across the world. Pinkerton detectives had killed or captured Jesse James, the Dalton gang, and the Wild Bunch. They had succeeded where so many had failed due to their ethics, their bravery, and their organization. Police departments all over the world mimicked their collection of mug shots and files. These days after the Great War, Pinkerton detectives mostly handled security concerns and the occasional cases for special interests, rather than engaging in the manhunts. In the last few years Arkham had seen dozens of seemingly unrelated murders, kidnappings, and disappearances. Statistics such as this would have been unsurprising in the previous century when the country was still wild. The days of the outlaws were passing into legend and dime store novels. For a small town thirty miles from Boston to have such a high death rate was perplexing. Perhaps, he thought, this might explain the strange case of Professor Michael Dyer.

"Your credentials have been verified, Detective Hunter," the short, sweating porter reported. "Doctor Hardstrom will see you now."

It was rare that any institution required verification from the home office for a Pinkerton detective. Hunter wondered if it was a stalling tactic to prepare the patient for public view.

Moans, groans, and grunts could be heard from behind closed doors as they briskly walked through the wing to the doctor's office. "Please excuse the noise," the porter said. "Some of the patients find it soothing."

The porter opened the office door and gestured for the detective to enter. The expansive office had a large circular window that overlooked the town and the Miskatonic River. There was a comfortable sofa and several bookshelves. He glanced at the titles that ranged from *Gray's Anatomy* to *Synchronicity* to titles in a half dozen languages. Sitting behind an impressive oak desk was a skinny bald man, dressed in a tweed suit and an oversized white lab jacket. "Welcome to Arkham Sanitarium, Detective Hunter," he said, extending his hand. "I am Doctor Hardstrom."

The detective accepted the hand and was surprised by how strong the doctor was, despite his appearance. "Thank you for seeing me at such a short notice."

"I apologize for keeping you waiting, Mr. Hunter, but we strongly respect the privacy of our patients here and, frankly, I was concerned that your presence might disrupt the treatment."

"Your patient killed seven men and allegedly consumed their flesh afterward," Hunter replied.

"You're very to the point, Mr. Hunter. So then you must also be aware that Mr. Dyer claims that he did not kill anyone. Of course, if he were truly innocent, I'm certain he wouldn't have engaged in the self-mutilation. His delusions are quite fascinating. I'm writing a paper on them."

"How pleasant," Hunter said wryly.

Doctor Hardstrom pulled a small silver case from his jacket pocket and flicked it open, revealing a row of Turkish cigarettes. "I'm afraid that I must warn you, he can be quite unsettling. You might just want to have me ask the questions you have."

Hunter thought back to the trenches of the Great War and shrugged his shoulders. "Doctor Hardstrom, I've lived through many unsettling times. I assure you that I can handle Mr. Dyer."

"At the least, you should have a cigarette," the doctor advised. "It will calm your nerves and it's very good for your t-zone."

Hunter accepted a cigarette, nodding gratefully "I haven't had one of these since the war," he said.

The doctor lit a cigarette and inhaled blissfully. "It's one of my few indulgences. Thankfully I have a deal with a trading company in Innsmouth," Doctor Hardstrom said. Hunter lit his Turkish cigarette and found the taste repugnant. It was a fine cigarette, and quite expensive, but all he could taste was mustard gas, sweat, and blood.

"Something wrong?" the Doctor asked.

"I'm fine, thank you," Hunter said, grimacing as he took another drag. "I'm just eager to question Mr. Dyer."

"I'm certain it will be quite the experience," the doctor said.

The doctor and the porter led the detective across the wing to a set of winding stairs. "Mr. Dyer is in our special care unit. Right next to Mr. Shelby," he explained as they descended. "Mr. Shelby is quite the fascinating case. He was a sailor that learned the tribal art of tattoo while in Haiti. It seems that he believes his tattoos come alive. He was caught after killing five women in Boston in 1919."

Although that case was almost four years old, Hunter remembered the agency attempting to crack it. Three detectives died trying to bring in Shelby. Hunter had never seen Allan Pinkerton so angry and despondent, even in the trenches during the war. He made a note to report back that Shelby had been secretly transferred. "I recall the case," he said. "I had assumed that he would be in prison."

"He was," the doctor explained. "But he quickly went catatonic and we have better facilities for taking care of the criminally insane."

The basement wing was quite different from the rest of the sanitarium. The floor and walls were made of black stone. The doors were steel and bolted. Three guards roamed the hallway with batons in hand. It was quiet as though their madness had made the patients mute. The only sounds were the echoing footsteps.

They stopped at the end of the wing. Doctor Hardstrom slid open a view portal and peered into the dark room. "Mr. Dyer, we're going to open the door. You have a visitor. I expect you to be on your best behavior," he warned.

"I told you that I don't wish to see her," a voice from the darkness whispered angrily.

"Your visitor is Detective Hunter. He has some questions for you."

"Very well," The patient said, satisfied. "If you must."

"Oddly, light seems to have a strange effect upon him. It's quite fascinating, especially with his condition. Dim light seems to be tolerable."

The guard lit a small, hand held oil lamp and handed it to Hunter. The end of the wing was illuminated. "Step back," the guard ordered.

The guard unbolted the three locks and slowly opened the door. Hunter peered inside. At a glance, it looked like a typical hospital room with a bed, a dresser, and a table with chairs. There was a small candle lit upon the nightstand. Michael Dyer sat upon his bed with his hands at his side. He was a lean, delicate looking man who appeared as though he had not eaten or slept regularly in a long time. From his description, Hunter knew that he was once a handsome man with brown eyes and wavy black hair. However, bandages and gauze now covered his eyes, his nose, and most of his hair. "What can I do for you Detective?" he asked, calmly.

Hunter wondered how Dyer could see with his eyes covered, and if they were covered how the light could bother him. "Does this extra light disturb you?" Hunter asked.

"As long as you place the lamp at the end of the room near the table, I shall not be too taxed," Dyer answered.

Hunter did as instructed, and then pulled a chair to the center of the room. "If you need anything, Detective," the doctor said, "yell for the guard."

Hunter resisted the urge to tell the doctor that he was armed and if need be he could slap down the gaunt patient. But he wanted to put Dyer into a talkative mood. "Thank you, Doctor."

The guard slowly closed the metal door. The clicks of the bolts seemed to echo in the stone room. "There is water in the pitcher if you are thirsty. I would offer you another refreshment, Detective, but as you can see I am without the means."

"No thank you," Hunter said. He bent over to put out the cigarette on the stone floor.

"Please don't," Dyer begged. "The doctor does not allow patients to smoke unsupervised. Seems he thinks we might be dangerous with matches. If you aren't going to finish that cigarette, I would not mind accepting that task."

Hunter grinned. It couldn't be this easy. "If you agree to answer some questions for me . . . ."

"I'll answer whatever questions you have, Detective. You might not like them, but I'll answer," Dyer agreed.

Hunter carefully gave Dyer the cigarette and stepped back. Dyer quickly took a long drag and breathed a sigh of relief. "I've very much missed these."

Hunter sat back in the chair, taking care that he had easy access to his pistol, snugged beneath his trench coat. "I suppose you are wondering why I am here."

"You are here because the families of the Mount St. Helens Expedition wish to have the bodies of the dead recovered," Dyer stated. "Some of them don't believe their loved ones are dead."

"How did you know?"

Dyer laughed. "Why else would a Pinkerton detective come to see me?"

"The families are very concerned. There are rumors that one of them has been spotted in Portland. If they are still alive, you would be released, of course," Hunter replied.

Dyer laughed coldly. "I can never be released Detective Hunter. And I assure you that those men are quite dead."

"Are you confessing to killing them?"

"Just because I say that they are dead does not mean that I killed them," Dyer answered. "It merely means that I know for certain that they are dead."

"How do you know this for certain?"

Dyer paused to take another long drag on the cigarette. "Do you know what true horror is, Mr. Hunter?"

Hunter knew this type—they liked to talk. And if you let them talk, they eventually tell you everything. The trick was getting them motivated. "I think I learned all that I needed to about horror from the trenches in France."

"Yes," Dyer replied. "I can see why you would believe that. I wasn't able to go, of course. But I can almost see it through your eyes: writhing, stale smelling lice; damp, chilling trenches; rats gnawing the eyes from corpses; the anticipation of waiting for the next charge."

Hunter began feeling queasy as Mr. Dyer described the very experiences he had lived through. It made him angry. "That's not a subject I'm prepared to discuss with you, Mr. Dyer."

He laughed again. It was hollow, mocking, and without mirth. "Detective Hunter, if you are unprepared to discuss such a trivial matter, then I humbly suggest that we stop here and now."

"Why do you care if I am ready or not?"

"As much damage as I have done, I would not seek to inflict this burden upon any other," Dyer said.

"Is that why you won't see your wife? Your file states that you have two sons."

Crazed, Dyer jumped from the bed to confront the detective. Swiftly, Hunter drew his service revolver from his long coat and pulled back the hammer with a loud click. "I could put a bullet between your eyes, and when I went home I'd get a bonus. So, sit back down."

Dyer's fierce scowl again shifted to a cunning grin. Slowly, he backed away from the detective, returning to his position upon the bed. "Right between my eyes, you say?" He whispered. "That would be interesting indeed. Tell me, Detective, what's it like being one of the Pinks?"

"It's a good job. Does a good service for the country," Hunter said.

"What is the motto again?" Dyer asked, clearly amused.

"We Never Sleep," Hunter answered.

Dyer cackled ferociously. When the laughing stopped, Dyer's smile faded. "And your symbol is the Great Eye within the Pyramid, is it not?"

"It is. The papers used to refer to our founder, Allan Pinkerton, as the Great Eye back in the day," Hunter said.

"And did he have 'the Great Eye?'"

Hunter shrugged. "Of course not. He had years of experience and knew people. He could read a case report and solve a crime a thousand miles away. He was that good."

"And what did the son of the Great Eye think of my file?" Dyer asked, clearly amused.

"You don't weigh enough to have fought and killed them by traditional means. We found it unlikely you would be able to shoot all of them or kill all of them in their sleep. They would have heard you and overwhelmed you," Hunter revealed. "However, as a Professor of Antiquities, you are familiar with the historical uses of poisons. Your employment at Miskatonic University allowed you access to several different chemical laboratories."

"If I poisoned them, then why did I take the risk and eat them?" Dyer inquired.

"We don't think you actually ate them. You certainly don't look like you could have eaten all of them within the short amount of time you were missing. That's why I am here. Their families want to bring their bodies back and bury them," Hunter revealed. "I don't know how much it really matters, but if I can give peace to those families, I will.

"There are no bodies for them to recover," Dyer stated menacingly.

"If you don't help us, another expedition will be sent and we'll eventually find the caves and the bodies anyway," Hunter replied. "If you help us, conditions will be improved. If they aren't really dead, then you are innocent and we can get you out of here."

"I am never leaving this place," Dyer stated grimly.

"Don't you want to see your family?" Hunter asked.

"More than anything in the world. That's why I have to stay here," Dyer revealed. "And that is why you must stop another expedition from finding or exploring those caves."

"If you can provide credible details of what happened, I'm certain that we can come to a mutually beneficial relationship," Hunter offered. "You have to give me something to tell these families."

"I've tried to block it out. Please understand that if I talk about this, there will be a price," he warned. "I'm not sure it's a price I'm willing to pay."

"You are the only person who knows that."

"I'll tell you what you want to know. You can decide what to tell the families from there," Dyer said. "But you will have to settle my affairs. Complete the work. I promise that it involves nothing immoral and that it will not harm any living soul."

"If I'm satisfied with your answers, I'll help you," Hunter promised. "But only if I am satisfied with the answers."

"Very well," Dyer said, wearily. "I suppose this is the last and only chance that I will get. What do you know for certain?"

Hunter pulled out his notepad and flipped through the pages. "Miskatonic University sponsored a geology expedition to Mount St. Helens in 1922. The team discovered a previously hidden series of caves within an old lava tube. They found some markings on one of the walls and requested your presence. The university agreed to sponsor your trip and you traveled there by train three months later. The expedition was out of contact for three months. You were found covered with blood and crazed on August 12th, 1922 outside Battleground, Washington where you confessed that the entire expedition had been killed. After you attempted to kill yourself in police custody, it was arranged for you to receive therapy at Arkham Sanitarium, so that you would be closer to your home," Hunter said. "Several local search parties were sent looking for the lava tube, but were unable to locate it. Professors Jack Abbott, Henry Sergeant, and James Cooper were never seen again. Professor Jacob Harden was spotted briefly in Portland, Oregon, but disappeared. The bodies of three locals were found near the remains of your base camp—their eyes were gouged out."

"Yes, the entrance to the lava tube has collapsed. Unless you know exactly where to dig, it is unlikely that it will be found anytime soon," Dyer explained. "And it's safer for everyone involved–"

"How is it safer?"

Dyer's reply was a hiss. "Don't interrupt me! You have no concept of what it's costing me to tell you of this. If you wish to know the truth you will have to be silent."

Hunter remained silent, waiting for the madman to continue.

"Very well. It is my great regret that I have to burden you with this knowledge, but your news that Professor Harden survived is most distressing. If he survived, then it's possible that the others did as well"

"Portland police didn't know he was considered missing when they questioned him. He was apparently a witness to a local murder," Hunter explained.

"You don't understand," Dyer cried. "Professor Harden died in the caves."

"Then who was it that's walking around with Professor Harden's papers and identity?" Hunter queried.

"I'm getting to that. The lava tube was long, and wide enough that several men could walk comfortably. It was, of course, very cool as they tend to be. There wasn't much remarkable about the tube itself. Its entire length was easily explored. What made it interesting was the series of caves that diverted to the south from the main lava tube. The expedition explored much of the caverns. There was one tunnel at the far end of one of the colossal caverns that was lined with strange, arcane symbols. Some of them appeared to be Egyptian hieroglyphs. Others seemed to resemble Arabic. At the end of the tunnel was a wall sealed with a single marking.

"It appeared to be a great fiery eye encased in a pentagram. Professor Harden had seen such a symbol before, but from where he did not reveal. When I first saw it, I had a queer sensation in my knees as if in the presence of a giant."

"What was it?" Hunter asked.

"Mystics and students of the occult across the world believe that some symbols have magic powers. In Eastern Europe, some peasants believe that a simple cross will chase away a vampire. Egyptians believed that the ankh possessed healing properties. The theory is that these symbols reflect astral light from the spirit world and that the shapes formed cause effects in the material plane."

Hunter frowned. He wondered just how insane the professor was. He'd heard wild tales before, but this one was a topper. "What does this have to do with Professor Harden?"

Dyer hissed again. This time the soft wet hiss didn't come from his mouth. It must have been Hunter's imagination, because he thought he had seen the bandages around Dyer's eyes pulse with movement. "Professor Harden believed that the symbols marked a possible entrance to a deeper cavern. He wanted to know if I could determine the meaning of the seal. But it was beyond anything I knew at the time."

"And he didn't wait, did he?" Hunter asked.

"Three days later, he ordered the wall breached. I'd not even had time to receive word from the university about the sketches I drafted. We expected stale air, but it was oddly clean, fresh. Harden was correct—there was another tunnel behind the wall. The tunnel went fifty yards before expanding into a small amorphous cavern. The ceiling was so high that only by tracing the outlines of the gigantic stalagtites could I find it. It was so vast that we could have fit the entire university inside the cavern and still *not* touch the walls. Every step seemed to echo endlessly. Our footsteps were quickly drowned out by a single high-pitched screech. Two others quickly followed suit from different directions. Although we searched frantically with our lamps, we couldn't find the source of the flapping and high pitched screeches."

"I imagine they were bats," Hunter interjected.

Professor Dyer smiled madly. "They may have been bats at one time. Some force mutated them into a horrid squamous blend of bat and man. They came from the ceiling, swooping upon us like hawks. Their claws ground into my shoulders as they lifted me off the ground. Abbott, Sergeant, Cooper, and Harden were also captured. The rest ran back to base camp in the confusion. We flew in darkness for quite some time before coming to the city of Hasad the Horrible."

Hunter rolled his eyes. *Mad as a hatter.* "There was a city beneath the mountain?"

"We cannot continue until you believe me," Dyer said, bluntly.

Hunter was about to reply, when the professor stood. Hunter aimed the revolver. Dyer did not advance toward the detective, but instead reached for his head, and commenced removing the bandages. The bridge of his nose appeared to have been smashed and widened. The skin around his eyes was bruised, bloody, and seemed to pulse with an uncommon autonomy. His eyelids blinked revealing black oozing slits. Small appendages poked out from the ooze and fluttered wildly.

Hunter scrambled from the chair, still aiming at the horrid figure. "What the hell happened to you?"

"I was taken to the city of Hasad the Horrible," Dyer said.

Hunter's hands were sweaty and shaking. The appendages seemed to beckon him with gestures. Mercifully, Professor Dyer returned the bandages to their place about his head. "Why didn't Doctor Hardstrom warn me about this?"

"He does not know. I have befuddled his mind. He believes I have gouged my own eyes out. I need my rest to fight what is happening to me"

Taking several deep breaths, Hunter tried to calm himself. "I believe you. What happened next?"

"We were taken to the city of Hasad, deep under the mountain. It's a strange honeycombed place, made of stone and flesh. We were taken to its epicenter, before a bubbling pit of gray filth and slime. Hideous tentacles rose from this pit, wrapped themselves around two great stone pillars, and then pulled forth an amorphous mass of terrible eyes around a single unblinking, relentless eye. Held motionless by the bat-like creatures, we were helpless and could only scream. The eldritch beast opened a loathsome maw, and from dozens of needle-pointed, ichorous appendages burst forth. Two of them wormed their way through the air to my face, jabbing under my eyelids. Never have I felt such abject agony."

Hunter's mouth was dry, and it suddenly became difficult to breathe. "What happened to your eyes?"

"Somehow, the tentacles injected my sockets with a vile putrescence that reacted with my eyes. The flesh burned and transmuted into what you see now. Yet, I could still see. The others were likewise infected, I knew.

"The infection came with images and ideas. The beast had planted a part of its soul into us. I can now see that astral light of which I spoke. It indeed comes from the stars, and others cannot see. I knew then that the symbol upon the wall was the Elder Sign and that it contained these beasts in slumber, and that soon I would be part of the wretched city we had uncovered. Our minds were implanted with commands. Hasad the Horrible hates the light of our sun. It prefers the cool of the darkness."

"So the five of you are infected?"

Dyer coughed. He began to lose his pallor and sweat profusely. "We were led through the tunnels to the lava tube by grotesque batrachian humanoids, not more than three feet in height, each with savage-looking teeth. The local porters were prepared to hike down to civilization to get help. We descended upon them like jackals, consumed their flesh, and howled at the moon with pleasure."

"How did you regain your sanity?" Hunter asked. "It sounds like you were possessed."

"While gathering my supplies, I happened upon a photograph of my wife and child. My mind's eye recalled the love I had for them, and for a few hours I was myself. When the others returned to the cavern, I determined that I would destroy the city. Harden had brought several sticks of dynamite with him. He didn't question my bringing them in my pack when we returned to the city.

"I had thought to attack Hasad the Horrible directly, killing myself in the process, if required. I hoped to see my wife again in heaven. But as we descended into the tunnels, I began to assimilate more of the memories. There is no heaven. I knew that there was nothing after death for those such as us. The only gods are hoary, terrible, and with no care for humanity. I am shamed to say that I was too cowardly to go through with it for fear of seeing them in the afterlife.

"Instead I detonated some of the dynamite in the egress tunnel leading to the open cavern. As I had hoped, it collapsed the entire tunnel. I duplicated the Elder Sign as best I could and tried to find my way back. My intentions were to find a cure for this infection," Dyer explained.

"What happened?"

"The memories and knowledge were too terrible. Hasad the Horrible knows more of this uncaring, unnerving universe than I could have imagined. By the time I found people I could not communicate. I was barely able to hide my affliction with a minor telepathic illusion.

"Over time, I pushed the police to returned me to Arkham, with promises of confessions once I was re-united with my family. My real hope was that the doctors here might give me access to the university's library. But it has since become restricted. And so here I wait and try to attain peace."

Hunter's instincts told him there was more—something unspoken. The idea frightened him. "Something's changed, hasn't it?"

"They escaped. That means they are carrying out their missions. Where I've been fighting the infection, they have been embracing it. Hasad the Horrible and his ilk can't walk freely upon the world yet. The stars and the timing aren't right, but they can work through agents. They can prepare the way."

"What can I do?"

"Find them and kill them, Detective Hunter. These four men are *still* men. They are men with tainted knowledge and grotesque powers, but men. Find them and kill them before they awaken the elder gods . . . ."

Somehow, Hunter knew this madman was speaking the truth. There was a horror in the world far greater than this gaunt professor. Even so, this wasn't a job that Hunter could do alone. He trusted his fellow Pinks with his life, but he couldn't tell this tale without proof. Maybe, he could show them? They had the skill and the contacts to find the men. "I'll need help from some others," Hunter said. "I'll bring them here to meet you."

"It will be too late," Dyer said.

"Can their plans be accomplished so soon?"

"No," Dyer answered. "I will be gone by then. You must kill me before you leave."

The lilliputian tentacles burst free of the bandages and crackled with eldritch energy. "Fight it, Dyer!" Hunter cried.

"This is the price I pay for speaking of such terrors," Dyer said, his voice burning with agony. "With the morphine and the quiet, I was able to block out Hasad the Horrible. Now, he grows in my mind, angry and cruel. If you let me live, I'll become his slave. Worse, I will do unspeakable acts in his name and I'll suffer for them. He is a master of the geometry of the soul. He will claim the greater share of mine and allow a small part of me to remain in anguish. *Kill me now!*"

Once, during the last days of the Great War, circumstances had forced Hunter to hold down an aware patient while the medic slowly, methodically sawed bone to amputate his leg. It had been the most terrible experience in his life. Observing this professor's humanity slip away to a loathsome creature quickly seared away the trauma of the war memories.

"Tell my wife and son I loved them very much!" Dyer begged, writhing in pain.

"I will," Hunter said.

The detective then fired three shots. Two guards frantically unbolted the door, swinging it open. Hunter stood over the dead body of Professor Michael Dyer, covering it with a sheet. "He had a weapon and attacked me," Hunter stated calmly.

The guards nodded, almost as if they shared a secret. Hunter knew that there was no remorse for the death of this insane killer. No one would question it. Justice had been served.

Doctor Hardstrom arrived minutes later with two nurses in a panic. "Did he hurt you, Detective?" the doctor asked.

"No. He just snapped, and I had to kill him. He tried to strangle me," Hunter lied. "I'll need to take the body with me for examination. Have your guards prepare a coffin. And I'll want to speak to the family of course."

"What?" the doctor said. "That is out of the question."

"Or I could make arrangements for this sanatorium to be examined from top to bottom. I have the feeling that Professor Dyer couldn't have gotten away with as much as he did unless there were several problems. I'm sure that the newspapers would be very interested to know how you got Shelby transferred here." Hunter said, menacingly.

Hardstrom's face flushed with anger, but he remained silent. "I'm certain that we can come to an arrangement."

"Yes, I just gave it to you," Hunter replied. "And we'll need all of his files by the end of the day."

Hunter was surprised how quickly Hardstrom conceded to his outrageous demands. He decided that the doctor must have dark secrets within these walls to be so willing to avoiding trouble. He called the home office in Chicago and told them to expect the body, and that he would explain when he arrived. With luck, he could convince his fellow Pinks that this menace did exist and that they should apply their skills and knowledge to the task at hand. Hunter knew that many of the Pinks felt listless after the Great War, lacking focus or purpose. There were no more cowboy outlaws to chase down, and there were the new national police agencies that could handle the man-hunts.

There were ancient creatures that slept waiting for the stars to change, waiting for the chance to rule the world. The Pinkerton Detective Agency had a motto known across the land—We Never Sleep. Perhaps, with luck, they could turn the Great Eye upon these secret horrors and give humanity another chance.

END